TAMING POISON DRAGONS

Taming Poison Dragons

Tim Murgatroyd

Myrmidon
Rotterdam House
116 Quayside
Newcastle upon Tyne
NE1 3DY

www.myrmidonbooks.com

Published by Myrmidon 2009

A catalogue record for this book is available from the British Library.

ISBN 978-1-905802-28-9 Hardback
ISBN 978-1905802-30-2 Export Trade Paperback

Set in 11.5/14.5pt Sabon by
Falcon Oast Graphic Art Limited,
East Hoathly, East Sussex

Printed and bound in the UK by
CPI Mackays, Chatham ME5 8TD

1 3 5 7 9 10 8 6 4 2

LOTTERY FUNDED

For my dearest Ruth, Tom and Oliver

Visiting the Temple of Accumulated Fragrance

I didn't know where the temple was,
pushing mile on mile among cloudy peaks;

old trees, peopleless paths,
deep mountains, somewhere a bell.

Brook voices choke over craggy boulders,
sun rays turn cold in the green pines.

At dusk by the bend of a deserted pond,
a monk in meditation, taming poison dragons.*

Wang Wei

* The poison dragons are passions and illusions that impede enlightenment. They also recall the tale of a poison dragon that lived in a lake and killed passing merchants until it was subdued by a certain Prince P'an-t'o through the use of spells. The dragon changed into a man and apologised for its evil ways.

one

'. . . No wise hermit, that recluse with shaking hands,
somehow sounding a ghost-white lute.

When he blinks, peers round, no one notices:
just the wind rustling twigs and memories . . .'

Western China. Spring, 1196.

Daughter-in-law chides me mercilessly.

'Honoured Father,' she says. 'Why do you not wear the flannel shirt I sewed for you? Did I blunt my best needle so you wouldn't wear it, heh?'

She betrays her lack of breeding through this casual 'heh', and I wonder if I chose a proper wife for my son.

'Your tender concern is a mark of true duty,' I reply. 'But Daughter-in-law's best needle rests against her teeth.'

Such ripostes keep her quiet for a while. She's working out my meaning.

'Honoured Father, you do not eat enough millet for breakfast. You will catch cold. And your bowels will suffer. Do not blame me when you run like Babbling Brook!'

'Give me the millet, woman. Don't you know it is my nature to babble like a stream?'

Eldest Son coughs. He has inherited my straight back and tallness but little else. Where my face is restless and given to many moods, his is round and bland as a full moon. He sometimes furrows his brow slightly when perturbed. Today is no exception.

'Be still, wife,' he warns, and for once she subsides.

We listen to the gibbons crying in the woods above Wei Village.

'Father, will you fish today?' he asks.

I cannot help myself.

'I've been a fisherman all my life, whether I go to Babbling Brook or not. Do you remember when I taught you *The Fisherman's Song*? You were just a boy.'

He clears his throat. He remembers. In ways I might not like.

'What news in the letter you received, Honoured Father?' demands Daughter-in-law. 'You promised to tell us.'

'Ah,' I say. 'That letter is like blossom. Who knows when it will bear fruit?'

While I scoop millet with my chopsticks I sense frustrated glances. One can be too distant.

'It is from my old friend, P'ei Ti. He promises to visit us soon.'

'Quite so,' says my son anxiously, weighing what is expected of him from such a guest.

Daughter-in-law flutters. She hates to be caught out, so I help her.

'You must set aside wine. No more is needed for old men. We like to drink and feed on our memories.'

'Just wine, heh? Is this P'ei Ti noble?'

'Of course!' rebukes my son. 'Have you not heard Father speak of him? His Excellency P'ei Ti is the Second Chancellor to the Son of Heaven. He has the ear of His Imperial Majesty!'

'Just wine,' I say, gently. 'The rest will take care of itself.'

In my heart I am less sure; and secretly ashamed of our simple life here, though I bear the title 'Lord'. So does every cock on its fence. It is no small obligation to greet a man like P'ei Ti at your door.

Our home, known locally as Three-Step-House, perches on the contours of a hill above the village. It consists of three large buildings, all of one storey, connected by brick-lined stairs cut into the hillside. The lowest building is fronted by a walled courtyard and gatehouse. The rooms are constructed of maple and pine, with red tile roofs. Terracotta lions, dragons and phoenixes decorate the eaves like guardian spirits. As a small boy I believed they came to life when I was asleep, hopping from ridge to ridge, conversing in the language of the Eight Winds.

For the next week Three-Step-House is invaded by an army of scents, marshalled by Daughter-in-law. She is preparing lucky sauces for the visit. Aniseed bears the scent of dignity; limes are tart as watchful marriage brokers, and as powerful. Daughter-in-law's angular face grows flushed as she works, determined not to be shamed. The maid and a girl from the village are her assistants.

Lame Fui, the wine-seller, delivers a dozen jars which I insist on testing for worthiness. That night I take down my lute and sing half the *Book Of Songs* before my son leads me to bed. He does not comprehend I am singing to the sickle moon, and that she doesn't care if I'm in tune. I might even labour my point in rhyme. Yet I sleep well for once, ghosts banished, and dream of nothing at all.

Waking brings a conviction that P'ei Ti will arrive today, and I tell Eldest Son. He nods gravely, then excuses himself to instruct the servants. Later he takes out his small bow and shoots fowl in the reeds around the river. Daughter-in-law anxiously watches the road climbing through Wei Village. She dresses with special care, her hair piled a foot high, held in place with combs shaped like peonies and swallows.

Even my grandsons are infected by the fever. I inflame them further by relating stories of P'ei Ti's illustriousness, and my less glorious deeds when we were young. I teach them an old song:

Yoking my chariot I'm merciless to the horse.
Ride like a prince through the streets of Lo.
In Lo Town everything pleases me!
High and low mingle like thieves.
The widest streets need lanes to join them.
How noble the houses of the royal counts!
A long feast keeps us young and thoughtless,
Casting no shadows for sorrow to haunt.

The children sing it over and over in high, excited voices. Eldest Son only dares to rebuke them when he thinks I cannot hear.

Later, my eye strays to the three bronze-bound chests I brought here when I returned in disgrace. Decades have darkened the wood. The varnish has cracked like lines on a face. I unwrap a bundle from my long, maple-wood chest and, with unsteady hands, take out my old sword. Its vermilion tassels have faded. It is too heavy for me to twirl as I once did. Gripping the hilt fills me with repugnance and a strange excitement, so I put it away, afraid of what I have become. When I look up my quiet son is watching from the doorway. I brush away tears and pretend to have rheumy eyes.

'Father,' he says, softly. 'Why not test another of Lame Fui's jars before we eat?'

A good son. I reward his thoughtfulness by reciting some of my poems. He stifles yawns behind a dragging sleeve.

A delegation approaches the gatehouse, holding their caps and muttering. I have watched them climb from the village through the morning mist, arguing all the way. Disagreeable visitors, I'm certain.

I descend reluctantly to the Middle House, sending a servant to fetch my second-best gown. I even run a comb through my thin grey hair and wispy beard. Once robed, I await the delegation, as Father received plaintiffs in his ebony chair. A tedious time. First they must get past Eldest Son, who I hear questioning them in the courtyard below. At last they are led before me.

All bow, as is fitting. I nod agreeably and clap for tea. The maids bustle away. This mark of condescension sets my visitors at ease. There is Guan the innkeeper, Li Sha who has done well for himself and leases three farms from me, Chiao Sung the blacksmith. All good men in their way. They stand uncertainly until Old Wudi, my bailiff and village headman, clears his throat. Wudi is short and round; people often remark on his resemblance to the Fat-belly Buddha.

'Lord Yun Cai,' he begins. 'We hesitate to interrupt your meditations. We would seek your advice, sir.'

I nod sagely.

'Lord Yun Cai,' continues Wudi. 'May we know if you have heard the rumours from the east?'

Li Sha interjects excitedly.

'Rebellion and civil war! It is said General An-Shu has raised an army of fifty thousand!'

Wudi calms him with a gesture. They wait impatiently for my reply.

'I have heard no talk of revolt,' I say. 'On what authority do you spread these rumours?'

'Li Sha was at Crossroad Market yesterday,' says Wudi, in his cautious way. 'He counted over a hundred people who had fled Chunming, camping by the roadside. They told him General An-Shu had fought a battle at Yunchow Ford and filled the dyke with His Imperial Highness's men. They said Chunming has fallen to the rebels. Those who refuse to kowtow to An-Shu are hung by their ankles from the city gates.'

This is grave news indeed. Chunming is only a hundred *li* from Wei. It also lies on P'ei Ti's route from the capital. I dare not imagine the consequences if he has been captured.

'An-Shu?' I say, flustered. 'Can we be sure?'

Wudi and Li Sha exchange a look. I sense irritation.

'Others have confirmed it,' says Wudi.

The tea arrives and conversation must cease. They sip from steaming bowls where they stand. At last the maid gathers empty bowls on a black lacquer tray and we begin again. The pause has given me time to compose myself.

'If General An-Shu has been victorious he will march on the capital,' I say. 'His best chance of success lies in speed. With each week that passes, His Imperial Highness will gather more troops from the frontier and prepare a counter-attack. However, if General An-Shu is defeated in battle or threatened by superior forces, he may flee back towards the mountains. Even then it is not certain he would choose to retreat through our district. We must await events.'

'What of the bandits higher up the valley?' replies Li Sha. 'A dozen deserters have joined them, demanding grain and wine from the shepherds, who have barely enough for themselves!'

'We must be calm,' I say. 'We have dealt with brigands before.'

'Lord Yun Cai will remember,' says Wudi, tactfully. 'That troops from Chunming chased off the last band of brigands. Yet all His Imperial Majesty's forces are either dead or have gone over to General An-Shu.'

'What are we to do?' demands Li Sha.

I am beginning to dislike the fellow, but that is unreasonable. Has he laboured twelve hours a day, all his life, only to be ruined by jackals? I feel helpless. All I can think about is P'ei Ti.

'I must consider,' I say. 'I will summon you when I have decided a course of action.'

The men mutter until my coldest stare reminds them of their place.

When they have gone I sit alone in the long, silent room. Rebellions are frequent in the Empire, yet this one is the closest to our remote district in over seventy years. It is my duty to ensure the villagers come to no harm: I am their Father, and must preserve even the most humble.

My own father's chair creaks as I stir. He would have known what to do. Perhaps I should invite the neighbouring lords to a banquet and suggest we raise a militia. But for over thirty years I have kept myself a stranger from my neighbours, who I find uncouth. For their part, they are mindful I live here in banishment, and avoid my bad odour.

Another fear gnaws. The last I heard, several years ago it is true, Youngest Son was rumoured to be serving in the army of General An-Shu. But of him I never think.

I sip cold tea and do nothing. Easier to feel weak and ashamed than stir. Finches quarrel in the eaves of the house. Shadows are gathering in the corners of the room.

Sunset brings rain. This is a wet region. At dawn and dusk, cloud rims glow between mountain peaks with an eerie light.

I listen to the rain as though to a great truth. It plays the earth like a festival of instruments. Drum tap on roof tiles, drip drip from twig and eave, click of tiny stick or hollow brass finger-cymbal. Day and night the river in the valley sings.

I step outside, look to the moon for comfort. How lonely she looks! Perhaps I detect my own sadness.

Far to the east, in the capital, Linan, the moon looked different when I was young. Cleaner, brighter, as I wandered the city thinking of Su Lin and her jade beauty, of the glorious man I would become. Surely I misremember. The moon looks the same everywhere, then and now.

I sigh, a little ashamed of my drunkenness when P'ei Ti might arrive at any time, possibly pursued by enemies. Yet only a little ashamed. Why should an old man be drier than racing clouds?

We have a visitor to Wei Village, and it is not P'ei Ti.

He appears at our gate around noon and sits beneath the old maple, glaring at the rain, protected by a leaky umbrella. As usual I have my chair carried out. A crowd of peasants and children gawp from a distance. Truly he is worth a stare.

Thousand-*li*-drunk is around my age but there similarities end. His face is round as a roaring lion's, tufted with huge black eyebrows and a general's bushy beard, filthy and be-draggled. The reek of wine seeps from all pores. He seems stupefied all day long, until you catch a red, sly gleam in his drunkard's eyes. No one knows his real name because he has never uttered it.

He has come early this year. Usually he passes – or rolls – through Wei Valley in the fifth month, carrying a bamboo basket with a rattling lid. He first appeared at Three-Step-House around the time I returned here from the capital, decades ago, shortly after my hasty marriage and Father's death.

Thousand-*li*-drunk's arrival provokes an uneasy holiday in the village. Within minutes a hundred people are following, whispering and pointing when they think he can't see. The village children are delighted and terrified by our visitor. They call him Thousand-*li*-drunk because it is said he has traversed the entire world seven times like an Immortal. Others claim he was once a high official in the capital and learned every secret. That is why he has taken to the roads, through pure disgust. Others say he should be whipped out of the village as a worthless beggar. Daughter-in-law is among them, though I point out all men possess a little good.

Thousand-*li*-drunk has many peculiarities and secrets. He refuses to eat any kind of grain. Instead his bamboo basket holds centipedes, spiders, and field crickets. These he impales on a cedar thorn, stripping away wings, legs, feelers, and stings, with every sign of relish. Finally he dunks them in cups of wine and swallows them whole, crunching and muttering. I once enquired about his diet and he replied that he prefers spiders because they make him feel like a high official. Crickets taste like peasants, except insects are fatter.

This year he seems out of sorts. After babbling that mountains are bones and eternity their flesh, he turns to me with a grave frown.

'I left Chunming as quick as I could. Hah! Soldiers on every street corner. Angry lice and stinging wasps. Hah! Is it not true that a certain Second Chancellor is on his way to visit you? So great a man for such a humble ant-hill!'

I am astounded, then realise he must have passed P'ei Ti's litter and escort on the road to Chunming. The man rocks on his heels, but refuses to answer my eager questions concerning P'ei Ti's safety.

'A fine lady remembers Yun Cai the poet,' he says, slyly. 'But Lord Yun Cai is so tall and handsome a gentleman! How could any lady forget him?'

Then he breaks into a song popular thirty years ago, one of my own. The way he sings is indescribable, beating out the time on his basket, more raving than music.

Avoid the reach of sharp swords,
Stay clear of tempting glances,
A sword stroke will cripple your arm,
A weak wheel breaks after ten yards,
One night of joy will scar your soul.

I become agitated and demand what he means. I have a strange thought he has been spying on me. Thousand-*li*-drunk roars with laughter, drains his cup, and swaggers away, as though he has merely passed wind at my gate.

Next year I might not be so welcoming. Having considered the matter, I believe he must have recalled my song from his youth, and poured it out. Words are how he retches. As for his reference to a lady, who is to say he was not referring to the moon? I must maintain composure.

I have convinced myself P'ei Ti will arrive today or not at all. Perhaps he caught wind of the rebellion in good time and fled back to the capital. Part of me longs to shelter him, whatever the danger. We might hide in some obscure monastery like hermits, drinking and talking of the old days until the storm passes.

I decide to walk to the lowest pasture of our winding valley. There the Western Highway passes, and I would be sure to meet him.

Daughter-in-law labours to persuade me I must travel in the family litter. I reply that an old man has earned his eccentricities. Besides, my legs, though unattractive and knobbly, are stronger than a frog's. Her concern has little to do with my health. She would consider it a great dishonour if I met our noble guest on foot, like a peasant. How little she understands men of our kind. It is true P'ei Ti always cared for display more than I, though that is another matter.

I finally agree to be escorted by my grandsons. We proceed through the village and people leave their houses to make obeisance. There are a hundred families and as many wooden houses in Wei Village, a few roofed with red tiles, most thatched with reeds. The lanes and streets are muddy at this time of year; they smell of dung, damp straw and chicken-droppings.

I instruct my grandsons to offer a present of rice to a widow. She lines up her children with their foreheads pressed to the wet ground, though I urge her to rise. Wudi rushes out of his courtyard as I pass and begs to accompany me. A refusal would humiliate him. He suggests I take a cup of wine so that his wife has time to prepare a basket of food.

'You are kind,' I say. 'But I am impatient to meet my friend. Why not send your sons after us when the basket is prepared?'

So my quiet walk turns into a procession. There's no help for it. One cannot clap with one hand. I lead, and my followers come a few yards behind, talking softly among themselves.

We pass hillsides lined with spruce and maple, dense thickets of fern. This early in the year, spring is more a promise than delight. Two troops of monkeys squabble for possession of a plum grove and we laugh at their antics. When I look back, the village is framed by mountains and peaks capped with white cloud. I gaze for a while, leaning on my stick.

Wudi's sons run up with laden baskets, panting like horses. A wry smile takes shape in my soul. I wouldn't be ashamed to meet P'ei Ti now, with grandsons and loyal servants around me. He might see I have not entirely frittered my early promise. Still I fear he might find me ridiculous, attended by bumpkins.

Disagreeable thoughts.

We reach the lowest pasture, the border of my land. Here, beside the High Road, the river forms a small lake called Mallow Flower Marsh. Wudi and his sons gather sticks for a fire to boil water and heat wine, using my excursion as a holiday. Grandsons play wrestling games and for a while I am forgotten.

I follow the lake's rim through a path lined with reeds. The earth smells of rotting things. Ripples flow toward the shore, stirring lily pads where insects flit. Turning a corner, I halt. And stare.

Deserters. Such they plainly are. Three dog-thin men crouching in a hollow by the lake, leather armour caked with mud, uniforms like tattered flags.

For a surprised moment we consider each other. My heart races. Desperate men, their hides not worth a grain of millet if caught. Hands reach for swords. Their hollow eyes strip me bare – the purse on my girdle, silk gown and boots – I might feed them for a month.

The reeds murmur and sigh in the wind. One of the deserters steps toward me, looking round nervously. Another follows. Then the third.

'Hey!' he calls. 'Old man!'

I back away.

'Don't make trouble, if you know what's good for you!'

A small stream surrounded by black, peaty earth lies between us. It might delay them for a moment, no more.

'I am not alone,' I call out. 'My friends are near.'

At this they pause, listen. I take two steps back. The leader curses, then rushes forward, his feet sinking in the bog. I wheel and stumble up the path. Hopeless flight! They are a third my age. I gain ten paces before they appear on the path behind me. Now they have sure footing and reach out their hands as they run. They do not even bother to draw their weapons. And that is what saves me.

For round a bend in the path I collide with Wudi and his sons. They clutch me as I slip in the mire, crying out fearfully. We fall silent. The deserters have stopped in confusion, a few paces away. They are outnumbered, and by burly, well-fed men. For a long moment both sides weigh their chances. It is fortunate Wudi's sons brought their staves; and the path is narrow, a bad place for swords.

The leader drags back one of his companions and runs for it. The other joins their flight. For a while we see reed heads waving, hear frantic crashing. They are gone. The lakeside resumes its calm.

All afternoon I wait anxiously for P'ei Ti, but the Western Highway remains empty. Not a single traveller passes, which is unusual even in the coldest weeks of winter. We see nothing more of the deserters. The way from Chunming is blocked. No one may reach through.

It is as though P'ei Ti has been swallowed whole. I withdraw to my room and read sheaves of poems we composed together during a hundred drinking parties, jousting with brush and ink. In this, at least, I was always victor. His faded calligraphy summons the man himself, the older brother I never had.

I read the letter announcing his visit to Wei until I know it by heart. There is no indication of his chosen route, except that he meant to travel through Chunming. That is bad enough. Worse are rumours of more fighting, a reverse for General An-Shu, who has retreated to Chunming so he may gather his forces.

I try to recall what I know of this General An-Shu. By repute, he is not a man for tepid measures. In Hunan Province he earned the title 'Butcher' An-Shu. Certainly, burying a thousand rebels alive might be viewed as an excessive punishment. And now, for all his previous zeal in the Emperor's cause, he has turned traitor. His soldiers are said to be the most disciplined in the army; such discipline stems from harsh inducements.

Where P'ei Ti might hide in such disorder, I dare not think. One thing is certain: the Son of Heaven's Second Chancellor would make a plump prize for General An-Shu, for he is familiar with His Majesty's most intimate affairs – and weaknesses. A shrewd rebel might make much of such knowledge.

Eldest Son comes to my room. He looks graver than usual, an achievement for him.

'Father, I have just returned from the village,' he says. 'Horsemen rode through this afternoon on the way to Hsia Pass. They looked like messengers.'

'Did they stop?'

'No, they rode in haste.'

'That is a pity. Did they wear the colours of General An-Shu?'

At that name, my son hesitates. His round face crinkles into an anxious frown. I know he wishes to mention Youngest Son. Inseparable as boys, he could never be angry with Little Brother, even after his disgrace. Now the troubled times offer a chance to relent. I could bend like the willows outside, but I have made my wishes plain.

'These are bad days,' I say.

He looks at me resentfully.

'What should we do?' he asks. 'Sit and wait like fattening pigs? More and more deserters have joined the bandits higher up the valley.'

'What would you have us do?'

'I do not know, Father,' he says. 'The whole family is afraid. My wife, the maids... They say soldiers looted Fouchow Village and dishonoured the headman's daughters. That is only thirty *li* away.'

Wudi won't like that last piece of news. Everyone with a position hopes it will protect them.

'A mountain lies between us and Fouchow,' I reply.

He nods and leaves. I am left helpless. It is no pleasant thing to disappoint your son. What does he expect of me? Am I some prince with an army to defend Wei Valley? It is written that the First Emperor buried a hundred thousand clay warriors in his tomb to fight again in the Immortal Land. I possess a few dozen earthenware storage jars to preserve us.

I rise at cockcrow, tired of itchy blankets. The servants are confused to see me about the kitchens so early. They bow and call out, 'Long live the lord!'

'Lord Yun Cai will protect us always!' declares the cook, no doubt intending to flatter. Perhaps he means to mock. By the look of him, half the food intended for my family reaches his belly.

His comment reveals the servants' fear. Rumours of Fouchow Village obsess them. Two hundred years ago, Wei itself was burnt by rebels and people round here forget nothing. One may still see the blackened foundation stones supporting many houses in the village.

'Continue as usual,' I say. 'All will be well.'

'What of Fouchow, Lord!' a few cry.

'A swarm of mosquitoes can sound like thunder,' I reply.

This old proverb seems to reassure them. Nervous smiles

cross many faces. Now they have brave words to trade among themselves, courtesy of authority. I turn to find my son watching, his mother's look of approval on his face. But then, she is another of whom I do not think.

I withdraw to my room and find my youngest grandson, Little Sparrow, weeping in the corridor. For a moment I recall another child, her vanished tears, jade drops of sadness. At first Little Sparrow will not explain his upset, then the words rush out: 'Middle Brother won't give me my wooden ball back! He says it's his because I lost it!'

Here is the philosophy of General An-Shu. I lay my hand on his head.

'You'll get your ball back,' I say. 'Now go and play.'

He dries his eyes and scampers away, passing from grief to elation in a moment. Not so my own feelings as I sit in my room, listening to the wind outside.

Headman Wudi arrives and we share a flask. This is a great condescension on my part.

'Lord Yun Cai,' he says, laying his hands across his Buddha's pot-belly. 'I beg to report knowledge you already possess.'

Meaning he knows something I don't.

'You are anxious concerning a high official, called P'ei Ti?' he asks, cautiously.

'Go on.'

'My wife's uncle is a fishmonger in Chunming,' he says. 'He has fled the town because of General An-Shu's rebellion. It seems the rebels expect their trout for free. He heard a rumour that a great official, called P'ei Ti, has been captured.'

I cry out, cannot stifle it. He waits silently.

'Is this true?' I ask, at last.

'It's what I heard.'

I lower my head. I know my faithful, honest P'ei Ti too well to doubt his loyalty to the Son of Heaven, and the reward he must reap for it.

Wudi hesitates.

'Are you angry with me, Lord?'

'No, no. . . You see, P'ei Ti meant to visit me. I am his host. And he is my dearest friend.'

He is uncomfortable at such frankness. From me, at least.

When he has gone I weep unashamedly. Only a brute would not understand my tears. It is hard for old men to cry, though they have more reason than the young.

All day I stare blankly at the wall. Eldest Son and Daughter-in-law flutter round me like helpless moths, attracted not to a lamp, but to my darkness. They have heard Wudi's news. Their anxiety is for themselves more than P'ei Ti, who is just a name to them. What if he tells General An-Shu of his destination in the hills? What if the General suspects our family of loyalty to the Emperor? What if he decides to make an example of us?

These fears trouble me, too. Mostly I try to convince myself P'ei Ti is still alive, a prisoner or honoured hostage. That he has escaped or persuaded General An-Shu to send him back to the capital with a message for His Majesty. Anything except the executioner's silken cord. His body flung into a ditch beneath the ramparts of dismal Chunming.

Fresh rumours have reached the village. The General is conscripting all men under forty for his depleted army. Any day now I expect soldiers and officials to arrive in Wei, seizing conscripts and animals, anything of value which might aid his cause. But the road stays empty. Our valley is remote, after all, and poor. Many of the peasants have barely enough, even during fat years. Such objections mean nothing to great men like the General or his advisers. To them we are merely ink on a map, and our feelings are stones to be trodden into the mud. We are simplified. Either useful or not useful. Our best hope is that the General decides to march south again soon, that way we might be left in peace.

Always the shadowy figure of Youngest Son haunts me, strutting among General An-Shu's regiments, perhaps thinking of us. I dare not assume his thoughts are fond.

In the hour before dusk I sit in the garden beside the highest building of Three-Step-House. My grandsons chase round ornamental rocks in the fading light, casting words and a wooden ball between them. Little Sparrow flashes me a grateful look. For a moment the vastness of the mountains reassure me, root my strength. If only I possessed the courage to act! Send a servant to Chunming, gather definite news of P'ei Ti's fate. Instead I sit with lowered head and watch the sun inch behind the peaks.

That night I dream of days when I was strong and never doubted my ability to endure, as young pines mock the fiercest winds of winter. Then the dream shifts. I see my wife's plump, reproachful face, and that of our daughter, Little Peony, and I wake to sorrow. Yet thoughts of hungry ghosts have given me an idea.

Sometimes what is obvious eludes us, whether through ignorance or neglect of truth. At last I see a way. A way which should have occurred to me earlier. It might even help P'ei Ti, if he still lives and is susceptible to good fortune.

I begin by summoning a geomancer to confirm that the day is propitious. He listens to my plan carefully, nodding approval when I voice my fears concerning unlucky orientations.

'Lord Yun Cai must proceed from west to east, not the other way around,' he concludes. 'Otherwise the spirits lack a means of escape and their fear may turn into anger.'

Wise notions I ponder for some time. I am determined to be more like Father, paying attention to every detail.

I send letters sealed five times with yellow wax to monasteries situated in a neighbouring valley; one Daoist, the other dedicated to the service of the Buddha. Letters written beneath a cloud of incense, in case demons peer over my shoulder. A small risk, given that I have warned the gate gods against intruders by whispering in their ears. I tell Eldest Son nothing of my plans. Surprise is worth an army of sorcerers in such a battle.

On the appointed day three travellers converge on Three-Step-House, each well-known to me.

Xia-Dong is a monk of thirty years standing, his organs unsullied by meat or fish of any kind, save for a fly he once swallowed accidentally. The other, Devout Lakshi, is blessed with innumerable secrets of the Dao. Nevertheless, Xia-Dong's companion astonishes me. None other than Thousand-*li*-drunk!

The learned monk informs me that, contrary to his usual custom, Thousand-*li*-drunk has spent the weeks since his visit to Wei in the monastery, from where he wanders as far as Chunming. This is a puzzle, yet in all other respects he stays true to his nature: still drunk, still dining on insects, and still unwilling to proceed further into my house than the gate. Xia-Dong assures me that his presence can only be beneficial.

'Madmen are often the incarnations of Immortals,' he advises.

Thousand-*li*-drunk watches my movements through bloodshot, cunning eyes, occasionally calling out strange riddles.

At dawn the next day I summon Eldest Son, Headman Wudi, and the rest of the household. For a moment I feel like Father, stern in his chair, quelling their murmurs with a fierce stare.

'These are bad times,' I announce. 'There is war in Chunming, and evil deeds blow across the valley like black seeds. I have decided that we must avert disaster.'

Eldest Son exchanges a glance with Daughter-in-law. For once I fear no reproach. I feel utter certitude.

Ceremoniously, like a general before the fight, I unroll a scroll prepared with the assistance of Xia-Dong and Lakshi. It sets out the position of my forces.

I read in a bold voice, so that any unseen listeners are aware of my resolve. For a moment there is a stunned silence in the room. They are unused to decisiveness on my part. Then Headman Wudi calls out: 'Long live our wise father, Lord Yun Cai!', and prostrates himself. All follow his lead. Some of the women sob with relief.

'Everything is prepared,' I say. 'Wudi, gather the village on pain of my displeasure, young and old, man and woman. The sick or menstruating must stay behind locked doors. See it is done within the hour!'

He bows his way out and rushes down the hill.

We use the hour wisely, proceeding to the ancestral shrine Father built in a grove above Three-Step-House. There I release white doves from a bamboo cage. The clattering of their wings echoes round the pine trees. Eldest Son can barely disguise his pride. My heart is glad.

When we reach the gatehouse, hundreds of the peasants await us. They roar with one voice as I arrive. In obedience to my instructions, many bear iron pots and gongs, clay drums and musical instruments. Others carry branches of willow, peach or artemisia, which they wave like swords. Eldest Son and my grandsons are armed with squares of paper bearing potent characters and spells.

We proceed on the route I have chosen. The uproar is continual. First we drive the demons and ghosts to the west of the valley, blocking their return with spells speared on twigs. The wind rises as if in approval, blowing invisible spirits before us like whirling leaves. And so through the cardinal points of north and south. At each I build a wall of sacrifice, burning incense on a brazier and pouring out sacred earth from the ancestral shrine. In the south, where Two-Face-Crag rises, Xia-Dong ladles out a jar of water while Devout Lakshi chants, transfixing sheep lungs on a stake.

I lead the procession to the village well. Here the Goddess of Wei Valley may often be glimpsed, smiling up at the villagers, especially on moon-lit nights.

By now wine flows through the crowd and jubilation is general. We march east, our final cardinal point. A frenzy of noise makes the valley echo. Peasants beat the air with branches, flattening bushes beside the road where stubborn demons lurk.

At last we reach the bend where the valley narrows between pine-clad hillsides. Monkeys scream and swing through the trees, alarmed by our approach. Meanwhile the remainder of our spells are fixed with iron nails onto the trees, effectively closing the gates on the hostile spirits who flee before us. Xia-Dong sets fire to branches of artemisia, thus satisfying the fifth element. It is done. Our valley purified. Finally, we spit prodigiously, for demons hate to be spat at.

In the strange way of crowds, we fall silent. People look around nervously. Mothers reach out for their children. A drumming of hooves approaches from the east. Cries of men in battle. I have heard that noise before, such wild shouts, long ago when I was young. Dread fills me.

'Wudi!' I bellow. 'Order the people into the trees! Quickly, to the trees!'

He hesitates for breath only.

'Follow Lord Yun Cai! To the trees! Leave the road! To the trees!'

Panic flutters through the crowd. We become a mass of elbows, heels, jostling bodies. The drumming of hooves grows louder. Before half the people have left the road, horsemen appear round the bend in the valley, whipping their mounts.

A dozen armoured cavalry wearing sky-blue cloaks, the emperor's colour, thunder through us. Dust and neighing fills the air, cries of children. Behind them come a larger group of horsemen on shaggy ponies. They bend bows and release a hail of arrows.

Screams amongst the scrambling villagers. One man falls, an arrow piercing his throat. Our crowd throws the pursuing archers into disorder. Horses rear and collide in confusion, rallying round a flag bearing General An-Shu's symbol. Though I protest that we should help the wounded, Eldest Son drags me away from the road, up the hillside, our silk robes tearing on thorns and brambles. I catch a glimpse of the mounted archers through the trees, milling in the road below. I know their kind from my youth. Barbarians, mercenaries from the steppes. They wheel and gallop back the way they came.

I have failed. My attempt to purify the village an utter misfortune.

Three children trampled by the mounted bowmen loyal to General An-Shu, and two peasants killed by their arrows. One of them was Wudi's middle son. A boy who grew to manhood alongside my own. His loss pierces my heart.

Worse must surely follow. The mounted bowmen abandoned their pursuit of the Imperial cavalry, perhaps believing the village ahead was hostile, and turned back to Chunming. If they tell General An-Shu that Wei is in revolt against his rule, we can expect swift reprisals. Of the Imperial cavalry, there is no news. They galloped further up the valley and disappeared, their presence a mystery in itself.

From my room I hear faint cries and wailing in the village below. Perhaps the villagers hate me for my failure. Xia-Dong and Devout Lakshi made off as soon as General An-Shu's horsemen fled. No one speaks to me or meets my eye. Oddly, only Thousand-*li*-drunk decides to stay, and goes so far as to beg an audience outside the gatehouse.

'Lord Yun Cai should be happy!' he cries, in his deranged way. 'All the demons have left the valley. The ceremony was a complete success!'

I regard him angrily. Is he mocking me? He winks.

'Thousand-*li*-drunk knows more than you!' he cries. 'Lord Yun Cai will be glad of saving a certain officer's life. All the demons are gone. Look around, can you see any? Ha! That is why Thousand-*li*-drunk is so happy!'

'What is your real name?' I demand. 'Stop your games!'

'Ah, no more games.'

His glee hardens into a sly smile.

'General An-Shu will never become the Son of Heaven,' he says, suddenly sober. 'The people have not turned against the Emperor. The Mandate of Heaven has not been withdrawn from His Imperial Majesty. Remember that, in your dealings with the cavalry who escaped.'

'Who *are* you?'

Taking a grasshopper from his basket, he pops it into his mouth and slowly chews. Gathering his small bundle, he wanders off without another word.

The wine-coloured light of dawn seeps through the shutters and paper curtains. My head spins from all I have drunk. Over half the jar still undrained. Yesterday seems far away – the horsemen and their cries, hooves sparking on the flinty high road, Wudi's middle son falling, a feathered shaft protruding from his throat.

I fumble into my outer garments and listen at the chamber door. No one hovering for a change, not even Daughter-in-law. I hide the wine jar behind a painted screen, in case someone punishes me by removing it.

The short corridor to the back entrance is deserted. I hear arguing and urgent voices elsewhere in the house, but these fade as I slip the latch and step outside, hurrying along a path bordered by stands of sprouting bamboo.

The path winds up towards our ancestral shrine, yet I will not go there. The dead stare as well as the living. Instead I follow a trail leading further up the valley, resolutely keeping my back to Three-Step-House and the village below. If I do not look they may as well not exist, for a moment, for eternity, such distinctions a dream. The path climbs round huge, lolling boulders whiskered with lichen, then crosses a stream over mossy planks.

I pause, soothed by the trickling water as it runs over stones and trailing ferns. When I scoop a handful, it tastes cold, flavoured with peat.

Further down the hillside, the path meets the road. Pines surround the highway, steep grassy banks. Here I sit to regain my breath, and fall into a pleasant doze, the wine swirling back to the top of my head. At once I enter a hazy dream and hear songs in the trees, the rustle of feet, whispered voices, distant and indistinct. To wake now is a great labour, yet I cannot help myself. My head jerks up. I look around. The road is no longer deserted.

I am surrounded by half a dozen villagers, talking in low voices. For a moment I blink, taking in details – a wheelbarrow, bundles on backs, frightened eyes. Then my gaze settles on a familiar face, one I least want to see in my bedraggled, sottish state.

'Ah, Wudi,' I say, and can think of nothing more.

He looks a long, scornful glance. His weathered face is set in a scowl of grief. The people round him include his wife and two granddaughters.

'I am sorry about your son, Wudi,' I say, with an effort. The slur in my voice shames me. 'Very sorry!'

Yet he does not even acknowledge my words. Turning to his family, he orders them on. They toil up the road, burdened by baggage and belongings, until out of sight. A desire to chase after him, beg forgiveness for not averting his loss, almost propels me to my feet. But I am too tired. And I do not blame him. He has every reason not to acknowledge me. Just as a bad emperor may lose the Mandate of Heaven through fecklessness, so may an inept lord lose the respect of those he has been set above.

A weary walk back to Three-Step-House. All the freshness and splendour of the morning has gone, trees and stones somehow lifeless.

At the gatehouse I find Eldest Son talking to men from the village. He frowns as I approach and I notice he does not bow. The villagers examine us both curiously.

'Do not stand and stare,' he barks at them. 'Go and keep watch on the road. At the first sign of travellers, send a runner to me.'

They leave us alone by the gate gods, and Eldest Son's face sags. I suspect he has had less sleep than me.

'Father, where have you been?' he scolds. 'The valley is full of brigands. And what about the horsemen who rode through yesterday? It is not safe. Where would we be if you were captured?'

Better off, I think.

'I met Wudi,' I say, sadly.

'Yes, he is taking his wife and granddaughters to a relative in Crow Hamlet. They will be safer there and he has promised to return by nightfall.'

'Wudi would not speak to me. I have known Wudi all my life. Yet he would not speak to me.'

'You must make allowances, Father. His son. . . I do not understand why our ceremony went so wrong! We have offended the Gods!' he cries, bitterly. 'They are ungrateful! We sacrifice to them with all propriety. What more do they want?'

'Hush,' I say. 'Lest they hear.'

'What are we to do, Father?'

There is something pitiful about his tone, as though he has never quite become a man. Am I to blame for that? I realise how hard he finds our present danger. He needs guidance, reassurance. I repress a desire to trail wearily back to my room.

'Should we send the children to one of the monasteries?' he asks. 'And our valuable clothes, the little chest of *cash*? They might be safe there.'

'We may need the money and cloth for bribes,' I say.

'Should we all go to the monastery, Father?'

'If the Lord flees, so will half the village,' I say. 'Your

Grandfather would know exactly what to do. . . Perhaps if we made a sacrifice at the Ancestral Shrine.'

'There is no time!' cries Eldest Son. 'The barbarian horsemen will be telling their tale in Chunming by now. They will burn our house to the ground! How long will it take for them to send troops here?'

'I don't know.'

'Should we all go to the monastery?' he demands again.

'It might be safer. But the village needs us. If we fail in this duty, we will forfeit all respect. Send only your sons, only them. They are children, after all. Besides, the headman has done as much. The rest of us must stay.'

'But my wife is with child!' he says, desperately.

This surprises me. I'm told less than half of what happens in Three-Step-House. I should feel happy at her fecundity. Yet good fortune can be a curse in times like these. So I say: 'That is good news. Yes, send her with the boys. We can pretend her pregnancy is more advanced than it is. . .'

I struggle to recollect something important. Thousand-*li*-drunk spoke of the Imperial cavalry who galloped through in their sky-blue cloaks, pursued by General An-Shu's men.

'What of the Emperor's horsemen?' I ask.

Eldest Son waves an impatient hand.

'They have been seen loitering further up the valley. It is typical of our misfortune! For some reason they wish to plague us.'

Again I recall Thousand-*li*-drunk's words. For all his air of mystery, he seemed certain the horsemen were to our benefit. Eldest Son interrupts my thought.

'You must go to the monastery as well, Father,' he says.

I peer at him. To go would be to resign the burden of my position as Family Head. I could drink wine and write poems all day with learned monks for company. A tempting prospect. But I have not sunk so far. Not quite.

'Do as I have said,' I mutter. 'Now I must go to my room to think. Have some food brought.'

'Father! Do you intend to get drunk?'

'What if I do?'

For a moment he blocks my way, bristling, then subsides. He bows. I sense that, however much I annoy him, he is relieved I am not deserting him for the monastery.

'Forgive me, Father.'

'Do as I say. That is enough.'

I stumble up to the topmost house and my room. At least the wine jar is where I hid it, and apparently undiminished, though it looks as though someone has been poking around. I dip the ladle and pour myself a cup, then raise it to my lips with two shaking hands. It does not taste so sweet as it did last night. Proof, perhaps, I have not had enough.

Tentative taps on the door. I start up, peer round. The taps become firm knocks, at once revealing my visitor. Everyone can be recognised by small signs, as one knows a friend in the distance by his walk.

'Enter!' I croak.

Daughter-in-law's head appears round the lintel. She wears no make-up, surely a sign of something. I motion her in. She adjusts her silken dress and cape; then, to my surprise, gets on her knees before me, paying homage. I blink suspiciously.

'Do I disturb Honoured Father's rest?' she says, for once not fixing me with her blackbird's eye. She seems almost afraid. Evidently I am to be spared advice concerning my most intimate ailments.

'Well, Daughter-in-law?' I say.

Her eyes remain fixed on the ground.

'I have come to say farewell, Honoured Father,' she says, sniffily. 'And to ask for your blessing.'

Then I remember. She and the grandchildren are to find

refuge in the monastery near Whale Rocks. At such a time I should give appropriate advice.

'You will be accompanied by some stout fellows,' I say. 'There is little danger. But you must leave as soon as possible. And obey the monks in everything. Remember you are their guest.'

It is the best I can manage.

'Why can't my husband guard me and the children on the road?' she asks.

'He is needed here,' I say.

She does not move to go.

'Are you displeased with me Honoured Father?' she asks.

'In what way?'

'You are sending me away.'

Now I see her anxiety. One of the five grounds for divorce, and the most common, is offending one's parents-in-law.

'No, foolish girl, it is not that. These are dangerous times. You are aware of our situation. I want you and the grand-children to be safe, that is all.'

Still she does obeisance. I grow uncomfortable.

'Something else is troubling you?'

'Yes, Honoured Father. It's someone I'm forbidden to mention.'

I can guess who.

'Yes?'

'My husband's brother. . .' she says.

'What of him?' I snap.

Then the dam holding back her tongue gives way.

'Old Mother Orchid in the village has heard through her niece that Youngest Son is a Captain serving General An-Shu. And *she* heard it through her second cousin who saw him parading in Chunming. They say he is a big man now and. . .'

'What's that to me?' I interrupt.

'He orders hundreds of soldiers about in Chunming and wears a fine uniform. And he has the General's ear. I heard he has been granted a house larger than our own, with a garden and a staff of servants, as well as. . .'

'Enough, woman! Again, I say, what is that to me? You know he is no longer my son. We have a document from the Prefect to prove it. Enough on this matter.'

Of course, she is right to worry. A roll of paper can be crumpled in a moment, an edict overturned by a whim. Her fear is simple. At present Eldest Son will inherit my estate in full. A special dispensation granted by the Prefect of Chunming has set aside the law stating property must be divided equally among all male children. Yet the Prefect of Chunming is currently hanging by his heels from the city walls, his eyes food for crows. He was a good man, in his way, and of respectable family.

'Honoured Father is always right,' she says. 'Still anyone can fret in times like these. I have to think of my sons, your grandchildren. What of them, heh?'

Her natural manner has returned. It comes as a kind of relief.

'I am not an astrologer. Anything could happen.'

'But we all remember Youngest Son from when he was a boy,' she continues. 'He has a temper like a bad dog. What if he gets it in that stubborn head of his, that he has been wronged? It's enough to make me tremble!'

She seems more outraged than terrified.

'And no one in the village wants such a hot-headed man as Lord. No one likes a beating. And the maidservants are frightened. Who can blame them? It's a disgrace!'

She is alluding to the reason I disinherited him. I might reply that people change. It is my dearest wish he has changed. Yet serving General An-Shu is unlikely to soften a man. I could tell her not a single day has passed without me missing him, that when I sent him away, half my heart departed.

'You should leave for the monastery now,' I say, wearily. 'And have faith in me. Did not the Emperor Wang Meng order his own son to commit suicide for mistreating a servant?'

'Eh?' she cries. 'Suicide? What's that got to do with us?'

'Concern yourself with women's business,' I chide. 'Be at the gates in ten minutes.'

She shuffles to her feet reluctantly, but remembers to bow on her way out.

Half an hour later I stand by the gatehouse with Eldest Son. She is escorted by a dozen retainers, including her serving women. If the brigands meet her party, what will they do? Rob her, for sure, perhaps rape the women. It is a risk forced upon us. The children cry to leave their home. All in all, a pitiful scene. I pretend not to notice the tears in Eldest Son's eyes.

'We have done what we can,' I say. 'The monks will send word she has arrived safely.'

He is desolate. It is not good for the peasants to see him like this. There is danger in growing too reliant upon one's wife.

'Have the watchmen reported any sign of troops?'

'Nothing, Father.'

'Then they will not arrive today. Perhaps we should expect them tomorrow. Order new watchers so the others may rest.'

I return to my chamber and what's left of the wine jar. Swallows flit around the eaves of Three-Step-House just as when I was a happy boy. I could be that boy again in a moment, if his heart had not flown away, season after season.

I wake at sunrise with my own words echoing from a dream: *Bring relief to those so sorely pinched*. I said them once, when I was young and earnest. At once I sense a bad day brewing. I have always been sensitive to energies patterning around me. Today, I am sure the soldiers will come.

When I appear in the hall Eldest Son is taking breakfast.

'Father!' he cries. 'You look. . .'

Indeed I do. For the first time since his wedding I wear the uniform of a man on the Emperor's Golden List, the vermilion girdle and tortoise-shell chest plate, the hat of black silk hung with four jade pendants. My cheeks are shaven and flecked with blood from the razor. On my feet, high-soled shoes, curling at the front. I am gratified by the impression my uniform makes. This bodes well. The outward and the inward in harmony with each other.

'Does Honoured Father require me to send for wine?' he asks, timidly.

Perhaps he thinks I have dressed so splendidly in a drunken humour. His offer is certainly tempting.

'No, send for the headman and command the servants to prepare a fine breakfast.'

I sit on Father's chair, hands tucked in my sleeves.

Half an hour later, Wudi arrives. He is as surprised as my son to see me. For a moment his resentful stare softens, but only for a moment.

'Ah, Wudi. Be seated.'

He obediently takes his place on the mat. Eldest Son hovers uncertainly beside him.

'I have concluded,' I say. 'That the troops we expect may arrive today.'

They watch me through narrowed eyes. I hate my confusion. Wine might make me bold, but if I started, who knows when I would stop?

'Are the watchmen at the head of the valley as I directed?' I demand.

Wudi nods.

'They understand their orders?'

'Yes, Lord,' he intones.

'Good. I have commanded that an awning be placed near the entrance to the village square. That way I shall be the first the soldiers meet. Then I shall welcome their officers.'

They watch me sullenly.

'Ensure the chair I am sitting on is taken down to the awning,' I say. 'Tell Lame Fui to set aside five jars and a dozen decent cups. Tell him I will pay.'

I turn to Eldest Son.

'You shall remain in Three-Step-House. At the first sign of fighting, you are to leave the valley and join your wife. I say this before Wudi, as my witness. It is my command. You are my sole heir and your safety is worth more to me than senseless heroics. Is that understood?'

'Yes, Father.'

I can sense them both quickening. For all my anxiety, I feel a flush of excitement.

'Wudi,' I continue. 'There is another matter on which I have given much thought.'

He stiffens.

'I refer to the loss of your son. Whatever happens I am determined he shall be remembered well. For that reason I have decided you should be allowed to construct a small family shrine on the outer perimeter of our ancestral shrine. Let your son's bones be placed within sight of my own, and my father's. By this means his soul shall mingle with his betters.'

Wudi looks at me calculatingly.

'Does Lord Yun Cai mean within the perimeter or outside its limits?' he asks.

'I mean, separate but adjoining. An intelligent man like you is well aware of the significance of this.'

A look of puzzled satisfaction crosses his weather-beaten face. He bows deeply.

'My son's spirit will rejoice to hear these words,' he says. 'We are honoured.'

So his family should be. One could imagine marriage growing from such proximity. Certainly he owns enough land to make his granddaughters worthy of my youngest grandson. In addition, Wudi possesses several farms in unexpected places, all of them fertile, as well as a watermill and tannery.

'First we must survive the coming days and weeks,' I say, lest his imagination run away with him. We have a saying in Wei: a dream at morning is forgotten by evening.

'Wudi, instruct the people to go about their business as usual.

And Eldest Son, draw up an inventory of grain supplies in the village and their value, in case we need to bribe the soldiers. Now I must descend to the village square. Only Wudi shall accompany me.'

So I take my place beneath the awning. Children and women gawp at me until I glare at them angrily. Flies buzz round the jade pendants hanging from strings on my hat. My silk robes are hot and uncomfortable. Indeed, they smell of mould. There is no help for that. The morning passes pleasantly enough. I read the poems of Po Chu-i to remind myself of a just man's courage. His voice strengthens my own. Eventually I fall into a doze.

By midday, still no sign of General An-Shu's men. A few of the village dogs adopt me, attracted by my lunch, which I share with them. I ask Wudi to send scouts to find out where the Imperial cavalry who rode through the village yesterday are hiding. Such information might give me power, and even avert a massacre. Women dragged from the houses, held down while raped. Man after man executed, the most senior first. Every store broken open, carried off by competing platoons. And the peasants beaten or simply stabbed should they protest. Finally, the smell of burning, smoke billowing up the valley, while drunken soldiers cheer. I saw such things in my youth. They are not unusual. They flow from war like dung from a sewer.

The sun reaches its zenith and I order cup after cup of tea, every sip scrutinised by the peasants.

An hour later, my test begins. One of the watchers runs into the village.

'Lord Yun Cai!' he cries. 'They are coming!'

'How many?'

He spreads out his hands in a gesture which means more than he could count. So we are taken seriously by General An-Shu. This is worse than I expected.

'How many are there?' I repeat.

He looks behind him nervously.

'They are coming,' he says, once more.

'Wudi!' I bellow.

The headman trots over from the well, where he was bathing his head with a bucket of water.

'Instruct everyone to remain in their houses, as should you.'

He dries his face on his sleeve.

'Perhaps I'll stand behind you,' he says. 'It won't look so good if you're by yourself.'

He's right, of course. And I'm grateful for his loyalty. Already in the distance I can hear the beat of drums, cries of command.

'This is not hunting crickets, Wudi,' I say.

He looks at me and grins, as he did when we were boys.

'My Lord is himself again,' he says.

That is when I grow afraid. For I know it is my destiny to disappoint him, and all who trust me. The marching feet grow louder. An officer shouts unintelligibly. Finally a column of men, five across, enters the village square. Their armour is burnished leather and they bear sword and halberd. These are not the rabble I expected, but superior, well-drilled troops. For a long moment everyone in the square stands still, assessing one another. I hear more tramping feet and the gallop of horses.

An officer on a fine, white charger rides into the square, his horse prancing. He is followed by a dozen cavalry bearing flags and drums, long lances tipped with pennants.

I peer short-sightedly. The heat haze blinds my old eyes. Horsemen trot toward me and I rise, puffing out my chest.

The captain's helmet is crowned by a jaunty red plume. Bronze armour covers the horse's head and flanks. Iron discs sewn upon the captain's blue leather coat glitter like angry eyes. His cloak is blood red. At his side a sword and bow. In his right hand, a double-pronged lance, trailing scarlet and yellow ribbons.

A dozen feet from me he reins in his horse. The beast snorts. My eyes are fixed on its rider's face, one whose changes I charted from birth. My soul lurches. Youngest Son.

two

‘. . . War’s infection spreads from the borders:
this year, last year, next – honoured rites of slaughter.

The phoenix flutters gaudy wings of sorrow.
When war is the plough, crops of bone must follow. . .’

Momentary balance, like a huge standing rock, its support of earth and shale eroded by seasons of rain. It could fall in any direction, crushing the unwary, or merely roll down the hillside to settle with a crash, throwing up clouds of dust. So it is in the village square. The rock of war could fall any way.

Youngest Son’s face! I cannot help staring. I recognise the colour of those eyes, his grandfather’s eyes, but not the haughty, military way he narrows his eyelids as though perpetually angry. That is something he has learnt from others. I know the shape of his cheeks, not the scar disfiguring one side, the battle which gave it birth. He is familiar, and undiscovered.

He sits on his white charger, still as a statue. I watch him, frozen by conflicting emotions. We share one thing, at least.

In all the years of his boyhood, neither of us anticipated this.

My glance passes to the soldiers rapidly filling the square. A desperate lot, and hungry by the look of them, their uniforms faded and tattered. Veterans ready for anything, looking no further than the next fight or meal. I pray they are still capable of discipline.

I turn my attention back to Youngest Son. He has followed my examination of his men, and perhaps reads my thought. He appears confused and resentful at the same time. His horse whinnies impatiently. It is thirsty and smells the water in the well. I wait, hoping my cap with its jade pendants sits straight on my head.

A flicker of vexation on his face. At last he seems about to speak. The officers around him are exchanging glances. I sense the fate of the whole village depends on his first words, for if he willed it, a general massacre would begin.

Then I realise he has no idea how to act, that my presence in the village square, especially dressed in the trappings of the Golden List, has surprised him. Oh, I have seen that expression before! I remember how he played as a boy, always leading the other children, his authority inexplicable to his elders, bubbling up as if from a hot spring. Yet sometimes I noticed the same doubt on his face. The secret doubt of all who strive for control.

Memories of him gather, pinpoints of reflected light on a lake in summer. His mother passing him to me, a tiny, red wrinkled thing, both of us joyful she had survived a difficult labour. Later, a boy wrapped in the folds of my clothes against winter draughts, while I told tales of Grandfather's brave deeds. His little face revealing tangled thoughts and desires – to be worthy of such an ancestor, to be important as any hero, and loved by me, how he longed for that. It touched my heart like a kind of grief. And then admonishing him when he bullied his older brother, his attitude of contrition belied by a curling lip, coldness of eye. Or flying a kite from Wobbly Watchtower Rock while I composed verses, crying out 'See, Father! See! Look at me, Father!', and my irritation at being interrupted, so the right word slipped away like an eel. Teenage years when the troubles began. My anger at the sloppy, careless way he composed his characters. Every smudge of ink seemed ingratitude and defiance. Anger at so many things.

Now, in the village square, neither of us bend. I place my hands in my sleeves, a casual gesture, and entirely deliberate, emphasising my uniform and status, that I represent a higher authority, while he is a mere soldier. Everyone knows no decent man becomes a soldier. It is a risk I must take, or choose to grovel before their gaudy flags, the dense, sweating weight of them. The officers around Youngest Son murmur angrily. He must do something now, or lose face before his men.

Still he hesitates.

Perhaps he remembers our last meeting. Perhaps that is what makes him pause. A hot night. Monsoon weather, the sky a lake of rain. He was on his knees then, full of excuses. I merely said, 'Because you are my son I will disgrace myself, and abandon all the principles I hold dear. Be content with that.' The next day he left for the Military Academy and I journeyed to the Prefect of Chunming to ensure he would never become Lord of Wei. Did that make me complicit in his crime? Certainly I have spent many hours of doubt. Even now I have no clear answer. But I wept until dawn on the night he left, and locked myself in my room for days.

Youngest Son is moving. As though dragged against his will, he climbs stiffly from his horse. A groom rushes forward to seize the bridle. Everyone in the square is alert. He brushes the dust from his clothes, then steps towards me. Now is the test. I sense Wudi shifting behind me. My breath catches.

Youngest Son lowers himself stiffly, first one leg, then both, until he is on his knees, paying homage to his father, as is only natural and fitting. Yet it is a feeble homage, as all must observe, for he does not bow, his back straight as a rampart. It is enough. For now the village is safe. I risk a glance at his men. They have visibly relaxed, and some dare to yawn. Perhaps they are disappointed. But their captain honouring his father changes them from conquerors to guests.

'Father,' he says. 'I have returned.'

'Youngest Son, are you thirsty?'

He nods. There are tears in his eyes, for I have acknowledged him as my child.

'Wudi,' I say, gently.

He knows what to do. Pouring out a cup of wine, he advances, and offers it.

Youngest Son gulps it in one. Emotion makes it hard for him to swallow.

'Ah!' he says, at last grinning his old, mischievous grin. 'Ah! I was thirsty, Father.'

'Then take another cup,' I say.

He drinks this solemnly.

'Are your officers dry?' I ask.

As far as I can judge, they seem a rough pair. One of them has the extravagant, bushy beard of a vain man. The other makes no effort to hide a sneer which, I suspect, is habitual.

'Yes, Father.'

'Let them drink, too.'

At this Youngest Son bridles. I must take care with him.

'If that is your will,' I add.

The two officers dismount and Wudi brings their wine. We stand awkwardly together. The officers bow in a perfunctory way. A breeze is picking up in Wei Valley, making the awning flap. The leaves of the mulberry trees shimmer and murmur. Birds twitter and sing.

The wine has refreshed Youngest Son in more ways than one. His bearing carries authority. He strokes his fine, curling sideburns and beard in a way designed to draw attention. Yet I am not a susceptible lady. To me, his whiskers seem absurd and common, far from the clean-shaven dignity of an examined scholar.

'You are evidently here on an important mission,' I say. 'If it is within your discretion, perhaps you could share its purpose with me, so I may be of assistance.'

Youngest Son raises an eyebrow. I can read his thought. *Father still speaks in the same flowery, annoying way.*

'I have been sent by His Highness to hunt rebels. That is all you need to know, Father.'

His Highness! General An-Shu is aiming higher than I expected. I refrain from correcting his confusion of titles.

'Ah,' I say.

The soldiers in the square are looking round. It takes no great wisdom to guess their thoughts.

'I have here an inventory of all the available grain in the village,' I say. 'Naturally, we expect your men will require feeding.'

One of the officers snorts. Youngest Son quells him with a glance.

'We shall only take what is needed,' he announces in a loud voice. 'Any who transgress this shall answer to me. General An-Shu protects the welfare of all obedient subjects.'

Subjects now! So the peasants are to be robbed of their food. Even Youngest Son looks uncomfortable. After all, he knows half the villagers by name, and is aware of their poverty. There's no helping it, for either of us.

'The General's kindness is well-known,' I say. 'We are grateful.'

Youngest Son is beginning to flush round the cheeks, always a dangerous sign with him. I have extracted what promises I can.

'Father should retire to Three-Step-House,' says Youngest Son. 'He will understand I must arrange bivouacs for my men.'

I nod.

'Perhaps Honoured Father needs a jar of wine after his exertions?' he asks, smiling slyly. 'I'm sure he does.'

Already the boy grows impudent. His officers chuckle,

indicating that words have passed concerning my weakness.

'Naturally, you shall join us to dine?' I enquire. 'You and your esteemed officers.'

He grunts, barely able to hide his satisfaction. I have traded my renunciation of him for the village's safety.

I leave the square, accompanied by Wudi, who carries my scrolls of Po Chu'i's poems and parasol. As we shuffle up the hill, I turn. Soldiers are scattering round the streets and lanes of the village, seeking the fattest billets. Youngest Son lolls like a lord in Father's ebony chair, *my* chair. Though I cannot see his expression, there is exhilaration and pride in the way he grasps the chair's arms, surveying his men as they scurry like ants. Anger is an emotion I can ill afford.

'Did it go well, Wudi?' I ask.

He scratches his chin.

'No one's drawn a sword yet,' he says. 'Not yet.'

He is right. I have bought only a little time.

'Did you discover where the Imperial cavalry are hiding?' I whisper, though there is no one to hear us except the crickets.

'In the side valley beyond Shady Wood,' he says, quietly.

'A good place. They are clearly well-led. But Youngest Son will be aware of it. General An-Shu must want these men badly. He has sent an officer who knows the district and at least two companies of his best men. Why are the Imperial cavalry so important to him? I still do not see why they came to Wei at all.'

Wudi shrugs, as if to say, *If you don't know, how should I?*

'Wudi,' I say. 'Are you prepared to risk another son?'

'I only have two left,' he says, dryly.

'If you are, send one of them to warn the cavalry. Tell them they should hide their traces and let their horses loose. Tell them to conceal themselves in the caves behind Heron Waterfall and not to come out under any circumstances, until they are told it is safe. Your son must show them the little entrance. The caves were discovered after Youngest Son's banishment, so he will not search there.'

Wudi scowls.

'Is it wise to get involved, Lord?'

'I believe so, in the long term.'

'It shall be done as you wish,' he says, reluctantly.

By the Goddess of Wei Valley, I hope I act wisely. Certainly she must be angered to have her wells and streams polluted by such a rabble. Yet my actions, perilous to everyone around me, are based on the words of Thousand-*li*-drunk, a notorious madman: *General An-Shu will never become the Son of Heaven. Remember that in your dealings with the cavalry who escaped.* Yet stranger changes of dynasty have occurred.

If my judgement is right, then my son, for all his fine uniform and whiskers, is to be pitied. If I am wrong, he is to be pitied a hundred times more.

As I enter the gate of Three-Step House, a solitary scream rises from the village below.

Three-Step-House is subdued. Even the sounds of chopping from the kitchen lack their usual vigour. The maidservants who did not accompany Daughter-in-law to Whale Rocks Monastery go about their work as if they have already been dishonoured, unmarriageable without a huge dowry to tempt future parents-in-law.

Eldest Son comes to my room. At once it is clear he has been drinking. Well, we are all acting out of character. If I'm sober, why shouldn't he be drunk? Perhaps wine might discover hidden courage in him. Yet I am ashamed for him. Some are fired by wine, others made ignoble.

'Did you see him, Father?' he asks, miserably. 'What did he say?'

'Only that he is hunting rebels and deserters.'

'Did he mention me, Father?'

'No. You must be calm! Drink as much water as possible and sleep for an hour. All will be well if you follow my instructions.'

He wrings his hands. A pitiful sight. And worrying.

'He's angry with me,' he says. 'Though it is not I who took away his inheritance.'

I realise then, he is not to be relied upon. His brother always had too much influence over him. Above all, Eldest Son must not hear of my dealings with the Imperial cavalry. I must remember to warn Wudi of this.

'He is not even angry with *me*,' I protest, gently. 'So this is my advice. Act like a simple-minded country lord's son. Talk only of the harvest and how lazy the peasants are and your favourite places to fish. Let his officers make fun of you as a simple type, and if they laugh at your expense, laugh with them. Above all, keep Youngest Son talking about himself without offering any opinions of your own.'

Eldest Son blinks at me stupidly. Will he recall any of this when it matters?

'Remember, our best defence lies in being agreeable,' I add. 'Personally, I am prepared to act the fool if it keeps us safe. You should do the same.'

He giggles hysterically.

'Everyone likes to feel superior,' I say. 'Why shouldn't we bumpkins oblige?'

'Father is wise,' he mumbles, though he doesn't sound sure.

'Go to your room,' I say. 'Remember you are my heir. And no more wine!'

'Yes,' he says. 'Thank you, Father.'

I'm left to examine shadows in the room. Finally, I take my own advice and lie down on the couch. Images of angry faces and Eldest Son's panic shimmer across my mind. But I am old and cannot help dozing, exhausted by my trial with Youngest Son. I listen to a cricket chirping insistently outside. A thin, clear, rhythmic sound. Then the past awakens, half-dream, half-memory. They say an old man's past is more real than his present. If the Lord Buddha is to be believed, both are illusions.

The cricket's chirp opens the door to this house, as it was, when I was a boy.

At that age I had many interests, but my great passion was crickets. The noble art of cricket-fighting was revered just as highly in our village as in the capital. Though I could not have guessed it then, those restless insects set in motion my long journey to the Imperial examinations – and all the fear and exhilaration which later haunted my ambitions.

Three-Step-House nourished many kinds of cricket, as a city sustains all sorts of people. I recall a sunny morning in the seventh or eighth month. Waking soon after dawn to birdsong and the chirrup of insects. My tiny bedroom lay in the corner of the highest building. Its window faced mountains capped with snow even in summer. A stand of bamboo nestled in the terraced field at the side of the house. I heard servants chattering in the courtyard below and cockerels crowing up and down the valley. Sweet scents in the air: dew drying, wood smoke, the summer pungency of plants.

I dressed quickly and padded down the central corridor, eyes and ears sharp for the slightest rustle of papery wings. By the front entrance I found Little Wudi, the bailiff's son, waiting for our daily hunt. In his hands a clay pot with a wooden lid and rope handle.

We skipped down the brick-lined stairs to the lowest building, for it was there we always began. The kitchen maids bowed, but I ignored them, my business more pressing than a palace eunuch's. At the faintest chirp or click we froze, searching like famished cats after mice.

In the courtyard dwelt a type of cricket which, though unattractive, was dogged and resilient. Because it fed upon household waste and chicken droppings it was often mean-spirited. The villagers called this plain, ordinary type Straight-Backbone-Wings.

Then Little Wudi and I made our way to the pigsty. It was built, as in most houses, beneath the privy so the pigs might benefit from their masters' waste. I was afraid of the pigsty, though I tried hard not to let Little Wudi see, on account of a story Mother had told me about the First Wife of the Emperor Goazu.

Empress Lu struggled for many years with her husband's favourite concubine, Lady Qi. Both women wished to have their sons proclaimed heir to the throne and for a long time the succession hung in the balance. Then came Goazu's sudden death – some whispered his First Wife had a hand in it – and Empress Lu's son ascended to the Heavenly Throne. At once the Empress poisoned Lady Qi's children and any other girl Goazu had favoured. She ordered the dismemberment of Lady Qi's hands and feet, gouged out her eyes, scorched her ears with red-hot tongs and crushed her tongue so that her old rival could only grunt. Then Lady Qi, once so exquisite, was thrown into the pigsty beneath the Imperial privy. The entire court was encouraged to demonstrate their loyalty by defecating on the half-mad woman crawling among the pigs. Empress Lu even invited ambassadors to view 'the human pig', as she named Lady Qi.

This story taught me bad dreams, and each time I visited the privy I peered nervously through the hole for Lady Qi.

Nevertheless the privy was home to a kind of cricket whose piercing chirps were like mournful gongs on a foggy evening, echoing from afar. One could only listen in wonder.

Leaving the courtyard, we climbed back to the Middle House. Here Mother and my sisters were already at work, embroidering gowns and coats so we might appear finer than our neighbours. A long, clean room where they laboured in silence, save for murmured instructions or rebukes. When I arrived

Mother would brighten. She always favoured me over my two sisters, who were older and on the cusp of marriage. That was natural. There's a saying in Wei: one son worth a dozen daughters. Unless, of course, your son turns out to be a feckless, disobedient wastrel.

Mother summoned me to the stool where she worked, brocade spread across her knees, and stroked the small tuft at the top of my shaven head. 'Did you sleep well?' 'Have the servants laid out a proper breakfast?' 'How much did you eat?' I was too impatient to answer, my business too important. At last she released me with a sigh.

Little Wudi and I scampered to the store chambers at the side of Middle House. Here might be found a white, bloodless kind of cricket living in the dark spaces beneath the eaves, known as Pale-Fragrant-Forehead, on account of its clammy body. A morose creature, it seemed too gentle to make a good fighter, but as they say, beware silent ones. I saw it leap upon green field crickets and crush them after a short struggle. Pale-Fragrant-Forehead detested any intruder in its territory, where it laid numerous sticky white eggs, like tiny beads. These it tended with fierce devotion. So to get the best from it, one had to collect a few eggs for it to guard.

The lumber rooms were mostly empty, although with each year more clutter filled the bare spaces. Our family owned little when Father first came here after his elevation. Mother put it about that our numerous ancestral possessions were lost on a boat which caught fire. Father always looked embarrassed when she recounted this tale to visitors, and rapidly changed the subject.

The truth was far more wonderful.

Father and his brother, Uncle Ming, were both self-made men. Of their parentage I know little. It was a subject everyone avoided. Sadly, none of our ancestors' bones lie in the family tomb that Father constructed at great expense. We are much weakened by this misfortune.

He became Lord of Wei as a reward for his service in the wars. Most notably, he leapt to the defence of General Yueh Fei when the latter had been unhorsed during the Battle of T'su Hu Pass, and found himself alone, surrounded by barbarians. At this desperate moment a humble lieutenant of the Glorious Destiny Regiment appeared by his side. He instantly slew two Kin warriors with his halberd and decapitated a third. Then he drew his sword. Bellowing like a frenzied bull, he swept away another four barbarians. By this time other soldiers of the Glorious Destiny Regiment had formed a protective ring around General Yueh Fei and my father had sustained enough wounds to kill a dragon, let alone a man. The proof was written across his body in deep scars until the day he died.

Those minutes of valour broke my father physically, but made him a gentleman. In gratitude General Yueh Fei granted him the title of Wei Valley and composed an elaborate curse lest any of his descendents seek to rescind it. I know, because the document is preserved within a hollow ox bone in my strongest chest.

As a boy I heard this story often. Father would relate it in the hall of the Upper House, his voice proud as plum wine. I sat at his feet and longed to be a hero like him. His words intoxicated me.

Yet in winter he hugged his old scars against the cold and might say nothing for days on end.

But I was remembering how we hunted crickets.

Finally I would lead Little Wudi to the topmost building, where our family slept and sat in the evening. Here dwelt the most ferocious of crickets, nesting between cracks in the walls. Crow-Head-Gold-Wings was the name of this doughty fellow. It had a green neck and purple-black wings streaked with gold. Its head was thick, body broad-backed, and its legs were long with muscular thighs. Crow-Head-Gold-Wings fed upon crumbs, shreds of fruit or flower stamens, but mostly other insects. Truly, a superior cricket! Yet rare.

I only found one fully-grown, lurking near Father's chair. In truth, I thought it so beautiful that, notwithstanding its fierce reputation, I chose never to let it fight. For a whole autumn it chirruped and sang in the cage above my bed, a sound so pure and hopeful it elevated my spirit. By the tenth month it was dead. I found it curled at the bottom of the cage, a crumpled, forlorn thing. Losing its companionship made me wail terribly. Mother ran to see what was wrong.

I felt guilty in the midst of my grief. As Crow-Head-Gold-Wing's master, was I not its father? Yet I had not been able to prolong its life.

My own father mocked my tears. He reproached me for losing face in front of the servants. Even Mother shook her head sadly, chiding me for being too sensitive, warning that worse losses occur in life. I was inconsolable.

'Trees may prefer calm,' she said. 'But the wind will not subside.'

In reply I composed a short poem in Crow-Head-Gold-Wing's honour, which I recited in secret to Mother. She listened carefully, then persuaded Father that I should begin learning my characters without further delay. A monk was duly hired from a nearby Daoist monastery for that purpose.

No poem could save Crow-Head-Gold-Wing, and I never found another like him. I wonder where the dust of his tiny, valiant body has blown, fragile as a lost day, fleeting as childhood.

One morning, Father ordered me to collect wine and a bamboo basket of food from the kitchen. I was ten years old. We left the house as a flight of geese passed noisily over the valley. Father leant on his stick and peered up, muttering to himself. Then he struggled out of the village toward Mulberry Ridge. I remember longing that people would see me being useful to him.

It was a slow journey. Often he gasped with pain. On the ridge he sat for a long while, regaining his breath. I crouched in silence, hugging my knees, gazing out across the plain, until his chesty voice startled me, as if from a dream:

'Little Yun Cai, what is it that fascinates you?'

Not knowing the required answer, I bowed in embarrassment. He grew impatient.

'What makes you stare?'

I wanted so hard to please him. Then I recalled an educated neighbour reciting a poem in our house. Father had seemed truly delighted. Closing my eyes, I spoke uncertainly at first, then boldly:

Green green the far off willows,
Far far the town of Chunming.
Beyond the horizon only future.
I must travel toward haze and mist.

As soon as the words were spoken, I wondered where they came from. Certainly a higher, better place than Wei. Yet I barely understood what the poem meant. Father shifted, uneasily.

'Who taught you that?'

'No one, Father.'

'Do not lie to me. Who taught you that verse?'

'Nobody, I swear.'

He glared at me.

'Father, I thought of the words because. . . to please you. I often hear songs and verses in my head. I'm sorry.'

He looked at me in wonder.

'You *did* make it up, didn't you?'

'Forgive me,' I said, fearfully.

To my surprise, he laughed his dry laugh.

'There's not a gentleman for fifty *li* with a son who can compose like that! So your mother is right about your true talents.

She was always shrewd. When you were born, I prayed that you would win renown in the Glorious Destiny Regiment. Now I see you are heading a different way.'

That afternoon he said nothing more, but drank his wine and ate his basket of rice and river shrimp. Though I did not know it, those lines of verse, crude and childish, but highly precocious, had determined my fate.

Everyone knows poetry is the key to wealth and office. Only those who can reproduce the wisdom of the classics through faithful imitation dare hope to pass the examinations and enter the Emperor's vermilion doors. Then the way to honour and esteem for one's family lies wide open, a road lined with envy and precious things. Father was well aware that scholar-officials were the real power in the land of Sung. The Son of Heaven distrusted military men, fearing his generals might attempt to seize the throne for themselves.

That same evening, Father summoned a monk to write a long letter to his brother, my Uncle Ming, in the capital, and set about waiting for the reply. He was good at waiting, as with everything else. Yet I sensed his impatience. For he had made up his mind I was to pass the Emperor's examination and become a high official.

Six months were all that remained of childhood, before I had to change from a spoilt, carefree boy to an anxious scholar. My time in Wei was drawing to its end. Mother hugged me frequently, and made me a suit of clothes far too big, as though she hoped to keep warm my future self. Sometimes she wept for no reason. Once she took me aside when Father was away in the village and whispered:

'You must promise me one thing, Yun Cai. Do you promise?'

'What is it, Mother?'

'Do you promise?' she repeated, fiercely.

By now I was alarmed.

'Yes,' I said, wide-eyed.

'When you reach the capital, you must never provoke or offend Honoured Aunty in any way. Do you understand? *Never*.'

Honoured Aunty was Uncle Ming's official wife. I nodded earnestly.

'Do not forget. She will always be mindful that you are my son. That is why you should keep on the right side of her. And do not mention any of this to Father.'

That night I dreamt of a cold, beautiful woman who I took to be Honoured Aunty. In my dream she was the Empress Lu, cruelly torturing the Lady Qi, who was Mother. I woke up screaming.

One month passed, then three, and four. Everyone in Three-Step-House began to treat me with new respect, even Father, as though I had been singled out for something auspicious and remarkable.

There is a huge boulder on the hillside above Three-Step-House, where I often sat at this time. I used to scramble up its side, nimble as a mountain goat, and resist Little Wudi's attempts to join me by poking a stick at him. We called it Wobbly-Watch-Tower-Rock. At the top I would settle and gaze west, a cool breeze stirring the tuft on my head. Crag and cliff rose against skies of earnest blue. Cloud like a dense plain broken by scattered peaks, snow-capped and enticing, waiting to be climbed. Those mountain-moods formed my soul.

Uncle Ming's eldest son arrived to collect me at the end of autumn. A long procession of camels and strangely-garbed men climbed up Wei Valley. At the news of their coming, Mother stood stock still, helplessly wringing her hands beneath long, trailing sleeves. She hurried off to a private chamber to compose herself.

Cousin Hong seemed a prince. He alighted from a litter lugged by eight sweating servants and his green silks glittered like polished jade in the sun. Gold amulets and charms to preserve him on the road hung from his clothes. His plump, pale face wore a smile of amused contempt. I glanced nervously at Father. To my amazement, even he seemed in awe of this strange, gorgeous fellow. It was our first glimpse of Uncle Ming's wealth, and instead of admiration, it taught shame. Our Lordship of Wei, which had seemed so bright with honour, suddenly paled. Many contradictory and unwelcome sensations contend within the breast of a poor relation.

Father's impatience for me to commence my studies meant I faced a winter journey to the capital. We left before dawn the next day, after a brief ceremony. I could not help weeping, and Cousin Hong made a great joke of my tears.

Days on road or river brought a thousand new sights and smells. Stooping peasants glimpsed in distant fields, boatwomen plying their oars, or high officials whose carriages dripped with silver – all fed my imagination in ways too subtle to conceive.

We travelled overland through a bare, wind-picked country, colours bled by the winter drought. Cousin Hong rode in his litter while I perched among the baggage on a camel's back, wrapped in a cloak of sheep's fur. At night we slept in village hostelries or small towns. They seemed vast cities to me. My senses and thoughts were in constant confusion.

I soon realised that Cousin Hong found me unworthy of notice. One evening, after we had dined in our usual silence, I recited the poem I had improvised for Father on Mulberry Ridge. No doubt I wished to impress him. To my surprise he grew angry.

'So you can bleat, as your father boasted! Understand at once, I am not interested. *My* father can hire a dozen poets any time he likes. He is only adopting you because he has a soft heart. You will fail the examination and be sent back to your hut in the mountains with a scorched backside.'

His outburst shocked me. No one had ever treated me in so low a way.

'*My* father saved the life of General Yueh Fei at the Battle of T'su Hu Pass!' I cried. 'We are noble, not common peddlers!'

Cousin Hong laughed dryly, but I could tell my words stung. Even he realised there are qualities beyond the reach of *cash* coins threaded on a string.

We were delayed by blizzards for several weeks and had to spend the New Year celebration a hundred and fifty *li* north of the capital, in a village whose name I gladly forget, a place where only the lice were energetic. Cousin Hong literally ground his teeth, and I started to feel sorry for him.

Holed up in a miserable inn, while a curious dog inserted its snout up his fine silk coat, he got drunk and poured out his troubles. I listened silently. As I came to learn, he was missing a fine time by his absence from the capital at New Year. Wine lent him eloquence.

He told me of the New Year markets where dishes of rice coloured green, red, white, black and yellow were auctioned. To eat them brought good fortune and he always bid the highest. He told me of painted door gods and paper streamers bearing lucky characters, covering the festival-city like blossom. Firecrackers and gongs and drums filled the streets with noise, so that only a fool bothered to think. Men dressed as gods paraded on stilts. Chimes and flutes chased misfortune round the Pond of Dragons, then through the Gate Of The Eastern Flowering, never to return.

'We must get back in time for the Feast of Lanterns!' he mumbled drunkenly, as though to a dear friend. 'Ah, Yun Cai, then you will see something.'

'Let us depart tomorrow!' I cried, in my high-pitched voice.

I should add that he had favoured me with a cup of strong wine, to 'float in' the New Year.

'What of the snow? Only a madman travels in snow. We would shiver all the way.'

'Let us shiver! Father marched in blizzards when he was an officer. Order the servants to prepare our departure!'

Cousin Hong bristled for a moment. Such decisions lay with him, not a boy. Then he laughed.

'You understand nothing. My litter is heavy. The bearers would sink in the snow.'

'Ride on one of the camels like me. Have the litter follow behind. That way, we shall reach the city in time for the festival.'

He belched.

'No wonder your father is called a hero,' he said, wonderingly. 'You'll end up a general for sure!'

But he did as I advised, and as a result we reached the capital in time for the Feast of Lanterns. Cousin Hong never forgot this episode and afterwards nicknamed me 'Little General'. It was good that I had one friend in Uncle Ming's house, even an unsteady one. I had need of any friend.

We caught our first glimpse of the capital as night was falling. Here I must win honour and esteem or scuttle back to the mountains, a failure in my own and Father's eyes. Cousin Hong had driven the servants forward all day with promises and threats. For several *li* the sky to the east glowed, as though from a great fire. When I remarked on it, Hong chuckled.

'Wait and see!' he cried. 'Just you wait, Little General!'

We were in a low valley full of roadside tombs, then the City of Heaven spread before us.

It seemed ablaze, but not consumed. Small flashes, like distant lightning, sparked across the horizon. A low rumbling filled the air.

We descended the hillside in haste and found ourselves beside a jetty on the shore of the West Lake. Miles of water glittered in the moonlight, covered with boats of every size, like fireflies scattered across a grey mirror. Each bore a lantern, some many, so they were beaded with strings of light. Cousin Hong leapt from his camel and rushed to the shore. By chance a fishing skiff was moored there, rocking alarmingly. Inside a couple were disporting themselves.

'Hey you!' he cried, apparently blind to what was going on. 'Hey you! Take us to the city and you'll earn three hundred *cash*.'

The young fisherman and his wife (assuming they were married, a large assumption at festival-time) fumbled with their clothes. Unabashed, Cousin Hong jangled three strings of *cash* coins, feverishly repeating his offer. He was a man possessed by demons. I believe he would have traded half his inheritance to enjoy the festival. Within a minute the bargain was settled. The fisherman stood by the large oar at the rear of his craft and we scrambled aboard. His 'wife' stood disconsolate on the shore. It was my first lesson that anything was for sale in the City of Heaven. Now Cousin Hong lolled like an emperor in the prow and I was left to gaze.

We passed dragon ships poled by men drunk and singing. Everyone tipsy and gay. Fast boats propelled by paddle-wheels formed a wake of moon-lit foam. Others were floating restaurants, crammed with talking, eating, laughing people, young and old, silk robes catching the light, hard faces softened by lamp-glow. We passed the decorous craft of nobles and outrageous barges full of coarse singing girls, enticing any who would hop aboard into curtained booths.

Cousin Hong triumphantly pointed out places of interest on the shore. Here, the Monastery of the Miraculous Mushroom where a junk was moored. He told me it was never launched because each time it set sail a storm followed. There, the famed pagoda on Thunder Point, an octagonal tower built entirely of blue-glazed bricks. It glittered that night like a barbarian's savage blue eyes. Huge statues of the Buddha carved into cliffs. Stands of willow or bamboo where parties could be glimpsed, dancing or revelling. Cousin Hong roared out coarse greetings to strangers as we passed.

In the midst of this uproar, one grey-bearded old man sat patient as a heron on the shore, fishing rod in hand.

At last we reached the Eastern Shore and disembarked. By now I was terrified and elated. Cousin Hong fell to his knees and kissed a handful of dirt. He summoned a wine seller, and bought a large jar, which he drank in one, wine dribbling down his chin. Passers-by applauded and cheered. His belch, when he finished, was like a thunder-crack.

'Follow me, Little General!' he cried. 'If you lose me, it will be your own look out!'

I took his warning to heart. The crowds jostled and shoved, remorselessly circulating. Not one of those people knew my name or had a reason to care for me. I clung to my cousin like a monkey attached to its owner's wrist by a cord.

Buildings towered. Houses lit by numberless lanterns, some made of glass with many facets, others of coloured paper. A million tongues were chattering until individual voices were lost.

Cousin Hong stopped frequently, stuffing delicacies into his plump face, downing cups of warm wine. His appetite seemed boundless. For all my confusion, I sensed he was anxious to be returning home.

Crowds gathered around acrobats, their faces painted like idols. We passed a show of marionettes, paper figures dancing on sticks. I stared at women wearing head-dresses shaped like butterflies. Precious, mysterious creatures compared to our homely mountain-girls. Ladies in dresses white as frost, accompanied by bellowing young gentlemen, lanterns hanging from long staves like dancing stars. Urchins burned pellets of coal-dust which flared beneath skipping feet. Fireworks of bamboo crackled and banged. I had never heard so much noise except during a storm. It was the roar of humanity, in a certain mood.

At last we reached a large, forbidding gatehouse and Cousin Hong instantly sobered. Statues of the gate-gods glared down at us, scimitars in hand. He turned to me and grinned. 'Little General,' he said. 'Now your new life begins.'

Uncle Ming's residence in the capital demanded many adjustments. My childhood freedoms were at an end, lost in a maze of strangers. I was utterly dependent on my relatives; not merely to fulfil Father's hopes, but for every mouthful in my bowl.

One must always begin with home. Uncle Ming's overlooked the Great Wine Market, adjoining the Imperial Way. Within high boundary walls, topped with metal spikes to deter thieves, were a dozen buildings where Uncle Ming's sway was absolute. At the rear of the enclosure ran South Canal, busy with boats and barges and the singsong cries of river-folk. I came to know it well, for my bedroom leant over the water, at the top of a low wooden tower.

Besides the house intended for his family, the enclosure contained warehouses and breweries, as well as accommodation for servants and apprentices. It was a place of constant bustle. Fermentation and the clatter of jars were continual. The sweet, heady scent of wine floated like a tender mist. Uncle Ming had many customers to satisfy, including nobles and the Imperial Court.

The front gatehouse gave straight onto the Wine Market, and for four days of the week thousands thronged there. Such variety! Simple stalls displaying a few home-brewed jars. Poor men hoping to sell wine by the cup. Fine merchants in wooden pagodas on wheels, where they conducted business, softening up customers with free samples. Soldiers and market-officials on the look-out for bribes, however small.

There were always dozens of drunkards, drawn like bees to an ever-open flower. Food-sellers tended charcoal braziers, crying out to passers-by. Steamed dumplings. Rice cakes. Pork fried with ginger, anise and bitter melon. Salt-fish spread in a paste on buns. Prawn sauce flavoured with lime. One man kept a kennel of panting, over-stuffed puppies behind his stall; I have rarely tasted meat so tender.

Uncle Ming's house stood on the shady side of the square. In summer this was a blessing and relief. The rest of the year we shivered, especially in the family apartments. There is nothing colder than fashionable, black lacquer furniture; or dull, conventional pictures of angry gods. Rooms swept obsessively until there was no trace of dust or muddle. These chambers were Honoured Aunty's domain.

Honoured Aunty was Uncle's first wife and the mother of his three official sons. Cousin Zhi, the youngest, spoilt and vain, clung to his mother in ways which made me wonder about their relations. He was short and wiry as a fox, and quite as dainty. Then there was Cousin Yi-Yi, a strapping, amiable fellow, but one that would normally be classified as an idiot. Finally, Cousin Hong, the first-born, and Uncle's heir.

Honoured Aunty ruled the family through force and guile. Her eyebrows were exceptionally long and curved, betraying an angry temperament. A short, dumpy woman, she had married Uncle when he was still poor, and hawked his wares on the street until freed by prosperity. Her clothes, though of the finest – and I soon became aware she took professional advice on matters of style – never seemed to quite fit. Her favourite haunt was a gilded, ivory chair decorated with carved dragons. She had ordered a similar throne for Uncle, though I never saw him use it. Around this cardinal point the servants scurried. Others came on business, including a sorcerer who had daily converse with demons. I was terrified of this old man, with his spells and brazier for burning animals' tender organs. One day he winked at me suggestively and said (he was inebriated at the time): 'I hope my mistress's enemies don't hear about the curses I place on them. They might wonder why they are always in good health.' After this I avoided him even more. His taste for young boys was notorious in the household, and Honoured Aunty sometimes insisted the prettiest of the apprentices satisfy it.

As for her attitude to me, I was grateful for indifference. Cousin Zhi was her obsession, leaving no energy for anyone else. Despite the edict that every son should follow the profession of his father, she had consulted the most expensive astrologers in the city, and determined he would pass the examination to become an official and gain the highest honours. Needless to say, Cousin Zhi was in complete agreement with this destiny.

I recall one interview with Honoured Aunty, a week after my arrival. She summoned me before her splendid chair and set about me with a bamboo-stick of questions. I knelt before her, head bowed.

'How many silk dresses does your mother own?'

'I do not know, Honoured Aunty. Forgive me.'

'How many servants do your parents have?'

'A dozen in the house. Then there is the whole village.'

This answer displeased her.

'What title does my husband's brother use?'

'Lord,' I said, simply.

'You seem very sure of yourself. Remember you are in my house now.'

Her tone frightened me. My position was precarious, without a single friend in a limitless, strange city. I remembered my mother's warning to never offend her.

'If I am at fault, Honoured Aunty, I beg a thousand pardons,' I said.

'How many pigs are there in your father's sty? I take it he eats meat once a week, or does he find it too expensive?'

And so it went on.

'Does your father travel by litter or walk everywhere? No doubt he cannot afford a horse.'

I forget the other questions. There were many. Finally she touched upon her true fears.

'They say you write good poems and this is why your father thinks you will succeed in the examination. Is this true?'

I shrugged modestly. Yet a note of defiance touched my voice, the tiniest trace, for I sensed her iron, vengeful nature. I sensed, too, she respected strength.

'In the City of Heaven,' I began, then fell silent.

'What? Speak louder!'

I recited a poem composed to impress my new teachers at the Academy. A formal, tiresome piece, yet exceptional from one so young. I have it still on a yellowed sheet of paper, my brush-strokes crude and earnest. It provoked amazement when I showed it to my teachers, for I had mimicked the court style of the Early Tang perfectly, through complex internal rhymes and an elaborate pattern of tones.

In the City of Heaven a thousand voices.
Urgent fluttering wings of cicadas.
Crickets sing until daybreak.
I must heed when teachers speak.

Honoured Aunty stared at me, for once confused.

'Enough!' she cried in a shrill voice, clapping her hands. 'Tell the servants to bring your Cousin Zhi to me at once.'

I scurried off gladly.

After that Honoured Aunty ignored me except for sideways glances when I entered the room. This was something I avoided at all costs. Yet I had only just begun to make her acquaintance.

Uncle Ming reminded me of Father, in that they differed in almost every way. In those days Uncle was at the height of his wealth. Fat hung in folds from his body. His pale, round face resembled the moon; especially his benign, empty smile. Honoured Aunty chose his clothes, so naturally they were extravagant and as ill-fitting as her own. This aspect of Uncle's appearance often worked to his advantage, particularly among the nobility, who at once felt superior to him, and at ease.

His appetites were tremendous, both for food and drink, but

also singing girls. He maintained a pavilion full of such beauties beyond the city walls. It was rumoured some of these girls had died or disappeared suddenly, as soon as they gained a hold on Uncle's affections. Naturally, Honoured Aunty was blamed. Perhaps she circulated these rumours as a way of saving face.

Even though I lived beneath his eaves, Uncle Ming remained a mystery. Having discharged his duty to Father by arranging for my education, he ignored me apart from beaming with goodwill. But then he smiled like that to everyone. At last, a week after my arrival, he summoned me. It was dusk, his office full of shadows. The room smelt of spirits and he had a coarse, earthenware wine cooler by his side. His eyes were over-bright, and his smile somehow too fixed.

'Ah, Nephew! Come! Come!'

I kneeled, touching the dusty floorboards with my forehead, aware he was watching. At last Uncle Ming leaned forward.

'When your father asked me to take you in, I could hardly refuse,' he said. 'You will find me quite generous, Nephew. Quite generous. But let us understand one another. You are here to pass examinations. Nothing else. That is what I promised your Father. Do not shame me by failing, or, Little Nephew, you shall find me far from amiable.'

I crawled out like a cowed puppy.

Another time our paths crossed in a way which made him notice me. It was a year after my arrival in the capital. I was wandering the streets and passed an alley notorious for a certain restaurant. It served an unusual, though by no means illegal, type of meat, cooked in the manner of lamb. All varieties of two-legged mutton could be bought there, from old to younger flesh, and each dish had a special name. In times of famine such restaurants did a brisk trade, but during plenty they were frequented only by connoisseurs. A banner hung above the entrance, bearing the words 'Lucky Bowl'.

As I hurried past a familiar figure emerged, bowed out by several waiters. He had a singing girl on each arm. Both girls were garlanded with pink lotus blossom. Uncle Ming took one look at me and his customary smile lapsed. He summoned me over and sent the singing girls on ahead. I flinched.

'Nephew,' he demanded. 'What are you doing here? Why are you not studying for your examinations?'

'Just walking, Uncle.'

He surveyed me unsteadily.

'I take it you have already forgotten my dining companions?'

For a moment I was confused. Did he mean the people he had dined with or on?

'You are alone, Uncle,' I said, quickly. 'I do not understand.'

His usual smile reappeared. Extracting a string of *cash* from his belt, he took hold of my hand and deposited the coins there. Then he slowly closed my fingers round the money, and patted my arm. His own fingers were greasy. As he leant forward, his breath fascinated and appalled me.

'Buy yourself something to eat!' he winked. 'I can recommend the Lucky Bowl, but don't tell Honoured Aunty. She might get strange ideas about who should be on the menu! Ha! Ha!'

It was the nearest thing to a joke I ever heard him utter. Of course, I followed his first suggestion and ignored the latter.

An ox must tirelessly haul the plough to earn its feed; a scholar must gain success to retain his distinctive blue robe. If the ox shows weakness, he is eaten, right down to his hooves. So it was for me. Once established in Uncle Ming's household my days formed a pattern of toil which endured for years, broken only by festivals or illness.

I would arise at cock-crow and struggle into my blue scholar's gown, ink-stained and threadbare at the elbows. After a breakfast of millet porridge and salty pickles, I hurried to the front gate. Here would be assembled an entourage several strong, supervised by Honoured Aunty, her face a mask as she barked out orders and rebukes. The entourage was not for myself, but Cousin Zhi. One flunkey to carry his scrolls bound with rhinoceros hide, another for inks and brushes, a third bearing a large wicker box containing meats and dishes known to nourish the brain. The fourth anxiously angled a huge, tasselled parasol. I would bow low, satchel on my back, and hurry past them to the wine market where my own escort awaited.

Why Cousin Yi-Yi chose to accompany me to the Provincial Academy each morning, I could not say. He was, however, a simpleton, so I didn't enquire too deeply. Yi-Yi had been blessed by nature in one regard only. Everything about him was outlandishly large, especially his amiable, misshapen face. I later heard his other organs were proportioned the same way.

We would proceed through the streets in silence, nimble boy and ambling giant, past bridge and canal, hawker and street-cry, scents of night-soil, wood-smoke, fried food seeping from buildings several stories high. Voices surrounded us like mist.

At last we entered the many courtyards of the government enclosure; soldiers and officials bustling, some with scrolls under their arms, others in polite debate. I should add we passed a palace where lesser courtesans intended for the use of visiting ambassadors were housed. Sometimes we spied a curtain parting suggestively, though we never saw the ladies themselves. I finally realised these glimpses were the sole reason Yi-Yi accompanied me. Cousin Hong once informed me – he thought it a great joke – that Yi-Yi would spend the entire morning masturbating in his room after seeing a curtain twitch. So for all his idiocy, Yi-Yi possessed imagination. He was faithful to the dominant sentiment of his family: desire.

Each morning I took my place in that long, bare room full of boys. All were from good families, or at least, wealthy ones. The fees were beyond most people's means, including my Father's. Only the goodwill of Uncle Ming enabled me to study at the Provincial Academy.

We sat on the dusty floor, writing blocks on our knees, mixing ink in preparation for the day's lesson. Teachers and their assistants prowled up and down with bamboo sticks, vigilant for murmurs or disrespect. Cousin Zhi sat near the front among a small group of merchants' sons, laboriously following every instruction from the teacher.

Beside me knelt a thin, feeble-looking boy with a sharp, inquisitive face who I came to know better than myself. His wide eyebrows were of noble proportions and his large nose indicated a formidable character. His name was P'ei Ti. I soon learned that, for him, the Provincial Academy and First Examination were a tedious formality. His family had been scholar-officials for generations, some achieving great honour. He never acknowledged me except to whisper among his friends the nickname 'Mountain Goat', in a voice loud enough for me to hear. The reason for his mockery was plain. Each monthly examination in the Five Classics ended the same way. I came first and he second, unless we were studying the *Book of History*, at which he excelled. From the start he showed an aptitude for governance.

Success gained me few friends, partly because of my strange accent, and also, I suspect, because P'ei Ti influenced the other boys. Who was I, after all? My father might well be a brave soldier (the tale of his heroism had even reached the capital), but in those days, as now, it was the fashion to despise soldiers until they torched your house.

Memories of our school-room... paper-winged flies... the drone of a voice reciting passages from the *Book of Changes* or the *Book of Rites*... moments of fear when students were beaten for falling asleep... copying characters outmoded a thousand years ago, every brush stroke charged with the exhilaration of magical power... squatting by myself in the courtyard for a midday meal of rice and salt-fish, while Cousin Zhi was served by his lackeys, poorer boys hanging round, hopeful for leftovers... angles of sunlight catching flocks of dust motes... the mid-afternoon gong releasing me into the city, a thousand fascinations, as I walked home.

All these things existed. And are no more.

Of course, there were those who wished to send me back to the mountains. My success had provoked Cousin Zhi's ill-will. His own marks were unexceptional. Indeed, he fluttered between pass and fail as a moth flaps round a lamp, scorching itself but never quite destroyed. Had I not been part of his household, he could have ignored me. As it was, my presence continually reminded him of disappointing his mother, an unbearable thought. Yet he dare not act against me openly because of Uncle Ming's protection. Thus he resorted to guile.

One midday break, before an examination for which he had prepared zealously, three of the lesser merchants' sons approached me as I sat eating. I had noticed Cousin Zhi whispering to them earlier, passing round a large basket of honeyed buns.

'Hey, Mountain Goat! Who are you to come here and insult our families!' the leader shouted. 'Go back where you belong! You're not welcome here.'

I continued to dip my chopsticks.

'I hear your father is too poor to own a pig!' squealed another, smaller boy.

The weak are always behind every fight. His companions roared with laughter at his wit and he seemed to grow an inch. Still I ignored them.

'Hey, I'm talking to you, Mountain Goat!' shouted the first. 'Explain yourself!'

I finished my meal and closed the wooden lid of my rice box. In truth, I was shaking inside. The punishment for fighting was five strokes of the bamboo. Far worse, I would forfeit my right to sit the afternoon's examination, thereby losing months of study. I didn't care to think what Uncle Ming would say. Cousin Zhi had set a cruel trap. It was obvious his friends wished to provoke me into throwing the first blow.

'I hear your father is a Mongol coward,' shouted the leader

desperately, looking over at Cousin Zhi for approval. The significance of his look did not escape me. Yet I was snared. This I could not ignore. I rose, my fists bunched.

'Pah!' I said. 'Cheap singing girl! For a steamed bun you sing anything!'

I prepared to follow up my words with a punch. Suddenly there was laughter all around us. P'ei Ti and his cronies had formed a circle.

'What do you say to that, Steamed-Bun-Singing-Girl?' he jeered.

The boy glowered at me, then turned sheepishly away. Quite unexpectedly, I had won. In a moment P'ei Ti stood beside me.

'Why didn't you hit him?' he asked, excitedly. 'He insulted your father.'

'Ah, but I did.'

And it was true. Ever after my persecutor was known as Steamed-Bun-Singing-Girl. That afternoon I gained a slightly lower mark than Cousin Zhi, so perhaps his plan worked after all.

When the gong signalled the end of our last lesson, I was free until supper-time. The City of Heaven lay at my disposal. Where did I go? A place Cousin Zhi or Honoured Aunty would never find me.

In any life, energy and contradiction form patterns you never choose. So it was with Su Lin.

It was summer when we met. The city panted in the heat. Dog-days without a single breeze to dispel torpor and freshen hope. I found her in an alley behind the Wine Market, where I had gone at twilight to escape the closeness of Uncle Ming's house. My spirits should have been high, having come first in another monthly examination, yet I was troubled by a sense of emptiness. Success came too easily. I longed to challenge myself in new ways.

She sat on a wooden doorstep, fanning herself as she sang,

her girl's voice sad and wistful, innocent and knowing. I might have passed by, except her song made me ache. It was a melody from the mountains, and her accent was my own.

As she finished a verse I began the next. Her mouth opened in surprise, then she laughed that light, scornful laugh of hers. I finished the verse, standing awkwardly. At last I noticed her beauty, and frowned, as though she had challenged me in some way. Her ivory skin covered a perfect, tear-drop face, made enticing by plump lips and almond eyes. Her breasts and legs and thighs, though hidden by robes of the cheapest pink silk, were easily imagined. I cleared my throat.

'It is too hot!' I said.

'Don't you mean, how is it I know the same songs as you?' she replied.

She was older than me, fourteen to my twelve. At that age such distinctions are worlds. She yawned and stretched. I peeped shyly at her chest.

'Seeing you interrupted my practice, small sir, have you nothing to say?'

'Only this,' I countered. 'Why have you so little politeness?'

She watched me languidly, her fan clicking.

'You are from Chunming Province,' she said. 'I can tell from your accent. So am I.'

I felt wrong-footed, and provoked. In truth, I suppressed an unaccountable desire to wrestle with her, to prove my superior strength.

'Of course,' I said, haughtily. 'I am the son of the Lord of Wei Valley.'

This seemed to impress her. Encouraged, I added solemnly: 'One day I will pass the Imperial Examination. That is why my father sent me here, that is why. . . I am.'

She looked at me pityingly.

'Is that all?' she asked.

'Yes, that is why,' I said, doggedly. 'My father sent me here to add to our family's honour.'

She sighed. Her pout fascinated me.

'Then we are just the same,' she said. 'When I was eleven years old, my father sold me to a broker, a most horrible man, who then sold me to Madam, who owns this house. I, too, must pass many examinations.'

Only then did I realise she was an apprentice singing girl.

'We are the same in that,' I conceded, lamely, and hurried on my way.

The next evening drew me back to the alley. Her doorstep was empty, the plain wooden door closed.

One cold, autumn morning Cousin Hong sent a servant to fetch me. He was enthroned in a small gatehouse at the rear of the family enclosure, alongside a table where a clerk was collecting rent from Uncle Ming's many tenants. They formed a respectful line right out into the street. The clerk's abacus clicked and *cash* coins clinked on the scratched wooden table. Cousin Hong was eating almonds from a silver bowl, dipping them in rice brandy for sauce. He airily offered me one.

'Eat it slowly,' he advised. 'It comes all the way from Tashkent.'

A miserable, sick-looking man shuffled up to the clerk's table. Wringing his hands, he bowed low and started to explain why he could not pay the rent. A shameful sight, and one I have never forgotten, though poor men were nothing new to me. Perhaps Cousin Hong's response fixed his pinched face in my memory.

'Pay or find your belongings on the street, you dog!' he roared. 'If you have a daughter, sell her! Get out, you thief!'

The line of tenants murmured anxiously. Cousin Hong motioned to dismiss the clerk. While we talked, the tenants waited in the wind-picked street. Cousin Hong warmed his hands before a small charcoal brazier, then wagged a reproachful finger.

'So, Little General, what is this I hear about you offending my brother Zhi? This will never do.'

'I have done nothing,' I protested.

'Ah, but you have. You should understand our ways here. As Eldest Son I will inherit Father's business. As for Yi-Yi. . . well, never mind him. But Little Brother Zhi is destined for great things. My mother has already decided which duke's daughter he will marry when he is a great official. It would be unwise to upset such plans.'

'How am I at fault? Please explain.'

'Little General, is it sensible to keep beating Zhi in the examinations? Of course not. Why not come second more often, then everyone will be happy.'

'Even if I came tenth, Cousin Zhi would not beat me,' I said. 'Is Uncle Ming displeased?'

'Not in the least. But that doesn't matter.'

His advice appalled my pride. Yet I knew he meant it kindly.

'My father sent me here precisely so I would pass,' I said.

'That is not my concern. Take this business with the boy who tried to pick a fight with you. My little brother complains he has lost friends because of it. It seems some of the other boys blame him for spreading rumours and causing trouble.'

It was true Steamed-Bun-Singing-Girl no longer talked to Cousin Zhi, but that was hardly my fault. Hong offered me another almond.

'And I hear,' he continued. 'You have made friends with boys of good family who should really be the companions of Zhi. One day those boys might be useful to him.'

'P'ei Ti has become a friend,' I admitted. 'At least we always talk at midday.'

'Exactly! Such a one should be talking to Zhi, not you.'

'But why?'

Cousin Hong considered, then shrugged.

'Why? There is no good reason why. Why was that wretch unable to pay his rent? Why are we enjoying almonds harvested by pretty barbarian girls with plump thighs and he is deciding which of his daughters to sell? Only fools ask why. Better to ask what is.'

I had never suspected Hong of philosophy, but all men need some principle to guide them. I also took the hint that I might end up like the poor tenant if I continued to offend Honoured Aunty and Cousin Zhi.

I wandered the streets in disgust for an hour, eventually finding myself in the alley where I had met the singing girl. The piercing, autumn wind could not reach me here. A pool of cold sunshine lit the doorstep where she had sat. As I passed, the door opened and, to my surprise, she poked her head out. I halted. We examined each other in silence. Then she smiled.

'So you have come back to see me!' she cried.

She was dressed in a gaudy gown and wore cheap, yet tastefully arranged jewellery. Her face had been painted and rouged. I felt like a child in comparison. Given the life she led, I was not misguided.

'Aren't you pleased to see me, eldest son of the Lord of Wei?' she asked, archly. Her coquettish look faded. 'But you are upset. Someone has upset you.'

She waved me to the step and we sat down. So close, her smell disturbed me. There was perfume, and a scent of wine, as well as something I could not name. Yet I poured out my difficulties, expecting she would find them incomprehensible. It was my first lesson to never underestimate her.

'Pah!' she said, finally. 'You must carry on as you have and take no notice of them. If it is your destiny to be first then all their tricks will never make you last. Besides, your uncle will keep them in order. The fact he sent his heir to fetch you from Chunming Province shows the regard he holds for your father. Such a sense of duty is not a twig, but a strong branch. Besides, only an envious spirit would not realise your success helps Cousin Zhi, for you are related and dwell in his household. Thus he gains honour through you. Your uncle will understand this. But you must keep your mouth shut, whatever the provocation. They are clearly a bad lot.'

I blinked at her, amazed by her shrewdness.

'What is your name?' I asked.

'Su Lin.'

'Thank you,' I said. 'Su Lin.'

A look of weariness crossed her face. She glanced around the alley as though seeking some means of escape.

'Do you like your life in the city?' I asked.

'No more than you,' she retorted.

'If I can help you, I will,' I said. 'Try me! I am faithful as a temple lion.'

She laughed at my earnestness.

'You don't want to be one of them,' she said. 'They never go anywhere, but just sit all day with their tongues hanging out. . . like this.'

She stuck out her own. I bridled at her mockery.

'I know things you don't,' I said, doggedly.

'And I know things *you* don't.'

Su Lin laid her hand on my arm.

'Do not be angry,' she said. 'I like talking to you. You remind me of home. And you. . . don't want anything from me.'

'Ha! That's where you are wrong.'

She recoiled a little. Her face hardened.

'I want to talk to you now and then,' I said, aware I was making a complete fool of myself. 'And you are from Chunming Province, like me.'

We sat for a while in the afternoon sunlight. The sounds of the city faint around us. A couple were arguing hysterically. In the distance a watchman called the hour.

'I do not like this house,' she said, gesturing behind her in disgust. 'Madam is cheap-minded and foolish. Already I can sing and play the pi-pa better than Madam. She teaches me nothing. I want to ride in a fine carriage and have servants and a pavilion by the West Lake, and my own barge for entertainments, and a garden with little waterfalls and flowers everywhere. The rarest, sweetest flowers! And I will fetch my mother and sisters and father from Chunming and look after them. Other girls have these things. Why not me?'

I could not answer that question. Cousin Hong's philosophy echoed in my ears. I thought of the man who was perhaps, as we spoke, negotiating a price for his daughter. As Su Lin's father must have done.

'One must always ask why,' I said, answering my own doubt. 'Otherwise we understand nothing. That is why I like to study. Without knowledge we are dust blown from one street to another, then back again.'

I subsided, embarrassed by my outburst, which had begun to take the shape of a poem in my mind, characters forming neat, balanced columns.

'I like it when you talk like that,' she said, wonderingly. 'Is that what they teach you at the Academy? Oh, I wish I was a man!'

At once I knew how to interest her.

'Can you read?' I asked.

She laughed mockingly.

'I can read what men want better than you ever will!'

'No, I'm serious. I could teach you. And to write. It's easy.'

Su Lin examined me shyly.

'That would be good, I would love. . . but you don't mean it. It is not nice to play games with a poor girl. Not nice at all.'

'I do mean it. I could come here and teach you. Then we could talk some more.'

'If you come here tomorrow at the same time I will know you mean it,' she said.

And the next evening I brought paper, ink and brush. Spreading a sheet across the door-step, I taught her to write her name. *Su Lin*. The characters for silence and forest.

*

For two more years I toiled like a termite, until my fourteenth year.

Each afternoon, once released from the Provincial Academy, I would hurry to my octagonal room in the low tower overlooking South Canal. Often, to appease low spirits, I practised the calligraphy which later won renown for its beauty. The strictures of Master Xie-He entered the fabric of my being and later served me well. That depictions should possess liveliness and be properly executed. That one must depict what is, using the right tones in the right order. Above all, harmony must be learnt by copying the masters, as one learns virtue from one's father. Luckily I had many masters to copy, all due to the generosity of Uncle Ming, though it cost him little.

I had discovered a large library of dusty scrolls, stored in the chamber beneath my bedroom, which he had forgotten he possessed. This library came his way in part-payment for a debt incurred by a scholar-official much given to wine and girls. Had Uncle Ming guessed the library's true value, I have no doubt he would have sold it, but contracts and accounts were the only written matters he valued.

At this time I also learned the lute, spending many hours in my room conversing with its gentle voice. It cured my loneliness, for a while.

Three or four evenings each week, I left my studies and wandered to Su Lin's alley. She had bought her own writing materials by then and I would teach her ten new characters each time we met. She learned fast, and greeted me like her dearest brother. Mostly we talked about our lives, or I did, for she never mentioned the business in Madam's establishment except through hints. I was glad of this tact. The thought of other men. . . no, I did not like it. No bond other than friendship lay between us, for I was young, and backward in that regard, and she never chose to lead me forward.

In one way I followed Su Lin's advice scrupulously. Each provocation from Zhi or Hounoured Aunty splashed over me like water on a stone. Naturally, they discovered my trysts with Su Lin and tried to discredit me with Uncle Ming. As a result, he summoned me to his office next to the brew house.

'Nephew, I hear bad things about you.'

He was lolling on a low, padded divan and had clearly been sampling his own wares.

'Forgive me, Uncle,' I said, falling to my knees. 'You are my father in this house.'

My instant submission pleased him.

'Honoured Aunty is not happy,' he said. 'You little rogue!'

'I beg forgiveness.'

'That's all very well. What's this I hear about you seeing a singing girl? I promised your father to make a scholar of you. Would you shame me?'

'Honoured Uncle, my teachers are very satisfied with me. I come first in nearly every examination.'

'So I understand. Perhaps that's the problem, eh? You little scoundrel, you!'

'Honoured Uncle, my relations with the singing girl are chaste. I am teaching her how to read and write.'

'Eh?'

'She's like a sister to me.'

This left him speechless.

'Are you lying to me?' he asked, at last.

'No, Uncle. Even the singing girl's Madam approves of my tuition.'

'Of course she does! It adds value to the girl. Have they ever asked you for money?'

'Never!' I protested.

By now I was fourteen years old and understood everything worldly, or thought I did.

'They are taking advantage of you,' he declared. 'I do not like this. It shows disrespect towards me.'

'I beg forgiveness,' I said, bowing once more.

'I'm not angry with you, Nephew,' said Uncle. 'Just *them*. The women. Next time you teach her, demand a proper payment. And a word of caution. I would be betraying your father's trust in me if I did not show you the right way. Slap her around a bit if she does not please you. She's not family and she's not reached a respectable position in her profession and she's not your wife. If you need some money to set things on a proper footing, here's a string of *cash*. Off you go, boy.'

I bowed my way out, leaving him well-satisfied, for whatever criticism may be uttered against Uncle Ming, he strove to fulfil his obligations.

Fortunately, I was spared further annoyance from Cousin Zhi and Honoured Aunty by a simple event. At last, after a failed attempt, he passed the First Examination. The celebrations in Uncle Ming's house lasted ten days and for the first time I saw Honoured Aunty laugh. The fact that I also passed, though two years younger than Zhi, was entirely ignored, apart from a letter to Three-Step-House in which Uncle expressed the utmost self-congratulation.

I celebrated by spending an evening in the back courtyard of Su Lin's house. She poured warm wine and fed me dumplings stuffed with pork and ginger. She sang gentle songs in our mountain dialect – of deserted wives and true lovers, of the harvest and hunt. That night I kissed her with passion for the first time. She made no objection when I buried my head in her breasts, their musky scent making me drunker than the wine. Their firmness in my longing hands, the discovery of her tightening buds! Is it unseemly for an old man to recall such things? I cannot help myself. Desire took hold of me, though I needed guidance to appease it. And surely I had earned that reward. Yet, to my surprise, Su Lin began to cry. She who never wept easily.

'I am so happy for you,' she said, between sobs. 'You have been the kindest of brothers to me. Oh, Yun Cai!'

Then she ran out of the courtyard into the house. There was a clicking of bolts. I reeled, too drunk to see anything but spinning stars in the clear night sky over the city. How I made my way home I do not know.

When I returned the next day I discovered Su Lin was no longer in residence.

'She's gone away,' said her Madam, curtly. 'I've sold her on to another establishment. But you're a good boy. Come back when you're older, any time! And if you want to teach another of my girls to write, that's fine with me.'

'Where has she gone?' I managed to croak.

Madam tapped my cheek with her folded fan and chuckled.

'Never you mind. You can't afford her now, that is for sure.'

I left like a beaten dog.

How long did my sorrow last? A week? A month? I cannot recall. Certainly it spoilt my triumph at winning a place in the Metropolitan Academy. More than a friend, I lost my capacity to trust wholeheartedly. I saw Su Lin's gay, artful conversation and affectionate words in a new, hateful way. Her anecdotes of life in Chunming and haunting mountain songs. Her slender hand on my arm, which seemed to promise so much. I had been used.

Would Su Lin practise her new-found ability to write by sending me a letter? No letter came. Or even pass a message through a porter or servant? No message arrived.

When I shared my hurt with Cousin Hong, expecting him to jeer (I wished to be humiliated for my folly, punished, I deserved it), he wagged a reproachful finger.

'This a valuable lesson, Little General,' he said. 'You won't learn a lesson like this in your precious Academy. Never pay in advance unless you can help it. If you'd used her services in instalments, everyone would be happy.'

I resisted such wisdom by reading and re-reading sheaves of love poems, learning dozens by heart until the bitter-sweet chime of their words echoed in my soul. Then I began to write my own, awkward, crude imitations, offerings to my distress, forerunners of my later success. For it is as a poet of loss and regret that I became best known.

For the first time I fell behind in my studies, and Uncle Ming's frowns suggested consequences I dared not contemplate. Honoured Aunty thoughtfully watched my discomfort until I wondered if she had a hand in my dear friend's sudden removal. It was as though Su Lin had died and I was in mourning. I never suspected how easily love returns from its grave.

three

'. . . *Evening discourses from a cold studio.*
All very well for Master Su Tung-po!

Enlightenment dredged from a deep wine bowl.
The moon's beauty worms away at my soul. . .'

I wait for Youngest Son and his officers by the gatehouse. Eldest Son hovers behind me. We have nothing to say to one another, our thoughts too full for words. I lean on my stick and examine the village below. Soldiers drift between the houses and an inordinate number of fires have been lit. Stray voices rise – our valley has a strange way of carrying sound – and all the dogs are silent. Possibly they are already on the spit.

I calculate we have been occupied by two companies of infantry, each a hundred strong, half armed with crossbows, the rest with halberd and sword. In addition, thirty or so cavalry, mainly mounted archers. Every day they spend devouring our hard-won stores increases the likelihood of famine. Wei Village and the surrounding valleys sustain hundreds of peasants, yet soon we shall be stripped bare. We have four, perhaps five days at most.

As dusk gathers, a small procession leaves the village, bound for Three-Step-House. At their head, men bearing General An-Shu's dragon banner, followed by drummers, and finally our honoured guests: Youngest Son and his three principal officers. Swallows dart above their heads, oblivious to the drumbeat echoing hollowly round the hills. It says much that my son feels such a show is necessary to dine in his family home. Eldest Son bobs uncertainly.

'Remember,' I say. 'It is important they feel obliged to us.'

An anxious evening lies ahead. I hope to placate Youngest Son, drown his past grievances in wine and food. Then I might extract assurances from him concerning the villagers' safety, so binding that he dare not go back on his word without great loss of face.

Up the hill they come. I raise a smile of welcome. Eldest Son's is more like a leer. Still, I have a few tricks up my official's sleeve. The first is deployed as Youngest Son approaches the gatehouse. I clap my hands and a servant rushes forward with bowls of flower-heads soaked in wine.

'Youngest Son,' I say, opening my arms. 'Welcome! Please make this offering to the gate-gods. I have no doubt they greet your return, and the presence of your esteemed officers, as I do.'

He seems surprised and tugs at his whiskers. He can hardly refuse. A period of bowing before the gate-gods follows, all forced into the role of dutiful, civilised men. Youngest Son pours the libation with every sign of reverence.

In this pious mood, we proceed to the Middle House, where a banquet has been prepared. Youngest Son nods stiffly to his brother but no words are exchanged. The household servants line the way on their knees. At the entrance, I pause.

'My honoured guests must make allowances for the dishes a poor, unworthy house can offer. As the venerable Lao-Tzu remarked. . .'

To my amazement Youngest Son interrupts me.

'Come Father,' he says. 'Let us not stand on ceremony. My men are hungry and I am eager to sit.'

Even the officers seem embarrassed by his rudeness. I understand his intention. He wishes to establish himself as host, not guest. I counter by pretending not to hear, and address the officers.

'You will notice, as gentlemen of distinction, the unusual shape of the rocks on the opposite hillside. They have often been admired by visitors.'

They peer obediently across the valley.

'Very unusual,' says one, older than the rest, with a sad, lined face. 'Very interesting.'

Youngest Son's eyes narrow.

'Please enter!' I cry. 'All are welcome.'

We kneel before the tables in our old-fashioned country way and the banquet begins. Youngest Son looks around, touched by predictable emotions. He has dined in this room a thousand times, knows its shadows and shapes, the feel of the mat beneath his knees. This was the last room he stayed in, on the night I dismissed him. Only fools deny the circular swirl of life. Perhaps he remembers his mother's presence here.

For the first few courses, little conversation. This suits me. When they are drunk I shall raise the village's safety, paying particular attention to the welfare of virgins. Servants bring in bowl after bowl on lacquer trays. Snails broiled in vinegar, little frog and noodle soup, then roasted quail and partridge, dry dishes followed by wet, each washed down by cups of wine. The officers are on their best behaviour, and even Youngest Son is restrained. It is only after the fifteenth dish that trouble begins. Appropriately, considering my guests, it is peppery pork. The servants light the lanterns, at once attracting a single, pale moth. Its fluttering wings change the atmosphere in the room. Youngest Son suddenly lifts his cup and cries out: 'To the health of His Highness, General An-Shu!'

His officers roar approval. I raise my cup thoughtfully, meeting the older officer's watchful eyes. Clearly something is expected of me, a declaration of loyalty, perhaps.

'The General's boldness will pass into legend!' I call out.

They murmur approvingly.

'He dares where other men only dream,' I add.

Thumping of tables, so the dishes vibrate.

'We hear little news in our poor valley,' I say. 'Youngest Son, be so kind as to share your deeds! We have much to learn.'

Youngest Son laughs harshly. He is drunker than the wine I have served warrants. Clearly he started before he got here.

'Where do I begin? Our glorious regiment (more thumping of tables) has earned its name of Winged Tigers! At Chu Ford we attacked across the water and drove back a whole battalion of our enemies. Do you see this scar, Father? The man who gave it to me floated away face down!'

His officers cheer. Beside me, Eldest Son is decidedly uncomfortable.

'I trust the wound causes no discomfort?' I ask.

'None at all! And when His Highness made a tactical retreat to Lu Pass, my company beat off three times its number.'

'So all goes well,' I say.

'Exceedingly! Even now we are gathering a force to march south all the way to the Dragon Throne itself. Many titles will be granted on that splendid day.'

He says this with the utmost significance. Is he referring to my own title?

'I am pleased Youngest Son is happy.'

'How could I be otherwise! Lieutenant Mah-Fu, what did you make of the Pretender's forces?'

The officer, barely more than a boy, frowns with concentration.

'Well, I'll answer for you,' continues Youngest Son. 'They lack the will to fight. That gives us a decisive advantage.'

Another officer breaks in, the one with a habitual sneer.

'Sir, you hit the target exactly! They have no stomach for their cause.'

Youngest Son frowns to be interrupted.

'Precisely. That's what I said. More wine! The servants have grown slow since I was away.'

I sigh, as if to concede we are simple folk.

'Glorious times!' he toasts. 'Already ambassadors have arrived in Chunming from one of the Western tribes, offering a host of mounted archers.'

'Barbarians are offering to serve the General?' I ask, surprised.

'Of course! His Highness is busy from dawn until dusk with homage. Who would have thought it in such a dull town as Chunming, eh?'

Who indeed? The idea is outlandish.

'A new dynasty is forming,' declares Youngest Son, tipsily. 'Mark my words!'

I grow pale to hear such treason uttered in my own house, and rage inwardly at the danger in which he places us. Yet I must be calm.

'Clearly great events,' I say. 'Here we think only of the harvest. And the early crop has been disappointing.'

'Never mind that, Father,' chides Youngest Son.

Such rudeness and disrespect to a parent is a kind of treason in itself. If his mother could hear it, she would weep with shame. He turns fiercely to Eldest Son. This is the moment I have dreaded.

'Brother! Why don't you join us? With my influence, an honourable position could be found for you. Look at the kind of men you'd be serving alongside! Doesn't that make you long for honour?'

His officers exclaim appreciatively. The room falls silent. Every eye is on Eldest Son. He seems troubled, spreads his hands helplessly.

'Someone must ensure the peasants tend the fields,' he says. 'Otherwise, how will the General's troops be fed?'

The youngest officer titters, yet I could hug Eldest Son for so obtuse a reply. Youngest Son seems nonplussed.

'True, true, but there's no glory in it.'

'Tell me again how you came by your scar,' I say. 'That is what we really want to know.'

For the next few minutes Youngest Son explains, blow by blow, and the crisis passes. More wine is poured. Evidently they have decided to make it a point of honour to get dead drunk. To my relief, the conversation moves away from us. Eldest Son and I are ignored. They talk excitedly about the march to the capital, how one good battle should settle the matter. More moths gather on the lanterns, their wings slowly opening and closing.

Wudi appears in the doorway like a ghost. I meet his eye and excuse myself.

Outside, we find a dark corner beneath the eaves.

'I have news,' he says, quietly.

'Be discreet,' I warn.

'The cavalrymen got your message.'

We glance involuntarily at the hillside above Three-Step-House. Clouds are passing, driven across the night sky. It will be windy tomorrow.

'Did your son speak to the commander?'

'No, I went myself.'

'What impression did you gain of him?'

Wudi laughs softly.

'He's desperate enough. He said he wants to speak to you.'

'Me?'

'Yes, Lord. He said to tell you.'

I try to understand, but cannot. My only hope is that it somehow stems from P'ei Ti.

'So the Imperial cavalry are well hidden?'

'I showed them to the caves behind the waterfall. The rest is up to them. I didn't want to hang around.'

'You are brave, Wudi,' I say.

'Or stupid,' he says.

'Go to bed now, old friend. Sleep here. It is not safe for you to go down to the village tonight. The soldiers might wonder why you're awake so late.'

He hesitates.

'I'm afraid,' he says. 'If any of this comes out. . .'

I need no reminding. After all, Wei Village has burned once before. Because of my actions, it might burn again.

'Tomorrow will decide that,' I say. 'Rest now.'

I relieve myself against a plum tree and take my place once more in the Middle House. The eldest of the officers, Lieutenant Lo, watches me closely. Does he suspect something?

'Lord Yun Cai,' he says, quietly. 'My wife has a scroll of your poems which her mother gave her. She likes to read them to me when I return home on leave.'

I cannot help flushing. It is a long time since I heard confirmation that my fame still lives.

'I am honoured,' I say. 'Your wife is an unusual woman to read so well.'

'She is of good family,' he says, proudly.

I sense a story behind his words, probably a sad one, given his current circumstances. I glance at Youngest Son, who is guffawing at the sly-faced officer's stories.

'Do you have a favourite poem of mine?' I ask.

Lieutenant Lo tugs at his lips. Despite the awkwardness of our mutual positions, I'm warming to him.

'No, all are very fine, as far as I can tell. There's one I like. . . how does it go? No, I have forgotten. I'll ask my wife when we next meet.'

His tone suggests the event seems distant.

'Send word to me,' I say. 'And I'll write it out for you. Then you can give it to her.'

He smiles sadly.

'I regret that is not likely. . . I remember now! The poem is about waiting by a lake. That's it.'

'Ah,' I say.

Then I close my eyes and slowly recite, characters forming neat columns across my inner vision:

The lake ripples as four winds will.
Fish rise, mouths gape like coins.
West Lake might as well be an ocean.
Heart's desire waits for shores to kiss,
No balance until they touch.

He looks hard at me, unexpectedly blinks back a tear.

'She's a soft-hearted wench,' he says, softly.

I realise the room is silent. When I look up, I'm met by their eyes, baffled or amused. In Youngest Son's case, confused. I sense the reproach his father's poem provokes. A reminder that, however great his hope, he ended up a mere soldier.

Eldest Son coughs. 'I like that one, Father,' he says.

I have no doubt he is thinking of Daughter-in-law. That's how it is with poems. Every man finds his own meaning, sometimes no meaning at all. They know nothing of the woman to whom it was addressed, her beauty, my restless longing when I was young.

A sergeant wearing full armour appears in the doorway, and enters with a deep bow. He seems out of breath, and anxious.

'The men are getting rowdy, sir,' he says, after receiving permission to speak. 'Some say that now the officers are away, they may have a little fun, sir.'

Youngest Son dismisses the news with a casual wave.

'My men are disciplined. They know better than to anger me.'

The sergeant exchanges a meaningful look with Lieutenant Lo, who frowns.

'Youngest Son!' I say, hurriedly. 'Surely, it would be wise to see if the good sergeant exaggerates? This brings me to another question. Perhaps an edict written by yourself, assuring the villagers will not be molested. . .'

'Father!'

Youngest Son lowers his cup to the table with a loud clatter. Wine spills to form a small puddle. The room is silent with shock.

'Father, there shall be no such edict! These are military matters!'

Lieutenant Lo clears his throat. I sense his embarrassment.

'Let me go down there, sir!' he says. 'Just in case.'

Youngest Son glares at him; snorts scornfully.

'We shall all go. It is late,' he says. 'Tomorrow is an important day. We have stayed here long enough.'

His officers rise at once, bowing gratefully for my hospitality. As distant shouts rise from Wei Village, they hurry into the night. Youngest Son's cheeks are flushed, never a healthy sign with him. Especially now, for he holds a sword above our heads.

I don't try to sleep. The banquet with Youngest Son has given me indigestion, more of the mind than body. One question troubles me above all others. Why did he not ask about the Imperial cavalry? I had prepared a dozen subtle evasions. It makes no sense. Who better to ask than the Lord, if you are seeking fugitives in his domain? Our valley winds round the lower slopes of two mountains and a dozen small valleys flow into Wei like tributaries. Without local guidance, even a force two hundred strong could spend weeks of fruitless searching.

I must assume Youngest Son did not ask for a reason. Perhaps he already suspects us. Maybe he is so drunk on his own abilities that requesting help affronts his dignity. Then again, he may already have the information he requires. Perhaps others in the village have betrayed the cavalrymen's whereabouts. Certainly, I believe he knows more about the intentions of the Imperial troops than I do, and always the doubt nags – are they connected to P'ei Ti? One could speculate until dawn.

There is a further possibility, one I desire to be true. Youngest Son does not wish to involve us, in case collective punishment against the village becomes necessary. However deep his devotion to General An-Shu, loyalty to one's family and ancestors must surely take precedence.

I look at my official uniform in the lantern light. Youngest Son has power now. Where has the eager boy I loved gone? How did his excited, high-pitched voice, like a flute, a sweet flute, grow harsh? He has become strange and daunting. Am I somehow to blame? And he is so young to be a captain. His officers evidently respect and fear him. I know the world well enough to understand he must have earned both emotions, probably in cruel ways. But even as a child he always led the other children. No surprise when a bough sprouts leaves.

As for his attitude to me – flashes of bitterness, lightning across a distant horizon. Yet I pity my lost boy. His mother would lament to see the danger he is in. He has planted every last grain of his future in General An-Shu's field, and should it wither, he will reap a rebel's end. A desperate man is ruthless. I must not allow myself to be blinded by sentiment. Wei Village will only be safe when he and his wolves march away. I must be balanced, too, for there are decent men among them. The older officer, Lieutenant Lo, might let slip information Youngest Son would rather I did not know.

Finally, a restless doze. When I awake the lantern has burned down. My room half-lit by dawn, Eldest Son beside my bed.

'Father!' he whispers. 'Wake up! Things happen in the village.'

I pull the coverlet up to my chin. It is cool. I can hear wind outside.

'What things?'

'The soldiers gather dozens of peasants. They're all in the village square.'

It takes little time to don my uniform. We hurry silently down the hill to the village.

There, the scene does not gratify. Youngest Son lolling in Father's ebony chair, surrounded by his officers, while one of his men is beaten for some breach of discipline. I assume it stems from last night's disturbance, and Wudi whispers in my ear that one of the village girls has vanished. Every time the bamboo cane strikes the soldier's naked genitals, he lets out a thin scream. The infantry stand on parade, weapons shouldered, watching expressionlessly. What troubles me is the sight of twenty or so villagers on their knees, in a huddle beside the well.

Youngest Son is evidently displeased to see us. No doubt that is why he forgets to rise, so I must stand before him, like an underling. A woman wails in one of the houses round the village square.

'Father,' he says, rising reluctantly. 'You should be resting. As I said last night, these are military affairs.'

I nod. Dust blows fitfully around the square. I feel invisible fingers tug my clothes.

'Your affairs are pressing,' I say. 'I merely wondered if some of the villagers have offended your authority. That would bring shame on us all.'

He follows my glance to the wretched group by the well.

'No, Father. Not yet. That depends on whether they co-operate.'

'I'm sure they will,' I say, smoothly.

'Let us see.'

He sits down in my chair and motions to Lieutenant Lo.

'Have those men brought before us.'

A few soldiers chivvy the peasants to their feet with halberd butts. They are pale with fear. The soldiers thrust them before Youngest Son. Several glance at me with beseeching eyes. Now I must prove a father to my people. My mouth tightens, yet I wait.

'Peasants,' drawls Youngest Son. 'All of you know the valley well, so don't pretend otherwise.'

They abase themselves, twice as respectfully as they do for me.

'You will lead my men to where the rebels are hiding,' he says. 'The first of you to provide useful information will avoid punishment.'

Dust blows around their foreheads, which they keep firmly pressed against the earth. None rise. At last, Yuan, the innkeeper, raises his head a little, and fearfully points up the valley.

'They rode through two days ago, Sir,' he says, his voice quavering.

I have to respect the man's courage.

'That I already know!' roars Youngest Son. 'You waste my time. Where are they hiding?'

Another man lifts his head. Li Sha, who leases three of my farms.

'I have heard, Sir,' he cries. 'They are camped in the valley adjoining Shady Wood.'

My heart twists with tension. Yet who can blame Li Sha for wishing to save his family?

We are disturbed by the clip-clop of hooves. The soldiers raise their weapons instinctively. Then a large, grey cavalry horse, still saddled, trots into the square. Men rush to seize its bridle and it rears in panic. Youngest Son examines the beast curiously. Only I and Wudi knows why it is riderless, that the Imperial cavalry let their mounts go free.

'What is *that* doing here?' demands Youngest Son. 'Do you mock me?'

The peasants cower. He motions and two soldiers drag Li Sha to his feet.

'How do you know the rebels are in the valley near Shady Wood? Why should they hide somewhere so barren? There is no grazing for their horses in that valley. Speak quickly.'

I step forward anxiously. Li Sha quivers, too frightened to speak.

'Hit him!' orders Youngest Son.

A single blow to the stomach. Li Sha lies groaning in the dust of the square. At last, between gasps, he manages to pant: 'My second cousin... a goatherd, Sir... saw them a day ago.'

'Only a day? Are you sure?'

Youngest Son motions again. Another dull thud, this time in the chest. Li Sha cries out pitifully.

'Sure, lord, I'm sure!'

'What about the rest of you?' demands Youngest Son. 'Use your tongues before I cut them out.'

At this, the wretches in the dust call out confirmation of the beaten man's words.

'Now we are getting somewhere,' says Youngest Son.

It is time. I take another step forward.

'Perhaps,' I say, tactfully. 'They know no more than this.'

Youngest Son glares at me. I meet his eye.

'After all,' I add. 'You know these fellows yourself. Surely you remember Yuan, the innkeeper, and Li Sha here! And what of Chiao Sung the blacksmith! All honourable men you've known all your life. And your old playmates over there, Turtle and Little Feng. None of them love a rebel, I'm sure. All are honoured to serve you, now you have returned among us.'

'Return to the house, Father,' he commands.

I have no choice but to obey, my dignity tattered. Slowly, sadly, I leave the square, feeling every year of my age. I fear he gains satisfaction from this scene, as though humiliating the village cancels the fact that once he was shamed here. The sound of further beatings and interrogation rise behind me, until dispersed by the quickening breeze.

I withdraw to my room and take to the couch. Memories swirl and merge, vapours of mist above a lake at dawn, the waters of the past evaporating. Pleasant to remember pleasant things. Not so, pain. Yet who has not suffered?

At the age of fifteen I graduated from the Provincial to the Metropolitan Academy, along with a thousand others drawn by fluttering banners of wealth and honour. We came from every corner of the Empire. Most of the students were the sons of scholar-officials maintaining family tradition, like P'ei Ti, or nobles seeking real power in the state. A few, such as Cousin Zhi, were from wealthy merchant families.

All gathered for the prize of office. If one graduated from the Metropolitan Academy, governorships and magistracies, posts with a hundred underlings might flutter one's way. Yet the test was hard. Just a few would negotiate the narrow tunnel of the examination and, of those, many succeeded only after a second or third attempt. Failure, of course, did not bring ruin. To reach the Metropolitan Academy required success in the First Examination. This alone earned the right to lesser office, a lifetime of dutiful clerking for one's superiors. But we all aimed higher, whatever the price. Ambition ruined many a young man's happiness.

The Metropolitan Academy stood in a broad park at the edge of the government enclosure. Pavilions and learning halls, gardens criss-crossed by artful streams to aid contemplation, shrines honouring His Imperial Majesty's ancestors and those gods favoured by scholars. Here were libraries and dining halls, dormitories where ambitious students lived like monks disgusted by pleasure.

Sometimes I considered requesting a place in the dormitories but always held back. For all its dangers, Uncle Ming's house offered freedoms undreamt of by those boarding within the Academy walls. And if nothing else, Uncle kept a good table. I could even bear Honoured Aunty's scowls when the alternative was waking at the exact time a thousand others woke, eating with them, vacating one's bowels with them, studying, performing the day's ritual, then more study and eating, studying once again, then sleeping. Every hour regulated by the huge, bronze gong beside the Chief Examiner's dwelling. At least the room in Uncle's octagonal tower was my own. I have always required a private ledge to perch on.

Su Lin gradually faded from my waking thoughts. Indeed, I was too busy to remember her. But at night she often stole gracefully through my dreams, and I almost smelt the heady musk of her perfume mingled with sweat, and awoke to find my thighs sticky, the bed empty. My room cold and dark.

One may meet graduates of the Academy who complain about its strictures. Who has not? The years of laborious study like clambering up a cliff lined with jagged stones, wearying spirit and body, parching youth beneath a merciless sky. Yet I rarely knew weariness. In those years I felt especially alive.

My joy was a love of knowledge for its own sake. My eagerness was to unlock significance through the keys I had been offered. Such intricate, fine, weighty keys! Naturally, the Five Classics dominated. But there were other writings, some dating back a thousand years and more. Ideas contending as flints spark fire, systems of thought which once regulated and confounded our ancestors, tradition a tangle of silken threads each generation must unpick, and re-weave to wear again.

P'ei Ti had graduated alongside me, leaving behind most of his former companions, who were incapable of progressing further. Again we found ourselves beside each other in lessons and this proximity grew into firm friendship. Often we left our studies to sit by the West Lake, discussing our teachers and fellow students before hurrying back to read scrolls by the light of flickering lamps until our eyes smarted.

We shared dreams of the future, too. P'ei Ti's were exact. He wished to advise His Imperial Majesty on matters relating to administration, which he believed could be improved through small, painless reforms, so subtle no one would notice until the benefit had been attained. My own ambitions were more diverse, and vague.

So three years passed until we were eighteen. One summer afternoon we lolled by the West Lake munching sunflower seeds. Shells spread across the water, then floated away. A hundred boats busy on the lake, fishing or carrying pleasure parties. Boatmen shouted greetings to each other. Ladies squealed elegantly.

'Yun Cai,' said P'ei Ti. 'In a year's time we will sit the examination. If you pass, what do you desire to become?'

'Ah,' I said. 'I wish to win the most beautiful courtesan in the whole city for my unique appreciation.'

He laughed, and punched my arm.

'As does everyone. What do *you* wish to become?'

'That's obvious,' I said. 'I will write poems so fine and in characters so exquisite that people will sing my words in disreputable taverns and tea-houses and on street corners. Oh, and I will drink a jar of wine for breakfast then spend the whole day wondering why the world is upside down.'

'That would be a proper answer if I were not serious.'

'So am I!'

P'ei Ti generally loved my mad, unconventional turns of mood, but not today.

'One doesn't endure the lectures of Old-Tufty-Beard on the venerable rites merely to get drunk. No study is needed for that,' he said.

'True.'

'Well then?'

I affected to yawn.

'I suppose I will serve the Son of Heaven, while I prepare for the final Imperial examination,' I said. 'Everyone must do something.'

'That is my plan, too,' he said, earnestly.

'I knew that already. First you will become Censor, then Chief Minister. Then the Empire will enter a golden age inspired by your wisdom.'

'Your mockery is only justified because I have not yet proved myself. But aren't you describing the duty all talented men owe, to both His Imperial Majesty and the people?'

'You are so grave today, P'ei Ti! It quite shames me.'

'I hope so.'

'As for me,' I said. 'I wish to pass the Imperial Examination merely to astound my father, who I have not seen for so long. Beyond that, I imagine no further.'

'It is fitting to please one's father,' said P'ei Ti.

His own father had recently gained the post of Prefect in distant Nanning, leaving wife and family in the capital for three long years. I knew P'ei Ti missed him deeply. His filial piety was unfeigned; an excellent virtue, all would agree. Certainly, I honoured him for it. Good people inspire goodness among those they meet, so I was happy my answer satisfied him. He would have been less impressed that I also longed to prove my worth to a faithless singing girl. Or to her memory. Such are the mind's contradictions. Wisdom and folly contend, yet somehow they rub along together.

'Besides,' I added, mischievously. 'I must pass the Imperial Examination for no better reason than it would mortify Cousin Zhi. Come to think of it, there *is* no better reason.'

We both laughed. Suddenly, in that way he had of knitting his brows into a determined frown, P'ei Ti announced:

'Then you and I, dear Yun Cai, must take earnest thought upon a crucial matter. I am sure you know what I mean.'

I flicked another sunflower shell to join the others spreading out across the lake.

'Look how slowly they float,' I murmured.

He sighed with frustration.

'Surely you have given thought to a patron?' he asked.

'None at all.'

'But passing the examination is not enough! Without a sponsor you could wait years for a worthy position.'

Naturally P'ei Ti was right. Merit and talent are feeble

without an influential patron; it was essential to win the goodwill of a highly placed official who might recommend one for a plump posting.

'You have someone in mind?' I enquired.

'Several. That is why I wished to speak to you. We must beat others to a great man's door or find his house already full.'

'But which great man?'

'Why, the most useful to us. And I have a plan.'

This did not altogether surprise me.

'If I use my family's influence to gather a list of names,' he continued. 'Then you can write poems praising their virtues. After all, it is a craft at which you excel.'

I caught his intention at once. P'ei Ti had always been an indifferent poet.

'If you give me details of these sponsors,' I said. 'Their titles and achievements, I could write enough poems for both of us. That way, to use my Cousin Hong's favourite phrase, 'everyone will be happy'.'

I sensed his shame at having to bargain for my help.

'You would be doing me a great favour,' I added. 'I would be forever in your family's debt.'

He nodded sheepishly.

'Then we have a pact,' he said. 'My knowledge will match your versifying.'

I smiled.

'Not if you take these great men at their own estimation, or even the world's!' I cried. 'Remember the words of Lao-tzu: *knowledge studies others; wisdom is self-known.*'

The next day P'ei Ti gave me a scroll containing information about six possible patrons and within a fortnight I had written a dozen verses lauding their sagacity, power, fame and exceptional virtue. Those I wrote on behalf of P'ei Ti were conventional and sincerely flattering, as befitted his character. They were written *old style*, and modelled on the greatest of the court poets. Those composed on my own behalf employed a bolder, dare I say it, more ambiguous voice to pay my respects. There seemed no point in pretending to be someone other than myself.

We spent several evenings perfecting our calligraphy and P'ei Ti's mother generously paid for the scrolls to be encased in sandalwood, embossed with the names of both recipient and supplicant. On a day declared propitious by an astrologer, we toured the wide city, presenting our gifts on bended knee, with many exclamations of unworthiness. In this, we had company. Outside one mansion a dozen other students from the Metropolitan Academy were queuing to present their own poems.

Afterwards I insisted we buy a flask of cheap wine, using the last of our cash. We drank perched on the city walls, gazing across the River Che as it flowed toward the sea. White birds wheeled and dived, their cries strangely exhilarating, and forlorn. We were like those gulls, except gulls seldom drown when fishing for the slippery eels of success.

A face swims into view, not arch and balanced like Su Lin's. More like my wife's, broad and prone to an uneasy grin. Her clothes simple and practical, sewn from hemp. She wore her hair in the fashion of servant girls in those days, combed forward to the front of the head, bound by ribbons of blue, red, yellow – any cheap dye – above a straight fringe covering her forehead. Her hair was black and thick. Her figure already full, though she was no older than me.

I had picked her out among the other servant girls, as one does, through the corner of my eyes. When she stooped to scrub clothes, singing a wash-song in a city accent, her wet arms glistened in the sunshine. Sometimes her eyes would meet mine momentarily, then return to her tasks of sweeping and polishing. One day I passed her as she was being admonished by Honoured Aunty, head hung in submission, yet I caught the brief glitter of her gaze. Evidently Honoured Aunty did too, for she paused in her harangue.

Not long after, I was rooting through a box of old scrolls in the room beneath my bedchamber when she entered, carrying a square wooden bucket slopping water.

'Sir, I have been ordered to keep this tower clean,' she said, in a high-pitched, slightly whining voice, very different from Su Lin's lively, delicate tone.

Welcome news. The place was grey with cobwebs and dust.

'What is your name?' I asked.

She glanced at me boldly from beneath her servant-girl's fringe.

'Peach Blossom,' she said.

The name suited her complexion. Unaccountably I grew confused.

'Carry on,' I said, sternly. 'Only don't spill water on the scrolls.'

Most days she came in the late afternoon, so she often found me with head bowed, absorbed by my studies after long lessons in the Academy. At first I pretended not to notice her. Then, by degrees, I found myself questioning her. Peach Blossom's father was a porter employed by Uncle Ming to carry wine. Her mother steamed rice balls flavoured with aniseed and sold them from a wheelbarrow beside Mallow Bridge. She never enquired about me, yet from unguarded slips I gathered she knew all manner of things concerning me. I found this vaguely flattering. When she bent over her tasks I was aware of being distracted, her scent a presence I could not ignore.

One summer afternoon she came early and appeared in my doorway. The city was sluggish in the heat, sunlight poured through the eight small windows of my chamber. There are wordless understandings. I watched her for a moment and she stood very still, her head bowed as though waiting. I felt my throat tighten.

'Put the bucket down,' I said. 'Please come here.'

She did so. Her obedience excited me. She stood a yard in front of me. Both of us were breathing quickly. Her head remained bowed. So close, her sweat possessed a hundred lures. I reached out and pulled her towards me. Her low moan acted upon my blood.

'Please,' I said, hoarsely, expecting a stream of angry words. 'Unbutton your blouse.'

She reached across and slowly unbuttoned the bone oblongs from the loops holding them. Her small, firm breasts were revealed. I began to kiss her face and neck, hardly daring to venture down. She took my hand and led me to the bed.

Over forty years lie between that moment and now. There have been many others since, but what of that? For an hour I knew nothing but intensity. Taste of her tongue, smell of her hair. My hand travelling up her plump thighs, encouraged by soft, insistent cries. Her own hands fumbling with my clothes, immodestly perhaps, though I did not care.

How long we grappled awkwardly in this way I do not know, until she was naked beneath me. I reached down and she invited me with her limbs. Emboldened, I edged forward, and release set me free.

After that our liaisons became an agreed thing, though a great secret. Uncle Ming would be angry to learn of a shameful liaison with one of his oldest employee's daughters. As for Honoured Aunty, I had no doubt she would dismiss poor Peach Blossom in disgrace.

Every afternoon, I would hurry from the Academy to my room and wait impatiently, imagining the warm, soft places of her body, our hurried, awkward conversation. Often she did not appear, assigned other duties in the house, and I would pace with frustration, sometimes missing meals in the hope of better food. My studies suffered as they had when Su Lin deserted me, and truly I was in a bad way. Yet my situation was worse than I guessed, as later became clear.

In the year preceding the examination, Cousin Zhi's animosity towards me grew alongside his fear of failure.

These were harsh and perplexing times for Cousin Zhi. All his life he had been assured of a particular destiny, confirmed by the best astrologers; above all by Honoured Aunty's expectations, repeated day after anxious day. Yet everything depended on passing the Metropolitan Examination, and there his troubles began.

As the months passed, his studies fell further behind, almost in proportion to the effort he expended. Never was there so earnest a student. Cousin Zhi listened with desperate diligence to every word from our teachers. When I glanced at him in lessons, I could sense the fingers of his mind groping out blindly, grasping a few confused concepts, then dragging them home, where they promptly dissipated like mist. Frustration etched itself upon his young face. A fixed, determined scowl, unrelieved by mirth. I have no doubt he felt utterly alone. Ambition such as his stands or falls by itself, for it seeks pinnacles, by their nature solitary.

I would like to pretend my offer to help him stemmed from goodwill. That would be a lie. First I became convinced he would never pass the examination. Then, that Honoured Aunty would find someone to punish, and who was closer to hand than myself?

One afternoon I waited for him at the end of our lessons. He ignored my greeting. Honoured Aunty had ordered he must be carried everywhere by litter, in order to preserve his essential breaths. We made a comic sight, me trotting alongside while his chair bobbed through the crowds on the Imperial Way, surrounded by sweating lackeys. On-lookers must have thought me one of them.

'Cousin Zhi!' I called. 'Please stop! I wish to speak to you!'

He looked pale and exhausted.

'What is it?' he snapped.

'I have an idea for our mutual benefit.'

His red-rimmed eyes narrowed as he bumped and jolted along.

'Why don't we spend some time together reviewing our studies?' I suggested. 'It would help us both.'

A sly, thoughtful look crossed his thin face.

'Ah, so you find it difficult,' he said.

'Not really. But I thought. . .'

'Why should I help you?' he interrupted, shrilly.

'No, it's not that. Can't you ask the bearers to slow down?'

He seemed enraged. Almost mad.

'Why should I help you?' he repeated. 'Your arrogance makes me laugh! Don't think you'll ever get the better of us! Look to yourself!'

The curtain of his litter fell and I was left breathless by the entrance to Ocean Market. My nostrils filled with the odour of decaying fish. Doubt touched me. Did he know about Peach Blossom? But that was impossible. I shrugged and walked home. Cousin Zhi's litter disappeared in the crowd.

Soon afterwards his nervous affliction took hold.

First he stayed at home for one, two, then successive days, missing vital lessons. A dark cloud settled on Uncle Ming's house, emanating from Honoured Aunty. A rule of absolute silence was imposed, lest laughter disturb Cousin Zhi's rest. Even the porters and brewers were ordered to conduct their business quietly. I witnessed one servant being beaten for giggling below his bedchamber. Uncle Ming disappeared more often than usual to his establishment outside the city walls and Cousin Hong walked around with an unusually thoughtful expression.

When Cousin Zhi's affliction continued, Honoured Aunty hired an army of healers. We have a saying in the mountains: plough too often and the soil blows away. So it was with Cousin Zhi's cure. All agreed his illness stemmed from disharmony among the separate virtues pertaining to health, especially the circulation of the breaths. That much was obvious. However none could agree which breath was deficient.

One learned doctor diagnosed an excess of cold and dry breaths, prescribing a decoction of thirty-two ingredients, including toad-venom, earthworms, spiders and centipedes, boiled and reduced to powder. A second devised a medicine of crushed rhinoceros horn, jade and ground pearls, so costly that Cousin Hong muttered about frittering his inheritance. A third doctor attempted simple acupuncture and massage, claiming Cousin Zhi's malady stemmed from an excess of the female principle, yin. Honoured Aunty sent him away after a single consultation.

Still he languished, and began to suffer fits of vomiting. Honoured Aunty resorted to more proven methods. Buddhist and Daoist monks were hired to chant spells and produce charms inscribed with potent characters, which Cousin Zhi wore continually, so his amulets clanked whenever he moved.

Finally, Honoured Aunty summoned her old familiar, the sorcerer who had frightened me when I first arrived in Uncle Ming's household. The intervening years had fattened him. His robes, paid for by Honoured Aunty, shimmered with gold and silver thread.

One night everyone was barred from the house at his command, even Uncle Ming. Strange chants and smells escaped through cracks in the windows, or when Honoured Aunty, unable to contain herself, bustled in to check her son's progress. The whole household crouched outside in the courtyard, waiting in appalled fascination. At dawn the sorcerer appeared, pale and exhausted, propped between two young boys, smears of sickly yellow powder on his hands. He swayed as if in a trance, screaming hysterically that an evil influence lay heavy on the family, and that until it was removed, no cure was possible. Then he stumbled from the house and would only communicate the demons' messages through secret letters to Honoured Aunty.

Cousin Hong cornered me and whispered: 'Ah, Little

General, the sooner you pass that examination the better for everyone. I have heard that the demons mentioned your name.'

I was so alarmed by this news I begged an audience with Uncle Ming. He saw me in his office. I got down on my knees and stayed there.

'Uncle,' I said. 'Have I displeased you?'

His customary smile had grown thin and fixed of late. Sighing, he poured himself a cup of wine from a simple, earthenware cooler which always stood by his divan.

'Do you see this wine cooler?' he asked.

'Yes, Uncle.'

'Do you know who gave it to me? Of course not. It was your father. When we were young we barely had enough food to get from one winter to another. The only reason I am here today is because your father shared half his rations. And they were little enough. Sometimes he gave me more than half, for I was feebler than him. Did you know that?'

'No, Honoured Uncle.'

'Of course not! Why talk of unpleasant things. He gave me a present when I married, this wine cooler. He advised I would need it. And though it is cracked and poor, and I could buy a hundred carved from the finest green jade, I still use it each day. Does that answer your question?'

My confusion must have been evident.

'Simply pass the examination, win the honour your father deserves, and I will consider this wine cooler paid for. Whatever befalls my youngest son will never make the wine I pour from it taste sour.'

'I understand, Honoured Uncle.'

'Good. Now leave me in peace. I'm sick of the lot of you.'

Afterwards I heard through Peach Blossom that the sorcerer had been set upon by unknown bravos and beaten to an inch of his life. I never again saw him loitering in Uncle Ming's house. Yet every time I met Honoured Aunty she examined me coldly. Deep thought lay behind her look.

A month before the examination, P'ei Ti and I received a summons.

I have often watched the wind pluck seeds winged with fine, downy strands from a flower, and wondered if destiny or chance determines their settling place. Our poems had not been delivered by chance. Unexpectedly, they sprouted leaves.

We found ourselves in the huge antechamber of a mansion on Phoenix Hill, dressed in our best clothes, clutching yet more poems of praise. P'ei Ti could hardly disguise his elation and anxiety. This was the game he had been born to play. My own feelings were mixed.

We were both chaperoned by uncles, our fathers being far away. Uncle Ming wore robes of exceptional splendour which seemed to make him itch. P'ei Ti's uncle, an official in the Imperial Treasury, exclaimed constantly about the value of the furniture and statues around us. We had been summoned for a test of worthiness, along with fifty others in the same expectant, awkward position, everyone competing to win patronage. In truth, Lord Xiao was merely looking us over, as one might a new wardrobe.

Lord Xiao. Chief Minister of the Imperial Finance, former Governor of Nanking and illustrious Foochow, author of a famous treatise on taxation which was notable for its rigour. While not of the Emperor's intimate council, he had access to the sacred ear. Hundreds in the Imperial Administration built their careers upon Lord Xiao's patronage, and through such obligations his influence spread far and wide in the Four Ministries. It was Lord Xiao's custom to gather new protégés each year from the most promising students in the Academy. By virtue of our consistent success in the monthly examinations, and our flattering poems, P'ei Ti and myself had attracted his secretary's interest, who had summoned us for an audience.

So we found ourselves waiting for our names to be called. P'ei Ti constantly straightened and smoothed his clothes. Every few minutes a major domo called out a candidate's name who he ushered to the nearby hall. Some returned downcast, others jubilant. In this way two long hours passed. My own attention wandered, drawn by a painting of waterfalls and sages on the wall, an original by my beloved Master Xie-He, as was proved by numerous seals of former owners, all illustrious. The painting itself must have cost a prince's ransom.

When my name was shouted out, I looked up in surprise. Uncle Ming poked me hard in the ribs, leapt to his feet and thrust me forward. At once I was nervous. A secretary led me to a high pair of purple doors. These opened onto a large audience-hall, its rafters painted in gay colours, walls adorned with frescos depicting the Son of Heaven's ancestors. I advanced with bowed head, not daring to look at the man who waited on an ivory throne at the end of the hall, surrounded by friends and relatives. The silence in the room broken only by my shuffling feet.

A dozen feet from his chair I sank to my knees and remained with head lowered. There was whispering around Lord Xiao, yet I could not look up. At last I heard him say out loud: 'Ah, that one. The poet. Very well.'

More silence. He was clearly watching me.

'I have heard of your father's deeds,' he said.

His voice was quiet and commanding, yet surprisingly high-pitched.

'Such loyalty in the father speaks well for the son.'

I bowed lower in acknowledgement.

'I also hear reports you are a poet. Indeed, I enjoyed your verses – and those of your friend. Loyalty to a friend also speaks well.'

My face reddened and he chuckled.

'You may look at me,' Lord Xiao said.

I saw a man in his fifties, in the prime of life, enrobed as befitted his position. His face narrow and, I thought, supercilious because watchful for disrespect. Fine lines ran in parallels across his forehead. Perhaps I stared, for he said lightly: 'Have you looked enough, young man?' His confidants tittered. My head ducked down.

'Let me sample some of this poetry I hear about from your teachers. No, not the poems you've brought with you. Improvise something.'

There was a murmur of amusement among Lord Xiao's followers. Here was the moment of trial. A verse in regular style at once shaped itself. I spoke hesitantly at first, then closed my eyes, possessed by words:

Outside doors taller than my father's I wait.
Whisper of suitors. Shadows shaping.
But my Lord's painting by Xie-He lends ease.
Sages and waterfalls blend wisdom,
Approving the virtue of Lord Xiao's house.

I waited, breathless, as though my fate depended on those words. In a sense it did. Or one possible fate, among many. For Lord Xiao could have yawned and sent me away without further comment, having decided I was no use to him. Instead he said: 'Interesting. So you noticed my Xie-He. Of course I own better, but that painting is certainly fine. Perhaps I should move it to a more prominent position. You may go now, Yun Cai. Yes, interesting.'

He had remembered my name! Without raising my eyes, I shuffled backwards, and out. Amidst elation, I felt a deep tiredness. Great men exhaust their followers; one can never be at ease with them.

P'ei Ti also gained Lord Xiao's attention at that audience. He was not asked to improvise a verse. Instead Lord Xiao questioned my friend concerning proper ceremonial procedure at a prefectural levee. Of course, P'ei Ti had pleasingly orthodox opinions on the matter, but also dared to offer an idea of his own concerning official uniforms for Third Grade clerks. The great man nodded, as though in approval. P'ei Ti repeated this story until I knew it by heart.

How often my life has resembled the absurd entertainments popular in the Imperial Pleasure Grounds! Certainly a bitter farce was brewing. Uncle Ming's household made up the cast of this puppet show. But we were live puppets, with hearts to break and bodies to waste away, the strings animating us barely understood. If we did not speak our lines in the shrill nasal voices favoured by puppet-masters, it was merely because we took ourselves too seriously.

Lord Xiao sent his secretary to test my respectability one morning towards the end of summer. Only two weeks remained before the examination. The whole household stood in readiness. Every room and warehouse had been swept clean. Bright banners bearing the name of Lord Xiao hung from the eaves. Uncle Ming was determined to make a good impression, even at the expense of his wife's good will. There was little enough of that. Honoured Aunty's scowl lingered from the moment she appeared, lightened only by a peculiar smile when she met my eye, which vanished as soon as it began. At once my natural anxiety doubled.

Lord Xiao's secretary was not visiting to discuss the price of hemp. His time was valuable, for it implied favour. His task no less than assessing my character through that of my family, the two being inseparable. In our case he needed to be vigilant. We were not scholar-officials of longstanding like P'ei Ti's relatives. Uncle Ming, though wealthier than most officials, was essentially *shang*, mere merchant, worthy of small honour. In my favour, it could be argued that Father was a Lord; but his elevation, so recent, bore a taint of vulgarity. I was walking a web of invisible threads whose strength I could not anticipate. Nothing was certain.

Uncle Ming met Secretary Wen at the gates, and ushered him with due ceremony to a room full of presents for the great man. In pride of place stood a complete rhinoceros horn, a princely gift, for it might save Lord Xiao's life in case of severe sickness. I knelt on the floor beside Cousin Hong, who risked a wink while the secretary was examining a casket containing a bolt of sky blue silk.

Truly Uncle Ming had invested in me. Or in his love for my father, which amounted to the same thing. Indeed, I believe it was the only love he felt deeply.

'I come in august of a greater presence,' began the Secretary. 'His name illuminates west and east. Millions are grateful for his wisdom.'

Uncle Ming shifted uneasily in his best robes.

'Lord Xiao,' he said. He seemed at a loss for words. 'Lord Xiao is a wonder.'

I cringed inwardly. The Secretary looked at him in surprise, then frowned.

'Of course,' he said. 'Such a one must not be associated with anyone base, lest his reputation suffer.'

Uncle Ming, who had no reputation to lose, unless it involved the quality of his wine, nodded wisely.

'I must ask,' continued the Secretary. 'Is your nephew of unimpeachable character?'

'Why yes,' said Uncle. 'He's a hard-working boy. He has read more books than I've sold jars, and that's saying something.'

If he expected the Secretary to soften, he was at once disappointed.

'I see. Is his body sound?'

Uncle Ming glanced across at me. Then at the presents.

'He's as strong as a rhinoceros.'

'No deformities?'

'None I've ever seen.'

'What of his breaths?' continued the Secretary. 'Are they sound?'

I awaited Uncle's reply with trepidation. Clearly he was struggling for appropriate words.

'They never smell anything but sweet,' he said. 'And he never gets short of breath.'

'That's not what I meant.'

Cousin Hong rose slightly and whispered in his father's ear.

'Oh, I see. Of course. Yes, his breaths are wholesome. Definitely wholesome. I'd vouch for every one of them.'

He spread his hands across his heart to prove his point.

'Hmm. That is well,' said Secretary Wen. 'What of hidden vices?'

'As I say, he's a good boy.'

'I must tell you,' continued the Secretary. 'While no one doubts this particular candidate's ability, there are questions, how can I put it, concerning the provenance of his, ahem, ancestors.'

A look of irritation crossed Uncle Ming's plump face.

'Honoured Secretary, let me beg a question of you.'

Our interrogator's eyes narrowed.

'That is not entirely regular, but please proceed.'

Uncle Ming waved to indicate the fine house in which we sat.

'Do you know how I gained this place?' he asked. 'But of course you do, for you have made honest, careful enquiries concerning me. All this I earned through hiring the right men. Men who are trustworthy and know how to work. I would hire my nephew and rely on him like the morning sun.'

The Secretary waited, for Uncle was clearly approaching another point.

'Come,' said Uncle Ming, softly. 'Let us take a cup. Talking is thirsty work. While we drink, perhaps you might honour me by opening the small casket to your left. It is an unworthy gift for yourself, Honoured Secretary. One man to another, you understand.'

At once servants appeared with warm wine flasks and *dim sum*. The room filled with delicious scents. The Secretary opened the casket. His breath hissed involuntarily. Inside lay a bar of solid silver. A year's salary to him.

'Why,' he said, slowly. 'Why, everything seems in order.'

Uncle Ming smiled his meaningless smile.

'I am glad you find us so,' he said.

Beside me, Cousin Hong coughed.

We left the chamber with the same ceremony with which we'd arrived. It was outside, in the courtyard, the trouble began. Honoured Aunty watched from a doorway beneath Cousin Zhi's bedchamber. The servants were on their knees in neat lines. Abruptly, one leapt to her feet. We all froze in astonishment. Everything happened with agonising slowness.

Peach Blossom was the servant. Who knows what terrible threats or bribes drove her to such desperate action? Her eyes were red with weeping and she clutched her belly. She wailed pitifully like a poorly-trained actress, and lurched forward.

'Yun Cai!' she cried. 'I am with child! Oh, I am with child!'

The Secretary gaped at her in amazement.

'What is this?' he demanded, angrily.

Then a figure beside me was moving. Cousin Hong had the girl by the arm and was shaking her so hard her teeth rattled.

'You whore!' he roared. 'Are you mad? What time is this to tell me such news!'

Then he dragged her sobbing to the house, shoved her through a door and slammed it shut. A stunned silence lay across the courtyard. To my amazement he came over and literally grovelled before his father.

'Forgive me, Father!' he cried, with every sign of distress. 'My concubine. . . she is afflicted, possessed by demons.'

Uncle Ming glanced across at Honoured Aunty, who met his gaze without flinching. At once I understood. If her favourite son could not pass through the Vermilion Doors, I should not.

'What is this?' repeated the Secretary. 'She used this young man's name.'

'It is my pet name with her,' cried Hong, from his position on the ground.

'I am shamed you have been inconvenienced,' muttered Uncle Ming. 'You have heard my son. His concubine, nothing to do with my nephew, that is for sure.'

'Ah, I see. The girl is perhaps mad?' offered the Secretary.

'She's not well in the head,' broke in Cousin Hong.

'I only keep her here out of charity,' added Uncle Ming. 'Which I regret because it has inconvenienced an Honoured Guest. Still, any act of kindness might help me in my next life.'

The Secretary examined each of our faces in turn. I could not meet his eye. At last, he shrugged. He was no fool.

Uncle Ming led him decorously to the carriage, bowing low as it drove away. Then, without a word to any of us, he swept to his office and did not emerge until late the next day.

Until that moment I had never truly understood the extent of my indebtedness to Uncle Ming. And now to Cousin Hong. For the first time I imagined the possibility of failing in the examination I took for granted; and my disgrace if I failed. A terrible realisation of folly stole the blood from my face.

'Let's hope Lord Xiao's secretary liked his silver,' said Cousin Hong, brushing dust from his clothes. 'Otherwise you'd better start looking for a new patron.'

I never saw Peach Blossom again. Nor was the incident mentioned, except that evening when I sought out Cousin Hong to thank him.

'You owe me for that, Little General,' he replied. 'And I always get repaid.'

But I did not forget. When the time came, I did not forget.

I often wondered what became of Peach Blossom. She was certainly with child. My child. Somewhere in the wide reaches of the Middle Kingdom there is a man or woman bearing my features, perhaps mourning an unknown father. Was that child's life ruined for the sake of an hour's pleasure? Perhaps he or she lives happily with children and grandchildren? One could speculate endlessly.

Poor Peach Blossom. I have no doubt Honoured Aunty failed to fulfil whatever bargain they struck. My shame is that I did not even seek to find out whether she was safe. She was only a servant girl. Such things happen every day.

At last, as with all longed-for and dreaded things, the day of the examination arrived. I was almost nineteen. Young to attempt such a rampart. Yet scale it I must, or suffer disgrace in Uncle Ming's household and endure the gloating mockery of Honoured Aunty and Cousin Zhi. Perhaps even be forced into a lowly clerk's position until the day I expired of boredom.

I was woken in the middle of the night, my room still dark. The servant, an old retainer of Honoured Aunty, held a lamp as I dressed in my student's gown. I was about to take the satchel I had prepared the night before, containing ink cakes and brushes, as well as food to sustain me through the trial ahead, when the servant coughed.

'I'd empty my bowels if I was you, young sir,' he said.

His eyes were yellow in the lamp light.

'Ah,' I said. 'Thank you.'

Then I retired behind a screen, his suggestion being easily fulfilled, such was my nervousness. Perhaps that is why I didn't hear my satchel rustle.

'Dawn is near,' he said.

I was about to follow him out when my eye fell on a small, silk bag on a chest. Su Lin had given it to me on the occasion of the First Examination, four years earlier. It had brought me good fortune then, so I stuffed it in the pouch at my belt. I also placed a lucky amulet round my wrist, a present from Mother and Father on leaving Wei. So armed, I followed the servant out.

At the gate my escort awaited, flaming torches in their hands.

Night lay across the city. A few stars formed unblinking patterns and mist swirled around our feet.

Cousins Hong and Yi-Yi were my only companions for the journey ahead. I could smell from their breath they had found a cure for the damp, chilly air.

'Have you breakfasted?' asked Hong.

'No.'

'Here.'

He thrust me a huge bag of steamed buns stuffed with egg, pork and shrimp.

'Eat on the way. See! The sun!'

And indeed the first pink fires of dawn were touching the horizon.

I became aware of movement above our heads. Glancing up, I saw the blinds of Cousin Zhi's chamber slowly rise. Two dark silhouettes filled the window, watching silently. One thin, the other squat as a toad. I felt suddenly feeble. Was she cursing me, using spells learnt from her sorcerer friend? I had no doubt of it. Yet my sole wish was to be loved. A sharp, contemptuous snort broke the silence in the courtyard. Then the blind fell with a rattle. The house was once again blank, its eye-lids closed.

'Let us go,' I said.

So, like resolute ghosts, we tramped toward the government enclosure at the foot of Phoenix Hill. Yi-Yi insisted on carrying my satchel of writing equipment. Each time a party of watchmen stopped us, Cousin Hong bellowed: 'Candidate for His Imperial Majesty's examination! Let us through!'

He, at least, seemed to be enjoying himself.

We did not go alone. Lights bobbed along the Imperial Way. Carriages rumbled on the stone flags, surrounded by friends and relatives, everyone quiet as befitted the dignity of the moment. Pomp and glorious ancestry could not aid the highest of the candidates now. The test awaiting us was a harsh garden where only the strongest seeds flourish, whether weed or precious orchid. Still we sought to plant ourselves, to weave the stems of our lives around the Son of Heaven. Ambition ever seeks the sun.

At last we formed a dense crowd outside the Examination Enclosure. It was still night, dawn swelling fast. The candidates left their entourages and gathered round the gates, where soldiers stood guard, halberds in hand, immobile as statues. The Chief Examiner emerged in his golden robes. All murmuring stilled. A thousand souls waited, clutching bags and satchels. All had been schooled in the ritual to come. Slowly, laboriously, the Chief Examiner pushed the iron gates open to their widest extent. My blood responded to this symbol. At once my fears faded into quiet determination.

I searched through the mass of expectant, nervous young men for P'ei Ti. No sign of him, though I recognised many from the Academy. I offered a silent plea to the gods we both favoured, wishing my friend good fortune, whatever befell me.

'Candidates!' announced the Chief Examiner. 'You shall enter one by one.'

Guardsmen flanked him, for it is well-known disorder may follow wherever a crowd gathers.

As we trooped past the Chief Examiner, he picked a token bearing a number from the sacred bowl, and placed it in our hands. Then scores of eunuchs led us into a large village consisting entirely of sheds, long rows of brick and tile sheds, four feet square, each numbered and set a uniform distance apart. My own number was seven hundred and thirty-nine.

Officials noted down my name and number, while more eunuchs examined my satchel and clothes for model answers. It amused me to think of P'ei Ti being searched in this way. He always hated to be touched.

I entered the shed and looked around. It contained a large water jar, a desk and stool, a lidded chamber-pot, and a high pile of paper.

I sat down and tried to meditate. The satchel across my knees felt strangely light. At last I heard the examiners outside the closed door, gluing a paper seal across the entrance. I was locked in that shed as if by chains. Then a roll of paper was stuffed under the door, containing the questions on which my future depended. Sighing, I opened my satchel to prepare my writing materials.

That moment of disbelief! It scorches me still. Fear is a deep wound. And some fears never quite heal. My own on that dawn moment was utmost despair. For however hard I looked, the cakes of ink and bundle of brushes I had so carefully prepared, were gone.

Finally I understood. What a fool I was! They had been removed by the servant sent to wake me, while I emptied my bowels at his suggestion. Honoured Aunty's revenge was complete. The door to my shed had been sealed. If I stepped out, I would be disqualified. Yet how could I attempt the examination without means to write?

I must confess that for long minutes I slumped with head in hands. Years of study and striving, cancelled in a moment! My heart beat unbearably. When it slowed I stared at the sky through the narrow window of the shed. How could I explain this to Uncle? He would assume that in my nervousness, or arrogance, I had forgotten the most necessary things. No one would believe my accusation against the servant, and what use was it anyway? Three long years must pass before the next examination. I would be despised as a wastrel, an utter fool.

Perhaps I should pack my bags and attempt the long journey back to Three-Step-House, except the thought of confessing my foolishness to Mother and Father was unbearable. Or I might ask Uncle if I could work for him until the next examination, studying as best I could in the evenings, all my dearly-won knowledge irrelevant to the selling of wine. Perhaps I should just weep forlornly, and starve myself to death, or shave my head and apply for a licence to become a monk. All these possibilities crossed my mind.

Nervously I picked at the pouch hanging from my belt. In the midst of fear came recollection. With trembling fingers I pulled out Su Lin's lucky pouch. It was a plain silk bag, embroidered by her own hands with the character for a successful candidate in the Imperial examination, a character I had taught her one warm, spring night while the city revelled around us. Inside was a cheap amulet, and more importantly, a stubby writing brush tipped with horse hair, and an ink cake, the best an apprentice singing girl had been able to afford. I laughed hysterically. The candidates in neighbouring sheds must have thought me crazy.

I can remember the exact feel and weight of that ink cake even now. So precious was it to me. It was small, but with care, sufficient. Not enough to write notes, but enough for hope.

My habit of visualising poems served me well on that cold, autumn morning. Closing my eyes I imagined answers to the questions as they would appear on the paper. Words and phrases to mark out my argument, flowing ribbons of characters. I had no leisure to contemplate the irony of my unexpected good fortune. Only later did I understand. What pains us most, and surely Su Lin had injured me deeply, may prove our greatest blessing. This idea ran through my answers that day, unconsciously, yet with the utmost relevance, for the Empire had suffered disastrous defeats at the hands of the Kin barbarians, and government policy struggled with the question of how to reverse our misfortunes. Indeed, every question gave scope for such a slant. I later heard His Imperial Highness had ordered it to be so. Even the Son of Heaven knew anxiety, and many an Emperor has lost his throne to uncouth horsemen from the steppes, with their singing, pitiless bows.

I wrote, crumbling and mixing my ink cake as a starving peasant ekes out his winter store to ensure the family do not starve before spring. I finished as darkness fell and slumped on my stool, awaiting the examiners. Then came a tearing noise. The paper seal had been broken. I stumbled out, took a lungful of fresh air, and vomited against the brick wall of the shed.

*

Weeks passed. The Bureau of Copying re-wrote every candidate's answer so that no one might recognise the handwriting. The examiners sequestered themselves in a pavilion guarded by crossbowmen, grading and re-grading the papers. My anxiety at that time can scarcely be imagined. I met with P'ei Ti each day to walk the city, seeking any distraction from the verdict awaiting us.

Then came a dawn, a long ago dawn. Once more I joined a crowd of excited young men outside the Chief Examiner's residence, for now the grain had been winnowed, husks blown away. His Majesty's scholars had all been granted vermilion silk robes and garlands. A worthy breakfast had been laid out on long trestle tables. Honey-coated lamb and chicken sizzling on braziers tended by eunuchs, cakes of a dozen kinds, rice-balls flavoured with shrimp, and fifty other dishes, all moistened by cups of wine. The sky a vast, inky blue, streaked by the emerging sun and a crescent of pale moon. P'ei Ti by my side, giddy as a bridegroom, laughing and clapping his hands at the slightest reason.

Then the Chief Examiner's gong sounded. Two hundred plumed guardsmen marched into the square, forming parallel lines. Musicians sounded drums and flutes. The cry went up: 'May His Imperial Majesty live a thousand years!', and we took our place between the lines of soldiers. At our head, the Chief Examiner and his staff. In our hearts, a pride never to be repeated in a single lifetime, for one can pass the Examination just once.

So we processed through the city, down the Imperial Way, crowds cheering on left and right, flowers paid for by the authorities thrown at us in handfuls. Oh, who did not envy His Majesty's scholars then! It is no lie when people say: 'The night of one's wedding and the day one's name appears on the Golden List!'

*

That afternoon P'ei Ti and I attended a pleasure party in the garden of Lord Xiao's mansion on Phoenix Hill. Both of us had written a sheaf of poems in his honour, as was customary, and for once P'ei Ti had written his own – although I made a few suggestions he readily incorporated. We were relying on Lord Xiao's goodwill for our first appointment. Naturally, after my long years of toil, I hoped for an easy berth. P'ei Ti, however, desired a posting in the Censorship, where the scent of power is most heady.

We arrived early and soon felt like drab pigeons among peacocks. We stood at the edge of the crowd, nibbling delicacies and sipping wine. Every so often some grand official deigned to notice us, making our acquaintance in case we might prove useful later in our careers. At last Lord Xiao himself appeared and we offered heartfelt gratitude for his acknowledgement of our worthless existence.

'Ah, Yun Cai and P'ei Ti! The two inseparables!'

His entourage tittered appreciatively. I took note that Lord Xiao liked to be considered a wit. Here was a way to win his favour, if one was that way inclined.

'It seems my faith in you was not misplaced. Congratulations! This is the finest hour in a young man's life.'

P'ei Ti bowed ever more deeply.

'Your example inspired me, Lord Xiao. So my success is actually your own.'

I was certain P'ei Ti had prepared that one in advance. In my perverse way, aided by too much wine, I found myself talking, too.

'Lord Xiao is generous,' I said. 'If we are to prove worthy of his faith, then I hope we bring relief to those most sorely pinched.'

I was alluding to the famine in the countryside. There had been a disastrous harvest that year.

I fell silent, having said too much for one in my low position.

I became aware Lord Xiao and his entourage were watching me curiously.

'A little earnestness is no bad thing in the young,' he replied. 'And you are not at fault, Yun Cai, to concern yourself with the hungry. Our task is to serve the Son of Heaven so he might bring happiness to the worthy. High and low, all fall within his care.'

I was deeply moved by his words. It must have shown on my face. Again I spoke when I should have been silent.

'Thank you, Lord. Already my education has begun.'

He laughed.

'Watch this one,' he told his friends. 'He wishes to make every peasant fat as a goose. A promising way to begin one's service! For a fat peasant has no thought of rebellion. Enjoy yourself today, Yun Cai. Your ideals will keep you working hard, at least.'

I bowed my head and when I looked up, he had moved on.

'You should learn to talk less!' hissed P'ei Ti, anxiously. 'I tell you because I want what's best for you.'

I did not care. There seemed no harm in mentioning what we all knew. P'ei Ti was greeted by a relative of his, and I wandered in Lord Xiao's garden to clear my head. It was an exquisite place in the fading light of an autumn afternoon, suggestive of delicate moods. We had been granted a warm day, perhaps the last before winter began in earnest. I found a bench beside a waterfall and watched swallows gathering for their eternal journey. My own journey was commencing. Growing old, weary and disappointed was something that applied to other men. From Phoenix Hill the city spread out like a banquet.

When I returned to the party, my elevated mood was rudely dispelled.

Lord Xiao, like all successful men, hired troupes of singing girls to entertain his guests. Several were performing as I approached. I idly scanned their faces until one made me stare. My heart quickened. For accompanying herself on the lute was Su Lin.

Resentment rose like bile, then became its opposite, enfeebled by feelings I could not justify or understand. She wore a gown of black and blood-red silk, hair held by coral combs glittering with silver. Her figure had filled out in the four years since our last meeting. Slender and graceful, her slightest movement as she sang fascinated me. At once I felt foolish, as I had that first time I saw her, practising a mountain song on a humble doorstep.

In confusion I sought out P'ei Ti. He was listening respectfully to a gentleman wearing the uniform of a senior official in the Censor's office.

As we left the party, I saw her circulating among the guests with the other singing girls, carrying trays of sweets and orchids. For a moment our eyes met. It was a long moment. Her tray wobbled slightly. I longed to approach her, relate in a rush how her gift of ink and brush had saved me from disgrace. I longed merely to hear her voice. But with all the fragile dignity of injured pride, I turned away. Even then, as I ruefully congratulated myself for being as stern and resolute as Confucius himself, I wondered how I might see her again.

four

'. . . Clouds drift through a maze of stars.
A fat autumn moon emerges from the mountainside.

In the valley lanterns bob like fireflies.
They are coming, as they did for Wang Wei. . .'

'Father!'

Reluctantly I open my eyes. A sour taste of sleep in my mouth. Eldest Son's beaming face is the first thing I see. With a jolt I recall his mother, and poor Little Peony, and confuse their features with Su Lin's, then the present reasserts itself.

'Father!' he says. 'They've captured the Imperial cavalry! Youngest Son has found them. Is it not good news? Now they will go away, for their mission is over. Our troubles are at an end, Father!'

I am pleased, for his sake, that he does not understand our true position. I fear it will be a brief respite

As the soldiers return, their drums beat a tattoo, suggestive of triumph. It is late afternoon, sun still bright. First shadows creep across the valley. My hope sinks with the sun. I have brought disaster on my people and those I love. The cavalrymen have been captured.

At last they march into view. If only these old eyes were sharper! They pass the stand of mulberry trees used by the women to feed silkworms, their column four abreast, weary from the day's hunt. Youngest Son rides at the head, implacable on his charger. General An-Shu's standard billows behind him. His success spells my ruin.

I tell myself, *Be brave, meet disaster with equanimity. Be the man you always hoped to become, the cardinal point at the centre of the Eight Winds. Did you imagine they would not blow? Does not every man's death argue for dispassion?* Yet I am afraid, and fear muddles the spirit.

The soldiers have entered the village now. Still their column marches. In the midst, twenty or so prisoners, stumbling forward, hands bound behind their backs.

'What is happening below?' I ask Eldest Son. 'I cannot see clearly.'

'They are parading in the village square,' he says. 'Now most of the troops are being dismissed. The prisoners are led away up the street. I can't see them anymore. Groups of soldiers gather round the houses. They seem to be looting the houses for wood to build cooking fires. That is bad, Father! But I am sure they will leave tomorrow. And see! The peasants who were seized as guides have been dismissed, too.'

'What of the prisoners?' I ask.

'I cannot see, Father. Surely it doesn't matter what happens to them?'

My hands, hidden by the sleeves of my robe, squeeze themselves for comfort.

'Go and tell the servants to prepare a good selection of dishes,' I say. 'Send word to Youngest Son. Ask if he will honour our dinner. Ensure this is done quickly.'

My son sighs.

'How strange you are today, Father!' he says.

He sets about my commands with alacrity, and soon a servant descends to the village. Within half an hour he's back. I watch him climb the hill as I sit by the gatehouse.

'Well?'

'The Captain says he has urgent business to attend to, and cannot dine with you.'

'Is that all he said? Did he not express his regrets? Did he not apologise?'

'No, my lord.'

'I see.'

The servant hurries off, glad to be in the safety of Three-Step-House. Raucous voices rise from the village and I try not to imagine the indignities my people are suffering. The girl who vanished last night has still not been found. It is strange to regard them as my children. When I first returned here I mocked them as rustics, resenting them for everything they were not. Yet now I am determined to offer myself for punishment when the blow falls. I must ensure those without blame are spared. It was my folly to hide the cavalrymen in the caves behind Heron Waterfall.

An hour passes. Still I hold my station by the gatehouse. Darkness confirms itself across the world. A moonless night, lit by a thousand stars. The wind drops so that the trees of the valley cease to murmur. Now is the time when malign, red-eyed spirits seek out mischief. They will find plenty in Wei tonight. A scent of burning in the air, roasting meat, the peasants' precious pigs and fowl slaughtered. All this I have brought on their heads.

Another hour. Youngest Son and his officers must have dined by now. Perhaps they are already drunk. Distant screams tear the dusk as the prisoners are questioned. Soon they will reveal that a villager told them where to hide. Perhaps Wudi is being beaten. Soon, for few resist torture long, he mentions my name, my orders. Youngest Son has no choice but to record his words, for Wudi is being interrogated before witnesses. Perhaps he feels horror, to discover his Father's life is forfeit, and that he, unwittingly, is the cause. Perhaps, even in the midst of distress, he senses opportunity. When I am gone there will be a new lord in Wei. What could be more natural than that the General should reward his loyal follower with my title? Eldest Son must be punished alongside me, his complicity taken for granted, his children disinherited and Daughter-in-law reduced to poverty. If the General decides to invoke the laws of collective punishment, even the children will not live.

I return to my room to await the summons, sitting fully dressed in the dark. I cannot eat. No appetite for anything, least of all sleep. Even my memories offer scant comfort. Bell by bell the long night passes.

At dawn Youngest Son issues commands. Our entire household is to descend to the village square at once. It is now the third morning since he returned. By my calculation, Wei's stores will be exhausted within another two days.

I lead a silent procession down the hill, servant girls walking arm-in-arm for comfort, the men cautious and wide-eyed. Only Eldest Son seems happy, convinced of our present release. I lack the heart to teach him otherwise. Lack integrity. Perhaps I simply cannot bear to see him lessened by fear.

At the foot of the hill I signal for a halt. We gather by the sty adjoining Chiao Sung the blacksmith's house. His hammer taps with unusual energy, ringing faintly on metal. The scent of pig wafts in the breeze, mingled with burning charcoal.

'I will instruct you how to act,' I announce. 'I believe we have been summoned to witness a trial. On no account must anyone disturb the proceedings. Some prisoners will probably be paraded and then taken away. A few may be executed.

Whatever happens, I repeat, *whatever happens*, you must remain still.'

My gut trembles and gripes, yet my voice sounds firm. I fully expect to be marched off to Chunming with the Imperial cavalry. My fear is simple. When the time comes, will I find the courage to offer myself, so the village is not implicated?

We enter the square and I am taken aback. The whole population has been assembled! Hundreds of peasants, men, children, women, even the infirm and old, kneeling in the dust, filling one side of the square. Facing them, over a clear strip of ground used for fairs and markets, two companies of halberdiers, standing at ease. The soldiers talk openly, a sure sign of ill-discipline. The peasants whisper under their breath, if they dare speak at all.

A sergeant bustles over to my household and indicates we should kneel with the rest. This indignity I must resist.

'Fetch a bench,' I drawl to my servants. 'Quickly. Go to the nearest house and place it here.'

The sergeant seems to recollect I am his captain's father. Prudently, he allows two men to carry a long bench from the inn. Eldest Son and I take our seats, reassured by this small victory. Now I have leisure to look around.

The awning and ebony chair stand as before, surrounded by a dozen bright standards, restless in the morning breeze. A few soldiers tend a brazier, heating iron tools, no doubt intended for manacles and chains.

I am reminded of the annual court when the Sub-prefect visits. He hears few cases in Wei. We are too poor to purchase his justice. A few of the younger peasants talk softly among themselves and, as the soldiers do not rebuke them, conversation rises, as it will where people gather. Eldest Son smiles at me, as if to say, *See, Father*!

I glance up sharply. A strange figure capers into the square, plucking grasshoppers from a bamboo basket and stuffing them into his mouth. Thousand-*li*-drunk! I am amazed by his folly.

Yet the man is deranged, as all can see. He bows left and right, roaring blessings for any brave warriors of the clouds who are not buried in an emperor's tomb. To my discomfort, he spies me and lurches over. The warm weather has not improved his odour.

'Lord Yun Cai is at a party and ravens prepare to duel! Ah, but he knows ten thousand magpies will fly down and eat up his honoured guests!'

As usual there is hidden sense in his words. Ravens and magpies are obvious symbols.

'Better for you to seek plump insects elsewhere,' I say, quietly. 'Go now, while the soldiers still find you amusing.'

Then Thousand-*li*-drunk is seized by a fever of scratching, as though devoured by huge lice! Even I cannot help but smile. The man is incorrigible.

'If I wait long enough,' he protests. 'Winter cold will kill them all! But now it is so hot they thrive, wretched dragons! I don't even like eating them, for they have dined on my blood! So I must wait patiently, like a golden pheasant.'

He fixes me with a hard stare. What is he trying to say? That I must wait, too? The golden pheasant symbolises a high official. I recollect P'ei Ti, imprisoned by General An-Shu in Chunming. My heart quickens.

Thousand-*li*-drunk stumbles through the peasants, scratching furiously, then slumps against a wall, where he appears to fall into a deep, contented sleep.

We are startled by a dozen drums. The square at once falls silent. The soldiers stiffen into parade positions. Drummers and standard bearers march into view, followed by Youngest Son at the head of his officers. He wears full uniform, pride in every strutting step. A fine-looking man! At once I feel cowed. My fears return. I count ten breaths and struggle to build calmness between them.

Youngest Son nods briefly to me. No bow! Even to his father! A bad sign. Many in the square look ill-at-ease. Such a neglect brings him no honour. He takes his place in Father's ebony chair, laying a plumed helmet across his knees. All watch expectantly. His face is blank as pressed earth.

'Bring out the prisoners!' he commands.

His eyes flick in my direction. Surely he knows! The cavalrymen have revealed my secret.

A group of manacled men are prodded with halberd-butts into the centre of the square. I blink. Squeeze my eye-lids together. Look again. My heart finds new courage.

These are not the Imperial cavalry I expected, but the deserters who fled up the valley at the start of General An-Shu's rebellion! They have been living in caves near the foot of Ying Mountain for a month now, causing few depredations. I stifle an involuntary laugh. Little decency in welcoming another man's ruin if it diverts one's own. I cannot help myself.

The deserters cower. A miserable lot. Many bear the mark of beatings, all have their hands manacled behind their backs. Once-proud uniforms hang in tatters. Their hair stiff and grimy, bare feet covered in mud.

I settle back on my bench. Soon this will be over. Youngest Son will rail at them to impress his men, then march them off to Chunming. A thorough whipping is the usual punishment for deserters, followed by a posting to one of the penal battalions. There is no helping what has always been.

Youngest Son slowly unfurls a scroll, and proclaims in a loud voice: 'By the new laws and express will of His Glorious Highness, General An-Shu, judgement is here passed on these cowards assembled today.'

He pauses, and looks over at the villagers.

'Just as my grandfather cleansed Wei Valley of bandits, I will do likewise. Let the prescribed punishments commence.'

This reference to Father offends me. All know the tale of how he apprehended a gang of cruel brigands by getting them drunk, and how the Sub-prefect ordered their strangulation. But there is no Sub-prefect here, no representative of He-Who-Rules-The-Five-Directions.

Youngest Son gestures with an impatient finger to Lieutenant Lo. The first of the deserters is dragged into the centre of the square. Soldiers push him to the floor, hold him fast. How young he is! His parents would weep to see him now. I lean forward curiously.

A fat soldier wearing a blacksmith's leather apron has taken a pair of large shears from the brazier. Sparks fly up. The iron jaws glow a virulent orange. He walks over to the prisoner, careful to hold the shears away from him, protecting his hands against the heat with leather mittens.

Stooping, the fat soldier positions the glowing shears over the prisoner's face, and with a sudden, determined grunt, cuts off his nose. The man's shriek pierces heaven.

All around me, the peasants cry out and recoil. Small children bawl and bury their heads in their mother's laps. It is the unexpectedness of the thing. But it is not over. The fat soldier shuffles round to the deserter's twitching legs. Another two guardsmen are summoned to hold him down, so that his bare feet protrude. The hot shears descend. First one foot, then the other.

The square has become a lake of distress. Luckily, the prisoner has fainted, and there are no more screams as his trousers are pulled away, genitals removed. The wretch lies on the floor, his external organs smoking faintly around him. Finally, the executioner takes up a heavy, two-handed sword. With two blows, the man's waist is severed. It is done. The executioner stands panting, leaning on his sword. I remember the Four Punishments, beloved by the tyrants of Zhou, a thousand years ago.

So this is General An-Shu's new law! Through tears I try to meet Youngest Son's eye. I should remonstrate, beg him to remember the kindness of his mother. His scarred face is utterly strange. Then I understand this is new to him, too. He is intrigued. He is learning.

The next man wails, yet I cannot watch. All is known now. The Four Punishments are orderly, fixed by ancient tradition. Still I try to catch Youngest Son's eye. He does not look at me, leaning forward on his chair, urging the executioner to make haste. Then the captain is angry because the deserters have tried to break free from their captors. Order is restored. And another man is brought forth.

To maim, and kill, twenty men in such a manner takes a long time. Two hours pass. At first the peasants weep or hug each other, then grow numb. I notice one winking at his friend as a particularly large set of genitalia are severed. There are dishes to suit every taste. I grip Eldest Son's hand, and command him to close his eyes as I do. He is shaking uncontrollably. If his little brother were not the instigator of this, perhaps he might view it with more composure. After all, we have seen executions before.

At last it is over. Our village square shiny with blood.

I watch through narrowed eyes as Youngest Son rises stiffly, pulling on his helmet with unsteady hands. It hangs askew on his head. He orders his drummers to strike up, and marches from the square. We are left to examine what remains. A few of the women begin to sob. Even the assembled soldiers seem restless. Many have been staring up at the clouds for the last two hours.

As soon as Youngest Son has gone, Lieutenant Lo hurries over to my bench. My official's robes are stiff with sweat.

'Lord Yun Cai,' he says, gravely.

I ignore him.

'Lord Yun Cai, it is over.'

My spirit rages against General An-Shu. That man has stolen my son from all affection. I look at him with accusing eyes.

'Since when are the Four Punishments applied except in the case of gravest treason?' I demand. 'Gravest, gravest treason. Those men were conscripts. A good whipping would have sufficed.'

'We must have no disorder,' he whispers. 'Any display of resentment would be rebellion.'

'At the very most, a simple beheading or strangling for the ringleaders, as an example to the rest,' I continue, ignoring him. '*That* would accord with natural practice.'

'Lord Yun Cai, I beg you! For the sake of your people.'

I come to my senses.

'What must we do?' I ask, wearily.

'Speak to the villagers. Order them to disperse quietly.'

I rise to my feet.

'Go home,' I say. 'Wudi! Where is Wudi?'

He appears at my elbow. I have never seen him so pale. Or relieved. It could easily have been us facing red-hot shears.

'Tell them to go home,' I say.

We separate the crowd into groups and dismiss them from the square. One has already left. Thousand-*li*-drunk vanished as mysteriously as he arrived. I frown and scowl continually. Let nobody imagine that I condone my son.

Lieutenant Lo insists on accompanying me up the hill. We exchange no words and he bows silently as I enter the gatehouse.

Watchmen have been placed on high ridges and outcrops all along the valley. Guards patrol the streets; no one leaves their home. A flight of geese form a ragged bow across the sky, and this gives me hope, reminding me of the day I accompanied Father to Mulberry Ridge. When the steward brings my wine, he says the soldiers have marched back up the valley, no doubt seeking their elusive enemy. I grunt in reply.

As soon as the door closes I ladle out a large cup. It is a mirror where past and present meet. A slight swirl of oil in the clear liquid, reflecting drops of light. I raise it to my lips and gulp, my throat lumpy with emotion. That will pass. How sweet it tastes! Ever since our troubles began I have avoided wine, restrained by duty. Little good it has brought.

The second cup tastes even better, thawing numbed sinews of self. Ah, how I loved to drink when I was young! Close your eyes, old man. See! The West Lake unfurls once again. You are nineteen, tall and eager, your heart full of expectation. Ladies glance at you coyly when you stroll down the Imperial Way. Bright, bright the sun... a scent of chrysanthemums in the air... and a hundred sorrows are yet to occur...

At Lord Xiao's garden party, I had hinted to my great patron that I cared whether the peasants starved. Also that I hoped for a posting which might allow me to aid their famine. My first position was entirely a matter of his whim. Perhaps he took the decision between sips of tea, or over a game of draughts. Either way, I was awarded a posting entirely suited to my talents, but completely at odds with my ideals. For I earnestly hoped to achieve great things for my fellow men.

P'ei Ti fared better in this game of offices. His dearest wish was for influence, the proximity of power, and he was not disappointed with the position of Secretary to the Lesser Censor of The Right Hand. While he might not determine policy, in such a post he could learn how one did. More importantly, he might gain important friends. Whereas I, fired by a thousand vague visions of the public good, was allotted an obscure berth.

How often those who intend the most are passed over in favour of those who intend least, and so attract the approval of their superiors! For change requires imagination and integrity, dangerous qualities in an official.

I found myself set aside from the great currents rocking the ship of His Imperial Highness' state, but in a position by no means ignoble. Indeed, I counted myself fortunate to be hailed as Under Librarian at the Hall of Imperial Records, a post worthy of several thousand *cash* a month. At the age of nineteen, I earned more than clerks who had toiled for forty years from dawn until dusk. It was no fortune, but enough to end my dependency on Uncle Ming.

Lord Xiao summoned me to his office in the Finance Ministry at the commencement of my post. Naturally, I abased myself, proffering half a dozen poems of gratitude I doubt he ever read. Certainly they were never mentioned again and I took no copies.

'So,' he said, peering down at my scalp. 'Is the son of the famous saviour of General Yueh Fei, pleased with his first appointment?'

I immediately understood Lord Xiao's mood was not balanced. Perhaps one of his many rivals had pleased His Majesty more than himself at the morning's Golden Audience.

'I am overwhelmed by my Lord's faith in me,' I said.

Did I intend irony? I'm sure I didn't know myself.

'One must start somewhere,' he said, yawning. 'Very good. Off you go.'

I left with all marks of submission. Whether it might be called arrogance or futile impudence on my part, his tone of voice (and he had a rather squeaky voice) rankled with me. Yet I owed Lord Xiao a thousand obligations. So you might simply call me ungrateful.

On the day I left Uncle Ming's house I surprised myself by weeping. It was a morning like any other in the Wine Market. Porters strained to balance jars suspended from poles. Hawkers of every degree proclaimed their wares. Smells of roasting meat mingled with the fumes of strong spirits.

My entire possessions filled a single handcart. Uncle Ming waited by the gate, a look of strange triumph on his fat face.

'Uncle,' I said, brushing away tears as rapidly as they fell. 'You have been a father to me.'

Even he, his core so hidden from the world, appeared moved.

'Nephew,' he said. 'You have brought me great satisfaction.'

'How, Uncle?' I asked, already knowing the answer.

His kindness, in truth, had never been directed at me.

'When I next meet your father,' he said. 'Whether in this world or the next, I'll have something to tell him.'

'Is the wine cooler paid for, Uncle?' I asked.

'You're sharp, boy! Of course it is! And that's why I'm happy.'

Then I turned to Cousin Hong, who waited behind his father.

'Little General, you're on your way! Who'd have thought it! I might even miss you, now and then.'

I knew how to please him best, and wanted to please him. For Cousin Hong had been a friend when I needed one most.

'Remember, I owe you,' I said. 'Write it down so you don't forget.'

He snorted.

'Writing is why we hire clerks. I prefer numbers.'

'Remember,' I said, clasping his hand.

'Of course I will! Don't be a fool, Little General.'

Then I came to Yi-Yi. He slobbered over my new uniform, and if he said anything intelligible, no one heeded it.

As for Honoured Aunty and Cousin Zhi, there was no sign. This time not even a paper curtain stirred. Yet I had not seen the last of them. Malice can endure as well as goodwill.

That brave morning, walking in advance of my handcart, I swam through crowds on the Imperial Way until I reached an estate adjoining the West Lake. Here, in the midst of a large park where short-horned deer fed at twilight, lay my first house, half-hidden by a semi-circular thicket of bamboo, pine and willow.

How do I remember Goose Pavilion so well? I might almost be there now, my bare toes padding across its earthen floors.

I had rented the place from a noble family fallen on hard times, their ancestry as glorious as their fortune was small. I never saw them, for they preferred to live cheaply in the country. The park was always quiet, their mansion empty except for a few old servants. In the midst of the greatest city on earth I might have been a country-dweller, and this suited me well.

The house was called Goose Pavilion because flocks of

waterfowl congregated on the nearby West Lake. It consisted of three small rooms. One for sleep, one for entertainment, and one for washing and cooking. Every room plain and simple. An old woman came from the mansion to fulfil my domestic needs each day and it was only later, in quite remarkable circumstances, I acquired a servant of my own.

Plain words describe rich feelings best. Oh, the first night I spent there, the pleasure of my freedom! Each room seemed to house a host of spirits, all smiling to greet me! I had escaped the coils of Honoured Aunty and Cousin Zhi, and was at last safe. When I leant against the lintel of my front door, the West Lake lay before me, forming ripples and delightful patterns until the moon's reflection danced.

Few appreciate good fortune until it has gone. Was I so? Certainly I recall moments of depression, yet my life was a circle of diversions, the most notable being my friends. How effortlessly one gathers friends when young! Later, they come more rarely, and always with reservations, for the years teach one to be suspicious. At nineteen, I was not so inhibited.

Confucius speaks of three advantageous friendships: with the upright, the sincere, and the man of much observation. I was lucky to find all three in a score of fellows my own age, many of whom later went on to gain high renown, their portraits hanging in the Hall of Assembled Worthies. At least, I assume they are. Decades have vanished since my final stay in the capital. Everyone has heard their names – Pan Ch'ao, Wang Chen, Cheng Kuo, above all, P'ei Ti – to recall but a few. I was considered in every way their equal. Perhaps they never think of me now.

We were blossom, bright and in our prime, promising to bear fruit one day. Or perhaps just butterflies, fluttering from one amusement to the next, dazzled by our superiority. Walks through public gardens where we improvised verses at the slightest provocation, praising an unusual rock or gnarled tree;

trips to theatre and tea-house; letters and poems exchanged to express eternal delight over a long-forgotten conversation; our exaggerated fondness for each other, and displays of sadness when official duties took a much-loved companion from our midst. In this we were entirely conventional.

Most of all I loved those parties where scrolls of poetry were removed from their boxes, ink mixed, brushes raised in amiable challenge. Delight at passing half a verse to be completed by a friend, then receiving it back, its rhyme subtly altered, back and forth until food and wine and paper ran out, or dawn surprised us. Sometimes we carried on into the morning, breakfasting on laughter. I loved, too, gathering in a monastery or pagoda to greet the moon. Naturally, we filled our vigil with ribaldry and song. I often took my lute and played gentle airs before passing it to the next man, who sought to embellish my theme. Or we would visit the studios of painters, vying to read as many symbols as possible in a landscape.

Twice a week I wandered to the Library of Imperial Records and set a few scrolls in order, before drinking tea with the Head Librarian. Then I would spend a pleasant afternoon reading whatever took my fancy while the eunuchs went about their business. Civilised pleasures, incomprehensible to a barbarian.

Years passed in this way until I neared my twenty-fourth birthday. By now P'ei Ti was already commencing the arduous studies required for the highest test of all, the Imperial Examination, and urged me to do likewise. Perhaps I might have turned my thoughts to the future had I not met Su Lin for a third, fateful time. Once again I had Lord Xiao to thank, though his generosity was far from intended.

It was Lord Xiao's custom to organise a large boating party each year for those who depended on his patronage. Several hundred officials and their principle wives, not to mention concubines, servants, musicians, jugglers, singing girls and acrobats, some of whom specialised in somersaulting from prow to prow without wetting their toes. Such a party required a fleet of craft. Lord Xiao would hire every available paddle boat on the West Lake, some a hundred feet long. Writing out the invitations was no small matter and, because my calligraphy was considered exceptionally fine, I was summoned by Lord Xiao's secretary to assist. For several days I toiled, copying out invitations on the finest paper, and even silk. Some were several pages long. Naturally, I had no choice. Refusal on my part would be shortly followed by a posting to some dismal province and a lifetime's reputation as an ingrate.

I used the opportunity to compose another letter requesting three months' leave to visit my parents in far off Wei. As usual, I received no reply. In truth, the long separation from my parents had begun to trouble my peace of mind. Sometimes I considered resigning my post and setting off for the mountains. Only fear of Father's reaction stopped me. Had he not spent a dozen miserable years on the frontier when he was young, dodging barbarian arrows and shivering in garrison towns? He would consider me a worthless puppy to throw away the career he had ordained.

So my mood was not one of gaiety when I boarded the paddle boat to which I had been assigned. I found myself among a sweating host of low officials and their gaudily attired wives. To my chagrin, P'ei Ti had been granted a place on a boat bearing a better sort. He waved across water churned by countless paddles and oars, evidently amused. It was the first indication that our destinies were diverging.

Still, the short trip was pleasant enough. We toasted Lord Xiao's health frequently, admiring the exertion of the boatmen as they cranked away at the paddles. A friendly clerk pointed out the best places to catch carp. Nevertheless, I felt snubbed.

At last we reached an island in the centre of the West Lake, hired by Lord Xiao for the day. Among clumps of willow and fine pavilions, food had been laid out and a dozen entertainments diverted his guests. Fire-eaters and jugglers circulated through the crowd, many on stilts. The island was full of musicians competing for tips, the low drone of a thousand voices speaking decorously, afraid of revealing too much, lest word get back to a superior. I wandered through the crowd, seeking P'ei Ti. I had already composed some amusing epithets about my fellow-passengers on the paddle boat, and could not wait to share them.

Then I saw P'ei Ti in an enclosure marked off by red, silken cloth. The more ambitious of Lord Xiao's followers watched from outside the barrier, occasionally bowing when a particularly fine uniform drew near.

I made my way to the entrance, joining a small queue. One by one, high officials and their wives shuffled up to a wooden gatehouse decorated with dragons, where secretaries consulted a long list, before granting them admittance.

Why did I assume entry? Was it the thoughtlessness of youth? Or merely arrogance? Yet when I came to the gate, the secretaries consulted their list and found my name missing. Decades have passed since that moment. I still feel the humiliation as if it was yesterday. Contemptuous glances from those in the queue. Frowns from Lord Xiao's secretaries, one of whom I recognised as Secretary Wen, who had visited Uncle Ming's house to assess me. How thinly he smiled at my discomfort.

I could have argued, but that would only double my shame. So I nodded with the muttered words, 'No doubt there has been some misunderstanding,' and withdrew a dozen feet from the gatehouse to compose myself. When I looked up, P'ei Ti was, thankfully, nowhere to be seen. But there was a familiar face watching from within Lord Xiao's enclosure, dressed in night-blue silks, her lute cradled on one shapely arm. Su Lin. And she had witnessed the whole scene.

My blush deepened. Never had I known such mortification. I

nodded a cold greeting to her, and hurried away. Finally I found a jetty made of rotting planks, concealed by a line of willows and bushes. There I sat and gazed at the distant hills, inwardly raging against Lord Xiao's secretaries.

Two hours later, my mood had mellowed a little. I had liberated a large flask of wine and a cup from a trestle table and was contriving my own solace. After all, the lake was full of light and shadow, the distant hills rimmed by fire from the setting sun. My soul opened its arms like the wind, to brush all it touched with a sigh.

I did not care that I must appear odd, sitting alone. Let them think what they liked. I had half-decided to resign my post and live as a hairy hermit in the hills, contemplating the Ineffable Dao. . .

'Yun Cai. Is that you?'

I looked round, startled. Dusk lay across the island. Soon it would be time for the paddle boats to return their cargoes of revellers to the city.

She appeared perfect in that light. Her oval face and high forehead like purest porcelain; her eyebrows subtly curved like willow leaves. She lowered her almond eyes at my frank gaze.

'I have been looking for you,' she said.

I said nothing. What was there to say? She had witnessed my embarrassment.

'May I sit beside you?' she asked, boldly. 'I am tired.'

She struggled in her elaborate clothes to sit, wobbling precariously on raised heels, so that I thought she might fall into the lake. I leapt to my feet and steadied her. Her smile of gratitude banished old resentment. I laughed.

'This jetty is almost as comfortable as a doorstep,' I said.

And then she laughed, too.

'So you remember Madam's back door,' she said.

'Most fondly.'

Something seemed to trouble her.

'Madam sold me hurriedly, you know. I had no choice. And

my new Madam was strict. When I asked permission to write to you, she refused, and I did not dare disobey her.'

I waved my hand nonchalantly, as if to say that fire was doused. We sat side by side in silence.

'Is that a flask of wine?' she asked, innocently.

'Do you know, it *does* look like one,' I said. 'In fact, it even smells like one.'

'And is that a bowl?' she asked, in the same guileless tone.

'Let me see. Well, it is certainly round and hollow. I believe you are right. It is a bowl!'

'May I have some?'

As usual her boldness filled me with admiration.

'I only have one bowl and I have polluted it with my foul, unworthy lips,' I said.

'Then we must share like good friends,' she said. 'We are still good friends, Yun Cai, are we not?'

I smiled and bid her pour.

'Why have you left Lord Xiao's enclosure,' I asked. 'Is that wise?'

'My duties are done for now. I was hired to play and so I have. For a while I can come and go as I please. Ah, this tastes good. And the lake is so pretty from here! How clever you are to watch the fire-flies instead of talking to stupid people.'

'There is something I must know,' I said. 'Are you Lord Xiao's concubine? If so, your presence here is a great danger to us both.'

It was an urgent question. Lord Xiao tolerated no trifling from his inferiors. There were rumours of underlings who had displeased him being sent to bandit-ridden provinces, never to return. Others were dragged before magistrates only too willing to apply the harshest punishments for imaginary crimes. Su Lin laughed gaily.

'Of course not! I am a singing girl, belonging to no one but myself.'

'I thought. . .'

'He asked for me by name when he hired the other girls. That is all.'

'Then you are not?'

'No.'

'Or . . ?'

'Not that either. Whatever it is you had in mind.'

Her reply pleased me to an absurd extent.

'Where do you live?' I asked. 'This is all so strange.'

'I am no longer an apprentice, if that is what you mean. Indeed, you should be very polite to me. I have my own little cottage now, and a maid to tend my make-up and hair, and strings and strings of *cash* saved up already. You really ought to treat me with some reverence.'

'But I do! Can't you tell?'

'I hope so. Or I will grow offended like the Empress Lu. Do you remember telling me about her? A horrible woman! Horrible! To answer your question, I live on the shore of the West Lake, near Turtle Hill Monastery, and a dozen other girls have cottages there, too.'

I was surprised by her news. Without doubt she had risen honourably in her profession. Turtle Hill Monastery lay near the foot of Phoenix Hill and one could not rise higher than that. Indeed, she probably earned more than I did.

'Then we are neighbours,' I said, and told her of my own small house. Even then the possibilities of our situation were apparent. Except for the small matter that I could not afford her services.

We sat in silence while she sipped. I sensed her tiredness.

'So Lord Xiao asked for you by name?' I said, at last.

'Yes, his secretary wrote to my broker. Perhaps he likes the way I sing *Wave-washed Sands*. It is always popular, especially at weddings.'

'You always sang well,' I said, lightly.

But the first traces of foreboding had taken root. A loud, sonorous gong echoed across the island. We glanced at each other. I contained a desire to reach out.

'How tiresome!' she said. 'I am expected to play in Lord Xiao's own barge all the way back to the city. And I was just starting to enjoy myself for a change.'

I found it hard to swallow.

'Do you still remember the characters I taught you?'

'Of course, Yun Cai! I am not stupid.'

'Then you will remember how to write to me. There is no strict Madam to stop you now, if that is your wish.'

Perhaps I sounded earnest. Yet she flushed beneath her white make-up.

'We shall see. I must go now.'

She hesitated.

'You are not sad about what happened today at Lord Xiao's enclosure? Pah! Such stupid men! I could have boxed their ears!'

'Not now,' I said, smiling. 'In fact, I am glad. Otherwise we would not have spent this hour together on a rotting jetty! I might even learn to prefer jetties to doorsteps.'

She giggled tipsily as I helped her to her feet. The gong sounded again and she hurried through the willows. I sailed home with a clenched heart. Sleep was impossible that night.

Later I heard my name had indeed been withheld from Lord Xiao's list by mistake, and that he was displeased by the error. After all, one does not rear a sow to have it not breed. He expected a return from all his two-legged investments, and gained nothing from us unless we rose. P'ei Ti was outraged on my behalf. Yet the fragility of my position had been revealed. A bitter draught I would not forget. Nor did I forget whose sweetness softened its taste.

P'ei Ti was right, of course. At twenty-four years of age I should have already commenced my studies for the Imperial Examination, moderated my incessant versifying, and paid countless visits to influential dullards who might further my career. Yet even he could be tempted from the steep path. I led him to areas of study his father, recently returned from a posting in uncouth Gunggu Shan, no doubt thought fatuous.

There were a dozen Imperial Pleasure Grounds in the city at that time, all in suburbs beyond the ramparts. They had originally been built to entertain bored soldiers, vast covered markets of amusement. Men of all classes visited them. They were no longer huge brothels, though that element still traded respectably. Instead, year by year, more sophisticated entertainments took root. I only visited a prostitute there once, and found the experience dispiriting, draining my essential breaths in a way mutual desire never did. As I recollect, the girl's pubic hair was long as a goat's beard and her breasts firm as over-ripe melons. Beyond that, little remains. She must recall me not at all.

My chief enjoyment in visiting the Pleasure Grounds was to marvel. How remarkable is humanity, considering we are P'an-ku's fleas! We take for granted our accomplishments, our diversity, our capacity to express the most subtle, and gross, permutations of mood. Blindness to assume wisdom or beauty belong only to the Classics, as we scholars are taught. The spirit creates a thousand ways to speak, all complementary.

Many would despise such unorthodox views. Part of me does, too, so deep did my education plough. Yet when I hear a simple folk melody, does not my heart respond as I might to the poems of Li Po, or my darling Po Chu'i, or my beloved Wang Wei? And did not the *Book of Songs* sprout from folk-ditties, watered by the people's experience? All seek meaning for their lives, often in unapproved ways. The test, I believe, is whether sympathy and kind thoughts are promoted.

The Imperial Pleasure Grounds combined wisdom and vacuity. In this they were like most men's lives, from birth to re-birth.

My favourite stood near the Gate of Elegant Rectitude. I loved the acrobats who performed behind silken barriers, wearing costumes of red or violet, yellow or blue, depending on their troupe. Tightrope walkers with poles on their shoulders, balancing jars of water and contriving to never spill a drop. I dubbed these 'High Officials', much to P'ei Ti's amusement. Musicians sang and capered. Little boys or girls struck spectacular poses on their shoulders. These I called 'Aspiring Families'.

How lute and pipe and drum stimulated the blood! I thrilled, too, or sighed, at the actors with their plays of ghosts and murder, tragic emperors and suicidal concubines. Performing ants always made me examine the crowd, unsurprised by the city-dwellers' fascination. Boxers, unerring archers, humorists spouting lewd tales, all found echoes in my soul.

One afternoon, when I had persuaded P'ei Ti to accompany me, we passed through the Gate of Elegant Rectitude and wandered beneath the awnings of the pleasure ground. P'ei Ti often grew uncomfortable and titillated in these shadowy, crowded alleyways. Here all rites and formalities were set aside. Low did not bow to great but brushed past heedlessly. This mingling of the classes lent excitement to the place.

That day I made two discoveries, one of which shocked me. The other, much later, at a time I could not imagine, except perhaps in nightmares, saved my life.

We had explored for an hour, downing cups of wine at alarming prices, when we found ourselves at the rear of the more respectable amusements. Here were booths and tents given over to boy-prostitutes. They paraded in thick make-up and silks thin enough to emphasise their buttocks. Pimps assessed the crowd, chewing sunflower seeds. P'ei Ti blushed fiercely and muttered that the law was lenient. Indeed it was, if you could afford the bribes. My own attention was drawn elsewhere.

A shooting gallery had been set up against one wall, marked out by military banners. At the near end stood a raised platform, surrounded by dozens of loaded crossbows. At the far end there was a thick stake hung with iron rings.

Suddenly a loud crack of gunpowder! The crowd murmured. When the smoke cleared, a heavily whiskered man, the very parody of military prowess, stood on the platform, hands folded across his chest. We fell silent before his glare.

'Who has vanquished the Kin and Mongol scum as I have?' he growled. 'Who has seen their cruel arrows fall like rain?'

He beat his chest extravagantly.

'No one! Yet for your entertainment, I have brought back a curiosity from the frontier. Do not all civilised men despise the cursed barbarians of the steppes?'

The crowd shouted its approval. For several minutes he harangued us in this manner until the entertainment took shape.

A hooded archer mounted the dais. Then an emaciated man, ten or so years older than myself, was dragged into view. A great show was made of attaching him to the stake by a thin chain, five feet long. He cowered miserably, yet I detected defiance in his lowered eyes. By now the 'general' was reaching a fever.

'Gentlemen!' he roared. 'What is worse than a traitor? For this wretch was born a son of Han, like any one of us!'

The crowd gasped. Drums began to beat, building in intensity.

'This dog was taken by the Kin and served them willingly for twelve long years! I tell you, he betrayed his own people until the day of his capture! Behold the Han-barbarian! Is he not an offence against nature? Is he not an animal, a bear? Now see the bear dance!'

The crowd bellowed. The drum reached a crescendo. Then the hooded archer was firing, aiming at the feet of the man. How he danced! Crossbow after crossbow twanged, bolt after bolt thudded into the ground. The Han-barbarian capered and lurched. The crowd roared with laughter. Here was victory, at last! Our all-powerful enemy humbled! Hot faces surrounded me, half-open mouths.

Abruptly the crowd fell silent. The archer, for all his skill, had fired too close. A bolt protruded obscenely from the target's waist. He tottered, fell backwards. I remember a sensation of disgust, for I could not hate this pitiful creature.

'Fifty *cash* for such a spectacle!' screamed the "general". 'See how he bleeds!'

His servants ran through the crowd, collecting *cash*. Finally I stood alone by the rope barrier, filled with a strange notion. And far too much wine.

'Is that fellow a slave?' I demanded of the mountebank.

'Yes, Honourable Sir. And I have a document to prove it, bearing the seal of Assistant Sub-prefect Wan Li himself!'

He was sweating from his exertions, cooling himself with a large, blue fan.

'He's not much use to you now,' I said.

'Don't worry, sir. Come back in an hour's time! I have a real devil from the steppes to replace him.'

'Is the wounded man for sale?' I asked.

'Eh?'

The "general" examined me with new interest.

'A dancing Han-barbarian is worth a lot,' he said, sternly.

'Not if he's about to die. I'll give a thousand for him.'

What possessed me to make such an offer, I'll never know. You might call it compassion. Or nobility of spirit. Was it merely to prove myself different, and better, than my fellows? I remember thinking how I would boast to my friends that I had saved a man, as a kind of joke.

We finally settled on two thousand and the "general" seemed pleased with his bargain. Well he might be. I'm sure I only agreed because I was drunk, and stubborn. I dared not imagine what Cousin Hong would say.

When the slave was carried out, he seemed more dead than alive. Then the responsibility I had assumed sobered me.

I looked round for P'ei Ti, but my friend had vanished. I was about to give up on him when I saw him emerging from one of the boy-prostitutes' booths, his face strangely flushed. In a moment I had turned away. I'm sure he never saw I knew.

*

My new servant was carried back to my pavilion in a hired litter, groaning all the way. He took up residence on a pile of blankets, and for several weeks contended with oblivion. Throughout this trial he rambled in his sleep, using a barbarous language I did not recognise. When awake, he would fix me with a feverish gaze until his eyeballs rolled. A most disturbing sight! I could not afford a doctor, so I bathed his wound in the water I boiled for tea. At the height of his sickness, I spooned rice gruel into his mouth.

His wound reeked of unwholesome humours. It was mottled with liverish oozes, green pus, enough to make any doctor curious. Yet I was no medical student. However, I did notice a dozen old scars on his thin body.

Of course my friends made fun of my eccentricity in nursing him. One, a stern supporter of the Ceaseless War party at court, chided me for showing lenience to the enemy. It was true that although the Han-barbarian looked like one of us, there was something suspect about the man. Something indefinably foreign.

Finally he lapsed into a coma. I had little hope he would awake. Two thousand *cash*! For nothing! I wasn't even sure where I would bury him. And I still didn't know the poor fellow's name.

In disgust, I took a flask of wine and writing equipment to a flat rock by the lakeside. It was early evening. Houses and pagodas along the shore, people-specks moving, softened by dusk. I paddled my bare toes in the water and forgot the Han-barbarian. My thoughts rolled across the lake to the far shore, where Su Lin's cottage stood. And my imagination spun webs of desire.

How clearly I pictured her, freshly returned from singing at a fashionable wedding. . . How she slowly disrobed, layer after silken layer, until naked. How she called to her maid for warm water, then yawned, stretched. Fine beads of sweat on her forehead and arm-pits. How she washed away make-up from her oval face with languid sighs. Water-beads dripped on her upturned breasts. Tiny rivulets ran down the flat of her stomach, to tickle her black rose. How she slipped her arms into a robe held open by the silent maid. The dense pile of her long, black hair loose around her shoulders. In a pleading voice, she summoned a cup of wine and took it to the window. There she sipped restlessly. Her almond eyes reached out across West Lake, seeking my house, wondering what I thought and felt. . . So I imagined. And longed.

Without pausing, I wrote a verse. Later, when it became hugely popular, some called for the poem to be banned, due to its provocative second line:

She washes kohl-lined eyes, almond eyes,
Make-up skeins of black in a jade bowl.
Pigments disperse as soon as friendship,
Making the water grey. Throw it away.
Wise heads have lived this before.
Is a dream of love all my reward?

I wrote feverishly that evening, dissolving my ink-cake in the lake water, filling sheet after sheet. When I arose, I felt light-headed. Embers of sun were fading behind the hills. I wandered back to my house and found a strange figure seated in the doorway, clutching his waist.

'So you have awoken!' I cried.

To my further surprise, he lowered himself awkwardly, groaning with each movement, and did homage. Befuddled as I was by wine and poetry, I did not know what to say.

'Sit down, you fool,' I said, after a pause. 'You'll re-open your wound!'

Slowly, painfully, he resumed his former position. We regarded each other.

'Are you hungry?' I asked.

'Had. . . the rice you left,' he gasped.

His accent was peculiar. I could not place it. I refrained from mentioning that, actually, it was my own dinner he had eaten.

'Tell me who you are.'

He would not reply. In the end, I helped him to his pile of blankets in the kitchen, where he straightaway fell asleep.

The Han-barbarian's recovery was slow and fitful. Apart from ensuring he was well fed, I was too busy with my friends to think about him. When I sought him out, he proved so taciturn that I wondered if he was a simpleton like Cousin Yi-Yi. I did eventually drag a name from him: Mi Feng. At least that was the name he told me.

One night, a month after his feverish coma had lifted, I returned drunk and singing from a party, to find Mi Feng chopping wood by starlight, each blow accompanied by a grunt of pain. He seemed to be enjoying himself, so I allowed him to finish, before saying: 'Mi Feng, do put the axe down. I really think it is time we talked.'

He examined me warily.

'Come, sit on the ground before me. I have a few questions.'

He did as instructed.

'Tell me a little about yourself.'

'You have saved my life,' he said, cautiously.

Now we were getting somewhere.

'That is right. But what kind of life have you led? That is what I want to know. And, in particular, how did you end up as target practice in the Imperial Pleasure Ground?'

Mi Feng had clearly anticipated this question. He launched straight into a fanciful tale of being conscripted to work as a labourer, repairing fortifications on the frontier. According to his account, the Kin barbarians captured his entire company and he was sold as a slave. After years on the steppes, he managed to escape and fled back to civilization, disguised as a

Jurchen warrior. Whereupon, he was declared an enemy by our forces and sold to the mountebank.

When he had finished, I raised a single, questioning eyebrow.

'Are you quite sure?' I asked, softly.

He bared his gums in a most alarming way and picked up his axe.

'I'm sure there is no need for that,' I said, hastily. 'Of course I believe you!'

But he had returned to chopping wood. I was kept awake for some while by his thuds and groans.

Another time I resolved to press for exact details of his past. By then Mi Feng was proving useful in unexpected ways. He could clean the house thoroughly and even prepare simple meals, though he muttered it was 'women's work'. In addition to chopping firewood, he displayed an aptitude for hunting. The bow and arrows he made – without my permission, of course – were remarkably effective. Soon I was dining on all manner of roasted waterfowl, which he shot in flight.

'Mi Feng,' I said. 'This really will not do. You are a mystery and I wish to know more about you.'

He paused in his work of plucking a duck, and sighed. This exhalation of breath, remarkably expressive, was intended as a warning. I pressed on.

'Mi Feng, how is it you are so proficient with weapons? If you were an innocent slave, as you claim, surely the Kin would not have allowed you to bear arms. And another thing. Your body is covered with old scars. War wounds, unless I'm much mistaken. I know this because I observed them while nursing you back to health. And, might I add, while saving your life.'

He flinched. For the first time he seemed truly unnerved.

'You did save my life,' he conceded. 'And you treat me honourably.'

'Well then, clearly I am your benefactor. As such, I desire a little frankness.'

He licked his lips. Quite unwittingly, I had trapped him.

'It might be that I've seen a little trouble,' he said, reluctantly. 'Never against the Emperor's men though!'

'Of course,' I broke in. 'For that would be treason.'

We fell back to our game of studying each other.

'Mi Feng, it is said that tigers and deer do not walk together. I trust that I can sleep safe in my bed tonight? If not, you have my permission to leave at once. I won't think the worst of you for it.'

A most surprising thing occurred. Tears filled his eyes.

'So you think I am without honour!' he cried.

He seemed genuinely distressed. It was as though I had called him the basest name in the world. I blushed. It is wrong to shame a man, even a dubious one.

'I'm sure you're very honourable,' I said, hurriedly.

I left him to his plucking. Handfuls of feathers flew. That night I half-expected to have my throat slit in revenge.

For a few more weeks we carried on in this unsatisfactory way. Then he asked me a question of his own. 'Sir, how is it you earn your living?'

A civilised question at last! And one deserving a full answer. I told Mi Feng of my noble position in the Hall of Imperial Records and of my poetry. I even recited a dozen or so of the longer ones, so he could get a flavour of my style. He listened with ill-disguised scorn. Of course, I was wasting my breath. After all, one does not climb a tree to look for fish.

'Is this Hall of Records,' he said, thoughtfully. 'Attached to the women's quarters?'

That evening I related our conversation to my friends, who laughed uproariously.

By now I was almost certain he would not murder me. It was high time we came to proper, regular terms, so I drew up a contract.

'Mi Feng,' I said. 'I have paid a large price to free you, but you are a servant not a slave. If you wish to return to your family, I will not stop you.'

A sly comment on my part. It seemed unlikely any family would want him back. He hugged his old wound.

'No, no. What place for me there? I'll serve you, sir.'

Then I mentioned my titles, that I was a Lord's son, and would pay a hundred *cash* a month, as well as food and lodging. I felt rather fine to deal in so open-handed a manner. Though I could not guess it, my open-handedness is the only reason I have a hand to write with now.

Mi Feng glowered at me when I offered him the contract, and tore it into many pieces.

'You have saved my life,' he said. '*That* is our contract.'

I nodded with every sign of sympathy. Secretly, I could hardly wait to share his latest outburst with P'ei Ti. Yet that night I slept soundly, knowing he was there to keep watch.

Mi Feng had many oddities. He insisted on rigging a curtained lean-to at the side of Goose Pavilion, like a kennel, claiming that buildings stifled him after his years on the steppe. I granted this, though it ruined the orientation of the rooms. His unorthodox lodging became a talking point among my friends, who visited me specially to view it. I was always happy to amuse them. Too happy, perhaps. Even then, some had begun to consider me an oddity in my own right.

When his breaths regained sufficient harmony, I sent Mi Feng paddling across the lake to Su Lin's cottage. Although by no means poor, I had only ordinary gifts to offer. Just the poems I had written on the night he woke from his stupor. A tiny jar of musk. A picture of a phoenix entwined round a peony, painted by myself. Of course, the phoenix represented the lover, and the peony she who was beloved.

He took my little rowing boat and I watched him ply its single oar. Fine silver droplets scattered like mercury across the lake. I held little hope Su Lin would reply. What would an ambitious girl want with a lowly Under Librarian? What was I, compared to such a one as Lord Xiao?

When Mi Feng, returned from his embassy to Su Lin, paddling slowly across the wide lake, I was waiting on the shore.

'How did she reply?' I demanded, as soon as he landed, rubbing his wound.

'The lady gave me a cup of wine, sir,' he said.

I ignored the hint.

'What did she say? Tell me at once!'

He seemed to consider for a moment.

'Her maid is a fine-looking girl,' he said, reflectively. 'She told me that her mistress has mentioned your name.'

'I did not send you to pursue your own interests with a maid! What did the lady say?'

'She said: "Such matters require much thought."'

Thought! When you blaze with feeling thought is disdain.

'Is that all?'

'Yes.'

'How often did the maid say that her mistress mentions my name?'

He spread his hands, as if to plead, *who knows*?

'So the Lady sent no reply, no message,' I railed. 'Nothing at all.'

Mi Feng shrugged.

'She smiled when she looked through those bits of paper you sent her.'

'What? Happily? Broadly? How did she smile?'

'You know, sort of. . .'

He bared yellow teeth in a hideous grin. I shivered.

'Go and clean the house. No, fetch me wine. And paper. Yes, brushes and paper and ink.'

I could tell he was amused as he hurried off. The wide world could laugh for all I cared, so long as she smiled on me. Naturally, I wasted the entire evening, and many days afterward, imagining a thousand things about her, desire and dignity contending like spurred cocks.

So I waited for her word. Words were everything to me in my twenty-fourth year. Poem after poem spilled from my brush, and I woke with one expectation, one goal. Indeed, I believe poetry kept me sane. When the brush was in my hand, all my troubles fled before its subtle edge: my sorrow at being denied leave to visit my aging parents; the frustration that while I held my position in the Deer Park Library, friend after friend gained preferment, climbing step by step towards positions of influence. One or two had even received important postings as Sub-prefects or Assistant Governors. Most were preparing diligently for the Imperial Examination, digesting dry, unpalatable tomes for regurgitation in neat piles of approved words. I was falling behind, and knew it. Yet fame, like light round a spluttering lamp, brightening as it gains fire, was gathering around me.

I had begun to frequent the weekly salons of the Society of the Western Lake. All have heard of it. Few are admitted. In those days, the best scholars in the city belonged to the Society, drawn by invisible threads of beauty, some satisfied with the web for its own sake, others aware that sticky nets may trap patrons and influence. After all, poetry is power. To move a person deeply is to influence them, re-align their co-ordinates. To win fame is to earn reputation. To be on everyone's lips, or at least the lips of those who matter, is to inhabit their thoughts, and so, their actions.

At first I knelt at the back with a hundred others and no one noticed me. Then I entered the monthly competitions, certain my very best poems would be rejected. The Esteemed Fathers of the Society sat on fine chairs at the front, while I expected to always belong on the ground, at the rear.

The first month confirmed my expectations. Others won the prizes for free or regular verse forms, and for poems set to well-known tunes. The latter were particularly popular at that time.

I strived again, seeking to imitate the winners. Again, I met no success. Others were praised, their words recited to the Society, their verses copied and distributed.

One night I shared my frustration with P'ei Ti. He had come to visit me at Goose Pavilion. Winter beat freezing rain against the roof. He had recently been promoted within the Censor's Office, and was sympathetic to my own position.

'What is the chosen subject for this month's competition?' he asked.

'The lotus,' I replied, gloomily.

'Which bears many symbols,' he said. 'You will be more aware of them than me.'

'Dear friend,' I replied, 'I have written poems expressing every symbol in the most honoured style, the most conventional terms, and still they do not answer!'

P'ei Ti daintily poured two cups of wine. He had a delicate way about him. Yet I knew his judgements in the Censor's office were considered harsh, even ruthless. Recently a corrupt official had been castrated at P'ei Ti's instigation.

'That's the problem,' he said, examining the wine in his cup like an oracle. 'Dear Yun Cai, you are not conventional! That is your strength and weakness. So I advise you, compose a poem from your heart, for it is a kind one. And all admire the kind-hearted. I advise, write what you consider true, and hope it will answer.'

So I did, as soon as he left, by the guttering light of the lantern. Two dozen couplets, set to the tune of 'Enduring Sadness', which I submitted to the Society in due form.

At the next meeting I sat at the back, anticipating nothing for myself when the winners were called.

How sweet to hear one's own name in such a place! I rose and approached the Esteemed Fathers of the Society, summoned by them to recite. All eyes were upon me, surprised by my youth. So I read my poem of the lotus, and received polite applause. For an hour I was the most envied of men. My poem pierced as surely as a surgeon's needle. Its theme: the pleasures which bound us to the city, as the petals of the lotus are bound together, and the strange sense of emptiness within the flower, the sense we might be plucked and trodden casually underfoot, as the barbarians gained strength on the frontier. A disquieting poem. Yet true. Above all, true. To voice a truth releases it, and fills the entire sky.

Later I heard that copies of my poem circulated widely, even being used to pay for refreshment in fashionable tea-houses, like a kind of currency. I have no doubt many copies ended in latrines, used for baser purposes – a great compliment! My poem was so widespread it became common as a *cash* coin, traded by many hands, yet still valued. Indeed, I know of no less than five melodies specially composed for the words.

At once I was invited to literary dinner parties by scholars alert for the latest man. You might imagine such attention brought only pleasure. Naturally, I was flattered, even excited. Yet I knew in my heart it was not me they sought – my virtues and foibles, humours and follies – but merely my talent. My value depended upon performance. The same may be said of any juggler.

One invitation brought me great disquiet. I had been summoned to a mansion on Phoenix Hill, although my host was little known to me. As always at such events I was expected to sprout words prodigiously, whatever the challenge. The company assembled in a room shiny with gilding and lacquer. Neat piles of fine, horse-hair brushes, exquisite inks, hundreds of paper sheets, all arranged in flower patterns. Delicate wines and a variety of dishes on the side, tended by watchful servants.

Despite being a nobody among the other guests, high officials to a man, my presence conferred a temporary equality, so that I felt as good as any. I displayed my calligraphy and won much applause. Then, when I was already half-drunk, the final guest arrived, having been delayed by business of state. It was none other than Lord Xiao, my patron! I bowed, perhaps with less respect than was prudent.

'Ah, young Yun Cai!' he drawled through his nose. 'What a surprise to see you in this company.'

I nodded politely instead of bowing again. As the most powerful man present, all deferred to Lord Xiao.

'Gentlemen!' he announced in his high-pitched way. 'You might wonder that I know our young friend, although his Lotus Poem is on everyone's lips. A very promising piece! I should explain, he is a protégé of mine. Indeed, I entrusted my secretary to sound him out, as we say, when he was only a little younger. Is that not so, Yun Cai?'

'Indeed, Lord,' I said.

Perhaps there was something about my tone he did not like. He slowly fixed his eyes upon my face, so that I glanced away in confusion, recalling tales of his cruelty to underlings who offended him. Then he chuckled.

'You were dwelling with your noble uncle, the wine merchant, I believe.'

Polite laughter at this jibe rippled round the table. The merchant classes have ever been distrusted and despised. Why he singled me out in this way, I do not know. Perhaps he had received a snub at court and needed someone to humiliate. Perhaps he sensed my antipathy towards him, such emotions are hard to hide. As a patron he had been a disappointment. I had been stuck in the same position for years, even denied access to my parents! Obligation must work two ways, or not at all.

'My uncle's wines have inspired a thousand generous thoughts, my Lord,' I said. 'And as many winds.'

The company laughed heartily at this rather crude joke. Lord Xiao smiled. Thinly. It is unwise to deny such a man the last word.

Then our host announced another contest, to compose a poem on. . . he could not decide the theme, so must consult Lord Xiao. Thus he could ensure his chief guest excelled, for

Lord Xiao could simply copy out something he had prepared earlier. The rest of us were forced to improvise.

'Very well,' said Lord Xiao, as though suddenly inspired. 'I propose the Fisherman!'

'But what form?' called another guest.

'Oh, a quintain, I think,' said Lord Xiao.

Naturally, all agreed. Heads bent over paper. Servants mixed ink furiously. Each guest strove to amaze with their wit. I alone did not write. I was thinking. I could see Lord Xiao casually copying out a poem he had composed earlier and memorised for just such an occasion. I decided on a bold measure. Instead of depicting the scholar-official seeking diversion from his labours on river or lake, as is customary, I wrote in a fever of meaning.

At last we settled. All read out their derivative pieces, copied from masters learned by rote at the Academy. Lord Xiao's no different, except that it drew on the words of a minor Southern Dynasty court poet to an alarming degree. I noted that his tones were inexpertly placed and the final rhyme was discordant. Worse, it was banal. Everyone proclaimed it a masterpiece. Then I recited my own:

He who gives life to the city is humble.
Salt him. Feed his family. Mix him with rice.
River textures are mirror and shadow.
The fisherman casts a net of heaven.
Droplets scatter, he hauls in the Way.

The company listened silently. Finally, my host, who had a reputation as a poet himself, sighed.

'Ah, the Way,' he said. 'Truly it may be glimpsed in a single droplet.'

'It is a drop of water,' said another, eagerly. 'What is tiny reflects the whole.'

An excited discussion followed, everyone quoting choicest

morsels of Lao-tzu memorised in their youth, when preparing for the Imperial examination.

So I stole Lord Xiao's thunder, though his poem was respectfully voted the best. I was glad of my impudence. Even then, I believe, Su Lin lay between us like an echo of the future.

Lord Xiao left early, pleading important matters of state the next day. As he departed, he smiled at me. There are many smiles.

At last I received Su Lin's reply. It was ambiguous in all respects save one. I still have the note in my middle chest, written on expensive paper, her characters untutored:

The Honourable Yun Cai's kind words to a poor girl have been read many times. Meet me tomorrow afternoon at the Gardens of Ineffable Solace if you would talk frankly.
Su Lin.

Never mind that she proposed our tryst for one of the few days I was expected to attend the Imperial Library. Mi Feng was swiftly dispatched to plead my indisposition. I dressed with particular care and made my way to the appointed gardens at the foot of Phoenix Hill, within sight of the palace.

I was absurdly early. An afternoon can seem wide as an ocean if you're waiting for one whose presence slows time, moment by moment. I found a bench beside a miniature waterfall with a good view of the entrance. Clouds formed kingdoms above the city. Early spring animated stem and leaf. Despite the beating of my heart, I could not help observing the antics of a thrush family. How they splashed in a puddle, squabbling furiously, all eyes and sharp beak. Perhaps that is why I did not notice Su Lin's approach, until she stood on the cinder path before me. Her voice startled me from my thoughts.

'Day-dreaming again, Yun Cai?'

I rose hurriedly. We both bowed. Whereas my own face was flustered, hers was elegant, and cold. I looked at her then. Words vanished from my lips.

Her cloud-hair shone like threads of black, glossy jade, held by combs of turquoise coral, fletched with silver and gold. Eyebrows long and thin, as befitted her character. She was the being in my eyes. Su Lin's own were lined with kohl, and glittered like meteors framed by the night sky. Her short nose hinted at desire.

She wore a short-sleeved jacket and long skirt, all of the dusk-hued colours which suited her best, alluring rather than obscuring the jade mountains of her breasts. Her girdle bore a silken purse, a sachet of scent, and a folded fan, red as dry blood.

Where now was the poor girl in the alley at the back of the Wine Market? Even in the months since our last meeting she seemed to have gained in wealth, whereas I wore my familiar green gown.

'Forgive me,' I said. 'I was indeed day-dreaming. But the sight of you makes me fully awake.'

She bowed again at this courtesy. A strange response for her! I expected a reply quick as a bright, mocking bird. Then I became aware she was not alone. A middle-aged woman with a dour, calculating face stood behind her. Su Lin followed my glance.

'May I introduce my former Madam to Yun Cai,' she said, delicately. 'Who I have invited here as my honoured chaperone.'

A chaperone! I struggled to digest her presence. We had been alone together a hundred times, what need for a sour-faced old woman? And the solemnity of her tone, so formal and distant! Su Lin and I never talked in this way.

'Honoured,' I said, curtly.

More bows all round. I was afire to speak my mind. Su Lin waited, her head lowered. Evidently I was expected to lead the conversation. For once, words slipped away.

'Will you walk with me awhile?' I asked, at last.

She nodded submissively and, staying two feet behind me, followed as I strolled, so that I had to continually turn to address her. Where was the freeness she once taught me, which I so admired, making her different from other women? She seemed encased in lacquer. All we had shared, it seemed, was to be forgotten. We were to begin anew, every remark between us constrained and foretold by elegant manners. I grew agitated.

'Su Lin,' I said, as calmly as I could. 'Why are you acting so strangely? Have I offended you in some way? If so, tell me what it is. I beg you, ask your chaperone to withdraw a little, so we may talk freely.'

Su Lin's face beneath its layer of cosmetics flushed. She stuck out her tongue a little, as a child does when afraid. She nodded to signify agreement, and her chaperone, scowling balefully, stalked a dozen paces behind us.

'What is going on?' I asked, at last able to tear down the dam in my breast. 'Is something wrong?'

Her eyes flashed angrily. Yet I was glad to provoke any reaction close to her heart.

'Yun Cai forgets himself,' she said. 'We are not husband and wife.'

Now I had something to work on, and seized my opportunity.

'Yet we are friends,' I said. 'Old friends, are we not? Tell me honestly, Su Lin. Did the poems I sent displease you? If so, I will burn them.'

Her eye-lids fluttered with confusion. We had reached an ornamental lake, and stood before an expanse of floating water-lilies. Clouds were reflected in the still water and foreboding gripped me.

'No, I liked them,' she said. 'A great deal, if you must know. It is not that. . . Oh, can't you understand anything?'

At last the fiery girl I loved was joining me! I pressed home my advantage.

'Teach me what I must understand,' I said, softly.

'Do you never consider the future?' she demanded. 'Or our mutual positions? For the first time in my life I have gained a respected place. Everyday I receive fresh commissions to perform for the very best families in the city. You know my dreams, unless you've forgotten them already. It is my duty to make a success of my profession while I am young and men still bother to turn their heads when I walk by. How else will I be able to support my family? Already they have come to rely on the money I send them. Because of my work, Father has been able to buy a small house. It is my duty, Yun Cai! Surely you understand.'

I had no answer to this. The disadvantages of my modest salary swam like hungry fishes before my eyes.

'I cannot offer wealth,' I said, haughtily. 'Yet I am richer than most in spirit.'

She clutched at the purse at her girdle. Let it fall.

'I know that,' she said, her eyes narrow with distress. 'Do not think I am not flattered you hold me in esteem. . . I presume you hold me in esteem, the poems you sent. . .'

She was silenced by embarrassment. Then I knew she cared for me.

'Those poems were written across my heart,' I said, slowly. 'All I needed to do was copy what was written there.'

She bit her lip.

'But this will not answer!' she protested. 'You are too earnest! You know I cannot be your sole concubine. You must be sensible, both of us must be sensible. One day your parents will assign you an honourable match. Have you forgotten what I am?'

It was true I could hardly marry her. My father would fall on his sword before allowing such a betrothal. Yet I had not seen my father in twelve long years.

'Marriage is one thing,' I protested. 'Love quite another.'

Again she wavered, until her face hardened.

'I do not wish to be any man's concubine,' she flared. 'Being ordered around by his official wife will never suit me! Do this, Su Lin! Fetch that, Su Lin! I would sooner live as I do.'

'You must not doubt me! How can you doubt me? This is madness!'

'Madness to love unwisely,' she countered. 'Did not your studies teach you that, at least?'

'My studies taught me a good heart is unstoppable,' I replied.

A poor argument. One may easily think of a thousand situations where that is not the case. We stood silently. The water-lilies floated serenely and insects flew from flower to flower.

'Is there another you esteem more than me?' I asked.

Was Lord Xiao in my mind? Why pretend otherwise. His wealth and influence eclipsed me as night drowns sun. I realised his mansion lay near the Gardens of Ineffable Solace, higher up Phoenix Hill. . . Was it possible she had come from his house to meet me here? Su Lin shook her head to my question. Yet I sensed evasion.

'I am free or I am nothing,' she said, stubbornly.

Foolish words! No one is truly free!

'Who is exempt from duty, especially the duty owed to one's heart?' I demanded.

'Do not talk like that!' she said, evidently hurt.

'Then you feel nothing for me.'

'Oh, Yun Cai! Why are you so cruel? You know that is a lie! It is only that I cannot belong to you as I know you would wish. As you deserve.'

'That must be some consolation, I suppose,' I replied.

I turned to meet her eye. For a long moment our souls were joined. But a moment is not a lifetime. All she wished to become rose like invisible hands between us, pushing us apart.

'If you change your mind, send word,' I said.

She nodded, her head lowered, then walked back up the path to join her chaperone. I did not look after her, but stared at the water lilies. Such delicate, implausible flowers, to grow on water rather than solid land.

As I left the public gardens, a familiar figure watched coldly by the gate. In my grief and discomfort I ignored him. It was Secretary Wen, the very same who had visited Uncle Ming's house to assess my purity, so many years before.

Through all these events, between the ages of nineteen and twenty-five, I visited Uncle Ming's household regularly, motivated by obligation rather than pleasure. Our worlds were too far apart, the distance wider with each passing year, yet they were still family, my only family in the city. And blood, as they say, is not the space between roof and sky.

My monthly visits assumed a settled pattern. I would arrive on the appointed day, often to find Uncle Ming absent, lodging in his establishment of concubines beyond the city ramparts. When he did admit me to his office he seemed tired, less jovial, than in my youth. I soon learned the reason from Cousin Hong. Taxes were rising year by year to pay for our fruitless war on the frontier. It was around this time that the Ceaseless War party persuaded the emperor to launch his ill-fated campaign of conquest against the Northern barbarians. All are familiar with the Battle of Hu River and its consequences, how our borders were rolled back yet further.

More damaging to Uncle Ming's prosperity was his own neglect. I believe he had wearied of his success years before, finding comfort in pleasures which drained his essential breaths. Perhaps he spent so much time away from his business to avoid Honoured Aunty. Certainly she was worth avoiding.

After my success in the examination, Honoured Aunty withdrew into a bitter world of her own. Her only diversion seemed to be tyrannising the household servants, two of whom committed suicide in a love pact. Even Cousin Zhi forfeited her interest. After this he made a miraculous recovery from his ailments, striving instead to become a rake in the town.

Needless to say, his attempts to purchase the goodwill of unsavoury companions depleted Uncle Ming's coffers yet further.

Only Cousin Hong tried to save the wine business. A year or so after I left to live in Goose Pavilion he had married a compliant, doe-like woman who more than tolerated his temper. They set up residence in the east wing of the house and at once produced little Hongs. Even these failed to stir Honoured Aunty's grandmotherly affection. Small surprise there, perhaps. But it disturbed me that Uncle Ming paid no attention to his heirs.

Over the years Cousin Hong often complained to me.

'Ah. Little General,' he'd say. 'I sometimes think you brought good luck to our house. Why don't you move back? Ever since you've gone trade has been on the slide. Take our contract at the Palace. A highly-placed eunuch decided our wine was worse than that bastard Chou-pa's and that was it! Order cancelled. After twenty years of getting drunk at our expense. I've no doubt the eunuch was bribed. But how can I buy people off unless Father authorises the payment? If it wasn't for the rents we get from our tenants, I could barely balance the books.'

'Have you explained that to Uncle?' I asked.

'Of course, but he's in a world of his own. Do those poems you studied hold any wisdom for a man in my position?'

I sighed.

'Only things which I suspect would annoy you. To view the world as a husk of rice. To cultivate detachment and contemplation, so one might be at peace with the Way.'

He looked at me as though I spoke a strange dialect.

'Little use that is!' he exclaimed. 'All your philosophers didn't have a wife and children to feed.'

'Some did,' I said. 'May I suggest that when the time comes, I teach your children to write. That will defray some expense, at least.'

'I'll take you up on that,' he grumbled.

After so many complaints and withering glares from Honoured Aunty, I was always glad to return to Goose Pavilion.

One night, soon after my meeting with Su Lin in the Gardens of Ineffable Solace, something acrid tickled my nostrils. It was not long after midnight. I stumbled half-awake from my bed and found Mi Feng outside, gazing across the lake at the city.

The whole horizon to the east glowed and the lake ripples ran red. Flames rose like distant signal flares in several districts. Fires were nothing new in the capital, each disastrous, for the buildings within the ramparts were packed close together, dense squares of wood and bamboo. In a single two-storey building dozens of families lived and cooked and lit lamps, the city crammed with peasants who had fled hunger in the countryside.

'A real blaze,' said Mi Feng. 'It reminds me of the time we burned. . .'

He stopped himself. I was too enthralled by the spectacle before me to enquire who *we* were. Billows of smoke rose into the clear night sky, rivers of sparks flowing upwards. Strangely beautiful. Such a thought shamed me. Loud cracks of collapsing buildings mingled with cries of distress.

'Mi Feng,' I said. 'We should do something!'

He looked at me laconically.

'Like what?'

'I don't know. Anything. It is our duty. Besides, I have relations in the city and there's another person who. . .'

I peered across the lake to where Su Lin dwelt. No sign of flame there. Mi Feng scratched his chin.

'Why not ask if the district where your uncle lives has caught fire?' he suggested.

'Yes! We shall go at once.'

'*We*, sir?' he said. 'Shouldn't I stay here and guard the house?'

He looked at me and laughed unaccountably.

'Maybe it would be best if I went with you.'

So we hurried down the high road into the city. I noticed that

Mi Feng had equipped himself with a short, iron-tipped cudgel, but took little notice. Perhaps he hoped to beat down the doors of burning buildings. A bucket would have been more useful.

Soon we entered a fog of smoke and fleeing people. Families clutched a few household possessions, their eyes dazed. Guardsmen from the palace were stationed on corners, watching the crowds uneasily. I coughed as acrid smoke blew down the street.

'What district is burning?' I asked a man, who was guiding his pregnant wife toward the safety of the lake. Their eyes reflected red sky.

'All around the Wine Market,' he said over his shoulder, hurrying on.

As I turned, Mi Feng had the audacity to clutch my arm.

'Dangerous,' he said, shaking his head. 'Dangerous. What good would it do?'

I shook him off, hurried further into town. When I looked round he was still behind me. The Imperial Way was crowded with people flowing in the opposite direction. Every house awake, its inhabitants gathered fearfully on the street. Sparks drifted like fireflies. It took an hour to reach the edge of the Wine Market. Soldiers and firemen from the district watchtowers ran to and fro before the blaze, spurred on by their officers. Here the blaze burned fiercest, timber roaring and cracking as it was consumed, the shadowy figures of looters fleeing with whatever possessions they could seize, obscured by dense rolling smoke. Had I wished to proceed further, I could not. Uncle Ming's house lay behind a barrier of flames and poisonous fumes. Heat engulfed us as the fire-wind picked up. Wherever fire met vats of plum brandy or distilled rice wine, loud explosions echoed across the square.

'We must go back, sir!' shouted Mi Feng, in my ear. 'We can do nothing until morning. We must go back!'

He was right, of course. We were choking fast, had to surface in air or drown. Smuts of soot covered us from head to toe.

How I regained my home, I barely recollect. Mi Feng carried me part of the way, for I had swallowed a floating ember and coughed, coughed like a beggar too feeble to hold out his cup.

The next morning I recovered sufficiently to re-enter the city and make my way to the Great Wine Market. The fire had subsided. Shells of houses still glowed, timbers charred and blackened, mourned by former occupants who stood or squatted before them, their eyes lifeless. At first I thought Uncle Ming's house had survived the firestorm. The brick boundary walls, though smoke-blackened, stood firm. Yet when I passed through the gatehouse, desolation awaited.

The family mansion was a long rectangle of smoking twisted beams. Even the low octagonal tower where I once dwelt, had been reduced to its foundations. The brewhouse and warehouse had simply vanished, mere rubble and ash. Uncle's office was no more. Somewhere amid the pile of embers and debris lay the wine-cooler Father had given him on his wedding day.

A few servants crouched near the gates, and I found Cousin Hong among them, clutching an elegant blue and white vase, which had miraculously survived the blaze. His face was black as charcoal, his fine silks stained and singed.

'Where are your wife and children?' I demanded, as soon as I managed to stir him from his exhausted stupor.

'At her parents,' he replied, dully.

'Thank heaven they survived. What of Uncle Ming?'

Cousin Hong blinked, wiped his eyes.

'Burnt, badly burnt. I had him carried to his house in the suburbs. Let us hope his girls tend him as they ought.'

'And Honoured Aunty?' I demanded. 'Cousin Zhi? Are they safe?'

'They have left the city,' he said, tonelessly. 'They have gone to a small estate my uncle bought in the country. They will be safe there.'

'And Cousin Yi Yi? Has he gone with them?'

Cousin Hong gestured angrily at the rubble.

'He lies somewhere in there. The fool wouldn't stop trying to put out the fire in his bedroom.'

'You should drink some water,' I said, gently. 'I will arrange it.'

After he had drunk half a bucket-load, Cousin Hong revived a little.

'We are ruined,' he said, simply. 'All Father's houses went up. Our income is at an end. We have nothing. Nothing!'

'You have your life. And children. And your faithful wife. Besides, there is still Uncle's house in the suburbs and the small country estate you mentioned.'

Cousin Hong laughed bitterly.

'One costs a fortune to maintain and the other provides an income of only six thousand *cash* a year.'

'You and your family must come to live with me,' I said. 'There is room.'

Although, of course, there wasn't.

I never saw Uncle Ming again. He died of his burns and a broken heart two days after the Great Fire. His former concubines stripped the house in the suburbs bare before Cousin Hong could reach it, and he gained small profit from its sale, for Uncle had used it as surety for a debt.

I spent half my month's salary on a fitting funeral for him, although there was nowhere to keep his ashes, the family shrine having perished with the house. Many notable wine merchants attended the ceremony, for Uncle Ming had gained much respect, in his way. Cousin Hong insisted we store his remains in the single vase he had reclaimed from the fire. I sent a long, mournful letter home to Three-Step-House, recording his auspicious career and brave end. As usual, only a brief reply came. I have no doubt Father grieved deeply to receive such news.

Honoured Aunty remained on her small estate on the borders of the P'si Marshes, and I never saw her face again, except in bad dreams. But Cousin Zhi found a different destiny, one which later became entangled with my own. Using the fact that he had passed the First Examination, he gained a minor post as an administrator of enforced labour on the frontier. This, at least, provided a small salary. Only a dozen moons were to fade before we met again, in circumstances. . . Well, why think of it.

Cousin Hong lived in my house for long months, filling my rooms with anxiety; though his children's spirits were surprisingly unaffected by the change in family fortunes. They loved the lake, viewing it as a great adventure. I taught the eldest boy to row and fish, as well as how to write his name, although he was a dull pupil. Cousin Hong and Mi Feng struck up a sudden friendship, of the kind one sometimes finds between men who share similar natures. Even his wife, who I had hitherto viewed as an empty jar (unless full of child), surprised me by her dignity. Sages are not the only springs of wisdom in this world.

I had never forgotten my debt to Cousin Hong. Although our characters were often opposed, I admired him for remembering how to laugh within a month of the fire. Perhaps no longer striving to hold the family business together brought a strange relief. It has always been the way of my family to relish setting out anew – with much grumbling, of course. Yet having such impoverished relatives cost me several fashionable friends. Only P'ei Ti stayed true, bringing toys and clothes, as gifts for the children.

Winter passed before I realised what must be done. Indeed I reproached myself for not thinking of it earlier. That same evening, I insisted on taking Cousin Hong to a restaurant he had favoured in the years of his prosperity. He looked me over shrewdly, as we tasted our first cup of wine. He sniffed it. Took a sip.

'What do you make of it?' I asked.

'Over-priced,' he said. 'Little General, where have you found the money to pay for this?'

'Do you remember telling me, Cousin, that you always reclaim your debts?'

He shrugged.

'I never remember a quarter of the things we prattle about.'

'Well, you did. I, at least, possess a memory. For instance, do you recall that Uncle Ming gave me all the scrolls he kept in the lower room of the octagonal tower?'

'No,' he said. 'Why should I?'

'Because some of those scrolls were very old and valuable. Since working in the Imperial Library, I have learned their worth. More than that, I have sold them and they fetched a good price.'

When I mentioned the sum he almost spilt his wine.

'You have enough to set up a business of your own,' I said. 'The money is entirely yours.'

Thus Cousin Hong bought his first wine shop, and my obligation ceased.

A week after Cousin Hong and his family left my pavilion for his new establishment, I received an unexpected letter, delivered by a gaudily-dressed man specially hired for the purpose. The letter read:

Most Honourable Yun Cai,
Your old friend sends respected greetings. You must excuse the badness of my characters. I have heard about the sorrows of your Uncle and his family. I am very sorry. I hear also that you have used all your wealth for your cousin's sake. This has given you great face among your former neighbours in the Wine Market. I heard about your deeds through my former madam, whose house survived the fire, and she hardly has a good word for anyone! Are you still angry with me?
Su Lin.

I replied:

Dear Friend,
Your letter arrived on the first day my orchids opened their petals wide. My house is strangely silent since my cousin and his children left for their new home. I was surprised to hear from you. Nine months have passed since our meeting in the Garden of Ineffable Solace. That is a long time. You ask, am I still angry with you? Of course, that is a stupid question, for I was never angry with you in the first place. Merely disappointed.
Your Old Alley Friend, Yun Cai.'

A few days later, I received another letter, carried by the same go-between:

Dear Old Alley Friend,
Your letter reproaches me for being stupid, but how am I to know your moods? Often I think of you, but don't know what to think. I remember your face and person very well, only I sometimes wonder if you remember me. Last night I heard a patron who had hired me to sing at his garden party, talking about a poem you wrote about the Great Fire. It sounded very fine, but I have not read it so I cannot say. No doubt it would be too complicated for a poor girl like me. Often I wish for someone to talk to. I have bought many fine dresses and a head-piece made of silver. But I like your last letter more.
Su Lin.

I took the letter to the Imperial Library, and replied after a thoughtful day's study, smiling as I chose my words:

Su Lin,
You will find enclosed with this letter a copy of the poem

you mentioned. I hope it is to your taste. Sadly, some have interpreted it as a criticism of the relief offered by His Imperial Majesty to the fire's victims, though that is not my intention. It seems my fate to be perpetually misunderstood. Never mind. Bamboo endures many winds. You say that sometimes you wonder if I remember you. Nature has granted me an exceptionally good memory (though I do not mean to boast) and so I remember you very well. But that is not the same as meeting.
Your Incorrigible Friend, Yun Cai.

Her reply:

Dearest Incorrigible Friend,
I have never had an incorrigible friend before. In fact I had to ask a learned person who I know what 'incorrigible' means. Where did you learn such noble words? No, do not tell me, I can guess. It is enough to say that they could turn a poor girl's head! I am glad you have a very good memory. Perhaps you will remember that it is my birthday on the thirteenth day of this month. Unfortunately I cannot think of anyone I wish to celebrate it with. So I am leaving that day free. It will give me a chance to wash my hair.
Your Friend Across The Lake, Su Lin.

The thirteenth was a fortnight away. I thought carefully before I replied:

Dearest Friend Across The Lake,
I was deeply troubled to learn that you cannot think of anyone with whom to spend your birthday. Fortunately, I have a solution. If you wait on the shore beside your house at the time of the second afternoon bell, some kind

of company may present itself. I say 'may' but I mean 'will'. Whether you choose to be there is up to you.
Yun Cai.

I received no further letters.

The time preceding the thirteenth day of the sixth month brought more anxiety than pleasant anticipation. My worries were endless. Firstly, the number thirteen is known as the Lord of Troubles for good reason. I expended a hundred *cash* to establish the propitiousness of the day, but the astrologer's reply was ambiguous, everything seemed to depend on paying him more to establish the true relationships of the heavens. So I was left in extreme doubt.

Then there was the matter of a suitable present. Again, modest means narrowed my hand. I finally decided on a silver girdle-charm depicting two mountains overlapping. The symbolism, I hoped was obvious. Both of us were children of the mountains. Then again, many love songs are called Mountain Songs, because a young man on one peak is supposed to sing to a comely girl on another, their voices echoing back and forth across the valleys. However, the quality of the silver-work shamed me. Finally, I worried about the weather, for my plan to delight her depended entirely on a fine day.

At last the day came. Quite appropriately, considering the date, low clouds rolled over the city, undecided between sunshine and rain. The air hung still and humid. Mi Feng, who had observed my preparations with silent interest, suggested I pack a thick parasol. I smiled at him thinly.

When I loaded my small boat with a basket of flowers, plenty of wine and delicacies wrapped in lotus leaves, the first bell of the afternoon sounded from Blue Dragon Monastery, rolling across the lake. A faint breeze ruffled the water, enough to give me wings. Then I rowed out from the shore, and raised the small sail. It flapped like a disconsolate sigh, before finding courage, and puffing out in the breeze.

Glorious hour of my life, to be young and excitable, to weave through pleasure boats and skiffs, until I sailed before the jetty fronting the cottage where she dwelt.

No sign of her on the shore. In fact nobody was around. Misgivings set in. Su Lin had sent no definite word she would meet at the time and place I had suggested. At once I feared my own rashness, ever a fault with me, and almost turned back, determined to preserve a little dignity. But I sailed back and forth a couple of times, as the low bell of a neighbouring tower intoned the second hour. Perhaps she was watching from her window. Perhaps she waited for proof I would really come. Abruptly, the door of a cottage opened, and my heart swelled like my sail. Su Lin stepped out alone, carrying a small basket. Straightening her dress, she proceeded by small steps towards the jetty as I guided my craft to the shore. We reached the jetty at the same time and regarded each other silently.

'Have you no greeting for me?' she asked, nervously. 'Does my appearance displease you?'

I laughed, and the tension between us flew away like a freed bird.

'My eloquence is in my eyes,' I said.

I climbed ashore and helped her into the wobbling boat, both of us smiling at the inappropriateness of her fine clothes. The touch of her hand lingered in my own as I loosened the sail.

'It is a delight to share your Feast Of A Thousand Autumns,' I said.

Su Lin laughed more uncertainly than she had when we shared humble doorsteps. For a moment I wondered if my desire was for someone who had vanished, for a dream. In part it must have been. Yet that bold girl stood before me still. Time had merely added to her; and if she lived long enough, yet more women would emerge from within her. There is no such thing as a single life.

'I prefer spring or summer,' she said. 'Autumn is so cold and dry! Though your kind wish is appreciated.'

'Is that why you are here?' I asked, pretending to fuss over the tiller.

'Perhaps.'

Her tone dangled something. I decided not to press for more. So we sailed wherever the wind took us all that hot, sticky afternoon. Above us, clouds knitted their brows, but we did not notice. Our talk was of gay, inconsequential things, gossip she had heard of great men while singing in their houses, her favourite songs (I begged her to sing a few, on condition we share a cup of wine for each song).

'What if it spills?' she asked.

'Then we will pour another.'

'What if all the wine runs away?'

'I have brought plenty.'

So Su Lin sang in her strong, clear voice and I listened, touched that she chose to perform a setting of my Lotus poem. She must have learned it specially. It could hardly have been part of her usual repertoire. A passing pleasure boat applauded and we laughed gaily. I smiled with pride to keep company with such clever beauty.

Sometimes doubts and fears are best unspoken. To fill my eyes with her was enough: to catch traces of her perfume amidst the clear scent of the lake, the oiled wood of the boat; to share hopes of the future, knowing they might never be gathered; to listen sympathetically and be heard in my turn – these things became world and sky, night and day, for a few hours.

Su Lin squealed at the first drop of rain. Absorption in each other had blinded us to gathering clouds. By now we were a good way from her house, even further from my own. I glanced round and spotted a small, wooded island I had often noticed, though never visited, on which stood a miniature pavilion. The sky darkened, hastening dusk. Yet for all the rain it was still uncomfortably hot. I drove my boat onto the island shore with a bump.

'Quick!' I cried. 'Take that basket!'

We gathered our belongings in haste and hurried up the mossy path to the pavilion. As soon as we had entered, the rain began to fall in earnest.

The single room was deserted, as was the entire island. Grains of rice from a previous picnic lay on the bench, which I took as a lucky sign. A faded mural covered one wall, depicting Zhong-kiu with his magic sword raised above his head.

'We are well-protected from demons here,' I remarked.

In the corner stood a low shrine, equipped with the means for visitors to make burnt offerings. I found flint and kindling and, after many failed attempts, lit the lamp. The room filled with soft, flickering light.

Strange we should be so shy of each other. First we exchanged and explained our presents – for in reply to my birthday gift, Su Lin had brought me peonies to show she wished me well, bamboo to honour my strength and fruit to promise fecundity. We toasted each gift with wine and shared our food.

'Well,' I said, when the meal was done.

She sat back on the floor, meeting my glance with lowered eyes.

'Well, what?' she asked.

'Who would have imagined this when I first heard you sing of the mountains?'

'No one sensible,' she replied.

'Must we always be sensible?'

My heart choked my voice. Without reassurance, even the strongest love recoils. For a long moment she seemed to consider.

'Not tonight, at least,' she conceded. 'For one night both of us may make an exception.'

And we did, our finest clothes strewn around the dusty floor for bedding. Her fragrances intoxicated me until dawn. I whispered to her, 'You are a flower re-born', but we both spoke more through urgent sighs than words. My heart strove to break from my breast as I touched and released her secret fragrance for the first time. Texture of skin and luxuriant hair spun frailest, firmest nets. Once not enough. Both of us hungered. And my most piercing joy lay in proof of her own. Some would call me unmanly for that. Yet her soft cries released all the ardour of my youth, tempting us to acts strangely free for new lovers. We did not care or feel shame.

With the first light of day we sailed from that island, curiously silent. Joy lessened by a certainty of parting, for I could not afford to keep her and my prospects were poor. To taste sweetness just once makes the pleasure cruel. I could offer only my heart and, as we passed boats laden with fine silk or oil or fish for the market, a faithful heart seemed little enough.

After our night in the pavilion, Su Lin haunted my smallest actions. We had cast down the defences holding us apart as surely as any city wall. But a wall is made of beaten earth. Our barrier was a compulsion toward different destinies. Earth is composed of grains where one might grow the sweetest flower. Petals may unfurl, day by day, heady with scent. If the soil is starved, only bitterness takes root. And that is a hardy plant.

Our first meeting after her birthday took place in the Garden Of Ineffable Solace. I insisted on it, for I wished to banish painful memories of the day we met with her ugly chaperone. This time we were alone. As ever, she filled my eyes, until I saw nothing else. Blindness made me awkward.

'Come with me,' I said, brusquely. 'I must show you something.'

I led her to the pond where the water-lilies floated. Five golden carp swam at their ease.

'Are we to be as free as those fish?' I demanded.

'How strangely you speak, dearest Yun Cai,' she said.

I blushed at my own intensity.

'My love, I only mean to ask, are we to swim as they do, disregardful of each other unless they brush occasionally, then swim away?'

'You speak in riddles!' she declared, in her best mountain accent.

I knew she understood my meaning exactly. She peered at the pool and said, almost timidly: 'But see, dearest Yun Cai! They can never be free for they are bound by the limits of the pond.'

I could not answer that.

'Sit with me,' I said.

We sat side by side on a stone bench, a decent distance apart.

'I often think of that night,' I said. 'Do you?'

'Often. Very often,' she replied.

'I cannot believe it ever ended,' I said. 'If you will come with me to my house, it could begin again. This afternoon could become our night.'

She slowly withdrew her fan from her belt, and fanned herself like a moth fluttering its wings.

'I am free this afternoon,' she said. 'I have no engagements.'

It was high summer. We lay together in the soft light of late afternoon and her skin glowed. As dusk fell, she had to hasten away, an engagement to fulfil. I sat by the lake with wine and ink, sampling both to excess until the quarter moon grinned. Then I recited a poem to the moon, my voice echoing across the lazy water.

Another time I met her at a restaurant near East Canal Bridge. We sat in a curtained alcove. Voices formed a lulling drone behind our conversation.

'It has seemed a long week since we met,' I said, once the waiter had gone, closing the curtain behind him.

'Yet a busy one,' she replied.

'For you, at least. My work in the Deer Park Library is so light, I feel compelled to present myself there several times a week, just for something to do. The Chief Librarian has grown suspicious of me, in case I'm seeking his job.'

Su Lin took a languid sip of wine. She dabbed her lips on a napkin.

'What do you do at the library?' she asked.

'I read. And read. And read. Then I think.'

'Is that all?' she asked. 'I am surprised you have not gone blind.'

'No, I do other things. I study all the approved authors to pass the Imperial Examination, though my heart lies elsewhere. I make no plans to sit the Examination, but study for knowledge's own sake.'

'If you are studying like that,' she chided. 'Surely you must take the test! One like you should possess such an honour.'

I shrugged helplessly.

'I read only what interests me,' I said.

She became grave.

'Ah, Yun Cai. That way years pass.'

'But with pleasure,' I countered.

'And little profit to yourself,' she replied.

'I cannot help my own mind. Sometimes I sit down intending to compose model answers. Then I look out of the window and I notice the way a leaf falls or a bird trills. And I grow distracted.'

She sighed.

'You must not. Are you to be content with a modest salary until the day you die?'

'No, I suspect not. But why are we so serious?'

So I poured her another cup and made light of ourselves, but I could tell Su Lin was somehow disappointed. It did not stop us ending the evening in each other's arms.

Another time I took her sailing once again on the West Lake. Perhaps I hoped to recapture the excitement of her birthday. If so, I heard more than I wished, for she opened her heart and I was forced to drink her words.

'Yun Cai,' she said. 'Do you never think of the future?'

I laughed.

'The future is a dream. Do you see how the breeze stirs your lovely black hair? In that moment, all past, present and future are contained. It makes me happy.'

'One day that hair will grow grey,' she said.

Su Lin did not take her eyes from my face. When I talked as I thought, she often listened with attention. Had she been born a gentleman, I have no doubt she would have composed poems. Instead, her own poems were the lilting, delicate songs required by her trade. This time, I could tell my words did not satisfy her.

'Does my answer displease you?' I asked, coldly.

'Oh, it is a fine, fine answer. But when you talk like that, much as I like it, I know your words float away.'

For all the brightness of the day, a shadow fell across us.

'I am afraid,' she said. 'You think that I am someone different from myself.'

'Then what are you?'

I let the sail go slack, so the boat drifted. A noisy pleasure boat passed by, full of young men who shouted ribald comments. I ignored them.

'Teach me,' I repeated. 'What you are.'

'What strange questions you ask!'

She took out her fan and opened it in agitation. Then she closed it, laying it across her knees like a rod.

'I will tell you, since you ask. I am an ordinary girl who wants ordinary things! Is that so wrong? Already my beauty is showing signs of age. When it is gone I shall have little value. Now is the time for me, the time when I must gather enough wealth to set me up for the rest of my life. Can you not see I have worked and worked to win just that? I should have the friendship of wealthy gentlemen, so I may use their presents wisely. I can almost afford a carriage, Yun Cai! Imagine it! Poor Su Lin from muddy Chunming, in a carriage! Poor, nobody Su Lin with servants and dresses as fine as any lady!'

I did not reply. It seemed better to wait for the worst.

'But when I am with you,' she continued, miserably. 'I forget what I must do. How can it be that the thing I take the most joy in, your company, threatens to ruin everything.'

'Ruin is a strong word,' I said.

'No, you do not see! I have set my heart on things you cannot give me.'

Then she began to weep. As the boat rocked gently, I took her hand, more like a brother at that moment than a lover.

'Oh, what is the use!' she cried.

She laughed with forced gaiety.

'Take me back to your house,' she said. 'And I will sing you songs and we shall drink wine and make love.'

So we did. And I tried to please her. I had persuaded myself each moment we shared would breed new moments. I could not think beyond her presence until she had gone, busy about her shrewd business. I even suppressed jealousy through a thousand subtle arguments; yet all the while it gathered in my heart like a clammy, black stone.

This was the time when I completed the West Lake sequence of poems, which became so popular one could hear them sung by servant girls and porters on the street, for they were written in the plainest terms, and many who heard or read them found mirrors of their own longing. I took much satisfaction from my fame. But, of course, it brought me no wealth. A poet's words, once released, blow like thistle seeds to the Eight Winds and grow where they may without any reward. Besides, I lived in a state of constant agitation. Bizarrely, those poems worked against me, for word got about of the singing girl who had inspired them and Su Lin was more in demand than ever.

One night in autumn, when the land was dry and cold winds blew east from the hills, Mi Feng announced a visitor. I was plucking mournful runs on the lute, the chamber lit by a single lamp, shadows dancing on the wall. Sound and shadow seemed one.

'P'ei Ti!' I exclaimed. 'What brings you here at so late an hour?'

He took a seat and the refreshments I offered, still dressed in his official uniform, for he had just left a long day's toil at the Censor's Office. His fingers were black with ink, his brow furrowed with care. As good friends will, we did not talk until he had poured himself several cups and shared the simple dinner I offered. Wind stirred the pines around my small house and sometimes the roof creaked. I watched as he ate. The boy I had known seemed far away, yet within him still. At last he laid aside bowl and chopstick, belching his satisfaction.

'Is that better?' I asked, gently.

He chuckled.

'It is always better when I see you,' he said. 'You help me to remember myself.'

'That's good then,' I said.

He settled back and looked at me frankly.

'I do not come on pleasant business,' he said.

'Oh?'

He belched again. Poured more wine. For the first time I realised he was nervous.

'Tell me, Yun Cai, is it not the proof of a true friend that he may counsel in an unwelcome way?'

'You are building up to something,' I said.

'Indeed I am.'

To my surprise, he rose and began to pace.

'You are in great danger,' he said. 'I would betray my duty to you if I did not warn you.'

'This sounds grave,' I said, pouring us both more wine.

'I beg you to be serious!' he cried. 'I must speak of painful matters. Perhaps it is best if I am blunt. Your love for a certain singing girl is well-known.'

My smile faded.

'What of it?'

'I must warn you that she has attracted another man's fancy, a man of great influence and renown.'

'Who is he?' I demanded, already knowing the answer.

'It is one you must not offend at any cost,' he said. 'Especially at so delicate a phase of your career. Your entire future depends on this man's goodwill. If you lose it, all hope of advancement will be at an end.'

I tapped impatient fingers on the arm of my chair.

'You must be reasonable!' he said. 'It seems this girl has caught Lord Xiao's fancy. He has made detailed enquiries into her background. And it is not in his nature to share.'

'Neither is it in *mine*.'

Such a protestation was a cowardly lie. For I shared her with anyone who could pay the absurd prices she demanded. I flushed with shame, and anger soon follows that emotion.

'You must forget her,' he said.

It was my turn to rise and pace. We circled each other like wrathful tigers.

'How can you say this to me?' I cried. 'Do you realise what you are asking?'

'I ask because I am right,' he replied. 'At least promise you will think about what I have said. Believe me, I do not wish to bring you pain.'

'Yet you have!'

I pretended to yawn.

'The hour is late,' I said.

He bowed stiffly. We glared at each other. We, who had been closer than brothers.

'Will you not at least consider my words?' he said.

We stood apart, staring at the floor

'I can promise that much. Goodnight to you.'

Our first quarrel as friends. It shook me terribly. One love seemed to have cost another.

The next day I received a summons. All friends of Lord Xiao were to celebrate the wedding of his eldest son, who was in his twentieth year and destined, it was said, for great advancement. The ceremonies preceding the wedding had been an acknowledged topic of conversation among polite society for some time, so splendid were the pre-nuptial gifts.

On the eve of the wedding I stood among a crowd of his clients and dependents outside the bride's home. It was a house of grandeur, the number of rooms tripled by the number of servants, all very visible. I have always hated waiting in line, yet I was comforted to see men of high position queuing before me.

We shuffled forward into the hall where the dowry was on display. We passed tables laden with jewels, ornate boxes, costly vases, finest wall-hangings painted on silk. The aim of this display was admonishment. Perhaps the powerful are insecure, for they need to find confirmation of their power in other men's eyes, as though glory depends on submission. In much the same way, it is said a deity loses its godhead when people cease to worship it.

Those were my thoughts. I was surrounded by conventional exclamations of surprise, for Lord Xiao had stationed secretaries at every trestle. Their task was obvious. To take note of anyone who did not display the required awe. I am sad to say, I could hardly stifle my yawns. P'ei Ti, who stood in the line behind me, doubtless passed the test with more credit.

The next day we were expected to gather at Lord Xiao's mansion. I joined the crowd outside his gatehouse when it was already several hundred strong. Late afternoon, a cold autumn wind ruffling the tassels and ribbons on the well-wishers' hats.

One may see many species of humanity in such a crowd. Those who accept their position without question, uncomfortable unless they demonstrate cheerfulness. Those who fulfil their duties like obedient servants, but retain their sense of self through unobtrusive grumbling. Those, like me, who find themselves in an uncongenial place, but cannot contrive to reach somewhere better. We were all there.

I stood at the fringes of the crowd, and so had ample opportunity to see the bridal procession as it arrived. First came a dozen singing girls, scattering handfuls of seeds, *cash* coins and cooked beans in front of the gatehouse, to avert baneful influences as the bride entered her new home. Urchins scrabbled to seize what they could. So did the more impecunious of the clerks.

Next came singing girls bearing torches shaped like lotus flowers. In their midst stepped the bride, dripping with finery and happy tears of jade. A plain, broad-hipped girl, ripe for children. Then I saw Su Lin.

My instinct was to hide behind a particularly fat official. I understood her presence at once. She had been hired specially for the occasion to play an honoured role, that of the Chief Singing Girl. She held a mirror and walked backwards in front of the bride, guiding her way. I say, 'walked', but 'floated' would be a better word.

That was a many-layered pain to me! To see my love serving another woman, however honourably, offended my pride. Worse was the evident enjoyment on Su Lin's face, her blush of excitement to be attracting so much attention. Her dress and hair-piece in the form of a phoenix, her supple figure, dignity and grace, all exquisite! What a gulf lay between us. I knew something akin to despair.

We followed the bridal procession into Lord Xiao's vast courtyard. The bride stepped on green-dyed matting and climbed upon a saddle shiny with silver, as is customary. Then she vanished inside, hardly ever to emerge again.

Did Su Lin see me? I did not believe so, and for that I was glad.

Our duties fulfilled, the crowd of clients and protégés dispersed, each to their own little house, each to separate feelings. My imagination raged. I saw the bride and bridegroom drinking their cups of wine before the consummation. Most of all, I saw Lord Xiao's attention to the flower that was Su Lin, his lust to force aside the petals of her being, and insinuate himself. It seemed no accident she had been chosen as the Chief Singing Girl for these nuptials.

I returned home disconsolate. What a thing it is to love! To own a heart scored by claw marks.

A few days passed. One afternoon I was lounging on the front steps of Goose Pavilion, watching the progress of a cloud as it journeyed inland, intrigued that it floated alone, a single-boat across the sky. My thoughts were fanciful. Did the Jade Emperor ride that cloud as his pleasure craft? Perhaps it was an Immortal's daydream, traversing the up-turned lands, mountain and valley, river and forest, just as a dream surveys all it would explain.

The sound of tinkling bells wakened me from this reverie. To my surprise a two-wheeled carriage pulled by a single horse was jolting down the pot-holed path from the high road. Inside, perched Su Lin and her maid, both clutching their seats to steady themselves. So this was the carriage she craved! The coachman whipped on the horse, its eyes staring, jaws flecked with foam.

As soon as she arrived, Su Lin climbed down and ran to my arms, where she sobbed.

'What is it?' I cried. 'Who has wronged you?'

Perhaps one of her clients had forced himself upon her. I went cold at the thought.

'Oh, Yun Cai! Take me inside, I must speak to you.'

This I did. Out of the corner of my eye I noticed Mi Feng bustling over to comfort Su Lin's maid, who seemed as distressed as her mistress.

'Sit down,' I said. 'Calm yourself. Tell me what is amiss.'

Her words were lost in tears, so that her elaborate make-up ran down her face.

'Dearest Yun Cai!' she cried. 'I do not know what to do!'

'You must be calm. Tell me what is wrong, so I can help.'

'Have you not heard?'

'What do you mean?'

'I have had a most trying afternoon!'

Again sense was stifled by weeping. I waited until she subsided.

'I must be sensible,' she said. 'You deserve that. Lord Xiao summoned me today and made me an offer. An honourable offer, I'm sure he meant it sincerely.'

My heart went cold.

'What were the terms of this. . . offer?'

'That I should become his official concubine! He said that though he has three others, I would be his favourite. He said a splendid house in his grounds, with its own gardens and ponds, had been prepared for me. He assumed I could not refuse.'

I clenched my fists.

'I must congratulate you,' I said, coldly. 'Now you have everything you have always desired. Fine clothes and servants and luxury. All will be yours.'

'Please do not be angry with me! I could not bear it if you were angry with me!'

'When do you join his household?' I asked mercilessly, as one might discuss a simple transfer of property. 'Or have you already?'

Su Lin gasped.

'You are cruel! I have told him I could not consent to his offer without careful thought. He seemed very displeased. I thought he might strike me.'

Hope formed a crack in my black mood.

'He wouldn't like that,' I conceded.

'No, he didn't. But I do not wish to become his concubine! I have heard his wife is a terrible woman, and besides, he is. . . though such an offer is a great honour, he is not to my taste. Yet who am I to offend Lord Xiao? The world will think me mad.'

'Perhaps it is the world which is mad,' I suggested.

'But what am I to do?'

I sat alongside her on the divan and took her hand. My thoughts whirled. I could speak of my own feelings, but they seemed strangely irrelevant. Su Lin had come to me for guidance. It was my duty to consider all aspects of the question, as a father might.

Firstly, Lord Xiao was powerful, and to scorn him would lead to consequences. He might discourage his friends from using her services, on pain of losing his good will. He might even hire men to physically harm her, or contrive some trumped up charges which brought about her ruin. But everyone in the city would know why and how these things had come about. He would lose much face for being so besotted with a poor singing girl that he took desperate, jealous measures. He would risk becoming a laughing-stock, an object of contempt among the fashionable men of the town. Worse than a cuckold, for at least a married man has enjoyed his wife. . . Yet still he might think it a worthy price to pay for revenge.

On the other hand, Lord Xiao was not without enemies. For all his influence, he had powerful opponents in the court, especially among the Peace-With-Dignity party, who opposed his calls for war against the Northern barbarians as a dangerous policy. After all, our armies enjoyed little success at the time. Such men would seize any opportunity to humiliate Lord Xiao. What could be easier than patronising the singing girl who had rejected his offer? Such an inducement might double the price she could demand. In addition, should Lord Xiao seek to use the law against her, his great opponents would have the means to frustrate him, thereby diminishing his status. Lord Xiao would be aware of this. It was a risk he would probably wish to avoid, for he was known as a cautious man, who preferred to strike from the shadows. Yet still he might think it a worthy price to pay for revenge.

Nothing was certain, but I inclined to think Lord Xiao would prefer the matter hushed up. Perhaps I was blinded by my own wishes. Yet my acquaintance with him had taught me this much: he hated to look small. What better way to avoid that, than to make light of his offer? I was sure that would be his natural way. Yet still. . .

'How deep in thought you are!' Su Lin exclaimed. 'What are you thinking?'

I ignored her. Sometimes women are tiresome, even those one loves. For I had discovered another possibility. Lord Xiao's wife was a notorious she-dragon. His position largely depended on the patronage of her family, for he stemmed from a weaker branch than her own. Her brother's influence at court was the main pillar supporting his power. If he offended her, he offended her family. For the husband to proceed on some undignified course of revenge against a common singing girl would shame the wife. A coldness might develop with his wife's relations, the same men he relied upon. They were said to be a proud clan, resentful of insults to their honour.

I looked up, and met Su Lin's troubled gaze.

'If you wish to reject his offer,' I said. 'I believe it will be safe to do so.'

Then I explained my reasons, elaborating on matters she could not be expected to know. When I had finished, Su Lin seemed reassured, for she was a worldly girl, in her way. Perhaps the intrigues at court resembled games played out among the singing girls. Certain passions are common to every class. Though the form differs, essential truths apply to all.

'But Yun Cai,' she said. 'I must tell you he mentioned your name. I believe that he thinks I hesitated because of my feelings for you.'

In my folly, I laughed, not without bitterness.

'I hope your feelings for me *do* hold some sway in your decision,' I said.

In a moment she was in my arms. If I required proof, she gave it that night. I did not allow myself to fear Lord Xiao's anger. Goose Pavilion had become a house of desperate love. So much so, that when I stepped out to relieve myself in the bushes, I heard Mi Feng busy with Su Lin's maid in the kitchen. The wind made the bells on her new carriage tinkle forlornly.

The following morning, Su Lin rejected his offer of concubinage in a grovelling letter I composed on her behalf. I thought myself very cunning to hire a scribe to copy it out, so Lord Xiao would not recognise my hand. It was received with the utter silence I had anticipated, and there seemed an end to the matter. How naïve I was! All my life I have expected men to behave as I might myself. But Lord Xiao was capable of schemes I could not conceive.

A week later the poisonous seed spread out its roots. I had broken the cooking cauldrons and sunk the boats. Now came the consequences.

It was a day when minor officials like myself were required to bear witness to the Emperor's negotiations on our behalf with Heaven. There were a dozen such ceremonies in the official calendar and all began the same way. The staff assigned to the Imperial Library of the Deer Park gathered before dawn, each in his uniform. Then we marched across the Emperor's Pleasure Grounds and lined up according to our degree, led by the Chief Librarian, until we entered the palace gates.

Here supercilious eunuchs held sway, at least for the likes of us. We joined other streams of officials, as tributaries swell a river, until we took our place in the huge square before His Imperial Highness's residence. Thousands were assembled, silent and fearful. As many torches lit the chilly darkness. The occasion, as I recollect, was the Dragon Son's sacrifice to his ancestors, so the Soil might be renewed.

First the Emperor left the palace in robes of darkest green, riding upon an ivory chariot. As he passed, all torches were extinguished, except those lining the way. We stood in darkness, craning for a glimpse of the cavalcade, aware of dawn gathering. Imperial Guards bellowed orders to each other. The earth itself shook with drum beats and the solemn, mournful sound of trumpets.

As the court musicians played the prescribed songs, His Highness mounted the altar steps, treading upon carpets of shimmering yellow gauze. So far away, I could barely see as he offered libations to Heaven on our behalf, to the august Earth, and finally to his ancestors. I could not hear as he read from the holy tablets, drinking the ritual Wine of Happiness. Yet the moment was replete with elation. We waited silently until he had changed his robes inside the shrine, and rode another ceremonial chariot back to the palace, surrounded by horsemen and cheering crowds on foot.

By breakfast time I thought myself done for the day and was looking forward to a nap. However, just as the staff of the Deer Park Library were preparing to depart, I felt a tap on my shoulder. I turned to meet the supercilious face of Lord Xiao's most intimate assistant, Secretary Wen.

'Come with me,' he said.

I bridled at his tone.

'By what authority?' I demanded.

Then he smiled such a smile. One he had learned from his master. Later I came to know it well, and always longed to cut it from his face.

'Lord Xiao,' he said, softly. 'Didn't you guess?'

I followed him through the dispersing crowd, men chattering as they will after a long period of enforced silence, until we reached the offices of the Finance Ministry.

He led me through long rooms where clerks plied abacus and brush, to an inner courtyard brightened by a tinkling fountain. Lord Xiao sat upon a high-backed chair, issuing instructions regarding the collection of taxes, his words recorded by a scribe. I waited at the side until his business was complete, then presented myself, bowing low. Lord

Xiao regarded me from his chair. I kept my eye on the earth.

'Why, if it is not Yun Cai of. . . I forget where. Some little place or other.'

The officials who sat around him laughed heartily. Clearly I was destined for rough treatment.

'So good of you to come,' he said. 'I take it I am not interrupting any of your fine poems?'

I lifted my head a little.

'My Lord is too gracious to enquire,' I said. 'But I am rarely inspired in the morning. My best time is evening.'

I could sense a dozen cold eyes upon me. No one laughed now.

'That is fortunate,' said Lord Xiao, in his high-pitched way. 'I would hate to interrupt your. . . flow.'

I waited. Indeed I had no other choice.

'You may be wondering why I have summoned you here,' he said. 'Of course, it is because I wish to promote you.'

Still I said nothing.

'Have you no reply to that?' he asked, sharply.

'Gratitude has left me speechless, Lord,' I said. 'Forgive me.'

He lolled back in his chair.

'Oh, I forgive you. But I am a busy man and this is not important. I might say, *you* are not important, so I'll come to the point.'

Yet he settled comfortably in his chair and watched me, as a cat might examine a tasty snack it has pinned to the ground with its claws.

'I've arranged a special job for you, Yun Cai. You are to be transferred. And I have no doubt you'll be pleased. You see, Yun Cai, I have considered your talents well. I resent those who I raise up meddling in my affairs, but surely that does not apply to you? Does it?'

I pretended to consider this.

'Not that I'm aware of, Lord.'

'A good reply! I take it you are skilful at adding up,' he said.

'Of course you are! That is why I have chosen you for a vital mission. In fact, I would entrust it to no one else. You are aware of His Imperial Highness's campaign against the rebels in the city of Pinang? Well, I have a little posting for you.'

If I had any doubts he was enjoying himself, the slow smile which spread across his face settled them.

'I am my Lord's grateful servant,' I replied.

'That is well. You are to join the Army of the Left Hand and there your duties will commence. I have arranged that you will hold a truly honourable position. Do you want to know what it is?'

'If my Lord wishes to tell me,' I said.

'But I do! You see, I require a detailed list of every man who perishes on that campaign, their name, place of birth, where and how they fell. As well as, let me see – age, yes, why not their age. In order to achieve this, you must accompany the troops at the front line. Think how exciting it will be! The sound of bows twanging and swords clashing! How stirring to the blood! And, after all, it is in your blood. Wasn't your father a common soldier?'

'Indeed, he was, Lord. And an uncommonly brave one.'

'Well, there you go! You can be brave just like him. You may take one servant with you, and I have assigned some clerks to assist you. You must leave the city at dawn tomorrow. Failure to leave at that time will result in a severe penalty.'

'Tomorrow, Lord? At dawn?' I asked, aghast.

'No delay is possible,' he replied. 'Do you like the sound of it, Yun Cai?'

I did not know how to reply.

'You seem at a loss for words,' he said. 'How very unusual.'

'It is simply I am overwhelmed by my Lord's generous nature,' I said, lifting my head so that I met his eye, for I had been provoked beyond caution. 'All men will say when they hear about my posting, that His Imperial Majesty's trust in Lord Xiao is not misguided.'

He glared at me.

'For one who is speechless, you have much to say. Do you know, I have a feeling you will never return from the frontier. And that grieves me, truly it does.'

If my mouth was dusty before, now it felt like a desert.

'Shoo!' he said, smiling. 'A hearty goodbye to you.'

His intimate followers, who had been silent before, slapped their thighs with mirth, a few of them even applauded. I left with the sound ringing in my ears. In truth, I can hear it now.

Eighteen hours were all I had before the Western Road must swallow me up. Eighteen hours to pack away a life – inform friends, write to my parents and relatives, quit my tenure of Goose Pavilion. Eighteen hours to say farewell to everything known and loved. My one comfort was that I had no time to be afraid.

Mi Feng met me outside the house, where he was chopping wood. Despite the bitter wind, he worked bare-chested.

'What's wrong?' he demanded, on seeing my sickly face.

'Mi Feng,' I said. 'It is time for you to find a new master.'

Then I told him the exact details of my conversation with Lord Xiao. By the end, tears were in my eyes. Mi Feng listened, his axe cradled in his arms.

'So, you don't want me to come with you?' he said.

I looked at him as though he had uttered a bad joke.

'Well, don't you?' he repeated.

'Do you mean this?' I asked.

'If you like, sir.'

'But why?' I cried. 'Are you mad?'

It was hardly a courteous reply to so noble an offer. He laughed sardonically.

'You did me the best turn a man can do when I was sold for

target practice,' he said. 'Fine gentlemen aren't the only ones who know about honour.'

'What of the danger?'

'What of it? You'll find I'm full of surprises, sir. And anyway, I reckon you need someone to watch your back. You know what this Lord Xiao meant when he said he doesn't expect you to come back, don't you?'

I understood only too well. But Mi Feng hadn't finished.

'If this Lord Xiao was a man, he'd sort it out sword to sword! And the man left standing would enjoy the girl that very night, any way he fancied!'

I was taken aback by his vehemence. His time among the barbarians had entered his soul more than I realised.

'No, I'll come along,' he continued. 'This city's pleasant enough but there are other places to live.'

And die, I thought.

We spent frantic hours. Above all I needed ready *cash*, as much as I could muster. I sold all my furniture and spare clothes to a wily merchant for a quarter of their value. My scrolls and books I could not bring myself to trade, for they seemed the best part of me, so I sent them to Cousin Hong. Mi Feng requested that I give him the money to buy horses. Naturally, I hesitated. What was to stop him disappearing into the city with all my wealth? Yet we needed horses badly, and other equipment.

'What do you know about horses?' I asked.

He didn't look up from fastening a bundle.

'More than you,' he said.

I couldn't deny that. And why not trust him? My situation could hardly be worse, even if he robbed me. I had a dozen letters to write, so I handed over the money with a sigh.

'Don't worry,' he said. 'I'll come back.'

Alone in the house, I packed forlornly for a while, then set about my letters. I was disturbed by tramping feet and hurried to the door. A sedan carried by four sweating men arrived, and even before it had touched the ground its occupant leapt out, looking round wildly. When he saw me he rushed forward, almost tripping on his long official's robe.

'I have heard the most absurd rumour!' cried P'ei Ti. 'Everyone has heard! Can it be true?'

I led him inside. Fortunately the merchant had not removed the furniture, so we still had somewhere to sit.

'It is true,' I said, gesturing at the small pile of bags on the floor, for we were intending to travel light.

P'ei Ti frowned, shook his head, then seemed to regain his calmness. He resembled the pictures of a stern judge one sometimes sees.

'Lord Xiao dishonours himself through this,' he said, stiffly. 'He abuses his official position for the sake of petty jealousy. He proves himself unworthy of high office.'

'Right now that is small comfort,' I replied.

'Have you told her?'

I shook my head sadly. In fact, it seemed better that Su Lin only discovered my fall once I had gone. I knew how she would blame herself, for she was tender, at least when it came to me. I had composed a long letter, urging her to forget me and get on with her life. Our best revenge, I had written, would be her continuing happiness and prosperity. I urged her not to abandon her dreams, and that I only asked she think of me fondly. Above all, I wrote confidently of my return, and that she should neither wait for me nor worry, for we would always be like the golden carp in the Garden of Ineffable Solace. No malice could ever change that.

'No, I have not told her,' I said. 'Please take this letter to her.'

'I shall,' he said.

We sat in miserable silence.

'Of course Lord Xiao's game is obvious,' he said, at last. 'He intends that you won't come back. You must be constantly vigilant.'

I was growing tired of this particular warning. My friends seemed to consider me an unworldly fool, his head buried up the backside of a lotus! Perhaps they were right. I could scarcely imagine what was to come.

'You must remember your father's example,' he urged. 'You must be ready to defend yourself when the blow falls. I have brought gifts which might help.'

He went outside and returned bearing a bundle wrapped in cloth. From it he took a sword with a plain hilt and scabbard.

'Oh, P'ei Ti!' I said, laughing. 'You are all kindness.'

'Do not be a fool!' he said. 'Look at the sword.'

I took it from his trembling hands, and drew it from the scabbard. It shone in the pale afternoon light. A wonderful, deadly sword, if one knew how to use it.

'This must have cost six months' wages,' I stammered.

P'ei Ti nodded.

'I asked the sword smith to put a cheap-looking hilt on it. No one should know its value unless you have to use it, or they might try to steal it.'

'You are thoughtful,' I said.

'I am serious. The only way you can repay me for this gift is by practising with it every day. Then, should the time come, you may strike back.'

'I promise to practise,' I said.

'And another thing.'

He withdrew a large bag from his belt, heavy with thousands of *cash*. Though I argued, he insisted that I accept it, claiming it was merely a loan.

As dusk faded to night, he helped me to write a dozen needful letters, assuring me that my parents would be informed of my posting. The hours of night tolled one by one, and I began to grow anxious for Mi Feng. If he fleeced me in so ignoble a way, I would make sure P'ei Ti hunted him down without mercy. He was good at anything which required persistence. So we waited, drinking the last of my wine, laughing too heartily and loudly at memories of happier times.

At midnight, both of us started to our feet. Horses were

cantering towards us. We rushed outside and saw Mi Feng riding a shaggy steppe pony, a second horse following behind, both saddled and equipped. He reined in at the last minute. His skill amazed us both: leaping from the saddle over the head of his horse to land squarely, still clutching the reins.

'Can this be your servant, Mi Feng?' asked P'ei Ti, in wonder.

Indeed he looked more like a barbarian than ever. It was then I understood that I did not know him at all.

At sunrise we rode through the city, followed by P'ei Ti's litter. Never had the broad streets and palaces, the markets and alleyways, the canals and lofty bridges, seemed more marvellous. People stared to see us pass, Mi Feng so nimble on his mount, while I struggled to retain my seat. Finally we reached the Gate of Eternal Rectitude, leading to the Western Road. There, I was not to be spared a most sorrowful parting. For waiting by the gate with her maid, was Su Lin.

Mi Feng coughed.

'I happened to send a message what time we were leaving,' he said.

I should have been angry with him for ruining my plan; secretly, I was pleased. I nearly fell off my horse as I struggled to dismount.

She had dressed simply, without make-up, and her downcast face tore at my heart. I gently lifted her chin so she could meet my eye.

'Why did you not tell me?' she whispered.

'Because I wished to spare you,' I said. 'P'ei Ti will give you a letter which explains everything.'

'All this is because of me,' she said.

'No, no, that is a lie! It is because of Lord Xiao. He is to blame for his jealousy, no one else.'

'Let me go with you,' she begged.

I smiled.

'Do you think I would take my sweet flower, my sweet,

delicate orchid, where she might be trampled? Come now.'

She began to weep silently. Then her eyes flashed.

'I'll get him for this,' she whispered.

'That is foolish talk.'

She took a small knife from her belt and, to my horror, before I could stop her, made a deep cut on the palm of her hand. She did not cry out as the bright, crimson blood dripped onto the road. In the mountains this gesture marked the commencement of a feud, for every time one saw or felt the scar, one would be reminded.

'Do not be so foolish!' I cried. 'You act as if you were a man.'

'I have the spirit of a man,' she said. 'It is only with you I feel like a woman, and that has been stolen from me.'

If I had not known better, I would have feared for Lord Xiao then. But she was only a singing girl. What could she do?

'That was a stupid thing,' I said, kissing her wounded hand. 'So beautiful a hand should be treasured with gentleness. You hurt yourself for no reason. Go home, my love. Read my letter. Make me proud of you, by being happy.'

I turned to P'ei Ti.

'Oh, my friend, watch out for her until I return!'

He bowed in grave assent. That bow reassured me more than a thousand words.

When I tried to mount my horse, the beast at once sensed who was master, and threw me to the dusty ground. A crowd of on-lookers had gathered, and they roared with laughter. Among them, watching with his usual small smile, stood Secretary Wen.

Mi Feng helped me into the saddle and we rode away. I glanced back only once. Su Lin and P'ei Ti were watching until I could be seen no more. Both were weeping. No magic potion of powdered jade and gold and dragon bones was needed to read their thoughts. It was strange to be considered already dead, when young and full of life.

five

'. . . The sly pheasant boasts six raw talons.
Our mulberry tree has countless roots.

The general's chariot tinkles with pendants of jade.
Rocks are our jewels, green bamboo our brocade. . .'

I am woken from my memories by a scraping noise, and peer round in confusion. I try to rise from the couch. The floor is no longer dappled by afternoon light, as it was when I began to doze. Hours have passed. Now dusk seeps shadow across the room. It takes a moment to locate the source of the scraping sound. When I do, it seems best not to move at all.

A tousled head slowly pokes through the window, pushing aside the paper curtain. The man's cheeks are grimy and pinched, starved of rations. Dark eyes glitter, searching the shadows. Then he spots me, where I lie on the couch. The fellow is a third my age, and four times as desperate.

I should stand up, shout for help, but I'm paralysed. His eyes flick anxiously round the room, falling on my three bronze-bound chests. Then with a slow, crab-like movement, he starts to clamber in through the window. Beneath his cloak I recognise a uniform – one of Youngest Son's rabble – and the hilt of a sword. At last, I find the courage to act.

'Eldest Son!' I bellow. 'Help! Come quickly!'

The looter hesitates. Once again he glances desperately at the chests. Perhaps he imagines they are crammed with gold and precious things, enough for him to flee into the mountains and set up as a landowner, far from the Winged Tigers Regiment and General An Shu's rebellion. Enough to purchase a wife and home. Enough to make him a proper man.

'Father! What is it?'

Feet can be heard in the corridor. Exclamations of surprise. For a moment the young soldier hesitates, casting a final, longing look at the chests. Then he slides back over the window-sill, jumping to the ground. I stumble after him, but all I can see when I reach the window is a bounding form, vanishing into the stands of bamboo beside Three-Step-House. I turn to find Eldest Son beside me, his face full of concern.

'Your brother cannot control his own men,' I say, feebly. 'Order the servants to bar all the shutters and doors.'

I am disconsolate over my dinner, and eat alone. This third day of occupation has been the most terrible – and still it is not over. First the Four Punishments in the village square, then the alarm of a desperate intruder. In addition, Wudi tells me that the girl who vanished from the village two nights ago, when the soldiers had their fun, has still not been found. We all fear the worst.

Eldest Son requested permission to retire early. The day's events have wounded him more than he possesses eloquence to express. He always counted it a blessing to dote on Youngest Son. Thus good becomes its opposite. Who can explain why the companion of his childhood exists no more, and has been replaced by General An-Shu's executioner? To do so would baffle a thousand sages. He must acquire acceptance in his own way.

The servants lay out plain dishes. Steamed rice. A sauce of soy and chervils. Cabbage flavoured with vinegar. Salt fish fried in garlic and ginger. The steward has informed me that, since the banquet for Youngest Son and his officers, our stores are sadly depleted. Soon we will dine on a handful of sprouting millet and be thankful for it – war is the enemy of the simplest satisfactions. There is no prospect of fresh supplies from the village. The soldiers devour like a cloud of locusts, and I do not care to think what will happen in a day or so when Wei is finally stripped bare. A hundred atrocities must surely follow.

Halfway through the meal, a servant sidles into the room and whispers to the steward, who also serves as my butler. Ever since the Four Punishments, my entire household is jumpy. My own servants fear me. After all, a word to Youngest Son and who knows what he might do? The steward edges before me.

'Lord Yun Cai, your son awaits your pleasure at the gatehouse.'

I blink at him.

'Which one?' I ask.

He struggles to find the correct title, poor man. His father was butler to my own father.

'Your youngest,' he says.

'Ah.'

I continue to lift rice to my mouth. Courtesy demands I leave my meal and greet him at the gate. Youngest Son has lost the right to courtesy.

'What message shall I give, Lord?' asks the steward.

'Tell him he may share my dinner.'

The fellow nods, hurries away.

A few minutes later Youngest Son enters the room. I do not look up from my bowl of salt-fish.

'Father!' he calls from the doorway.

Without further acknowledgement, I gesture at the food with my chopsticks. Youngest Son clanks across the room, wearing a hauberk of iron squares sewn on leather. A sword hangs from his belt. I am surprised he didn't feel the need to bring a loaded crossbow.

He waits for me to speak. At least it is within my power to deny him this satisfaction. After a minute he takes a seat and the butler rushes forward to fill more bowls. Neither of us chooses to speak before the servants.

The meal is finished. Still ignoring him, I belch and sigh; wipe my lips with a napkin. Then I gaze out of the window. Cloud banks are gathering over the peaks we call Three Widows, threatening rain if they blow this way. Crows wheel high above the valley, circle slowly then descend towards the village. No doubt they hope to peck for morsels in the square. I sense Youngest Son's restlessness beside me; he has never been one to benefit from silence, though I often advised him that silence is where a wise man hears the most. At last he scowls.

'Father,' he says. 'I can tell you are angry about the justice meted out today. That is a great fault in you.'

I can contain myself no longer. Let him administer the Four Punishments on me, for all I care!

'Who are you to tell me I am at fault?' I demand. 'On what authority? Have you no respect, no decency, to address your own father in this way? You have shown me discourtesy after discourtesy since returning to Wei. Do not talk to *me* of fault, when you embody it!'

He is taken aback, but soon bridles.

'You are wrong again, Father. A man's first loyalty is to the state, and the ruler of the state. This duty over-rides all others. General An-Shu is wise. All will acknowledge him as their father, even you. I have merely been doing my duty.'

I snort.

'What of your family? *That* is an upright man's first duty.'

He shakes his head, no longer angry. How soon his moods

change direction, like a hot wind! Youngest Son leans forward eagerly, and I realise he wishes to correct my errors, to offer me instruction.

'General An-Shu has taught all his officers to expect incomprehension,' he says. 'That is only natural. *Where ignorance runs deep, many will not understand*, he has said. The General warned us to expect this, so I do not blame you entirely, Father.'

'What nonsense you have been taught.'

'Not nonsense, Father. These are new ways, new times.'

I drink a cup of wine with unsteady hands.

'There you show your ignorance, boy. The General's ideas are old and stale. They date back to the tyranny of Shang in the time of Zhou. Their author, Shang Yang, was beheaded for his troubles and the world clapped its hands for joy. Did the general tell you *that*?'

He nods happily.

'We have been told everything. Not that, exactly, but everything we need to know. It is our destiny, His Highness' destiny. All will learn this! Can't you see the future, Father? Can't you feel it gathering around you? Why, the General will seize the capital and proclaim himself the Son of Heaven! Then he shall no longer be General An-Shu, but the founder of a dynasty to endure a thousand years!'

His voice lacks balance. Has he been drinking? Perhaps he is drunk on something more dangerous than wine. I must counter with calmness.

'Were the scenes in the village square a foretaste of his great dynasty?' I ask.

'Of course! Only through the harshest punishments may order be maintained. One's duty can be painful, but only the disloyal flinch.'

I do not mention that he seemed to enjoy his duty today.

'Peace will never come from such a system of rule. If you had studied history thoroughly, instead of believing the words of a. . . of the General, you would know that repression breeds only sorrow, cruelty merely engenders more cruelty, until the tyrannical state chokes on the blood it has shed and expires. There are patterns to history, as in nature.'

Youngest Son tightens his fists. He is not used to hearing his precious truths disputed. Good. It is time the boy learned how civilised men weigh ideas.

'Take the Four Punishments,' I continue. 'I assume you were acting out the General's commands?'

'Of course,' he says, haughtily. 'All deserters are to be punished in the severest way. That is the new law.'

'Are there to be no exceptions? Or courts? Or evidence? Or shades of wrong? Just terrible punishments?'

'They got what they deserved,' he says.

'Did they truly deserve that? Look into your soul! There you will find the truth. Subtle, baffling, glimmers of truth. Does not your heart tell you that the new law, in this case, is excessive?'

'Men's hearts are bad!' he exclaims, angrily. 'Only through punishment, the harshest punishment, will order thrive. Everyone knows that.'

'Should we not encourage virtue by watering it like a tender plant?' I reply. 'There is goodness in all souls. Indeed, evil deeds often flow from a man's circumstances, or companions. We must maintain the natural way, then men are not led towards evil.'

I could point out that when he committed a crime, a capital crime, those who loved him averted the law. I could mention we hoped he would learn gentler ways, that we believed in his essential virtue. But I forebear.

'Look at my men,' he continues. 'They obey every instruction because they know what will happen if they don't.'

'If only this were true!' I sigh.

Then I tell him of the intruder in my bedchamber that afternoon – the Four Punishments did not deter *him*. Youngest Son blusters that he will post a guard around Three-Step-House, yet I do not speak my thought aloud: who will protect us from such protectors?

He bolts down a cup of wine. Then another. The conversation has clearly taken turns he did not anticipate. I press my advantage.

'Your dear mother had a kind heart,' I say, gently. 'Do you remember how she helped those who were needy, whether they deserved it or not? Think of the seasons. Winter's punishments are accidental, and wholly a consequence of the Way.'

'I have heard enough, Father!' he snaps.

'But consider. . .'

'No! I will listen no more. Your words border on treason. No wonder the General has warned us to distrust adder-tongued scholars.'

I sigh, settle back in my chair. I cannot hate him, though his instincts have grown hateful. His precious General is the one I detest. Vile corrupter of youth, thief of my son.

'Your views sadden me,' I say. 'When you are older, I believe they will seem strange to you. I dearly hope so.'

'Then you hope in vain,' he says, rising to his feet.

His sword knocks a bowl off the table. It clatters and breaks into shards.

'I am disappointed, Father. This should have been a glad meeting, for I bring happy news. Before I left the temporary capital at Chunming, I persuaded one of the officials to summon you to court, so you might pay homage to His Highness. Perhaps he will grant you an official position.'

'What!'

'I see that the influence I possess surprises you!' he continues.

'You took it upon yourself to offer me as one of the General's officials? Are you mad, boy!'

'You should be grateful, but you are not!'

'I'm not grateful, that is certain.'

'Have you no pride, Father? Do you not resent the Emperor's lackeys for banishing you? I cannot understand you.'

I shake my head vigorously.

'Long ago I reconciled myself to my banishment. This news

alarms me deeply. Send word at once to Chunming and have the summons rescinded.'

'That is not possible.'

'Tell them I am sick. Tell them I sit in a corner all day dribbling. I will help you to compose the letter.'

'I will not disobey my orders,' he counters. 'Besides, my officers have witnessed your good health. They would report my lie and that I had wilfully defied an instruction.'

'Then tonight I shall catch the plague!' I say.

'No, Father. I will not fail in my duty.'

His voice has grown obdurate and proud. Finally I realise the truth. Youngest Son would burn the whole of Wei to possess the glorious future he imagines for himself. But there may be other motives.

'So this is how you punish me,' I murmur.

He is already half way across the room, his horseman's boots echoing.

I sit, hands folded on my lap. For the first time I am truly afraid. Heed your own wisdom, I tell myself, inhabit what is, not imagined fears.

The night-rain enters my dreams, running down the eaves in tiny rivulets, hurrying drops, a constant whisper. My dreams are angry, full of eyes. The deserters dismembered once again in the village square until they form a mound of limbs and torsos and organs and grinning heads. Though I protest in a strained, querulous voice, the body parts begin to move and re-assemble – head to arm-socket, leg to severed nose – crawling in confusion like startled ants.

'This is not natural!' I rail. 'This is an affront to the Way! Oh, when will we learn?'

Their strange dance continues. Then I realise I am not in Wei at all, but on the large parade ground before the Prefect's residence in Chunming!

I wake covered in sweat. The room is dark. A smell of rain

seeps through the rafters. I listen to its irregular tap, opposing distress with measured breaths, emptying my mind until a space is formed where sleep gathers. The hours drag towards sunrise.

It is the fourth dawn since the soldiers marched into Wei Valley. I watch from the gatehouse, pleased to see them march away. But they are only continuing their search for the cavalrymen further up the valley, not returning to Chunming. Perhaps I should be pleased. When they finally leave for Chunming, I must go with them.

Youngest Son is at their head, as usual, implacable on his white horse, drummers all around him. How he loves a loud noise! Perhaps he hopes to frighten away evil spirits. Or thoughts. Certainly he is surrounded by threats, some made worse by his own actions. Instead of wasting a whole day on fancy executions, he should have been scouring the valley. Now everyone is too terrified to offer him information. Should it prove wrong the consequences are unthinkable. Even his strictures concerning the necessity for harsh punishments work against him. If he fails to capture the cavalrymen, to succeed in his essential mission, General An-Shu's code allows no mercy.

I am reminded of an anecdote related in a Legalist text I once perused in the Imperial Library. It concerned Prince Chao of Han, who got drunk and fell asleep on a bitterly cold night. The man entrusted with bearing his crown placed a coat over him. When the prince awoke he enquired who had covered him against the cold. On hearing it was the crown-keeper, he ordered the man's execution. The coat-keeper, whose job it was to keep his master warm, was merely castrated. Prince Chao's reasoning? To transgress one's duties of office is worse than simple negligence. Thus the crown-keeper deserved the more severe punishment. One might view Youngest Son's decision to waste a vital day in this light.

As I recollect, the author of this text also fell foul of his Emperor. After suffering the first of the Four Punishments until without nose, feet, or genitals, he was whipped and severed at the waist, all his family – parents, brothers, wife and children – were executed in strict accordance with the principles he had spent his life propounding.

By such ironies one may judge the prudence of espousing any system. Can such antique ideas really hold sway in Chunming? Youngest Son's words seemed to indicate so. One might call General An-Shu a desperate man indeed. Or simply bad, unfit for the Mandate of Heaven.

Thoughts of law send me rooting about in my three chests for documents. I gather up the charter granted by General Yueh Fei to my father, confirming our family's Lordship of Wei in perpetuity. Other papers, too, concerning our property, for the estate has grown over the years, despite my neglect. My wife's dowry, then Daughter-in-law's, added swathes of unproductive hillside and woodland, some of which Eldest Son has managed to bring to profitable cultivation. We are not rich as a result. Yet we have much to lose. Finally, I send for the steward and ask him to fetch Eldest Son.

He arrives unshaven, a beaten look about his eyes. If I had any doubts about what must happen next, his gaunt appearance settles them.

'Sit beside me,' I say. 'We have much to discuss and little time.'

'Father!' he exclaims miserably, once seated. 'I have heard the news that you must go to Chunming. Why does my brother hate us so?'

I purse my lips.

'I suspect it is not hatred. More a kind of confusion. There may be some anger, certainly, but we must try to think the best of him. We must assume he means well.'

Or pretend he does. I do not wish Eldest Son to hate his own brother. Such feelings can ruin a man's peace.

'I wish to talk seriously for a while, and you must listen,' I say.

'Yes, Father.'

'I have not always paid you the attention you deserve...' I wave my hand to silence his protests. 'When you were young, my head and heart were full of other things. But if I can, I mean to do well by you now. See that bundle of papers? I want you to take them to Whale Rock Monastery and join Daughter-in-law there. My will and all our deeds are in that bundle, so ask the monks to guard them well. When you get there, do not return home. It is too dangerous for you to stay here. I could not bear it if harm befell you.'

'But Father, who will look after you?'

My eyes flash.

'I can look after myself quite well.'

'I wish to accompany you to Chunming,' he says, doggedly. 'It is my duty.'

'And I wish the opposite,' I reply. 'That is *my* duty.'

He sighs and lowers his head.

'You should go at once. Thankfully your brother has neglected to enforce an embargo on all travel within the valley. Yet another mistake on his part. If you are stopped, point out you are the Captain's brother and that you have been sent away on urgent family business. Tell them he will be angry. That should settle the matter.'

'Are you sure I must go, Father?'

'Do not question my instructions! Now I will say something grave. It is very possible I may never return from Chunming. You know that, don't you?'

He nods.

'So I want you to know this. I am very proud of you...'

'How can you say that!' he exclaims. 'I was always too stupid to pass the examinations! I have disappointed you.'

'Once that was true,' I concede. 'Since then I have learned better. You are my pride and heir, do not forget that. If I do not return, tell my grandsons about me, and my poems.'

'Father, do not keep saying you won't come back! It will bring bad luck.'

'Perhaps. Now leave Three-Step-House. Delay only to put on your shoes. Take one of the servant boys with you. Go with my full blessing, and tell Daughter-in-law I am particularly satisfied with her conduct.'

He hovers. I suspect he wishes to embrace me. His tears make my own eyes itch.

'Go!'

An hour passes. I sit with hands folded on my lap, for once empty of thought, though not feeling. A knock on the door. It is Wudi. He appears pale and anxious.

'Enter!' I cry, relieved to have company.

'I'm not alone, Lord,' he says, hurriedly. 'I didn't know what else to do.'

He glances nervously over his shoulder, and bundles a large, heavily-cloaked man into the room before hastily latching the door. I look at my visitor curiously. I have seen him somewhere before. Then I remember, and my mouth goes dry.

'I had no choice,' whispers Wudi. 'I found him hiding beside your family tomb. I'd gone there to measure up where I can build my own tomb, as you promised. There are soldiers all over the place!'

I meet the man's eye. He is young and, by the look of his cheeks, hungry. My one comfort is that he does not wear his uniform, though no one would mistake him for a peasant.

'Why are you here?' I croak.

He lowers himself to his knees and cries: 'Ensign Tzi-Lu, sir!'

'Quieter!'

'Of His Majesty's Guard! I was instructed to pass a message to you alone, sir!'

He looks at Wudi meaningfully.

'You may speak in front of the headman,' I say.

'That is against my orders. . .'

'Damn your orders! Speak quickly, then leave my house before you bring it tumbling round my ears. What is the message?'

The Ensign Tzi-Lu nods stiffly, bringing his fists together in a salute. He rises suddenly, listening for movement in the corridor. The house creaks ominously. Then he resumes his kneeling position and lowers his head. When he speaks again, it is in the sing-song tones of a messenger who has learned his message by heart:

'Should the Second Chancellor to the Son of Heaven, His Noble Excellency P'ei Ti, arrive at the gate of Yun Cai of Wei, in Chunming Province, His Imperial Majesty expressly orders that his servant should return at once to the capital, without delay of any kind, and that this command be confirmed by the seal carried by this bearer.'

The Ensign Tzi-Lu proffers a small jade seal, carved with intricate characters and fletched with gold. There is a reckless courage about the man. No doubt that is why he was chosen for so insane a mission. Yet travelling through General An-Shu's armies to Wei calls for guile as well as bravery. At last I fully understand P'ei Ti's importance.

'I am grateful to you for saving my life, ' he adds. 'And that of my men.'

'You are still hiding behind the waterfall?'

'Yes. The rebels have searched the area twice, but without success. Lord Yun Cai,' he says, passionately. 'Please know that I have been commanded to save His Excellency at any cost. Any cost at all!'

A knock on the door – one I know well – my steward.

'Do not enter!' I call. 'I am indisposed.'

I motion fearfully that the cavalry officer should hide behind my dressing screen.

'Lord!' calls my steward, outside the door.

'What is it? I have told you I cannot see anyone.'

How long has he been listening by the door?

'Lord, your youngest son has arrived in the hall. He won't have a moment's delay. He told me he wishes to see you.'

'Tell him to wait in the hall.'

I hear the steward's hurried footsteps padding down the corridor.

'Go at once!' I hiss. 'Wudi, get Ensign Tzi-Lu away from Three-Step-House! I will occupy my son.'

'Your son?' asks the officer.

'Is one of General An-Shu's captains. Oh yes, now you know my predicament.'

He stiffens with suspicion.

'Leave at once. For all our sakes.'

Wudi opens the door and peers around. The corridor is clear. He gestures to the officer who hurries after him. The door closes and I listen to the scuffle of their feet. All is silent once more. Then the sound of heavy boots in the corridor, and my door swings open without even a knock.

Youngest Son stands glaring in the doorway.

'Father,' he says. 'Didn't the steward tell you I was here?'

I fan my face with the first piece of paper to hand. A copy of the lake poem I have prepared for Lieutenant Lo.

'What is the matter, Father?' he demands. 'You seem unwell.'

I cough uneasily. It is essential I detain him in my room for as long as possible.

'Ah,' I say. 'Sit! Sit yourself down! I am just tired. Are you thirsty?'

He glances round the room suspiciously.

'There is no time for that. One of my guards saw a stranger approaching Three-Step-House. The fool lost him in the bamboo grove! Have you seen any strangers?'

I gesture at the empty room. Smile blandly. It is a shameful thing when one is afraid of one's own son.

'Doubtless he saw a villager,' I say.

'No, Father, he reported a man of military bearing.'

'Really? How curious.'

Youngest Son paces up and down. He seems to fill the room with his armour and cloak, his long sword rattling in its scabbard.

'I take it, His Imperial Majesty's soldiers have not been found?'

He stops pacing. Scowls.

'You should not refer to the Usurper like that!' he says. 'Only General An-Shu deserves such a title. You must remember that when you are in Chunming, or. . .'

Or else? Well, he hardly needs to explain. I must keep him talking, win time.

'Perhaps your enemies have left Wei. In which case you search in vain.'

'That is not possible,' he snaps. 'The exits to the valley are guarded.'

'You should know there are numerous routes in and out of Wei.'

'No,' he says. 'I *know* they are still here. I can feel it. I must capture them, Father! It is essential for me to capture them! I have assured His Highness it will be done.'

'Sometimes we all fail,' I suggest. 'What matters is how one learns from it.'

'I will not fail!' His voice is slightly hysterical. 'I have not failed!'

It distresses me to see him like this. Yet the more he talks, the better hidden my unexpected visitor will be. I have no doubt Wudi is too wise to leave Three-Step-House. As a boy he learnt every corner on our cricket hunts, surely he will find a quiet hiding place for our guest.

'What am I doing here?' cries my son. 'The house must be searched! Wait here, Father.'

Now my anxiety doubles.

'Surely that is not necessary,' I say. 'Let me call for wine. You can tell me about the situation in Chunming. I mean, the Temporary Capital.'

Once more he looks at me suspiciously.

'Chunming is indeed the Temporary Capital,' he says.

'Of course. Sit yourself down! We have much to discuss.'

For a moment I think he will oblige. Then he remembers his intention and, without another word, stamps out of the room. I hear him bellowing orders. The sound of soldiers' feet and clumsy hands opening doors, frightening the servants, shifting furniture and barrels. Youngest Son's shouts rise above all. He is in a frenzy, the fever of a desperate man. Should I pretend to be an old dotard and try to frustrate them? Or should I stay here and anticipate the worst? Few know Three-Step-House better than Youngest Son. At any moment I expect to hear shouts of triumph, the sound of the Ensign Tzi-Lu being dragged forth.

Finally I can bear it no longer and make my way to the Middle House. Everywhere soldiers and their sergeants. They stand aside to let me pass, knowing I am their captain's father, but that will be small protection when the Ensign Tzi-Lu is found, as surely he must. I walk down to the Bottom House, where kitchens and storerooms surround our courtyard. A squad of guardsmen by the gate. Truly, we are trapped. Suddenly Youngest Son emerges from the privies, which are built above the pig-sty. He fumbles as he straightens his clothes and armour. Perhaps the excitement of the hunt has loosened more than his temper.

'Well?' I ask, trying to feign unconcern.

He stares at me.

'You seem nervous, father.'

I laugh hollowly.

'My home is full of soldiers,' I say. 'People will think I am a rebel against the General.'

He looks from side to side. Even as a boy, this gesture signalled he was thinking.

'You are right,' he says. 'My soldiers will remain here as guards until the rebels are found. Go back to your room now, Father.' He wishes to concede something. 'Though I am glad you try to help.'

I do as I am told. I sit in my room and anticipate the discovery of Ensign Li-Tzu. Where can he be hiding? Why has he not already been captured? Perhaps he is in the rafters, or beneath a bed. I cannot imagine where else he might be. After a while, a knock on the door. Wudi enters without ceremony and sits heavily on my favourite divan. He looks decidedly grey.

'Well?' I whisper.

He blinks at me.

'He's in the pigsty,' he murmurs. 'Do you remember the tiny chamber beneath the privies, with the low doorway for the pigs to enter?'

'Ah, where we hunted the cricket with a piercing cry, like gongs! When we were boys!'

'I don't know about that, Lord, but he's in there. Rather him than me on a hot day like this.'

I settle back. What can we do but wait? Minutes pass. It must be an hour since they began searching.

'Join the servants in the kitchen,' I say, finally. 'I don't want my son to find you with me. It might make him suspect something. Tell the steward I have ordered you to collect a sack of rice from our stores in anticipation of my journey to Chunming. He'll understand that. If we can, we'll give it to the Ensign for his men.'

Wudi raises his thick eyebrows.

'But if they find your. . . guest?'

'Then pray he does not reveal your part in this.'

Wudi grunts.

'I'm off to the kitchen then.'

So I am left alone, and close my eyes. I can hear the soldiers continuing to search and a sergeant's raised voice.

At last it is evening. Stars gather in eternal shapes above the earth; but down below, in Wei, the campfires are brighter. Red, merciless eyes looking us over, assessing what we have left to take. Little enough. After four days we have been stripped bare, yet still they want more. Who can blame the common soldiers? They do not belong here, feel no loyalty towards us. All civilians despise them. We are just one more larder, and when the food runs out other meat will present itself.

Wudi comes to my room after the lighting of the lamps. Neither of us is inclined to talk. I gesture towards the wine flask, fan myself. He pours himself a cup and drinks it in one. Then he anxiously kneads his Buddha's pot-belly as though he were alone.

'I have heard bad news from the village,' he says.

'Regarding our guest?' I ask.

'No, Lord. Our *guests*.'

'You mean General An-Shu's rabble?'

He looks around nervously.

'Someone may be listening by the window,' he pleads.

'What of that?'

'You have been drinking, my Lord.'

'That is true,' I say.

'This is not the time, perhaps?'

I laugh bitterly.

'What of our *other* guest?' I ask.

'Still in the same place, as far as I know.'

So we are safe for now.

'And your bad news? You mentioned bad news.'

Wudi scratches his bald head, a sure sign of distress with him.

'The soldiers are getting out of control,' he said. 'I have heard they dragged the landlord Li Sha's daughter from her home and held her down. All because he refused to tell them where he had hidden his seed corn.'

I digest this development. So the food is finally running out in the village.

'Is she the only one?' I ask.

'No, there have been others.'

'And your own relatives?'

'Safe so far, Lord, but I am frightened. It is not good.'

It takes little imagination to recognise that rape may lead to massacre. But if they devour the peasants' stock of seed for planting, another kind of massacre must follow, slower perhaps, but as deadly. Our whole province is threatened with famine and that worsens our danger. We can expect no assistance from neighbouring districts as badly pinched as ourselves.

'Youngest Son has lost mastery of his own men,' I say. 'That is the worst news of all, for everyone knows that only the stupid, criminal or poverty-stricken enlist as soldiers. Such men require a firm hand.'

Wudi shrugs. 'What are we to do?' he asks.

I sense weary fear behind his question. He is a peace-loving man, a peasant at heart, ill-suited to the risks he has taken on my behalf.

'First, we must say farewell to our unwelcome guest.'

'Eh?'

'You know what I mean.'

He sighs heavily.

'Very well, my Lord, I will do it. But there are still a dozen soldiers around the house.'

I wag my finger. Perhaps I'm drunker than I imagine.

'Leave it to me,' I say.

'Forgive me, Lord, but I think it would be best for all of us, if I went with you.'

We are disturbed by voices in the corridor. I place a finger over my lips. There is a tap on the closed door.

'Forgive the late hour, Lord Yun Cai.'

We relax. My steward's voice.

'I have a gentleman with me who insists he must see you.'

Again we grow tense. My life has begun to resemble the farces I remember being performed in the Imperial Pleasure Grounds! They, too, were full of unexpected entrances.

'Then show him in,' I call.

The door opens. Instead of Youngest Son returning to admonish me further as I expected, a more genial face, though by no means welcome. Lieutenant Lo, in full uniform. I peer behind him for a squad of soldiers but he is alone. So we are not to be dragged off, just yet.

'Welcome, Lieutenant,' I say. 'Please be seated while I finish with my servant.'

He sits down awkwardly.

'Ensure that not a *cash* coin of my rents goes uncollected!' I chide Wudi. 'As for that other business I mentioned, wait until I have entertained my honoured guest before proceeding further.'

Wudi bows, sidles out.

'Forgive me,' I say. 'I have much to arrange before I am conducted to Chunming.'

Lieutenant Lo looks embarrassed. I have no doubt he guesses how I feel about General An-Shu's summons.

'Your son, I mean, the Captain, sent me here with an urgent message.'

I raise my eyebrows.

'He requests that you gather all the possessions you require for the Temporary Capital without delay, and that you should be ready to leave before cock-crow.'

'That is. . . soon.'

Lieutenant Lo scratches his chin.

'A messenger arrived an hour ago from the General himself. We have received orders that all companies must assemble immediately. It seems the Emperor, I mean, the Usurper. . .'

'I know who you mean,' I say quickly.

Lieutenant Lo meets my eye and an understanding passes between us. After all, the man is not a hot-headed youth or complete fool.

'It seems,' he continues, with his mournful smile. 'A second army is preparing to march on Chunming.'

'Ah,' I say. 'Tell me, did you defeat the first army with ease?'

He spreads his hands.

'We defeated them, Lord Yun Cai.'

'And did you lose many men in the process?'

'Quite a few.'

We both nod, conversing, as they say, without words.

'And is the Emperor's, I mean the Usurper's, second army larger than the first? No doubt he has had time to summon reinforcements from the frontier.'

'You'd expect such a thing,' says Lieutenant Lo. 'On the other hand our own forces have been swelled by many conscripts.'

'But has there been time to train them?' I ask.

'The time has been short,' he concedes.

Lieutenant Lo rises to his feet, and bows.

'I must get back to the village,' he says. 'There is much to organise.'

'Perhaps your presence will restrain some of the more, how can I put it, ill-disciplined, of your men? You understand that, as Lord of Wei, it is my duty to shield the villagers from harm.'

I am assuming too much with him. But what have I to lose? It appears I do not misjudge him.

'You are their father,' he says, simply. 'Rest assured I will try my best, even if it means no sleep for me tonight.'

'Then you will gain my eternal gratitude, Lieutenant Lo.'

He rises to go.

'One moment!' I call. 'You may recollect that I promised you a copy of the poem we discussed on the first night you came. I have it here. Honour me by presenting it to your wife.'

He looks puzzled, then smiles sadly.

'*Waiting by West Lake*,' he says.

'That's the one.'

I pass over a rolled parchment. The edge of the paper flutters in the night breeze entering through the window.

'I'm obliged,' he says.

I wait a respectable time for him to leave, then search out Wudi. I find him by the entrance to the Middle House.

'Do you have the rice?' I whisper.

He taps two bags at his waist.

'Then accompany me.'

It is securely dark. Few of the servants are around and I order those we meet to their rest. No rain-clouds obscure the stars filling the valley with soft, sweet light. Even the village below seems at peace; men laughing and singing, though the wisest among them must realise what awaits them back in Chunming. Looting, or worse, could still break out in a moment. Night insects chirrup. Fireflies flit around Three-Step-House. This is my last evening here, possibly forever, and I would enjoy my old home if I could.

We reach the privy.

'Wait outside,' I murmur. 'If anyone comes, cough.'

I enter and close the door. It is black within, yet no eyes are needed to sniff out the wooden seat with a round hole cut into it.

'Psst!' I whisper. 'Ensign Tzi-Lu! It is I, Lord Yun Cai.'

Silence. Then the sound of a slight movement.

'Can you hear me?' I whisper.

The stench is nauseating. I fight back an urge to vomit. To have spent a whole day among such smells and textures might haunt a man for the rest of his life. Perhaps he has been overcome.

'Yes,' comes a muffled reply from below.

I sigh.

'Wait for a short time,' I say. 'Then make your way to the entrance of the sty. Be careful to make no noise, there are guards patrolling the house. Do you understand?'

'Yes,' once more.

I rejoin Wudi.

'We must meet him below,' I say, pointing at the floor of the privy.

As silently as two old men can, we shuffle to a side-gate and listen. The sound of voices. Two of the soldiers pass, talking quietly, and we wait in a pool of shadow until they have gone.

'Quickly!' I breathe into his ear. 'Before they come back.'

The gate creaks alarmingly, then we are outside, beside the lower enclosure. No sign of guards. Away from my familiar room, I feel strangely exposed. We shuffle to the entrance of the pig-sty.

I smell our guest before I see him. His long day beneath the privy has streaked his clothes and hair with a whole day's traffic. His only companion has been a truculent sow. From the rents in his trousers and tooth-marks on his legs, she has not welcomed his company. He staggers out.

'Can you walk?' I whisper.

'Yes,' he grunts.

We hurry up the side of the house toward a stand of bamboo. At least we reach it! Then the bamboo rustles and a soldier steps out, tightening his belt. We are saved by his surprise. Before he can raise the alarm, a heavy figure knocks me to one side. In a moment Ensign Tzi-Lu is upon him, panting as he stabs repeatedly, his hand held over the man's mouth. The struggling figures disappear into the bamboo. For a moment the stems rustle wildly, then settle. Wudi and I waste no time in following.

The Ensign is on his knees, easing the man to the earth. His eyes flash white in the darkness. I am shaking. Wudi passes wind loudly beside me.

'What are we to do?' he whispers. 'We can't leave him here.'

'Hush.'

We freeze. The two guards are returning. One of them calls out:

'Hey, Shao-Ao, you lazy Turk! Where are you?'

They stand half-a-dozen yards from us.

'I bet he's in the village. Some of the lads are talking about a bit of fun tonight.'

'More likely he's having a sly nap. He's past it for that kind of fun.'

'He'll catch it if the captain finds out.'

'Ah, but he won't, will he?'

'Let's go round the house and look for old Shao. If we find him asleep, we can get a week's pay off him to keep our mouths shut. If we ever get paid, that is.'

They set off again, debating this fine point.

'Now,' I say. 'Pick up the body and follow me. We must hide him. They'll think he's deserted if they don't find him by tomorrow. Besides, they won't have time to search for him properly.'

Wudi looks at me dubiously.

'As my Lord says.'

First there is the matter of a hiding place. A man's corpse is no small thing. Once deprived of motion, it grows heavy as a large sack of millet or a dead pig. Then there is the matter of his weapons, which we find in the bamboo. Slowly we labour up the hill, looking round constantly for watching eyes, until we reach the small wood where Father built our Ancestral Shrine. A strange idea grips me, one so sacrilegious my instincts recoil. Yet it is the only certain place.

'Hide him in the shrine,' I whisper.

They look at me in amazement. Wudi shakes his head.

'Do as I say.'

I am sure Father would approve. He was no stranger to expediency.

'I hope your ancestors do not blame me for this,' grumbles Wudi.

I fumble with the latch and they carry him in, gasping at their load. The darkness is complete.

Who is this nameless soldier, to lie among the bones of his betters? Will his spirit leave his body, look around in confusion, and haunt my family for eternity, bringing malice and misfortune?

Outside, I turn to Ensign Tzi-Lu, who is wiping his clothes with handfuls of leaves. He looks desperate enough, smeared with pig-filth and blood from the dead soldier. A faint echo of thunder sounds in the east, the direction of Chunming. Clouds are advancing towards us. With luck a shower will wash away our traces.

Wudi sits on his haunches, peering at the distant horizon.

'A lot of rain for this time of year,' he says. 'Perhaps the real monsoon will be delayed.'

I turn to Ensign Tzi-Lu.

'You must go now. Hide in the woods for at least a day. The soldiers are returning to Chunming and after they have gone you will be safe. Seek out Wudi then, and he will explain my position.'

He nods.

'Lord Yun Cai has saved my life for a second time.'

'Remember that this family is loyal to the Emperor, even if one of my sons is a renegade. Remember that fact when His Imperial Majesty is victorious, and I will be repaid.'

'I shall.'

'And another thing. Tomorrow I too must go to Chunming on General An-Shu's orders. Tell those who sent you that I do not go there willingly. My family are not traitors. They must not be punished, however things appear.'

'Your actions prove that.'

'Then ensure they are not forgotten. It is all I ask.'

He bows stiffly, and fades into the darkness.

'Wudi,' I say. 'Somehow we must enter the house undetected.'

Two weary old men, we creep through shadows down the long hill.

In the hour before dawn I pack a few possessions with the aid of my butler: spare clothes and shoes; my official uniform;

writing materials; a few precious scrolls to comfort a dark hour – Lao Tzu to remind me of the Eternal Way, my beloved Wang Wei and Po-Chui, their poems ever-burning lamps across time. There is circularity in this choice. These same books were my companions when I was banished to the frontier long ago. They brought luck, of a twisted kind, and solace. Perhaps they may do so again. My steward arrives with a large sack of food and wine. My favourites, he informs me proudly. I try to smile.
'We are done,' I say.

Unexpectedly, both kneel, their up-turned faces grey in the light of dawn.

'You have provided good service,' I say. 'So I will speak frankly. It may be that I never return from Chunming. If I do not, you must serve my son – my Eldest Son, that is. He, and he alone, is my rightful successor as Lord. Wait half a day after I have departed, then gather the servants. Pass on my words to them. Tell them also that I am pleased with their loyalty. When I am gone, that loyalty must be shown to the new Lord, or I will see from Heaven, and grow angry.'

They do not raise their heads.

'May the Lord live a hundred years!' they murmur.

Which Lord do they refer to? Either will do.

My baggage is carried down to the gatehouse, where I watch the sun rise over Wei, perhaps for the last time. Thickening light reveals bustle in the village, soldiers forming lines in the square below, officers and sergeants bellowing orders.

Wudi appears beside me.

'Your baggage has been loaded on a wheelbarrow,' he says. 'Shall I order it to be taken down to the village?'

'Yes, I will go with it.'

'Then I shall accompany you, ' he says.

I shake my head.

'Keep your distance from me,' I say. 'Who knows what will befall.'

'But, Lord!'

'It is for the best, old friend. To you, I owe many thanks.'

I extract a folded letter from my girdle.

'Give this to Eldest Son,' I say. 'It instructs him to ensure your family shrine adjoins my own as we agreed. Let your son be buried there. In addition, the best of your granddaughters shall be betrothed to my youngest grandson. You have grown wealthy, Wudi, and I rely on your good sense to ensure the size of the dowry matches the honour your family gains from such a union.'

'I. . . I am speechless.'

'Good, then we will waste no more words.'

So I descend the hill slowly, more slowly than necessary, for I have decided to feign infirmity. That is not hard. The last few days have strained all that I am. In the village square I find Youngest Son preparing to mount his white charger. He hesitates, then strides over.

'Are you ready, Father?'

I sense many eyes upon us.

'I am ready,' I say, in a feeble voice.

He frowns.

'Then you shall ride beside me,' he says. 'I have a horse prepared.'

I sigh, regretfully.

'Such an exertion would be too much for me.'

'Could you not sleep?' he asks, peevishly. 'I must tell you that one of the guards assigned to Three-Step-House disappeared last night. Did you hear any strange noises? Unfortunately, I do not have time to investigate the matter as I would wish.'

'No doubt he deserted,' I say.

'He was a reliable man. Perhaps I should leave a dozen guards to search for him.'

'Did not your orders state that all available men are to return to His Highness's temporary capital? Orders must be followed to the final brush-stroke.'

I let the thought dangle. He bites back angry words.

'Lieutenant Lo!' he bellows.

The lieutenant canters over.

'Order space to be found on one of the wagons, for my father and his baggage.'

So I leave Wei like a prisoner in a two-wheeled cart, perched upon piles of crossbow bolts and smoke-blackened cauldrons, free only in that my hands are not bound before me. Drums beat and the cart jolts, whipped on by a surly fellow with his cap askew. Dust rises from the road, stirred by hundreds of marching feet. We pass a gibbet where a dozen peasants sway in the wind, among them the landlord, Li Sha, his tongue already turning black. I notice a few frightened eyes peering through half-lifted blinds. Several of the houses have broken doors and a plume of smoke rises where a building has been set ablaze. If Youngest Son notices this outrage, he shows no sign. Yet I comfort myself I have averted destruction, even massacre, for my people. Most have escaped with their lives.

My eyes are drawn skywards. A few of the soldiers cry out and point. A bow-shaped line of geese fly over the marching column, honking gaily. They fly as they flew in Father's time, when I was a boy. This thought gives strength. The geese may fly all the way to Chunming and, with luck, peck out General An-Shu's eyes.

six

'. . . I dreamt of riding a giant heron,
gazing down from Heaven at insect armies –
ant-sting lance thicket
                    gnat-swarm arrow cloud.
But the tears of the widows
were as vast as Lake Poyang. . .'

As we leave the mountains for the foothills, we journey towards heat. I bump along in the back of the wagon, sweating profusely. The air humid. The sky alternating between fine, mist-like rain and blazing sun. Such unseasonable weather surely signifies something, perhaps a judgment of Heaven on our troubled province.

Youngest Son remains at the head of the column and rarely deigns to notice my presence. I cannot say it grieves me. So much unspoken distrust between us it seems better not to speak at all. Each night we camp in villages stripped bare by war.

Many of the peasants have fled and those that remain stare at us with mournful, hungry eyes.

On the afternoon of the third day our column approaches Chunming. One moment we are toiling up a hill, then the city lies before us, hazy in the distance. It is customary to feel pride in the capital of one's province. If so, my own feelings are perverse. Chunming has always bored me, its streets and attitudes stiflingly narrow. Now I view the town with fresh interest. If Youngest Son is to be believed, Chunming is the seed from which a glorious dynasty will sprout.

As we approach, I notice soldiers dotted like black ants on the earthen ramparts. Military camps surround the city, villages of tents and pickets, lines of soldiers drilling beneath the merciless sun, and the size of General An-Shu's army surprises me.

Youngest Son canters up. He is excited, his mask of sternness forgotten. I am reminded of his unspoiled, boyish face, before he learned to frown continually.

'Father!' he cries. 'We have reached the Temporary Capital.'

I look at him gravely.

'Is that something to make me glad?'

At once his youthful enthusiasm hardens.

'I trust you are glad,' he says, doggedly.

'Then I shall be glad,' I reply. 'For your sake, if not my own.'

He pretends to rein in his horse, which rears obligingly.

'You will see, Father,' he calls over his shoulder, galloping back to the head of his troops.

Why he is so excited I cannot say, seeing he has failed in his mission in Wei.

Li by *li* we approach the city gates. As one would expect, a few corpses dangle, unsavoury after weeks of close weather. We enter streets crowded with soldiers and prostitutes, food-sellers and labourers carrying supplies. I strive to keep my fears at bay. Lieutenant Lo rides up and regards me from his horse.

'Lord Yun Cai must go on foot now,' he says. 'Your son has instructed me to take you to your lodgings. You must stay there until summoned to pay homage to His Highness.'

It shames me that my own son does not take this duty upon himself.

'Who shall carry my bags?' I demand in a shrill voice, for I would retain some dignity.

'That shall be done,' he says.

And it is. We walk a short way through the streets until we reach the walls of Golden Lotus Monastery, a place I have often visited over the years.

'Am I to stay here?' I ask, relieved.

The monks, at least, are capable of civilised conversation.

Lieutenant Lo does not answer. He speaks sternly to the soldiers at the gatehouse, who usher me inside. The tall gates close behind me with a thump. At once my nostrils twitch.

'Where are the monks? Where is Abbot Ssu-Ma?' I ask, as I am led into the main courtyard. My guide does not reply. Why should he? It is obvious what has happened to the monks.

The monastery is crammed with prisoners, every available space occupied. Some sitting, others standing alone or in groups, leaning out of windows or huddling wherever one may find a corner of shade. Hundreds penned here, their voices forming a low, constant murmur. Most distressing is the sweet, sickly aroma of sweat and faeces, urine mingled with boiled cabbage. I turn desperately to my guard.

'There has been a mistake,' I say. 'My son is a captain of the Winged Tigers Regiment. He would never expect me to lodge here.'

The soldier looks at me dourly.

'All newcomers to the city must stay here,' he says. 'Until they are properly registered and assigned other quarters.'

'Then I should be assigned other quarters at once!' I protest.

'Be quiet!' he says. 'Follow me.'

I am led through the monastery, rooms full of men sprawled out on mats or squatting against walls, strangely silent as they watch us pass. We reach a small courtyard also packed with men, and as nauseous, but here the prisoners are of a slightly better degree. Some have small piles of possessions beside their sleeping mats. A few wear fine silks, begrimed with sweat and dirt.

'There has been a mistake,' I repeat.

'Think yourself lucky, old man,' replies the soldier. 'This is the best room in the inn!'

Then he turns on his heels and leaves me standing, my baggage scattered around my feet.

It is night. The stars glitter even above our courtyard. I lie on a bed of clothes, sweating amidst a hundred rank breaths. A few sleepers groan as they dream, otherwise the courtyard is silent. No one has spoken to me since I arrived. All hug their own dignity, apart from a small group, merchants by the look of them or members of the same clan, who sit muttering together. I am hungry. And thirsty. Too tired to think clearly.

Did Youngest Son really want this for me? Perhaps he hopes to point out the consequences of defying General An-Shu. Yet I assure myself he has no control over my place of captivity. And that may be the most alarming thing of all.

At dawn I queue beside the single latrine, clutching a bag containing my most valued possessions. I have observed this is the custom here and conclude that theft must be rife. I void my bowels as quickly as I can, trying not to notice the stench and the fat, buzzing flies. Angry voices urge me to hurry up. No means of cleanliness is provided, so I am forced to use some of my small stock of precious paper. A most unpleasant occasion.

When I return to the corner of the courtyard where I spent the night, the remainder of my baggage has disappeared.

At first I panic, ask the men around me whether they witnessed the theft. Heads shake, shoulders shrug. Though they surely know, no one says a word. Miserably, I assess what I have left, making sure I am unobserved: a few hundred *cash* still in my purse; a knife; ink and brush; a sheaf of paper; the top half of my official uniform, minus the hat. Best of all, I retain my scrolls of Wang Wei, Po Chu'i and Lao Tzu.

My neighbours watch curiously as I unroll *The Way and Its Power* and sigh as I read the words: 'Keep hoarding gold in your house, and you will be robbed.' Sometimes philosophy is a most grating comfort.

Impossible to breathe air already sieved by a hundred men's lungs! I'm gasping. At midday we each receive a bowl of rice gruel and a ladle of brackish water. Now I understand the inertia and hollow eyes of those around me. For we are being slowly starved.

Late afternoon. Youngest Son appears at the courtyard entrance and I almost sob with relief. At last a chance for more water. He frowns as he glances over the crowd until he spies me, then marches over to the wall where I rest.

'Father, are you ill?'

I sigh.

'We are not being given enough water,' I say. 'Already I have seen a dozen men carried out.'

He glances round fearfully.

'I did not expect this, Father,' he says. 'While I was away, the General issued a new edict. All strangers to the city must be detained here pending confirmation of their innocence.'

'So I am a prisoner?' I ask.

Youngest Son stares at the ground, obviously embarrassed.

'I have been informed you cannot be released until you have paid homage to His Highness, and that may take many days.'

Then he rises to his full height.

'Let me take your things, Father,' he says. 'This place will not do. I should have come sooner. Please accompany me.'

He clears a path to the entrance and throws the bag into the guard's arms.

'This man does not belong here!' he barks. 'What is your name?'

The guard shrivels before him. I am led through the crowded rooms and courtyards into the street. No one tries to stop us. Finally, Youngest Son helps me down a steep lane until we reach a tall house beside the city walls. Another soldier stands guard by the door. He leaps to attention at the sight of a Captain.

'Admit this man at once!' roars Youngest Son. 'And ensure he receives food and water.'

The soldier rushes forward. Youngest Son looks at me nervously.

'This is not as I intended,' he repeats. 'But you shall be safe here until you are summoned before the authorities. I have no doubt you will be offered an honourable position at that time. Now I must return to my regiment.'

So one nightmare ends, and a lesser begins.

I have been in the house by the ramparts for two days now. It, too, is full of prisoners but we are a more select gathering. Everyone speaks in whispers. Clearly, it is the safest way.

Occupying a valley in the foothills, Chunming is an odd-shaped town. Instead of the neat, regular square favoured by Heaven, it follows the contours of the land, the streets snaking up and round hills, clinging to the central gorge through which the Green River flows. Of course, such a muddle leads to unfortunate consequences.

Firstly, the lack of order drains the city's virtue, so that the citizens of Chunming are famous for being cantankerous, churlish, and prone to bad luck. Secondly, it is hard to mount an effective defence in the event of a siege. This has never been a problem before. No commander in five hundred years has been foolish enough to trap himself here.

Another consequence of Chunming's unpleasing shape is that

many houses are built several stories high, as is the one I find myself in. I have been allotted an attic room which I share with four others. From the small balcony-window I can see over the Prefect's residence and enclosure to where General An-Shu has planted his court. So I witness what transpires there.

Soldiers and messengers come and go. Yesterday a dozen men suffered the Four Punishments, observed by the General and his officials, as well as a small party of ladies. Whether they enjoyed the show, I could not tell, for their features were a white blur in the distance. I was surprised by my equanimity as I watched. That is the worst of men like General An-Shu. They make the unacceptable normal.

We are adequately fed. Two small, plain meals a day, and water is plentiful, as the small garden at the rear of the house contains a deep well. A sweet relief, for the city continues to brood in the heat.

When I consider what I have learned since arriving in Chunming, it seems almost nothing: that the General is awaiting reinforcements from his brother, who is a military governor somewhere up north; that his Chief Adviser, a shrewd and cunning orator, is called Yuan Chu-Sou – I started at the name, remembering a lawyer I knew when I was young. But he must have died long ago, and it is a common enough name.

I also hear that the General is besotted with his concubine, who styles herself the Lady Ta Chi after a great lady from antiquity. A strange choice of name, for the original Lady Ta Chi was the lover of the last Shang king, Chou Hsin, and abused her power abominably. As for General An Shu's official wife, it seems she ate a bad meal and has been paralysed ever since. I also hear that the future Son of Heaven heeds his concubine and chief adviser to an extraordinary degree.

No one mentions P'ei Ti, and I dare not ask. I think of him hourly and of how I might discover whether he is a prisoner in Chunming. There is a large prison on the west side of the Prefect's enclosure where captives are regularly brought during the day. Many enter, yet no one seems to leave. Perhaps P'ei Ti is held in there.

Two more days pass and my spirit dwindles with the hours. I'm stifled by resignation and dullness. We have been forbidden to leave the house by the ramparts on pain of severest punishment, and only a madman would risk it.

From my vantage point on the balcony I witness preparations for war in a large encampment outside the city ramparts. They have constructed a parade ground where regiment after regiment drills beneath the midday glare. Any soldier who faints is severely beaten. Clearly much training is necessary. Perhaps this explains the General's reluctance to advance east. Perhaps, if the frantic entertainments I observe each night are to be trusted, his advisers are having too pleasant a time to hurry from Chunming.

Yet the General cannot be faulted for his diligence. Every day he inspects the troops, riding an ivory chariot modelled on the one used by the Emperor at the New Year ritual. When he passes, all except the highest officers press their foreheads to the earth.

I think at such times the General's ambitions are not in vain. Why should he not conquer? The Emperor is inept when it comes to war, as was his father. Perhaps now is the time for a man of iron to sweep the Kin barbarians from our land. Can the Mandate of Heaven be granted to General An-Shu? When I witness the fearful loyalty of his troops, I begin to comprehend Youngest Son's faith.

I am in this mood when he calls upon me. He is in full uniform, upright with youth and strength, his armour and plumed helmet seeming to double his size. As I shuffle into a private chamber where he waits, his greeting expresses utter confidence. He has just left a parade. Indeed, I glimpsed him on his fine horse amidst a forest of flags, while the General's chariot rolled past.

'Father,' he says. 'Please be seated.'

So he is my host here! He shows none of the small, yet comforting, gestures of respect I crave. In the General's new dynasty, perhaps such courtesies are to be abandoned as effeminate and impractical.

'I bring good news, Father,' he says.

'So I may return home?'

He regards me sourly.

'I am surprised you should say that, Father. All must see that our task of renewal is about to commence.'

He seems rather proud of this fine phrase.

'What's your good news?' I ask, curtly. 'But whatever you do, I beg you not to mention 'renewal' or 'sweeping away the old'.'

Youngest Son looks around anxiously.

'That is a dangerous way to talk,' he says. 'I thought your day in Golden Lotus Monastery would have taught you the consequences of foolish, ill-advised talk! I trust you do not speak like that when others might hear you.'

'Rest assured,' I say. 'I reserve honesty for when I speak with you.'

He sighs, as if confronted with a truculent child. Indeed, there is something of that in our relationship – on both sides. I must strive for moderation to retain my authority.

'Tell me your fine news,' I sigh.

He becomes enthusiastic again.

'Father, I have reminded one of the Chief Minister's secretaries that you are here in Chunming, and capable of useful service.'

He waits expectantly for my reply.

'Is that it?' I ask.

'Are you not pleased? What is the point of wasting your days here? Surely, now is the hour when all must prove their worthiness.'

Can he really have blinded himself to my true feelings? Yet he's surrounded by other young men who share his faith and strengthen it daily. No doubt he thinks I'll fall into line when the time comes, like the other conscripts.

'That was considerate of you,' I say. 'But there is something I must ask. Have you heard of a high-ranking prisoner called P'ei Ti?'

He looks confused.

'There are things one does not discuss,' he says.

'Then it is true, he is here?'

'Perhaps,' says Youngest Son.

'Where is he being kept? In the prison adjoining the Prefect's residence?'

'You mean *His Highness's* residence,' snaps Youngest Son.

'Quite so. Is he there? Do not tell me a lie!'

'Why on earth do you wish to know this, Father?' he counters. 'It will not help you gain a suitable position in His Highness's administration.'

I lean towards him and he recoils a little.

'Because P'ei Ti is a friend, an old friend. Even in your glorious new dynasty, friendship must count for something.'

'Of course! As long as it does not conflict with duty. In this case, Father, I am afraid it does. You must give up all thought of this wretched P'ei Ti. I can confirm there is a prisoner of that name. It is best not to mention him. The Chief Minister is personally interrogating him.'

Given my old friend's position as Second Chancellor to the Son of Heaven, it is not hard to see why. Perhaps they hope to discover secrets which will swing the rebellion General An Shu's way.

I settle back in my chair. I do not care to consider the vile cell P'ei Ti must inhabit. The daily wounds to his noble spirit. Enough that he is alive. That, at least, argues for hope.

'Father, you are lost in thought.'

Indeed I am. A wild, foolish thought that, perhaps, with much cunning and luck, I might bring about P'ei Ti's release.

'Father! You are acting strangely. I bring you good news, yet you do not appreciate it.'

'Oh, I know what I must do,' I say.

Youngest Son rises.

'I am glad, Father,' he says. 'When you gain high office in His Highness's service, it will bring great honour to our family.'

Finally I understand him. He dreams of gaining influence through me! Me, of all people! A fantasy so misguided, I could weep for him.

'It is your mother's birthday tomorrow,' I say.

He suddenly seems mournful.

'I will honour it,' he says.

And I believe he will. That is the worst thing. I believe he will.

Midnight, and I listen to a dog barking. Its warning charges the night with urgency, then fades. I cannot sleep because I am thinking how I may pass a message to P'ei Ti and how he may reply.

If I were wealthy, I could bribe the guards. If I could somehow compromise them, it might be possible to gain his release through blackmail. If I was a great warrior, I might hack him free with a sword. But these are the taunting speculations of a powerless man who dreams to keep himself sane, as if an imaginary thing will become real through the act of being imagined. These are the hidden sparks which flicker behind submissive eyes, the vengeful daydreams of an abused clerk.

The reality is this: I lie on my pile of blankets, stifled by the close, unmoving air in the room. Yet I have tasted more fear than most men, and memory urges me back, through the long sleepless night, to when I was young and wayward. Riding out of the capital on a horse I had not learned how to master, and with a sword I had not learned how to use. Mi Feng beside me, when I was young, I was young. . .

Biting wind may freeze a man's bones. Snow and hail may chap his skin. In each case, given warmth, his wounds will mend. But nothing quite thaws a heart frozen by fear, corners of soul burdened with ice. So I discovered during my first hour in the besieged city of Pinang. Yet it was fire, not frost, which caused the mischief.

We emerged from the mountain passes quite suddenly, late in the afternoon, and the whole dismal scene spread before us. First the city, with its high, mud-coloured walls and towers, surrounded by camps and siege lines. Pinang lay in a basin, encircled by low, dusty hills. It was roughly square in shape, several *li* on each side, protected by marshes to the south and exposed plateaus to the north and east. It had been laid out according to the usual grid design, hundreds of years earlier, during the Tang dynasty.

Pinang's purpose was three-fold: to act as a market, a regional court and, most of all, an outpost to protect the Southern Silk Road. Many caravans paused here on their long journey, watering beasts, replenishing stores, perhaps undertaking a little trade, before the final stretch to civilization. For all its fine defences, Pinang remained a provincial backwater, long past its prime, yet still populous. And it was here the rebels, led by the self-styled King of Western Peace, Wang Tse, had proclaimed their capital.

As we toiled down the steep road to Pinang, it was not the city itself that chilled my heart, but my first glimpse of war.

The Imperial forces had lined up twenty huge siege engines on the west side of Pinang. Their design was simple. High wooden frames on which a pivotal arm rested. At one end of the arm, a cup to hold boulders or incendiary bombs. On the other, a hundred long ropes pulled by as many men. Thus large projectiles could be hurled at the city. Naturally, I knew of such weapons from Father, but had never witnessed them. Our strategy was obvious. Batter the walls and set the place ablaze.

As we neared, orders were screamed out and missiles curved towards the walls, where they exploded in clouds of smoke and dust. It seemed to me nothing could withstand such force. I reined in my horse and Mi Feng halted beside me.

'The rebels can hardly have expected this treatment,' I said.

Mi Feng examined the siege lines but did not reply.

'See!' I exclaimed. 'The best they can do is hurl barrels! Let us hope they are not filled with wine, or our celebration when the city falls shall be a dry one.'

And it was true, the rebel artillery were replying with nothing more deadly than casks of water! A dozen landed harmlessly in front of our siege engines, with a loud splash. Our soldiers laughed and made obscene gestures at the ramparts.

'Look at that tower,' said Mi Feng.

I peered across the battlefield. Flags of different colours were being raised and lowered on a watchtower.

'What of it?'

'An observer up there is guiding the artillery behind the walls,' he said.

'What nonsense!' I scoffed.

He glanced at me, then shrugged. Yet as he had predicted, water barrels began to fall among our artillery, several landing in the crowds of men hauling at the ropes. A few unfortunates were instantly crushed, a terrible end. But the casualties were light.

'Come now!' I said, less certain.

A fresh flight of projectiles curved up from the city. These trailed smoke. Down, down they came with a loud whoosh. Some exploded in mid-air, others hit the earth. Wherever they fell pandemonium broke out, for instead of water, the barrels contained burning powder, jagged pottery, and flint.

As long as I live I shall remember it. Those striking the siege engines at once destroyed them, roaring like enraged dragons. Wood and clouds of smoke rose amidst the screams. More terrible were those fire-barrels falling among the conscripted peasants as they hauled desperately on their ropes.

When the smoke cleared, scores lay dead or wounded,

twitching pitifully in piles. Wailing filled the air. Yet any peasants who tried to flee were beaten back to their posts by soldiers.

Again a flight curved like fiery geese from the city. Again, explosions made my horse rear. Mi Feng watched impassively from his saddle. Within half an hour, our once-proud siege engines were either burning or mere piles of shattered timber. Scores of men lay on the dusty earth, many still alive as they smouldered. My nostrils caught the aroma of roasting flesh. To my shame, for we had not eaten since dawn, I thought of roast mutton. Immediately I retched and Mi Feng had to steady my horse. Bile choked my throat and nose.

It was merely a foretaste.

Our journey to the North Western Frontier had prepared us for the possibility of defeat.

We had left the capital in late October and made good progress on the road. Su Lin filled my thoughts. I was subdued and morose even in my sleep. Mi Feng, however, became more alert with each *li* we travelled. At his insistence we shared a room at night and he made a point of wedging the door with blocks of wood he had carved for the purpose. After a week on the road I mustered sufficient spirit to question such precautions. For the first time since my misfortunes began, he grew angry with me.

'Are you a child?' he snapped.

I was speechless before his impudence.

'Don't you realise you're not meant to return from the frontier?' he roared. 'How do you know Lord Xiao hasn't decided you won't even reach there?'

'That is ridiculous,' I blustered. 'It would be murder!'

'Get off your horse!' he commanded.

We were on an isolated stretch of the highway.

'I do not answer to a servant!' I shouted back.

Then, to my amazement, he leapt from his mount and

dragged me to the ground. He stood in front of me and whipped out a long knife from his belt. To my horror, he grabbed me by the chest and held the blade to my throat. Its point tickled my fluttering windpipe.

'Yun Cai is dead!' he cried, then let me go and stalked back to the horses.

I stood on the dusty road, panting in consternation.

'Are you mad?' I stammered. 'Of course you are!'

'Yun Cai is dead,' he repeated, furiously. 'You have a fine sword and you can't even defend yourself. Pah!'

He spat at my pony, which shied nervously.

'Paper is my shield and ink is my sword,' I protested, loftily. 'I am a scholar, not a barbarian, you dog!'

'That is why you are dead,' he replied.

It is said a good friend's advice hurts, a bad friend's never. Though I longed to dismiss him there and then, I must confess, I dared not. As suddenly as it had arisen, his flare of temper faded. He got on his knees and, shame-faced, pressed his forehead to the road.

'Forgive me, sir,' he said. 'I have done wrong. But you scare me. You're too, too. . .'

In a fury, I struggled onto my horse and rode away. When he caught up, I did not discharge him, but steadfastly refused to acknowledge his existence. Indeed, I sulked like a boy. That evening, as we rested at an inn, I asked timidly if he knew how to use a sword. Foolish question. Whatever he had learnt during his captivity among the barbarians seemed to involve some kind of weapon.

So he became my tutor. When we paused on our journey, he made me brandish P'ei Ti's gift until my arm ached. And if I didn't scream like a madman as I hacked the wooden targets he constructed, Mi Feng would grow surly and mutter: 'Yun Cai is dead.' If I showed the proper spirit, he chuckled and urged: 'That's it! Cut deep! Stamp on his face! Doesn't it feel good?' And I was alarmed to discover it felt very good. Most gratifying, indeed! Lord Xiao's body received a thousand imaginary gashes at my hands, and with each blow I experienced a thrill of power. Afterwards, however, I felt ashamed.

The inns near the frontier were full of strange rumours concerning the rebels. Now it was Mi Feng's turn to suffer, for he was inordinately superstitious.

It seemed the rebellion of Wang Tse was no ordinary uprising. The initial cause was banal enough. The local Prefect had embezzled money and grain, starving the city of Pinang and its garrison until neither could tolerate the abuse. A mob stormed the Prefect's enclosure, slaughtering all they found, adult or child. In Wang Tse the rebels had chosen an admirable leader. Many believed he was not just a soldier, but a sorcerer.

Everywhere we heard tales of his forbidden powers. It was said that, even as a common Captain of Artillery, Wang Tse had married a sorceress who taught him many useful spells. His wife's father had owned a magic mirror and when her mother decided to burn it, appalled by its dark promptings, the ashes whirled around her and she became pregnant. The fruit of this unnatural conception, Wang Tse's wife, was no less than a fox fairy in human form, able to conjure up soldiers and cavalry from paper and beans. Certainly his forces never seemed to diminish.

Of course I smiled at such fanciful notions. The idea that demons would raise a rebellion in out-of-the-way Pinang seemed absurd. Why not choose the capital itself? Then we learned the first army sent to crush the rebels had been slaughtered almost to a man, mainly because of a mysterious sandstorm, for Wang Tse could conjure wind and weather. Still I pretended to attribute the disaster to natural causes.

At last we reached the mountain passes leading to Pinang and joined a train of fifty wagons carrying supplies to the front. The roadside was littered with white bones, for the region had endured many battles during the previous Emperor's reign, as he struggled to maintain the Silk Road's flow of wealth into the Empire.

By now every man in the army had heard dark rumours concerning Wang Tse's power. Most kept a constant watch over their shoulder, for the sorcerer's wife sometimes flew above our troops at night, scattering an invisible ink which caused premature death by painting unlucky characters across a man's forehead. One sergeant, who had been at the siege from the beginning, told me a strange tale:

'I was with the first army,' he said. 'We got as far as the city gates, when suddenly we were covered in a fog of sand and smoke. A most devilish wind was blowing, sir! We were driven into the marshes on the south side of the city. Well, everyone knows the rest. I'm lucky to be talking to you, sir! We lost two-thirds of our men, sir! That's why they've sent a new general to take charge.'

'What's his name?' I asked.

'Field Marshal Wen Po,' replied the sergeant.

Of course the name was familiar. Who had not heard of Wen Po? Less well-known was that this same illustrious Wen Po was Lord Xiao's cousin. If my tongue hadn't been parched from the dusty mountain road – it was a barren range, all rock and sandstone crag, populated by vultures – it would have gone bone dry. The web Lord Xiao had spun around me tightened yet again.

Later that day we arrived at Pinang, and witnessed the burning of the siege engines. Could sorcery have guided Wang Tse's missiles? It is hard to doubt what everyone knows to be true.

We were guided through a large encampment to a wind-picked hillside overlooking the western ramparts of Pinang. By now I was sufficiently recovered from my queasiness to look around. The roads were full of wounded men hobbling back to their camps. Down below, in front of the ramparts, siege engines still burned and acrid smoke billowed. I was surprised to notice many of the dead were simply left to smoulder where they had fallen.

Yet I needed to clear my mind. An important event awaited me. For I must meet the clerks who were to be my underlings.

'With all due respect, sir,' advised Mi Feng. 'You've got to show who's boss right from the start. Find a reason to slap one of them about.'

'I have never beaten you,' I replied. 'Yet you seem to respect me.'

He considered this for a moment, then concluded: 'Even so, it won't do no harm.'

Of course he was right. I dismounted beside a latrine and swapped travelling clothes for my official uniform, much to the amusement of several cooks squatting in the trench, who shouted ribald comments, while pointing up the hillside at the Bureau of Fallen Heroes.

Then we rode up the steep slope to a small, miserable hut. As I looked across the basin of hills enclosing the city, hundreds of campfires glittered in the dusk. The cold wind moaned and an eerie, desolate light lit the mountain peaks, so that the winding Silk Road glowed as it uncurled westwards, vanishing into the distant horizon. Pinang was dark and silent below us, except for a few torches on the city walls.

I dismounted stiffly and smoothed my uniform. An orange glow shone through the open doorway of the hut, and I could hear voices muttering. I approached quietly and glanced through the low entrance. Within lay a scene of wretched disorder. Here was my office, an outpost of government, yet it would have disgraced a slovenly thief.

Three men in threadbare uniforms crouched round a small fire, built within a circle of stones. Their faces were gaunt and unshaven. More like brigands than honourable clerks dedicated to His Imperial Majesty's service. On a low table were piles of documents. As I watched, one of the clerks, not much older than myself, reached up and took one of the scrolls. Tearing a strip of paper, he rolled it into a taper and used it to light a small lamp. His eyes wandered to the doorway, and he froze. I glowered into his startled face. The others followed his gaze. The room was silent except for the crackle of dried ferns and brushwood on the fire. They exchanged nervous glances. Finally, I said in a quiet voice:

'Bring me that paper you have used to light your lamp.'

The young man rose and brought it over sullenly. His fellows did not move. A bad sign. Given my uniform, they should have been on their knees.

I plucked the paper from his hand and slowly unrolled it. Then I glanced over the writing. An inventory of ink cakes used during the last year. He cringed a little at this proof of negligence, but only a little. Now was the moment when I either gained their respect or became their pet. So without a word, I slapped him as hard as I could across the face. After my recent sword practise it must have been a fine blow, for he keeled over with a cry.

'Get out!' I roared. 'The lot of you!'

They scrambled to their feet and lined up outside. For the next few minutes, I harangued and railed, conscious that Mi Feng was watching with approval. Then I ordered them to collect their blankets and find somewhere to sleep, promising they would be thoroughly questioned at dawn. Mi Feng arranged my own bedding and we spent an uneasy night, disturbed by the low muttering of the wind, and the clerks, outside.

Lord Xiao's written instructions were clear. I should supervise The Bureau of Fallen Heroes. A fine title for a petty office! Our duty was to record all losses among the troops, either through battle or disease, with due reverence to the proper military authorities. 'As and when the opportunity arose', we were to send full reports of our progress to the capital.

The pointlessness of this mission was obvious. Firstly, such a task belonged to the military administrators, who naturally resented our presence. Not least because many claimed the wages of dead soldiers while pretending they were still alive. Secondly, our reports would end up in a great mass of paper in the Finance Ministry, unread and unregarded.

Of course the real function of the Bureau of Fallen heroes was to punish any underlings who displeased Lord Xiao. Perhaps I should not have been so hard on the clerks for we were all cranking the same wheel. Yet I was determined to vanquish Lord Xiao's malice by a most ridiculous method. I would fulfil my mission, however meaningless, with exemplary diligence and vigour. In this way, I reasoned, pride might be retained, my worth confirmed for all to see.

The next morning I summoned the clerks into the hut, one by one, and grilled them. Each entered half-frozen from a miserable night beneath the stars. I had not intended them to be terrified, yet they were.

One had been exiled here for answering back to Lord Xiao's secretary (this was the scroll burner). The second had been drunk when Lord Xiao unexpectedly inspected his office and had broken into a tirade about the conditions under which he was expected to work. The last had offended Lord Xiao by giving him the nickname 'Squeaky Rat Voice', which his childhood friend treacherously reported in order to gain a promotion.

I learned that my predecessor as Bureau Chief – who had made the mistake of protesting about financial irregularities Lord Xiao wished to cover up – had died for no apparent reason within a week of reaching Pinang. His official hat and robes hung forlornly by the door. Since then they had drawn their weekly rations of millet and rice and tried to stay inconspicuous. Their main duty consisted of guarding against soldiers from the neighbouring camp who, as I was told solemnly, 'were ten times worse than any rebels'. Not a single list of the fallen had been compiled.

'Clearly,' I said. 'You have drifted into bad ways.

Nevertheless our duties are important and we shall fulfil them with pride. If you work hard, I'll let you sleep in the hut. Otherwise you'll sleep outside.'

It seemed the worst punishment I could threaten. Strangely, they nodded with approval. Habits of unquestioning obedience do that to a man, as a much-beaten dog looks around wistfully for its cruel master.

I began by introducing myself to all the relevant military administrators, for they held the key to the whole business. I rode from regiment to regiment on my shaggy pony, while the clerks followed in full uniform, carrying bundles of scrolls. It soon became obvious our presence was viewed as profoundly unlucky. Many reached for charms and amulets, to prevent their name from appearing on one of our lists. Some soldiers even shouted out: 'There go Wang Tse's spies!' as we passed. It was essential to reverse this situation as soon as possible. The best way seemed complete frankness.

'Honourable Sir,' I said to the first official who agreed to meet me, his lower jaw jutting with hostility. 'I fully appreciate how annoying our presence must be. Let me assure you, sir, we have no choice in the matter. If we had our way, we'd be back in the capital drinking wine and admiring the bosoms of fine ladies. But as we are here, we have duties to fulfil. So, if you would be so gracious, my clerks will note the casualties on a daily basis and we shall send back our reports. I must assure you, Honoured Sir, that no one ever reads them. Nevertheless, we are determined our dispatches will bring us great credit. Who knows, if we work hard enough, we might even get recalled and you'll see the back of us.'

The official's mouth twitched. For a moment he tried to frown, then roared with laughter.

'Bosoms, indeed! Drinking wine, indeed! All right, young fellow,' he said. 'Just keep out of everyone's way.'

I proceeded from camp to camp in this manner. While I can

hardly say we won friends, there was no doubt we lost a few enemies.

Father always told me: 'Hard weather makes thorns put out their spikes.' He meant, of course, to teach me the best way to be a man. Never did I need guidance as much as that first month on the hillside above Pinang. For the weather was indeed hard; and I entered a strange world with stranger rules.

I had little choice except to put out spikes against the wind. It blew night and day from the barren steppe-lands, piercing layers of clothes and, finally, the very spirit. My soft hands and face became chapped and raw. Often I woke shivering beneath my blanket. We had little fuel for fires and our rations were barely adequate. Our one blessing was a small spring at the rear of the hut, so we did not lack water. Not everyone in His Excellency Wen Po's army was so lucky and I was not surprised when we were roused one night by our neighing horses.

Mi Feng and I charged outside waving our swords. Fortunately, the thieves – a few crossbowmen – melted into the darkness, heading for the nearest camp.

We quietened the horses, wind tugging at our hair and their manes. I glanced up at the stars, intermittently shrouded by racing clouds.

'Sir,' said Mi Feng. 'I think they wanted our beasts for the pot.'

This was too obvious to deserve a reply.

'Why not give the weaker one to the captain of the crossbowmen camped yonder?' he suggested. 'We could ask him to make sure his men don't touch the horse we have left. Then everyone will be happy. Besides, there's not enough fodder to feed both animals until spring.'

This seemed an excellent plan and the next morning it was soon accomplished. The captain, an excitable fellow from Nanning, sealed the bargain with a cask of salted fish. That night the Bureau of Fallen Heroes dined like palace eunuchs, each shred of fish melting on our tongues.

Often I leaned against a sheltered wall of the hut, gazing out across Pinang. At least fifty thousand men were besieging the city, outnumbering the rebels many times over. Yet, as the Eleventh Month commenced, we seemed no nearer victory, despite regular assaults on the ramparts. So each day my clerks returned with the names of the dead and our list lengthened. Every week I visited the regimental headquarters to meet military administrators and nourish goodwill. Heaven knows we needed it. It was on just such a venture my misfortunes began in earnest.

I was trotting back to our hut when the steep, twisting road was blocked by a large party of horsemen. Naturally, I hurried off the road to let them pass. They were arrayed in full armour and carried a dozen bright flags. Behind the cavalry came a litter carried by eight sweating guardsmen. Within reclined Field Marshal Wen Po, a stout, bearded man approaching his fiftieth year, famous for cunning stratagems. I stayed on my knees, clutching the reins of my pony. But instead of passing by, His Excellency barked out a command and the whole procession halted. I found myself gazing up at his implacable face. He leaned forward in his litter and frowned. It was obvious he recognised me. I understood at once my presence had been communicated to him by his cousin, Lord Xiao. No doubt the letter contained delicate hints about the fate I was expected to suffer.

His Excellency Wen Po regarded me for a long moment. It was not an angry look; indeed he appeared thoughtful, as though contemplating a necessary but unpleasant duty. Then he gestured to his bearers and the procession continued on its way. A large crowd of officers and officials came behind, mostly on horseback. A few were carried in sedan chairs by barefoot peasants. They had almost gone by when my attention was caught by a thin, pale face in a particularly fine litter. At first I refused to acknowledge the evidence of my eyes. His own gaze fell upon me. A gasp of astonishment replaced the familiar sneer on his bloodless lips. Then he was swept along behind His Excellency Wen Po and turned a corner.

Cousin Zhi rode in that litter! Cousin Zhi who I had last seen years earlier, before the Great Fire. And now he was in His Excellency's entourage! Normally one is glad to meet a relative, especially in a time of need, but this was Cousin Zhi. Yet why shouldn't he have changed for the better? Even in this dreadful place a man might still improve.

If Wang Tse, King of the Western Peace, hoped His Excellency Wen Po would despair in the face of winter and heavy losses he was to be disappointed. A subtle opponent always has eggs to hatch.

His Excellency's next stratagem involved the thousands of labourers who accompanied the army. His plan was to build an earth wall parallel to the western ramparts, a mere dozen yards from the battlements. When the wall was high enough, he could clear the fortifications using archers and crossbowmen. Meanwhile, picked units of swordsmen would mount siege ladders and pour over the city walls, dispatching any rebels who remained alive. Pinang would lie open like a hen-coop with its door ajar.

A sound enough plan, and well-tested. Its disadvantage was that thousands must perish to accomplish it. His Excellency evidently accepted that price.

One dawn I was watching the preparations before Pinang when a splendidly attired messenger galloped to our hut. The man took a single glance at the Bureau of Fallen Heroes and dropped all pretence of courtesy.

'Which of you lot is Yun Cai?' he demanded.

I stepped forward, straightening my grimy uniform.

'Have you never seen a graduate of the Golden List before?' I replied.

My clerks chuckled appreciatively. They hated any sign of weakness on my part. I was their father here. And their hope. The messenger raised his eyebrows.

'Here!' he said, thrusting a scroll into my outstretched hand. Then he cantered away.

'Where's my bow?' muttered Mi Feng beside me. My servant had acquired such a weapon and taken to shooting at passing birds or wild dogs to supplement our pitiful rations.

'Don't bother,' I said. 'He would taste awful.'

Again the clerks applauded my wit. I was beginning to see why great officials require sycophants. Yet I resembled a beggar more than a scholar-official. My robes threadbare and unkempt, my hair lank in its own grease. The plump, glowing cheeks Su Lin had once so admired, were pinched and covered with stubble, like hairy leather bags.

My one consolation was that I had managed to send a splendid report to Lord Xiao, boasting of our diligence and good health. A foolish gesture, as I soon came to learn. Yet truly I believed he had long ago given us up for ghosts swirling round the barren mountains, and so would never read it.

Wearily, I unrolled the scroll. From the prim style of the characters, it had evidently been dictated to a secretary. It read:

Bureau Chief Yun Cai, His Excellency Field Marshal Wen Po has received a memorandum from the capital regarding your work. Lord Xiao is concerned that your reports are niggardly and delayed. He has requested you should personally attend the foremost scenes of battle, in order to collect information at first hand. Accordingly, this is His Excellency Wen Po's command: Bureau Chief Yun Cai is to proceed daily to the Western ramparts, there to fulfil his duties. May His Imperial Highness live a thousand years!

It was signed by Wen Po's secretary.

For a long while I sat alone on an outcrop of rock. The clerks and Mi Feng kept a respectful distance. I stared sightlessly to the south-east, in the direction of the capital. My spirit rose in a mournful sigh, flying over mountain and plain, through stalks of bamboo withered by winter, over the roofs of dull provincial towns, ships plying turbulent rivers, far far to the south where Su Lin would be bathing in tepid water poured by her maid. Perhaps they chattered about the day ahead: her engagement at some wedding or a trip to purchase new clothes. Then she would yawn, stretch, practise her lute for a while, gently sounding the strings, her plump lips pursed in concentration. Perhaps the maid brought out her chest of cosmetics, brushing rice powder on her face.

Did she think of me in my extremity? I had thrown away my entire future for love of her. Did she think of me as she looked out across the West Lake, and recall the pleasant hours we spent together? Oh, I had to believe it was true. Nothing made sense unless it was true. For two months since my arrival in Pinang I had been too dispirited to even compose a couplet! I was the worst of all failures – an ex-poet. Did she read the poems I had dedicated to her and sigh? Poems people sang on the street. What honour I had brought her!

Perhaps my words seemed foolish now: a dream that was over. Nothing much. Perhaps she clutched another lover in the dark of night, breathing his breath, sharing her fragrance. How could she betray me so abominably? Tears rolled down my cheeks, the first I had allowed myself since arriving in Pinang. How Lord Xiao must be chuckling at my discomfort! I felt too defeated even to hate him.

A rough hand gripped my shoulder. I was met by the grizzled face of Mi Feng.

'Sir has had bad news?' he said.

He listened carefully as I read the scroll aloud. Our eyes were drawn to the earthworks rising by the Western rampart. Even from this height, we could see arrows falling among the assembled labourers and soldiers. Shouts and screams were carried to us by the wind.

'Do you know,' he said, thoughtfully. 'I reckon Lord Xiao is afraid of you.'

I laughed bitterly, drying shameful tears on my sleeve. To my shame I could not contain them.

'Leave me!' I stammered. 'Save yourself, Mi Feng. Get away while you can. I am cursed!'

'Think about what I'm saying,' he urged. 'He goes to the trouble of posting you here for the sake of a skirt. Then he writes to his cousin and forces him to send you where the arrows are thickest. He's afraid you'll come back.'

'Little chance of that,' I said, trying to smile.

The effort made me both sob and giggle hysterically at the same time.

'Maybe, maybe not. Look at it from his point of view. There he is, stuffing his face on a breakfast of roast swan and a report arrives from you. . . He reads it and goes cold because you might not die for his pleasure after all.'

'But I am doomed, Mi Feng!'

He shook me by the shoulder so hard that I winced.

'You're going to disappoint him, aren't you?' he said, icily. 'What kind of fool is this Lord Xiao? He doesn't know Yun Cai like I do!'

Crazy talk to make me feel better.

'You wait,' he gloated. 'You'll be enjoying your girl before you know it and laughing at Lord Xiao as you ride her!'

'Do not forget your place!' I said, shocked.

'No, sir,' he said. 'And don't forget yours.'

Was there ever such a servant? Sometimes I wondered who was the master. But he had revived my spirits and for that I was grateful. I wondered what Father would do in my situation. The answer seemed obvious. Resort to guile, dressed up as courage and decency.

Later that day I descended to the siege lines with my clerks and halted beyond arrow range. The brooding walls of Pinang stretched before us. Mi Feng handed me several shields lashed together that he had begged from the captain who had eaten our spare horse. As an afterthought he had lent me a helmet and armour for my legs and arms. He offered more, but I could barely carry what I had.

My prospects were far from encouraging. Field Marshal Wen Po's earthworks were rising, layer upon layer, built by swarms of conscripted peasants, busy removing soil from a long ditch and piling it high. Teams of men ran up walkways, pushing laden wheelbarrows. They dumped the soil as quickly as possible, then scurried back for more. Meanwhile the defenders poured down a steady hail of rocks and arrows, countered by our crossbowmen, hidden behind wooden palisades. At such close range Wang Tse's huge catapults could not easily throw boulders or bombs at our men.

Already the earthworks were approaching the height of the lowest battlements, but at a terrible cost. As we watched, several labourers fell with arrows protruding from stomach or back. Even our crossbowmen were severely harried. A steady stream of wounded were carted away in wheelbarrows.

'Clerks!' I announced, in my gruffest voice. 'You are aware of my orders. It is the duty of all to obey their superior without question. I have been instructed by Lord Xiao to station myself in that wretched trench over there and record all losses as they occur. You will stay under cover here and compile the numbers I bring.'

I staggered towards the siege works behind my outlandish shield. Almost at once I was rocked by the thud of a crossbow bolt piercing the edge of the wood. How I ran! A minute later, I was cowering in the ditch while shafts and rocks fell around us.

Aside from the bodies, the trench reeked of excrement and urine. Positioning my shield as best I could, I drew an abacus from my belt and began to slide the beads, each click a wordless prayer for a man's soul, just as a Buddhist prayer wheel ceaselessly clicks and revolves. Every few hours I retreated like a crab to my clerks and they duly recorded the numbers of fallen. Needless to say, both soldiers and labourers viewed my antics with complete incomprehension.

Several days passed in this way before I could skulk in the ditch beneath my shield no longer. The constant sight of blood and corpses had begun to gnaw at my sanity. I found myself chuckling or singing unaccountably. I conducted lengthy debates with myself about all kind of topics, or simply curled up in a tight ball. Each night sleep came hard; harder still to drag myself back to the siege lines the next day. Yet disobedience would be mutiny, instantly punishable by death.

By now the ditch was littered with decaying bodies. Rats scurried and crows stalked from corpse to corpse. Flies and maggots feasted. And still our rampart rose.

That morning I borrowed a wheelbarrow from my friend the captain, filling it with a water cask and strips of rag made from the uniforms of the fallen. Instead of advancing behind my shield, I charged over to the earthworks, pushing the barrow. Arrows skipped around me. Once in the scant safety of the ditch, I doled out water to the wounded, who lay groaning in the dirt, waiting for night to bring a chance of escape. When the water ran out, I went back for more, and so more days passed.

My tendency to shiver and mutter faded. No pleasant thing mopping the brow of a man writhing on the ground, yet it was preferable to inactivity. Now I had no time to be afraid. As I worked, I recollected the beneficial effect of good deeds on my next reincarnation. Surely I would be reborn nearer to Nothingness, a blessed abbot or hermit, untroubled by the misery and illusion of this world. Never again a love-deluded poet. Never again a weary scholar with ink-blackened fingers, striving for knowledge when the Way may only be inhabited without thought.

All the while dying men surrounded me, crying out for their mothers. How hard it was to tear soul from body, to step from one room to the next. Some faces carve themselves on the hillside of one's spirit, like giant stone Buddhas.

One day, as I pushed my empty water cask wearily back to Mi Feng, I noticed His Excellency Wen Po in the distance, watching my progress from his horse. He followed me like a tiger anticipating the heart and liver of its next meal. Impudently, for by now I was past caring, I stared back, until a flight of arrows sent me scurrying forwards.

Then, almost unexpectedly, the ramparts were complete. We retreated for the last time as twilight fell and I found my path blocked by a dainty youth in yellow silks. He was so out of place in dreary Pinang that I almost took him for an Immortal. He smiled at me.

'Come with me, Honourable Yun Cai,' he piped in a dreamy, mincing voice. 'You are invited to dinner.'

The youth led me toward Wen Po's headquarters, situated in a village above Pinang. At first I feared punishment. My crime? That was obvious. I was still alive. Yet it seemed strange that an austere man like Wen Po would send a catamite as his messenger, unless he intended it as a joke.

We were an odd pair. My guide anxious to avoid dirtying his silken clothes and slippers, all the while eyeing the soldiers we passed like a less-than-coy girl. And then myself: Yun Cai, pitiful Yun Cai, stinking of sweat, dried blood and soil. As I staggered through lines of marching men, a few bowed or called out my name, for my wheelbarrow of water had made me a curiosity among the besieging army. A few even seemed to know the reason for my presence in Pinang. Why should they not sympathise when most had been conscripted against their will? Besides, I flattered myself that my poems were known even here. At least I wished to believe so.

'How sad you look!' tittered the youth.

I peered at him. His elation was too brittle to be natural. It made me think of the drugs used in the decadent days of the Han to make one impervious to sorrow.

'I have every reason to be sad,' I said. 'That's natural sometimes.'

'You need someone to make you glad,' he replied, coquettishly.

I glowered at him.

'Who exactly has invited me to dinner?' I asked. 'It is evidently not His Excellency Wen Po for we have just passed the way to his headquarters.'

'Yun Cai will see!' cried the youth, covering his face with perfectly manicured hands and peering through the gaps between his fingers.

We reached an encampment constructed beside fetid marshland on the south side of the city. A small village of tents and pavilions stood in the centre of the camp, lit by red and blue lanterns. Soldiers in the white uniforms of a penal battalion, wearing death's colour because their lives were forfeit, guarded the entrance. Beyond a low palisade of reeds gathered from the marsh, huddles of men lay on the chilly ground. Here thousands of conscripted peasants were bivouacked, those who raised the earthworks each day, cheap fodder for war's senseless teeth to grind.

As we weaved through their silent ranks, my guide hummed a dance song I recollected from the capital. By this means he hoped to forget the miserable wretches around him. I could not resist a cruel urge.

'You are afraid you will join them, aren't you?' I said.

He twirled on his heels like a dancer.

'That will never happen!' he cried.

Then he sang in a high, clear voice:

'*Oh, never will the wind part the rushes, my love!*'

'Who is your master?' I demanded again.

'*Never will the wind part the rushes*,' he sang. '*Never will the wind blow east, or west!*'

A low, restless murmur rose from the conscripted peasants hidden in the darkness. I, too, found his song disturbing. I shivered as the wind unfurled its icy breath.

We picked a way through to the pavilions, protected by a ditch and an earth wall six feet high. I was inclined to think these defences were not meant for Wang Tse's rebels, but to keep the conscripted peasants from murdering their overseers. Certainly a large contingent from the penal battalion guarded the gates.

I was led to the largest of the pavilions and my guide bowed low, evidently relieved to arrive home.

'Enter!' he said. 'You are welcome.'

I stepped inside. The tent was carpeted with dozens of thick rugs of the kind one finds among the nomads. A small charcoal fire glowed in the centre, roasting a stuffed piglet on a spit. A piglet! Roast pork! At once my mouth drooled shamelessly and I felt light-headed. Incense burners scented the air with pleasant perfumes. A lute accompanied by wisp-like bells tinkled lulling melodies from a darkened corner. Was I dreaming? I screwed my eyes shut. When I opened them again I saw Cousin Zhi lolling on a wide bed of furs, watching my confusion with evident enjoyment.

'Cousin!' he said. 'Welcome to my humble home!'

He was still wiry and delicate although he had acquired a dainty, waxed moustache and goatee beard. I looked round and laughed.

'Not so humble,' I stammered.

'Perhaps not, perhaps not.'

He rose and hurried over. Taking my hands, he patted them earnestly. His touch felt hot.

'What a terrible time you are having!' he cried. 'Sit down! Rest! I insist on it.'

He clapped his hands and half a dozen servants appeared from the shadows. Two began to turn and baste the roasting piglet. Others brought me a cup of warm wine. How I gulped! I had thought to never taste such a pleasure again.

He motioned that I should sit on a divan beside his bed and I obeyed in a daze. Smiling, he took up his former position.

'You do not look quite as you used to,' he remarked.

'Neither do you,' I replied.

His robes were splendid. As fine as when he had followed the life of a foppish rake in the capital. He possessed a new confidence and, yes, power, for strength may shine from a man's face. Cousin Zhi waved at the gorgeous tent, its statuettes and wall-hangings, with feigned embarrassment.

'I must beg forgiveness for my poor hospitality,' he said. 'But in times of war. . . Well, what can one do?'

Where had he learnt such fastidious manners? Frankly, I preferred the old, resentful Cousin Zhi of my youth. At least I'd known what he was thinking. More wine appeared in my cup and disappeared down my throat.

'How did you gain. . .' I gestured around me. 'All this?'

His smile widened and he curled up his knees.

'Through my own merits,' he said. 'How else? Actually, I inherited my position from my predecessor, who found me useful in all sorts of ways. Regrettably, he had an accident involving some of our labourers and I was appointed in his place. I'm surprised you have not heard of the incident.'

'What exactly *is* your position?' I asked.

'Why, I am in charge of this labour brigade! Come now, you must know that. I cannot believe you have not heard my name mentioned!'

He seemed piqued.

'And what is *your* position?' he asked, more in his old style.

'Chief of the Bureau of Fallen Heroes,' I said. 'A more melancholy duty than you can imagine.'

He sipped his wine.

'Oh, I can imagine,' he said.

'But Zhi! Look at you! You have become a great man.'

'Of course,' he said, wagging his finger as though chiding me.

'In a normal battle the labour brigades are little regarded. They transport stores, dig a few ditches, all the glory belongs to the fighting men. But in a siege, Yun Cai, in a long siege everything is different. Take the earthworks I have constructed: who could raise them for His Excellency except I? No one. You may wonder how I achieve this, but the answer is simple. The peasants out there,' he gestured beyond the tent, 'either dig or die. You see, Yun Cai, you need to know how a man thinks.'

He tapped his forehead significantly and peered at me from his elevated couch.

'Of course, I know why you've been sent here,' he said. 'So don't bother to pretend. I know *everything*. Oh, Yun Cai, how could you cast away all those years of study, even your honour, for the sake of a worthless girl?'

I gulped another cup. It coursed right through me.

'It is strange how things end up,' I said.

Cousin Zhi gestured impatiently to the servants and at once his own cup was filled. It seemed better to change the conversation.

'How is Honoured Aunty?' I asked. 'I take it she prospers?'

'Never mind her,' he said, his voice slurring. 'Actually I never think of her. Do such unfilial sentiments shock you?'

He obviously wanted me to be shocked.

'No,' I said.

'Well, I don't. Honestly, I don't.'

'Yet she is your mother.'

'Why should I think of her?' he demanded, shrilly. 'Do you know that if I succeed here, I have been promised a Sub-prefect's position? Oh yes, even though I have not passed the necessary examinations! Mother will be proud of me then! I might even allow her to live with me.'

He threw down his cup and began to pace before the roasting piglet. For the first time I wondered if he was entirely sane.

'You haven't changed at all,' he said. 'Still as arrogant as ever! But this is no monthly examination you can cheat at. Your life hangs on a thread, Yun Cai! A single thread! Tomorrow His Excellency will launch our final attack on the walls and Pinang will fall. A victory I alone have made possible. You realise, of course, that you will be expected to accompany the first wave of troops.'

The possibility had not occurred to me.

'Casualties will be high. Very high. It is likely you will be among them. But dear Yun Cai, I could prevent that!'

I listened carefully, drunk as I was.

'How?'

'Never mind how. Just trust that I can. You see, I can have anything I want here. That is the beauty of this place. Your life is in my hands, Yun Cai! But there is a price.'

He returned to his bed and lolled, snapping his fingers for more wine. I watched him, appalled. Had I really treated him so badly that he could play with me like this? I was family, his own blood.

'What is your price?' I asked, dully.

He patted the bearskin rug where he lounged.

'I have waited for this moment. Can't you guess?'

For a moment I was confused. Then I noticed the catamite who had led me here, grinning in a corner. And the final triumph Zhi craved became obvious.

I imagined his crab-like body on my back, thrusting and yelping. His hot breath on my neck. A revolting prospect. Yet for a moment I hesitated. How precious is life! To dine on succulent meat and giddy wine, to sleep on a soft bed when I was tired, so tired. Surely life itself was worth a little dishonour? I wavered only for a moment. No longer. Just long enough to sow seeds of self-disgust. They have been rotting in me ever since.

I rose unsteadily and swayed.

'Cousin,' I said. 'If Uncle Ming could see us now he'd be glad to find us talking like old friends. But I really must go.'

Cousin Zhi rose, too.

'Tomorrow you will die,' he said. 'Think! I have great influence with His Excellency.'

I turned toward the exit.

'Yun Cai, come back. I should have given you the pork, then you'd have. . . It was stupid of me. Stay a while!'

By now I was walking and soon found myself in the cold night air. Somehow I made my way back to our hut, though the siege lines were dangerous after dark. Mi Feng was waiting by the door. I lurched past him and collapsed onto my bed where I dreamt of Honoured Aunty, cooing as she felt around beneath my clothes.

There is an old song from the days of the Han: 'We fought for the South of the Walls, we died North of the Earthworks'. The whole army was singing it with one voice as we advanced on the Western Ramparts. Drums beat incessantly. Flags ordered regiments to their attack positions. I clutched my abacus and inkpot as I walked among them, carrying my lashed up shield. Mi Feng had insisted on accompanying me, armed with weapons stolen from corpses.

For the first time I wore P'ei Ti's sword at my belt, though I harboured few illusions about my ability to use it. One gains confidence among so great a host. Surely the enemy's arrows will find other bodies before your own.

A strange, warm wind blew in our faces as we took up position. I feared some new sorcery from Wang Tse, and many must have shared my thoughts for all around me men were fingering amulets and charms.

Reserve battalions had formed up in good order on the hillside above the city. Field Marshal Wen Po's staff were gathered round a tent ringed by huge standards bearing the symbol of Heaven's Son.

We halted, awaiting the signal to attack. The silence from Pinang was unsettling. Where were the clouds of arrows and missiles all expected? Our dense ranks provided a perfect target. I turned to Mi Feng.

'Something's going on,' I whispered.

He did not reply. Trumpets began to bray. Then with a loud cheer, thousands of crossbowmen charged up our earthworks, taking positions with a clear view of the ramparts. Behind them, regiments of our best men crowded into the long ditch, readying hundreds of long ladders. We, too, waited in the vile trench where I had endured so many hours.

Still the rebels did not attack, as our crossbowmen took up aim. Then came disaster. All along the city walls, strange devices, in the shape of large bellows, reared ugly heads like the snouts of dragons. Instead of fire, they sprayed out vast quantities of oil over the dense lines of crossbowmen. Mi Feng clutched me, raising my shield above both our heads.

'Do not let the oil touch you!' he cried.

By now, more oil was falling on the regiments of swordsmen in the ditch. For a long second we seemed to draw in breath, then the cry went up: 'Naphtha! Naphtha!'

Flaming torches curved from the ramparts and the naphtha ignited with a loud whoosh of flame. Suddenly the earthworks were covered with burning men. The air grew thick with crossbow bolts and arrows directed from the city walls. Hollowed out gourds filled with burning powder landed among us. They needed no fuse to light them for everywhere our troops were on fire. Explosions echoed. The air swirled with smoke and an indescribable stench.

Ten thousand screams and wails! Above them rose the voices of our officers: *Attack! Attack!* Those who still lived and were unburned surged up the earthwork. I was carried with them, Mi Feng still clutching my arm. At the top I was greeted by an incredible sight: hundreds of our troops were rolling on the earth, trying to extinguish their burning clothes. Beside me, several soldiers were swept aside by a huge boulder, fired from the walls.

But Wang Tse's trickery had not ended. Out from the battlements swung long wooden arms, dangling barrels with smoking fuses from thin iron chains.

Mi Feng hurled me to the ground, dragging a corpse to shield us. At once we were buffeted by the roar and force of a huge explosion. For many minutes I was too dazed to move. My ears rang as if with a hundred gongs. I struggled to breathe.

'Pretend you're dead,' whispered Mi Feng in my ear. 'Pretend you're dead.'

I might as well have been. Through the smoke I glimpsed reckless men trying to place their siege ladders, casting away their lives for the sake of a gesture. The remnants of our forces were fleeing the accursed earthworks, large stretches of which had collapsed from the devilish force of Wang Tse's explosions, burying alive scores of the wounded.

'Now!' gasped Mi Feng.

He dragged me back down the steep side of the earthworks, slippery with mud, blood, smouldering naphtha, the limbs and faces of men crushed underfoot. We joined the general rout and, gasping for breath, regained safety.

I collapsed onto the stony earth, consumed by a thirst I have never known since. Wen Po's magnificent siege works, built at the cost of so many lives, lay in ruins, covered with blackened bodies. Cheering reached us from the city. Beside me, Mi Feng chuckled with relief.

'A few more to add to your lists,' he said. 'But not us! Not us!'

I scarcely noticed his callousness. For I wept, as did hundreds around me.

After the disaster we settled in for a long siege. By some miracle of influence at the Imperial Court, Wen Po was not recalled to atone for his failure. Perhaps his reports persuaded the Emperor that he faced an enemy armed with more than mortal weapons.

Field Marshal Wen Po resorted to the feeblest tactic in any siege – starving out the enemy. He had little choice. Our forces were exhausted, the best men dead or wounded. Perhaps Pinang was indeed hungry. If so, it brought us little comfort, for we were hardly better off ourselves. One cannot appease hunger by painting a cake.

His Excellency concentrated on ensuring nobody entered or left the city other than his hired spies or assassins. The intensity of his longing for Wang Tse's head can scarcely be imagined. Yet each attempt to infiltrate the city resulted in fresh corpses dangling from the city gates. Finally a dozen magicians were summoned from the capital. They could be seen discharging clouds of red or blue smoke in the direction of Pinang, or inscribing spells on pieces of coloured paper to avert magical assault. Feverish efforts were made to prevent Wang Tse from exploring our dispositions while invisible, as he was known to wander round our camps at will. Others consulted horoscopes and almanacs to reveal the weak points in the enemy's defences.

I sent a lengthy description of our losses back to the Finance Ministry, without commenting how they had occurred. This dispatch caused me great disquiet, as it would signal to Lord Xiao that I was still alive. There seemed no alternative. A direct order had been issued, stating our reports were too infrequent. To disobey a superior would expose me to severe penalties.

The eleventh month dragged into the twelfth. By now the land was dry. Even the blessed spring beside our hut shrank to a feeble trickle. Wind from the steppes whipped fiercely, blowing dust clouds which caked clothes and stuck in the throat. Everyone cursed Wang Tse for conjuring this new misfortune, although Mi Feng, usually the most superstitious of men, declared it was perfectly normal for the time of year. With the wind came unrelieved cold. If there had been any moisture in the air, snow and blizzards would have assailed us. For days on end we shivered in our hut, sick of each other's company. Sometimes I struggled to compose couplets, but the words would not come. Each failure cast me into depression, until I tried again, with the same result.

Our rations, though reduced, continued to be doled out from the heavily-guarded granary attached to His Excellency's headquarters. Yet I believed we would have succumbed to famine if Mi Feng had not persuaded me to spend my remaining strings of *cash* on food. Even in a siege, luxuries such as dried fish or pickled vegetables can be purchased at inordinate prices.

I shared what I could with the clerks, who loved me for it. Who does not wish to be loved? They addressed me as Young Father, and I liked that too. There was little else to enjoy.

Sometimes I considered appealing to Cousin Zhi for help, but the thought was distasteful. I could not help remembering my moment of weakness in his pavilion. Then I would blush and rail at the clerks for some imagined fault. He sent me no message, yet I suspected he was maintaining a baleful watch, awaiting his chance for revenge.

One bitter afternoon as New Year approached, we were lounging in our hut, awaiting the despondency darkness brought, when we heard marching feet. I looked up from peering at a favourite poem of Po Chu-i's in the dim light. I could scarcely read the characters. No matter: I knew the poem by heart. The clerks halted their noisy game of chequers. Mi Feng stopped sharpening his long, curved knife, an activity like meditation with him, then spat on the blade.

I sighed and put away my scroll. Before I could reach the door, Mi Feng blocked my way. He pointed at my belt. I picked up P'ei Ti's sword and followed him out. As usual, a sand storm whipped our faces. A small squad of guardsmen were carrying a message: attend His Excellency Field Marshal Wen Po, instantly.

Half an hour later, I was led by an orderly into a farmhouse used by His Excellency as a headquarters. Wen Po rested on a straight-backed chair beside a bronze tripod full of burning coals. Four guardsmen lined the walls, staring into empty space, as though on parade. Perhaps the rumours that Wen Po lived in constant fear of assassination were true. Perhaps he believed Wang Tse might use sorcery to enter his chambers invisibly. Perhaps, after so many defeats, he simply didn't like to sit alone. Certainly he looked tired and lonely, a map of Pinang unfurled across his lap. I thought it prudent to get on my knees.

He glanced up and coughed.

'Yun Cai,' he said. 'You may lift your head.'

I did as instructed. His face was troubled. Indeed he had aged since I last saw him.

'I have received another letter from my cousin, Lord Xiao, concerning you,' he said. 'It appears he is still gravely displeased with the frequency and quality of your reports. This surprised me, as I understand from my officers that you are diligent and send your dispatches regularly.'

I waited, unable to think of a reply not bearing the taint of insubordination.

'Well then,' he barked. 'Explain yourself!'

'I have strived to fulfil my duty,' I stammered.

Suddenly my eyes filled with tears.

'When you commanded me to accompany the troops, I did so without endangering the clerks under my care. I have strived, Your Excellency.'

His face softened.

'You are not quite what I was led to expect, Yun Cai. I expected a sly fop. But you are either very sly indeed, or neither. Is it true your father was the saviour of General Yueh Fei?'

'He was.'

I did not conceal my pride.

'Then your courage before the ramparts can be explained. Tell me, why did you take a barrel of water for the wounded each day? A strange action for a gentleman, surely?'

I shook my head.

'I do not know, sir. At the time I told myself it was to ensure a favourable rebirth, for I expected to perish. But now I think it was merely to be of use.'

'Of use? Quite so. One may be useful in many ways. Yet you gained honour from it. Was that your motive, to gain honour?'

'Excellency,' I said. 'All my life I have longed to be worthy of my Father's example.'

He nodded vigorously at this noble sentiment.

'All decent men dream of earning their parents' respect,' he said. 'Well, Yun Cai, you shall have other opportunities. Because you seem an honourable young man, I shall entrust you with a secret. Do you know how to keep your mouth shut, as well as how to ladle out water?'

'I believe so, Your Excellency,' I said.

'For your sake, let us hope so. In two weeks the New Year will fall. Now for some time a tunnel has been dug with great secrecy. It now approaches the city walls. I expect it to be finished at the height of the New Year festival. Then. . . Well, we shall see what happens. Of course, I have reported this to my superiors at court, which brings me to Lord Xiao's latest letter.'

I waited silently.

'It seems news of my tunnel has reached Lord Xiao,' he continued. 'And he has found time amidst the busy affairs of state to request that you accompany the initial sortie into the city. You must understand I can hardly refuse such a request.'

'No,' I said, tonelessly.

'He has even sent two. . . how can I put it? *Bodyguards*, to protect you when you are inside the city.'

The room was silent.

'There's no more I can do for you,' he said, coldly.

I bowed so my forehead was a few inches from the ground.

'I am grateful for the warning, Your Excellency.'

'Well, prepare yourself as you see fit.'

He watched me in his expressionless way.

'I hear you have powerful friends in the capital, who are making much of your presence here,' he said.

Again I was nonplussed.

'Your Excellency, I have no idea who these friends might be. I have always lived a secluded kind of life.'

'Well, it is all one. You are dismissed.'

I edged backwards and left. Mi Feng waited outside the headquarters, holding my horse. He looked at me quizzically.

'It is time you sharpened my sword,' I said.

His Excellency Wen Po's revelations filled me with confusion. I went about my daily tasks as though in an unpleasant dream. Day after day dedicated to sword practice, for the discipline I had learnt when studying could be applied in other ways. Although I did not reveal Wen Po's secret, Mi Feng sensed my fear and spared me none of his wisdom.

'If you are to fight, who will walk away? . . Watch his eyes, not his arm. . . If he wounds you, let it prick you on. Finish him, before you weaken. . .'

A hundred things to teach me the proper spirit for killing a man. Still I expected to disgrace myself when the trial came.

The clerks watched silently as we clashed. They thought I was dishonouring my position, for no true gentleman-scholar engages in crass military matters. That is what soldiers are for. My instinct was to agree with them.

Even in extremity a man will make much of the New Year. We had no wine, but could sweep and water the doorstep, hanging streamers coloured with precious red ink round the lintel. My clerks offered dishes of millet to the god of our hearth, instead of the usual vegetables and soya beans. He had protected us well and deserved great thanks. Then, while they played chequers or word games, I sorted through a pile of old scrolls, trying to set everything in order for my successor. I thought it unlikely I would live to see the morning.

The clerks must have sensed my mood, for frequently they begged me to honour them by joining their game. I could not. There seemed too little time. But I sent out Mi Feng with the last of my strings of *cash* to buy whatever could be found to raise our spirits. While we waited, I turned to the robes and hat hanging by the door. My predecessor as Bureau Chief had been a large man if his robes were any guide. They hung heavily as though padded. No one had touched them since his death; out of respect, certainly, but also because his robes acted as a kind of gate god, preventing the entry of demons.

The previous chief had been known as a pious, honest man, his only fault being a fanatical adherence to rules which he interpreted in the narrowest way, regardless of the consequences to himself or others.

It is usual to clean or replace the images of the gate gods at New Year, so I felt no hesitation in giving his robes a dusting. As soon as I took hold of them, something felt wrong. They were too heavy. Curious now, I rummaged in the folds of cloth, discovering a large secret pocket in the lining. Inside were three tightly rolled scrolls, each no more than a palm's length. He had obviously thought them valuable, for they were protected by a thin leather bag.

I took the scrolls outside and perused them in the dwindling afternoon light. I expected a religious text, or perhaps an anthology of writings he found inspiring. But all three contained the same thing: column after column of figures accompanied by notes written in what appeared to be a kind of code, for they made no sense otherwise. Strange documents for a man to hide upon his person. I recalled that my predecessor had been banished to Pinang for offending Lord Xiao over a question of suspect accounts. It seemed probable the scrolls were relevant to that affair.

I was distracted from further speculation by Mi Feng. He returned with pickled vegetables and steamed buns, all he had been able to buy for a sum which would have hired an entire banqueting hall in the capital. I did not care to speculate what meat the buns contained. Yet we feasted as best we could, toasting the New Year with cups of water from our trickling spring. For an hour all was gaiety – a little food is like a barrel of wine to a hungry man – and then we lolled around the hearth, where a few scraps of scavenged wood and dried horse dung smouldered. All the time I was waiting for a summons. His Excellency Wen Po had taught me what the New Year festival would bring.

My waiting ended early in the evening, with a loud knock on the wooden door.

'Yun Cai! Message for Yun Cai!'

I rose and turned to the clerks.

'Stay here until I return,' I said. 'And if I do not come back, then carry on as you have been taught.'

Before they could reply, I stepped out into the night, buckling P'ei Ti's sword to my belt. I was in no mood to explain myself. In any case, I had sworn not to mention Wen Po's secret tunnel to a living soul.

A single rider waited in the gloom, his horse's breath steaming.

'You must accompany me to the Glorious Dragon Encampment at once,' he said. 'That is all my message.'

I nodded. Before I could depart, a rough hand held my arm.

'Where are you going?' asked Mi Feng.

'I have promised not to reveal that,' I said. 'Go back inside, Mi Feng. Sleep well and wish me luck. You have been more than a servant to me.'

I hesitated.

'Mi Feng, despite the gulf between us, and without doubt it is considerable, I have come to trust you as a friend.'

He hand stayed on my arm.

'I will go with you,' he said.

'But you have done enough,' I protested. 'No, I would not have your death on my conscience.'

The messenger rattled his bridle impatiently.

'You are in danger,' said Mi Feng, accusingly. 'And you wish to leave me behind!'

'Believe me, it is for your own good.'

'My own good!' he replied. 'It is I, Mi Feng, who decides what is for my own good! You are in danger, and that is enough for one like me.'

Honour takes many forms. Always its weakness is wounded pride. He disappeared inside the hut and I motioned to the messenger to wait. In a moment Mi Feng reappeared, carrying his long knife and bow.

So I did not go alone to the Glorious Dragon Encampment. Within a few short hours I was glad of it.

We travelled right round the besieged city, past camps where soldiers celebrated New Year with wrestling matches and mournful songs, or capered in the flickering red light of bonfires to the solemn beat of war-drums, the shrill encouragement of flutes. Flags fluttered in the cold night air; artillery companies used precious gunpowder for firecrackers.

The Glorious Dragon Encampment was especially festive. Frantic lion dances were cheered by hordes of troops. Acrobats performed dazzling leaps, musicians played at full pelt – for even common soldiers possess talents their betters can only hire. But I noticed neat piles of weapons marked out by banners bearing the colours of particular companies, guarded by officers and sergeants. Within minutes the revelling soldiers could be marshalled for battle, and this was clearly Wen Po's intention.

Pinang, despite the New Year, lay in darkness. Only round the Prefect's residence, where Wang Tse had set up his court, might one glimpse light and fireworks. What he and his followers had to celebrate, I could not imagine. It was hardly likely our forces would melt away with the New Year and the coming of spring. Unless the rumours were true of an infernal alliance between Wang Tse and the Kin barbarians to the north, the rebellion seemed doomed. Yet those who are advised by demons think differently from ordinary men. They have an eye on their own glory, their place in history, and seldom hesitate to let others bear the cost.

Our guide led us to a fenced enclosure at the back of the encampment, concealed by earthworks. Here no lights burned, and our noise was masked by revelry from the camp. Guards dressed in black waved us through to a hidden courtyard within the earthen walls. Hundreds of men sat in eerie silence on the ground, swords across their knees. Many had long ropes coiled round their bodies.

'Over there,' whispered our guide.

We picked a way through the waiting troops to a small group of officers. I bowed respectfully, for among them were several of Wen Po's highest commanders. And someone else, too, dressed in a tight suit of black silk: Cousin Zhi. He waved me over, and said in a low voice:

'Well, Cousin, this is a little different from our last meeting.'

'Thankfully,' I replied.

His eyes glittered in the darkness.

'You have been assigned a bodyguard of two men,' he said. 'But such is my regard for you, I've added another pair from my own Penal Battalion.'

I said nothing.

'Who is that rough-looking fellow with you?' he asked, sharply.

'Just a servant.'

'You will not need a servant where you are going,' he said.

'Where exactly is that?' I asked.

Cousin Zhi smiled and pointed down at the earth. The scent of sandalwood and musk from his perfume filled my nostrils.

'You will see soon enough – and marvel! I have presented a miracle of engineering to His Excellency, and before the New Year is out, I shall be rewarded with the title of Sub-prefect. Think of that while you can, Yun Cai. You should have accepted my offer of help.'

I shook my head.

'When the King of the Infernal Regions comes to weigh our souls,' I said. 'It is you who will remember this night. And then you will howl with despair.'

He sniffed contemptuously.

'Foolish old stories to scare children into obedience! Farewell, Cousin.'

He motioned to four burly figures beside him. We were led away and curtly ordered to sit with our 'bodyguard' around us. I could see Mi Feng examining them closely. He bent forward and murmured, like a breath of wind in my ear: 'These men are the danger you fear?'

I nodded. A salvo of firecrackers in the neighbouring camp allowed him to whisper unheard.

'When the time comes, do exactly as I say.'

He settled back on his haunches and began to hum a low tune. Above us the moon danced between flowing clouds. At last an order circulated among the men.

'Gags! Gag your neighbour!'

Crude hands took hold of my head. In a moment, a stick of bamboo wrapped in cloth stopped the possibility of speech. I gasped to breathe. More whispered commands from the officers: *Now! Now!*

Squad after squad of men were lining up to creep into a black hole in the earth. We followed and found ourselves in a narrow earthen tunnel, without light of any sort. My only way forward was to clutch the back of the man in front, and be clutched in my turn by the man behind. My head reeled. I struggled with a desire to snatch the gag from my mouth and moan or scream, to fight a way back through the river of men behind me, out to the clean air. The tunnel was foul. Those who had dug it had abandoned their faeces where it lay. I could hardly breathe. I closed my eyes, useless in the dark, and shuffled along, almost bent double, spine and legs aching. Yet one could not pause to rest.

The tunnel gradually descended, then levelled out, and now small guttering candles appeared every dozen or so yards, like glow worms guiding us forward. Timber props held up the roof, and I dared not consider the tons of earth pressing down. Every so often a hand or leg stuck out from the earthen wall, proof that many miners had perished to dig this hell.

How long may a nightmare last? As long as its terror grips you. So it might be said that particular nightmare has never ended, for whenever my breath is short, or I feel trapped in a narrow space, I am back in Wen Po's tunnel. Yet somehow it came to an end and I stumbled out, covered in dirt and filth, into a well-tended garden.

I sucked in huge lungfuls of air, too dazed to look around. When I could take in my surroundings, I discovered we had emerged ten feet or so inside the city walls. No sounds of fighting. Dark figures swarmed along the battlements, taking up positions and lowering ropes. We had achieved complete surprise, the few guards on the wall having been quickly dispatched. Officers stood round the entrance to the tunnel, directing men to their positions. When they saw myself and Mi Feng emerge, evidently civilians, followed by our ruffianly bodyguards, they were taken aback.

'Over there,' whispered a young officer. 'By the wall. And if you get in the way or make a noise, you'll pay with your tongues.'

We hurried to do as directed. For the first time I got a proper glimpse of the men Lord Xiao and Cousin Zhi had assigned to take care of us. They seemed ordinary enough. Each was armed with a sword and knife. If they were frightened, they showed no sign. I wanted to pretend to myself they might be what they seemed, allies, protectors, but only for a moment. I noticed that Mi Feng had boldly positioned himself so they did not surround us, and I copied his example.

Moments crawled. I examined the abacus strapped across my chest, the satchel of paper and ink hanging from my belt.

Foolish talismans. Yet the touch of paper gave me a kind of strength. Mi Feng crouched beside me, his hand on the hilt of his knife. He seemed to think we were safe here, sheltered by the city walls, dozens of soldiers all around us. Any attack against us would have many witnesses. Then a cry went up. Our troops had been discovered. At once the sound of clashing swords echoed through the night air. Within minutes trumpets were sounding the alarm all around Pinang. The battle had commenced.

How soon Wang Tse mustered his forces! The fighting in the district by the wall continued through the long hours of the night. More and more of our troops were scaling the ramparts, fanning out into the streets, until a wide bridge had been formed into the heart of Pinang. Still we waited in the garden by the ramparts.

My bodyguard sat patiently. Their stillness filled me with dread. These were not inexperienced men. When they decided the time was right, I would join a long, secret list. The man nearest to me chewed continuously on a dark root I did not recognise, his eyelids fluttering. I became aware Mi Feng was watching him from the corner of his eyes. He nudged me as a commotion broke out to our left. A small group of Wang Tse's rebels were being pursued by our troops into the garden. He leapt to his feet and drew his long knife.

'Rebels!' he bellowed.

Instinctively, our bodyguards also rose, turning in the direction of the fight. Mi Feng shoved the root-chewer so hard he fell across his comrades, throwing them in confusion.

'Run!' he cried, streaking off towards the dark opening of an alleyway.

I followed with a fleetness I scarcely imagined possible. There was no pursuit. The rebels had run straight into our bodyguards. I heard the sound of clashing swords and cries behind us.

The alleyway terminated in a flimsy wooden door, for this was a poor area of town. The sickle moon lit the sky between the houses. Mi Feng applied a sharp boot and the door broke inwards. Inside the single room, illuminated by a small fire and a few coloured lanterns to celebrate the New Year, a family cowered.

In a fluid motion, Mi Feng sank to one knee and drew back an arrow. For a long moment we waited, the family whimpering behind us, then our pursuers charged into the alley. Straight away he loosed. One arrow, then another. There was a high-pitched scream, the sound of something heavy falling.

'Quickly!' he hissed, slamming shut the door and barricading it with a table.

He ran to the front door, for we had entered by the rear, and cautiously opened it.

'Draw your sword like a man!' he spat.

I hastily obeyed, feeling foolish with the weapon in my hand. Mi Feng peered out of the front door. A narrow, silent street lay before us.

'Get out!' he commanded the family, who were still cowering.

They scrambled past us into the street, the children wailing pitifully. A loud crash shook the barricaded back door.

'We'll do the last thing they expect,' he whispered in my ear.

He was so calm! And furious at the same time. It lent me courage.

'What shall we do?' I stuttered.

He grasped my arm and met my eye.

'Fight,' he said.

He must have seen my fear, for he laughed.

'Fight, like your father,' he said. 'Then we'll gather their heads.'

The back door splintered open and the first of our enemies rushed through. He was met by a twang from Mi Feng's bow.

For a second the man carried on, clutching the shaft in his throat, then fell with a gurgle and rolled on the floor, scrabbling at the broken arrow shaft. The two remaining men charged through, towards the front entrance, where we waited.

Mi Feng's plan was obvious. Only one of our opponents could emerge at a time. But they were not fools. Instead of rushing onto our swords, everything went still inside the house. I could hear the sound of fighting in nearby streets, screaming children, the panting of our breath.

Finally a chair flew through the doorway, making us duck aside, and they surged after it onto the street. Instantly, we were fighting, Mi Feng with his long curved knife, me with P'ei Ti's sword. I had no time to think of my servant. My entire self was concentrated on the opponent before me. Time slows at such crises. Your life like a spinning mirror, ready to fall one way or the other, to break or remain intact. Thought is no longer a virtue, what matters is cutting and parrying.

At once it became obvious I was outmatched. I faced the root-chewer, and he beat back my sword effortlessly, taunting me as he did so. He found me a kind of sport. Then he struck at my chest and I leapt back. The blade struck the abacus strapped across my breast and by some miracle, some absurd chance of war, the tip of his sword caught in the rows of beads. I was merely buffeted by the blow, my skin scratched not pierced. He tried to withdraw his sword but it had stuck.

With a desperate scream, I lunged P'ei Ti's sword. I'm sure I aimed for his stomach. Instead the blow fell on his groin. It didn't matter. His startled grunt tore the night air. He staggered back with a high-pitched whine, dropping his sword and clutching his wound. I stepped towards him and hesitated. Enough had been done. He could hardly harm me now. He was gasping, staring at me through wide eyes, begging wordlessly for mercy. I lowered my sword. Then, gripped by fury, I struck him with all my strength across the neck so that he crumpled, his head at a strange angle.

When I finally took my eyes from his corpse, I saw Mi Feng bending over the body of his opponent.

'No!' I cried.

For he was in the process of removing the man's head. Mi Feng rose reluctantly.

'Better make sure of the others,' he muttered, disappearing back through the house. When he came back his long knife glistened.

All night the fighting continued. A hundred small battles fought in the dark. Capture a house, kill its defenders, then be driven back in your turn, and capture the house once again. Wang Tse's rebels fought with the desperation of doomed men. The streets filled with the fallen. Near dawn it seemed we might be forced out of the city when the sorcerer broke our ranks with a charge of horses and bullocks maddened by firecrackers tied to their tails. Finally superior numbers told, the beasts were cut down amidst scores of crumpled men, and a desperate charge of our spearmen drove the rebels back.

Somehow we found our way back to the garden by the ramparts. I set up my shattered abacus and a sheet of paper, P'ei Ti's sword thrust in the earth beside me. By this means I hoped to prove my official status, and perhaps it worked, for we remained unmolested until the first rays of a red dawn lit the eastern horizon.

I slept for an hour, my head on Mi Feng's shoulder. We were like two weary brothers propped against each other. He, at least, seemed proud. Killing three enemies in a single night proved him a formidable man.

I, too, should have felt only relief. Yet how my heart fluttered and ached! The man I had once been lay among the dead assassins. On my hands and clothes, droplets of blood. I felt unclean. If I was to die then and there, I had no doubt my rebirth would take the form of a wolf or an ever-hungry stoat or cold-eyed bear.

By late morning, Pinang had been subdued. Our entire army thronged the city.

One may justify what followed, I suppose. Perhaps one could cite the anger and excitement of troops crazed by months of defeat, suddenly drunk on victory. Or one could argue Heaven was taking its just revenge on the rebels for trafficking with demons. Perhaps one might shrug and say: well, such things happen in war. I cannot justify what I saw. Families dragged from their houses, crying out for mercy.

Naturally the women and girls received special treatment, yet all ended up the same way, littering the streets. Blood has a peculiar, pervasive stench, oddly reminiscent of iron. Many have commented that the officers lost control of their men. That was true in some cases. But I witnessed officers engaged in foul acts, little better than Jurchen or Mongols off the leash. By midday the slaughter abated and we were left to behold the consequences of victory. It is little wonder the phrase, *Pinanging a town*, has entered our language.

I left the Western Gate with Mi Feng by my side and climbed wearily up the hillside to our hut. It was deserted, the clerks having descended to the city, no doubt hoping for a share of the loot. The encampments around us, once so crowded, were also empty. Everyone was in the city. Yet we found a horseman waiting outside our hut, splendidly attired and equipped. Both mount and rider seemed exhausted. He came alive at the sight of me and stepped forward eagerly.

'Where may I find Yun Cai?' he demanded. 'I have been told he dwells here.'

I could not blame him for mistaking what I was. I doubted that question myself.

'Is Yun Cai in the city?' he asked.

Mi Feng and I regarded him silently.

'I have ridden all the way from the capital with an urgent message for the Honourable Yun Cai! Where may I find that gentleman?' he asked, desperately. 'My message cannot be delayed.'

'You have found him,' I said.

He looked at me suspiciously.

'Are *you* Yun Cai?'

'I am what's left of him.'

Something in my tone must have held authority. He advanced towards me, his hand on the hilt of his sword. Mi Feng and I reached for our own.

Then he sank on one knee and extracted a scroll from his messenger's satchel, and presented it. He seemed quite moved by the moment. Heaven knows what he had travelled through to deliver this message.

'Who is it from?' I asked, harshly. 'Of course! Lord Xiao has fresh duties for me! Well, my friend, you can ride back the way you came and tell him I resign my position. My government service is at an end.'

He looked up at me, puzzled.

'My message is not from Lord Xiao,' he said.

I waited, looking past him to the hut. Nothing seemed important. I simply longed to sleep. Again he proffered the scroll. I turned away in disgust.

'You ought to read it, sir,' said Mi Feng.

'I don't care to,' I replied.

'Come now, sir,' Mi Feng said, as though to a child. 'You are just weary.'

'I don't want to read it,' I replied, peevishly. 'And I won't!'

My servant frowned, stepped forward and plucked the scroll from the messenger's hands. Then he placed it in my own and stalked off to the hut. The door rattled on its hinges behind him. There seemed no point in refusing a second scroll the messenger also offered.

I studied the first letter, perched on a rock. It read as follows:

Dearest,
I write in the same room as another dear friend of yours. Though you are far away, you are not forgotten. Who is that friend? Of course, you can guess. It is none other than P'ei Ti, who has laboured ceaselessly on your behalf since the cruel hour of your exile. I will say no more about him, for I know he wishes to send a message himself.

Dearest Love, how I have thought of you each day since you went away! Morning finds me desolate. And so it is at evening. I cannot forget what you have sacrificed for me. The memory of your affection makes me feel constantly ashamed. I am afraid to be unworthy of it. Yet, as you shall hear, I have used the little power at my disposal to hasten the day of your return. If I was a man, your enemies would soon regret what they have done!

My poor head is all a flurry. I have been assured I can write as much as I like, and that it shall be delivered into your own hands. Naturally, there is a price to pay. Yet I am willing to pay anything for your dear sake, and when the time comes you must try to understand.

None of this probably makes sense. I have chosen to write as I think. As though I could talk to you in the same room. Are you not proud of the way my writing has improved? I have hired a tutor and spend an hour each day copying out difficult characters.

But I must be sensible. I have important news and do not know how to begin. Since you left the capital a great deal has occurred.

Are you aware how many secret friends you possess? I suspect not. Soon after you left a great, important man – P'ei Ti tells me I must not write down his name in case this letter falls into bad hands – has taken up your case, accusing Lord Xiao of abusing his power. P'ei Ti assures me it is safe to mention Lord Xiao's name, so do not be alarmed, because all this is well-known. This great man, who I cannot name, asked for all the details and, for your dear sake, I held nothing back. It was a great honour for me, as you can imagine. I received many engagements from this great man's friends as a result.

His complaint is that Lord Xiao is misusing the Emperor's funds to pay for a petty revenge. You would be amazed to hear that even common people are offended by your exile because of your poems, which they love. So you may see that Lord Xiao's reputation has suffered. I am told there is much more to this than meets the eye. P'ei Ti comprehends it all. Perhaps he will explain when he writes.

We are not entirely without news of you, dearest Yun Cai! The great man I have mentioned receives regular reports of the siege against the sorcerer. Through him I heard how you took barrels of water to slake the thirst of the wounded. You cannot imagine my pride. I long to prove it to you.

How is your health? I can scarcely imagine your sufferings. This pains me whenever I think of you. When you return I shall hire a dozen cooks to make you fat again, and twenty tailors to dress you in the finest silks so you may be warm, and a hundred musicians to heal your spirit. I shall dress in any way which delights you and learn every song you care to hear. At night I shall wrap you in my arms beneath the thickest quilts so you may never feel cold again. Do you think these promises mere talk? Only come back and you'll find out.

Just come back, and do not let the enemy scratch your sweet body. How I hate them! Yet I know you are always brave.

Before I finish my letter, I have strange news. I would

hesitate to mention it, except I know you have shown your servant, Mi Feng, great trust. I must tell you that my maid is bearing his child. Will it displease you to hear that I have not dismissed her? I believe you would want that, for you are always kind and generous. I long to know if you think I have done wrong.

So, my dear one, I must finish. P'ei Ti tells me the messenger waits, ready to depart at once. I do not wish to stop writing these words. I could talk to you all afternoon, and never stop! That blessed hour will come. You must believe that, beloved Yun Cai.

Your Doting Friend, Su Lin.

Such a letter should have brought tears to my eyes. Yet I read it dully, incapable of feeling. Then I opened the second scroll, which was much briefer and more elegantly written:

Yun Cai,

It is unsafe for me to say much. When you return, you shall find conditions more favourable than you imagined possible on that wretched morning when you departed through the Gate of Eternal Rectitude. If I was a hero of old I would resign my office and gallop north to aid you. But my oldest friend knows what I am – and what I am not. Rest assured I strive on your behalf using the means I know best. The capital is a dull place without you.

Your old friend, P'ei Ti.

I staggered to my bed and lay down, the scrolls clutched to my chest, as though they might cancel out all previous misfortune. It was too late for that. Yet their words countered hellish images of Pinang, commencing the process by which all men reconcile themselves to terrible things. On the other side of the room Mi Feng was already snoring.

'Wake up! You must not sleep any longer.'

I moaned pitifully in the hope he would go away.

'Sir! Wake up! This is no time to sleep.'

'It doesn't matter,' I mumbled. 'Nothing matters.'

I was shaken vigorously and my eyes jerked open. Naturally, it was Mi Feng, showing scant regard for my person. Any protest was stilled by the look of pure alarm on his face.

'You must see this,' he said, and hurried out of the hut.

The pale light seeping through the door spoke of dawn. Outside I could hear voices raised in argument. Their tone infected me with fear. I scrambled from my pile of blankets and stepped outside.

The Bureau of Fallen Heroes had gathered near the entrance, squabbling furiously. Each of my clerks clutched items looted from the fallen city. One held a gilded birdcage containing a sorry-looking sparrow. Another a bundle of silken clothes. The third, less fortunate than his fellows, had a young girl attached to his wrist by a cord. None seemed particularly pleased with their spoils. Mi Feng stood alone, staring across the steppes to the north, where the Silk Road flowed to the edge of the world. I followed his gaze.

'What is that?' I asked. 'A dust storm?'

The clerks became aware of my presence and apprehensively sank to their knees. I ignored them.

'What is that?' I demanded, addressing Mi Feng.

The dust-cloud formed a line, several *li* wide.

'It is an army,' he said, simply. 'See! There is the centre, and on either side, slightly forward of the main force, are its wings.'

Mi Feng continued to look north like a hawk.

At once the truth struck me. For months we had heard rumours from captured prisoners that Wang Tse had appealed to the Kin Emperor for help. It is not the kind of possibility one cares to consider too deeply. The Kin were our foremost enemy then, as now. Indeed, only the heroism of the great Yueh Fei, he whose life my father had saved, had prevented their conquest of all China a generation before. Yet the threat had never abated. Wherever we were weak, one might find the Kin eager to seek an advantage.

For many years they had concentrated on the eastern seaboard, striving to conquer the Chiangnan. To find them so far to the north-west defied all reasonable foresight. Yet had not Sun Tzu written long ago in *The Art of War*: 'Attack the enemy where he is unprepared, and appear where you are not expected.' And certainly our army had been enfeebled by its winter siege. Why should they not anticipate an easy victory? The reward, too, was worthy of risk. Pinang would grant them control of the Silk Road and its vast revenues. The Emperor would be obliged to pay heavy tribute to keep the trade flowing, thereby humiliating and weakening us further.

All these thoughts crossed my mind. My feelings were less orderly – like the clerks, and even, I suspect, Mi Feng, whose blood generally resembled ice-broth, I panicked.

'This is merely a reconnaissance party,' I declared, quite willing to deny the evidence of my eyes.

We had suffered too much hardship to deserve more. No one had seriously doubted our final victory over Wang Tse, despite his alliance with demons. The only question was its ruinous cost. But the Golden Army of the Kin struck fear in all sober hearts. Inexperienced in war as I was, I knew the dust-cloud on the horizon could not be explained by infantry, but only by waves of Kin cavalry, famed for wild, inexorable charges. And their contempt for prisoners.

Meanwhile streams of our men, many exhausted by drink and fighting, were hurrying back to their encampments with armfuls of loot.

'Surely they should be taking up position to the north,'I said. 'Or manning the ramparts. Mi Feng, what is happening?'

He glowered at me.

'Do you wish to discuss strategy?' he said. 'Well then, I see it like this. Either we run for it or fight. If we get trapped in Pinang, we're done for.'

The prospect of changing from besieger to besieged unnerved me. The city was denuded of supplies. We had no time to drag our artillery inside the walls. Pinang would become a cage from which few might walk away, except as slaves.

'As for me,' he said. 'I'd sooner run for it.'

Would Field Marshal Wen Po think the same way? His choices were stark. Attempt to gather the army and fight before the ramparts, or abandon the city which had so grievously reduced his reputation as a general. Perhaps the choice had already been made for him. When the illusion of power dissolves, one often glimpses a frightened, ordinary man beneath.

I paced up and down, uncertain where my duty lay. One thing, at least, was clear. I turned to the clerk with the girl attached to his wrist. It was the young, insolent fellow and I was glad for a chance to punish someone. I struck him across the face so hard that he staggered.

'We are liberators, not barbarians raiding for slaves!' I admonished. 'You, my friend, need to take this girl back to her family.'

She crouched on the ground, staring around her, no more than twelve years old. I got on my knees beside her.

'What is your name?' I asked.

She peeped up at me, shivering in the harsh wind. I ordered the second clerk to pass over the silks he had looted and wrapped them round her.

'We are going to take you back to your family, little princess,' I cooed.

I must have made a ridiculous sight, for Mi Feng snorted.

'What is your name?' I repeated.

She told me. I forget what it was. Eventually I teased out where she lived, all the while glancing fearfully at the approaching dust cloud. There was no time for this! I slung her on the back of our faithful pony and cantered down the hillside through soldiers struggling to turn our artillery in the direction of the Kin. Outside the city gates, I lost my nerve. Brusquely I tried to set her down, yet she clung to me.

'Take me with you!' she begged, pitifully. 'Take me with you!'

I shook her off. Indeed I was desperate to rid myself of her and return to the hut.

'Find your family,' I ordered.

Then I rode away.

What became of her I can scarcely imagine. Did she find her family still alive where so many had been put to the sword? It is little comfort to tell myself I acted for the best. Perhaps my kindness caused miseries she would otherwise have avoided. Who can know? They say no good deed ever goes unpunished. One day I may chance upon her spirit in the Infernal Regions, and if she points accusingly at me across the Lake of Ghosts, I will know for sure.

By the time I had whipped my horse back to the hillside, those regiments capable of order were forming up beyond their camps. Trumpets blared a medley of confused commands.

I was about a *li* from the hut when fresh misfortune struck. My pony sank a hoof in one of the many holes dug by rodents on the slopes, and I was thrown. The pony stumbled, rolling over itself. I was lucky not to be crushed. I lay winded on the hard ground, whooping for air. When I finally stumbled to my feet no bones were broken – unlike the poor pony. It lay on the ground slavering, a foreleg snapped, eyeballs rolling in pain. I should have ended its misery at once – another reproach – instead I scrambled up the path to where Mi Feng waited. He was angry.

'I hope the girl was worth it,' he snapped. 'Now we haven't got a horse. And look!'

Lines of Kin cavalry were recognisable now, filling the horizon. I could even see the glint of sun on steel. Behind them, a long way behind, thousands of infantry advanced across the plain.

Would my father have stayed to fight? Probably. I entered the hut and gathered my meagre possessions. The clerks had already fled, only Mi Feng and I remained of the Bureau of Fallen Heroes. I was about to leave the hut forever when I recalled the three, tightly rolled scrolls I had discovered in my predecessor's robes, and stuffed them into a satchel.

Mi Feng waited impatiently outside. The trumpets were sounding a general retreat.

It seemed the only way. Pinang was lost to us. Perhaps that is why Wen Po decided the city should burn, for plumes of smoke were rising from every district, scenting the air with ash, forming dense, billowing clouds. A good strategy. Smoke would delay the Kin and mask our depleted numbers. Perhaps Wen Po could not bear the thought they might possess what he had lost. Fires leapt from house to house, and there was a low rumbling, as wooden buildings collapsed in on themselves. The surviving population were rushing from the gates and gathering in ditches below the ramparts. I hoped the girl was among them.

Of course we had no idea what to do. So we followed the retreating army, clutching our possessions. Now I felt the loss of that horse. We stumbled among a crowd of soldiers, choking on smoke, until we found ourselves south of the city, before the wide pass leading home. Here, Wen Po had decided to take a stand. We joined a dense river of men, straggling through the marshy ground, glancing fearfully over our shoulders.

I cannot imagine what rigour it took to halt the army and turn it around. But halt it did, to await the Golden Army of the Kin. I crouched beside a huge boulder and shivered, trying to calm the beating of my heart. My forehead and hair were damp with sweat. Mi Feng sat beside me.

'We should not stop here,' he said, motioning towards the mountain pass. 'That is the way to safety.'

I was too exhausted to take another step. The fall from my horse had weakened me more than I cared to admit. Besides, I was hungry and thirsty. A whole day of frightfulness had passed since my last solid meal. Surely it was safe to rest for a while. Marshy ground lay between us and the enemy, confounding their ability to charge.

'Leave me,' I said. 'I cannot go on.'

I expected Mi Feng to berate me. Instead, he sighed.

'As you wish.'

Yet he did not move. So I caught my breath, while thousand upon thousand of Kin horsemen flowed round the city walls, entering the fog of smoke still pouring from Pinang. Meanwhile Wen Po steadied his lines of troops, a pitiful remnant of the force which had marched out six months before. The terrain was entirely in our favour, but at the sight of the advancing cavalry, I began to doubt.

'Let us climb higher up the pass,' I said, and Mi Feng was only too willing.

A short way up the path several guardsmen stopped us.

'Get back into position!' roared a sergeant.

I blinked at him. For a moment I felt the rage of a thwarted child. Then, without thinking, as a child quite artlessly plays a role to get what it wants, I reached into my bag and extracted the first scroll to hand. Su Lin's letter, bound in sandalwood and filigree silver. Certainly it looked impressive. I waved it. The sergeant scowled and I was sure he would beat us back down the track to join one of the miserable regiments waiting in line.

'Get me a horse, sergeant! I have lost my horse! I have a vital communication for His Excellency Wen Po's cousin, the illustrious Lord Xiao! You must find a horse for me!'

All around us, fleeing soldiers were being driven back by snapping bullwhips.

'His Excellency's cousin?' said the sergeant. 'But I am ordered to turn everyone back, sir.'

That 'sir' revealed his weakness. I leapt on it.

'What is your name and regiment?' I demanded, waving the scroll as though I might stuff it down his throat. 'You will answer to His Excellency for this delay, damn you!'

I must have been convincing. I had even convinced myself!

'Let them through!' he ordered, and we wasted no time, climbing up the pass until we joined a horde of straggling men, conscripted labourers for the most part and many other civilians who accompanied the army. The sound of fighting below made us turn.

It was the kind of sight one never forgets. Wen Po had mustered at least ten thousand men. They formed interlocking lines, blocking the Kin cavalry's progress to the pass. Yet they were outnumbered two to one by the advancing horsemen. Onwards they cantered, mounted archers at the front, spreading to outflank our infantry. Then the first wave of armoured cavalry charged into a shower of crossbow bolts. Their losses must have been dreadful, for they halted and wheeled away. Then a second wave attacked, riding over their fallen comrades. And a third. Finally they overwhelmed our lines of infantry and all hope of an orderly retreat died.

'Flee!' said Mi Feng.

Why he said it, I do not know. I was already several paces ahead of him.

Even uphill a man on foot is soon outstripped by a horseman. As we ran our progress was impeded by a column of the retreating army. All dignity lost, we cursed and shoved each other aside, caring only for our own skins. For several *li* the enemy did not attack us, as they regrouped their forces. We struggled up the broad pass in our thousands, following the ancient Silk Road. Then a cry went up: *Kin! Kin!*

Scores of horsemen were riding along the bare slopes beside the road, loosing flights of arrows. They could hardly miss. Mi Feng manoeuvred me into the centre of our retreating column. On the edges, dozens fell, arrows piercing their bodies. We had no means to fight back.

Up, up the pass we surged until the steep valley narrowed. In the distance I glimpsed the highest point of the pass, protected by an ancient rampart. If we could reach there we might be safe, for the cavalry, however numerous, could not ride beyond. Even a hundred determined men could hold such a stronghold. Still the arrows fell among us. I trampled the bodies of wounded men in my eagerness to escape.

Here the road was elevated by a ravine on one side. We were but a *li* from the ramparts. I found myself beside a bobbing litter. Within, clutching the sides in sheer terror, rode Cousin Zhi. He was carried by six of his conscripted labourers. I had never seen such exhausted men. They were whipped on by a handful of white-uniformed guards from the Penal Battalion. At first I thought he might not notice me. Then he cried out and summoned the leader of the soldiers.

Who knows exactly what he said. I can only imagine his motive for what followed. Indeed, I have considered it many times. I believe he knew Lord Xiao desired my head. Perhaps he hoped to trade my life for a Sub-prefect's position. Perhaps he simply detested me. Whatever the reason, he ordered the soldiers to apprehend me and I can hear his voice now: 'Get him! That one, yes, that one! A thousand *cash* for whoever throws him to the barbarians!' He was beside himself.

The soldiers clutched at me and I fled through crowds up the high, narrow road. In that moment Cousin Zhi's litter had lost its bodyguard. Perhaps he realised his folly. I heard him crying: 'Come back! Come back!'

At last unguarded, the peasants carrying his litter lurched to the edge of the road and tipped it over into the ravine. At the fall of their master, the soldiers halted, trying to fight a way back to him. A futile effort. Like us, they were carried forward by the retreating column.

I reached a bend in the road, and paused.

What I saw then, I cannot forget.

Cousin Zhi's litter rolled down the steep side of the road, round and round, with him shrieking inside. At last it came to rest, upside down. Half a dozen mounted archers broke away from their main formation and galloped up. They leapt off their horses, dragging Zhi from his litter until he lay pleading on the ground before them. He must have seemed a gorgeous, delicate creature, dressed in the finest silks, rattling with jade ornaments. I knew my father would have drawn his sword and rushed to save his cousin. Yet I turned away like a coward. The last glimpse I had of him – bare white legs waving as they tore his silks aside – and then I was swept away up the road. Cousin Zhi had gone.

A fresh cloud of arrows filled the air. I had waded unharmed through naphtha and crossbow bolts on Wen Po's earthworks. I had even survived the superior swordsmanship of a hired assassin. Now the last thread of my luck snapped. An arrow smashed into my shoulder, knocking me to the ground. The blow emptied me of breath, and in the moment before I fainted, I felt heavy feet trampling my chest. I regained consciousness almost instantly and found Mi Feng dragging me to the side of the road. Hot tongs of agony squeezed my right arm and shoulder.

For a while we crouched in the dirt, fearful of more arrows. Then somehow, in an indescribable weariness of pain and shock, I stumbled the short distance to our fortifications.

Beyond the ramparts at the head of the narrow pass we finally found rest. As the last dregs of our army streamed through the gate the mounted archers of the Kin withdrew, their work accomplished. No fresh waves of attackers rode towards us. We had been washed onto an island by the raging torrent.

Hours passed, and it seemed the Kin might be satisfied with the capture of Pinang. Certainly no attempts were made that day, or afterwards, to penetrate further into the Middle Kingdom. In this they showed moderation, not entirely characteristic, yet eminently wise. The Silk Road was secure. Our mountainous frontier was dangerous terrain for an army whose strength lay in wild cavalry charges. And Wen Po's victory over Wang Tse had delivered them a great prize, burned and ruined as Pinang was, for the price of a few thousand dead. Why risk these advantages by pursuing further conquest? Every scorched house may be re-built. New people would occupy the streets emptied by war.

I shivered on the bare mountain pass, faintly delirious. Mi Feng had extracted the arrow head with some skill – clearly not the first time he had done so – washing and binding the wound. How it ached! My mind was full of strange dreams in which I wrote endless lists of names, all the while complaining that I could compile no more, that numbers and lists sickened my soul. Then my thoughts would clear for a while and I was forced to consider the hopelessness of our situation.

How we might return to the capital without money, food or transport I could not imagine. Su Lin's letter had promised the warmest of welcomes and I could always be sure of lodgings with Cousin Hong. Better still, P'ei Ti himself had hinted the situation with regard to Lord Xiao was vastly improved, that I had unknown friends capable of protecting me from his spite. Yet none of that mattered if I died of starvation and frostbite. When the lips are gone, the teeth are cold. Mi Feng brought me fresh water from a nearby mountain stream but we had nothing else to appease our bellies.

In this miserable condition I watched Field Marshal Wen Po riding among the defeated army, seeking to reassure and raise spirits. He reached the outcrop of rock where I lay sheltering from the wind. My only blankets were the few spare clothes in our shoulder bags. My pillow was a cap.

Wen Po appeared gaunt, his face a mask of worry-lines. I tried feebly to get on my knees as he reined in his horse.

'Stay seated,' he ordered, looking down at me. 'You'll open your wound.'

I remembered saying the same thing to Mi Feng when he had been prostrated by an arrow wound.

Mountains rose all around us. Wen Po looked small on his fine charger, set against cliff and peak. He must have known his career was at an end. No more would the Field Marshal ride at the head of unquestioning regiments, his merest word signalling life or death. No more would his name be praised for cunning and subtle strategy. The toadies and hangers-on would make excuses, then find themselves a new Wen Po to feed on.

He had joined the ranks of failed generals, those one finds in treatises on the art of war, shining examples of how not to win. With luck, a great deal of luck, he might evade a command from His Imperial Majesty to commit suicide and retire to a country estate for the remainder of his days. Or, more likely, he would find himself arraigned for incompetence, on trial for his life, while old friends at court crawled away from him like lice from a dead body.

'So you have survived, Yun Cai,' he said. 'I'm glad, though I can think of those who will not share my feelings.'

That much was evident. I nodded, wincing over my wound.

'What happened to. . . the bodyguards I warned you about?'

'Your Excellency, their names have joined one of my little lists.'

He squinted at me in surprise, then guffawed.

'Little list! I like that!' he said. 'I like to see a bit of spirit!'

There was something faintly hysterical about his laughter. Given the circumstances, one could see why. Maybe that joke saved my life. Or he simply felt the need to be magnanimous now his power was draining away.

'Send your servant to my secretary in an hour's time,' he said. 'On my authority, you are dismissed from further service in the Army of the Left Hand. My secretary will give you a letter to this effect, ensuring that all Imperial Inns grant you lodging on your journey back to the capital. I cannot spare horses, so you shall have to walk or beg other transport.'

I bowed gratefully, but already His Excellency was riding to the next huddle of men. Mi Feng got up from his knees, brushing off the dust.

'Well, sir,' he said. 'From now on they'll have to call you Yun Cai the Lucky.'

I looked at him through narrowed eyes. If this was luck, then what was misfortune?

I am falling upwards. My spirit rises from a young man gasping over his wound, Mi Feng helping him walk a stony road. Rising up, high above a barren valley littered with bodies. Over a mountain range, rivers spreading out like silver braids of hair. Pinang burns, tiny and insignificant. Up, up into feathery clouds. . .

I cry out. Scatter my blankets. Beside me squats one of my fellow prisoners, his plump face all concern.

'You have been dreaming,' he says.

I blink. Sourness in my mouth.

'You have been tossing and muttering all night,' he says. 'I thought it best not to wake you.'

I rub my eyes. For a moment I glimpse Cousin Zhi's white, terrified face.

Commands are being shouted outside, movement disturbing the stillness of dawn.

'What is going on?' I ask.

He gestures at the balcony.

'See for yourself. I doubt we'll get breakfast today.'

I drag myself up and lean on the balcony rail. At last, General An-Shu's army is on the move. In the courtyard before the Prefect's residence, a band of cavalry are gathered, their horses covered with glinting mail, their riders similarly protected. I recognise them as the General's bodyguard.

Beyond the ramparts, regiments of infantry and their supply

wagons are taking up position. Dust rises as officers gallop along the lines. Everywhere the sound of tramping feet and cantering horses. Trumpets, drums and flags signal. Bright banners bearing the General's symbol hang limp. In the streets companies of men are marching toward the East Gate.

For a moment I wonder if I am still in my dream. Is this the lost army I knew in Pinang, or another? In what way do they differ? They could be any army marching out to die or triumph, war upon war. . .

'What's happening?' I ask.

My fellow prisoner is combing his thin, straggly beard.

'The General has decided to march east,' he says.

It takes several hours for the army to march away. We chatter excitedly, certain the General will grant an amnesty and that we will be allowed to go home. Yet the door is still locked and guarded; and I can still glimpse soldiers from our balcony.

Youngest Son has not contacted me. Perhaps he was allowed no time, too busy arranging the disposition of his troops. It is possible I may never see him again. I feel his silence more deeply than I should, considering all he has become. Or, to be more exact, all he has failed to become.

As the hours pass, our mood lightens. Faces relax for the first time in weeks and I am relieved to hear laughter. We are interrupted by running feet on the stairs. The door is thrown open. A guard stands breathless, one hand on the hilt of his sword.

'Quick!' he calls. 'Put on your shoes. Everyone must assemble outside the house at once.'

There is something about the soldier's manner I do not like. He seems frightened. We do as we are bidden. The guards take up position around us. They are unusually well turned out; another bad sign.

'Don't just stand there!' shouts the sergeant. 'Get them moving!'

We are hustled down the street and meet another column of

prisoners, herded by halberds and rude blows. We are silent now. Many of the captives can barely walk, exhausted by thirst and hunger.

We are led to the large courtyard in front of the Prefect's residence. Hundreds of us have been gathered, surrounded by watchful troops.

Then a large group of high-ranking men from Chunming, some of whom I know well, are led into the square. They take up a position away from the humble prisoners, all dressed in their finest clothes. Several sniff perfume bottles and flutter gaudy fans. Others whisper to their neighbours.

For an hour we wait in the unrelenting sun. A few weaker prisoners collapse, but we are offered no water. The soldiers seem as anxious as those they guard. General An-Shu's flags hang in front of the Prefect's residence. As I grow weary, their colours and symbols blur before my eyes.

Another hour passes, and still our reason for being here is no clearer. An acrid scent drifts across the square. Men relieve themselves in their own clothes, a safer course than breaking ranks or trying to argue with the soldiers, who represent the dregs of General An-Shu's army, one of his many Punishment Battalions. Usually such units are reserved for the most desperate fighting. Strange to hold one back to guard a friendly city.

By the third hour my own bladder is causing discomfort and I feel dizzy. I am stirred from lethargy by a blare of trumpets. An absurd cavalcade enters the courtyard.

At the head, riding General An-Shu's ivory chariot, is a slim, youthful woman dressed in shimmering, silver silk. Her make-up forms an expressionless white mask. Her beauty – for she is beautiful – is that of a goddess, remote in its perfection. The officers at once leap into action, ordering everyone to their knees, amidst a flurry of scrambling.

The chariot and its attendant horsemen halt before the Prefect's residence. General An-Shu's concubine, the self-styled

Lady Ta Chi, rises to her full height in the chariot and looks over the crowd.

By chance I am near her, and catch the dull, black glitter of her eyes. Depthless eyes in a white mask. Eyes without passion, yet capable of awakening at a moment's notice.

She gestures to a gorgeously-attired man in a seven-brimmed hat. From his bloated face, he is evidently a eunuch. He swaggers forward and prostrates himself before her, flat on his belly as though she were the Dowager Empress herself. Then, with great ceremony, he unrolls a scroll and clears his throat. When he speaks, his voice echoes like an actor's.

'Let Chunming hear His Highness's will! He who is the Most Glorious Lion and Dragon. He who is the Son of Heaven.'

At this, there are gasps from the ranks of prisoners. Astonishing that General An-Shu should assume such a title! Either he has the soundest reasons for his confidence, or he is deluded to the point of madness.

One of the local dignitaries goes so far as to rise to his feet in outrage. The Lady Ta Chi turns slowly to gaze upon him. For a moment he stands firm, then quails, and gets to his knees. But the damage is done. Guardsmen are directed into the crowd and he is dragged off, protesting that he has a bad back and could not help himself. When the square is silent, the eunuch continues:

'He who is the Son of Heaven, the Chosen Centre of The Five Directions, has decreed the following. First, that Chunming shall remain under military rule. All existing curfews are to continue until further notice. All prisoners are to remain in their places of confinement until their guilt has been determined. All who enter and leave the city are to be counted in and out.'

'His Highness makes this further command. He appoints the Lady Ta Chi as his sole representative in the City of Chunming. Whatever Her Highness commands is his command. Whatever she wills is his will. To disobey the Lady Ta Chi is treason.'

No one murmurs now, except inwardly.

'Chunming is the most honoured of cities!' he continues, his voice rising. 'Under the ineffable rule of Her Highness Ta Chi, universal peace shall reign!'

He lowers the scroll and glares at the crowd.

'Raise your voices in gladness!' he commands.

The crowd is silent. All eyes are upon the young woman in General An-Shu's chariot. The eunuch looks around angrily.

'Raise your voices in gladness!' he repeats.

Still no one moves or calls out for her blessing. There are a few pitiful cheers, which soon die away. From the back of the crowd comes another sound, that of scornful laughter. The tension in the square mounts. For a moment I wonder if the soldiers will be ordered to attack us.

Lady Ta Chi squeals a command to her driver and the chariot rolls out of the courtyard, disappearing behind the Prefect's residence. The officers bellow for silence. The square is full of men eagerly discussing what they have just seen.

'Someone will pay a price for this,' mutters a man beside me.

From the look of insane fury on Lady Ta Chi's face, I suspect it will be all of us.

seven

'. . . Otters cannot stop catching carp
and so we pursued our pleasures.
Drum and flute set us dancing all night
to the tune *Telling of Innermost Feelings*.
When the gong's echo faded
dawn revealed our delusion. . . .'

No news of home for weeks now. Sometimes I fret whether Three-Step-House is intact, whether Wudi protects my interests while I am away, whether the gallant Ensign Tzi Lu and his small band have a safe place to hide.

Often I wonder how Daughter-in-law and the grandchildren fare in Whale Rocks Monastery. Do they feel like prisoners, too? Daughter-in-law must be pleased to have Eldest Son beside her, unless the stupid boy has disobeyed my instructions and returned to Three-Step-House. Surely I worry needlessly. The war is being fought out far to the east. Yet to love is to worry: they are ladle and bowl.

Today our house of prisoners receives odd news. The Lady Ta Chi has been granted a new title: Empress-in-waiting. I am tempted to joke about Temporary Empresses in Temporary Capitals.

We also hear that she has introduced a new punishment for rebels and grumblers, known as 'the heater'. The criminal must hold a red-hot bar of iron to the count of ten without dropping it. Should he let it fall, his sentence is doubled.

The long hours drag, and my mind dances with impossible schemes to save P'ei Ti.

I stand in the garden, observing a stem of grass, rooted high up in the brickwork walls of the ramparts. A single seed must have blown there and taken root. Now the stalk is heavy with a crown of new seeds. That humble plant might teach us much.

A guard summons me over.

'You've got visitors,' he says, unsmiling.

The men waiting in the vestibule do not smile either. One is the Head Eunuch who announced General An-Shu's proclamation outside the Prefect's residence. The other two are soldiers from the Punishment Battalion.

The Head Eunuch examines me curiously.

'You are required,' he says, fanning himself with a turquoise and gold fan. His nails are exceptionally long and curved. It is strange to find a high-ranking eunuch in simple Chunming. They belong in the Imperial court, which is no doubt why General An Shu acquired him.

'Don't look so alarmed, old man,' he says, raising an eyebrow.

I follow him down the street and across the square to the main entrance of the Prefect's residence. Soldiers lounge by the steps. I take the opportunity to examine the prison block where P'ei Ti is held. Behind its blank walls, broken only by tiny, barred windows, my friend must crouch in shackles. I dare not ask my guide for news of him. There is an entrance at the side of the prison leading to a heavy, barred gate in the enclosure walls. No guard stands by the gate. If one could somehow leave by the side entrance and unlock the gate it would be possible to escape from the Prefect's enclosure, unobserved by the soldiers in the main gatehouse.

I am led through the hallway to a door decked in yellow silks. Young men in tight-fitting robes whisper to each other. They pause to assess me as I pass. When I stand outside the yellow door they fall silent, every eye upon me. I gather the folds of my dignity.

'Her Highness is expecting you,' says the Head Eunuch, laconically. 'Go on in!'

Still I wait. It would hardly do to march in unannounced.

'Oh, very well,' says the Head Eunuch.

He raps out a complicated pattern on the door. It opens to reveal three guards, all eunuchs, carrying long executioner's swords. They abase themselves before my guide, who smiles thinly.

'It is a good thing you have nice manners, old man,' he says. 'Ssu-Ba-Loh here – that's all three of them, by the way, we find it easier to address them by one name – have strict orders to deal harshly with intruders. Isn't that so, Ssu-Ba-Loh?'

They look at him, then each other, and bow again.

'But I forget, you won't get a sensible answer from Ssu-Ba-Loh. All three have had their tongues removed. Can you guess why?'

I blink at him, quite determined to act the old fool.

'It is so they cannot prattle about what they witness,' says the Head Eunuch. 'A fact you would do well to remember.'

With a twitch of his silken gown, he floats down a long corridor and I am hard put to keep pace – or pretend I am. We soon reach another door, for the Prefect's residence in Chunming is no palace, whatever they call it. He knocks cautiously. The supercilious smile has left his face, replaced by a mask of servility. Ssu, or perhaps it is Ba or Loh, stands so close behind me I can smell onions on his breath. No chances are being taken against assassins. A wise precaution given the Lady Ta Chi's popularity in Chunming.

I follow him into a long chamber smothered with turquoise and pink floor coverings. Silks waft inwards through the open window, softening the light. It is a room to lull the mind. A small jade fountain tinkles in the courtyard outside. The perfume in the air is subtle, yet pleasing, like a spring morning. A young lady is giggling as she plays with a cat, tempting it to leap after small cubes of meat. I look again and realise the creature is a tiger cub. The lady is Ta Chi herself. She perches delicately on a mound of golden cushions. So close, her beauty makes me stare. Her features, smooth and balanced, seem scarcely human, almost divine. She has meteor eyes and shining cloud-hair. Her cherry mouth reveals wide, even teeth, fertile as pomegranate seeds. My own mouth opens. I cannot help it.

Astonishment makes me slower in getting to my knees than is prudent. Yet I detect, from an upward glitter of her eyes, that she understands the reason for my delay and is not displeased. She must be accustomed to such reactions.

'Oh, Little Goldhair is getting naughty!' she says, addressing the Head Eunuch. 'What am I to do with him?'

He lifts his head from the floor.

'Perhaps if Your Highness fed him a little less heart and spleen,' he suggests. 'Goldhair might be more obedient.'

'But he's so sweet and little! How can I refuse him anything? Oh, I suppose you are right.'

She turns with a gentle smile to me. I struggle with a desire to gaze brazenly at her.

'This cub,' she says. 'Is a present for His Majesty when he summons me to join him in the capital. I do so want the little chap to make a good impression. Perhaps you can advise me what to do?'

The Head Eunuch doesn't welcome my inclusion in the

conversation and the Lady Ta Chi senses it. She looks innocently between us both.

'Your Highness,' I say. 'If His Majesty does not understand the nature of a tiger, I would be very surprised. May I venture to suggest that he will not condemn Goldhair for wanting as much meat as possible.'

She claps her hands with delight.

'A fine reply! You are more than you look, Lord Yun Cai! Did you hear that, Head Eunuch? Now, I'm sure you couldn't have said that.'

Actually, I'm surprised he didn't. He simpers regretfully, glaring at me from the corner of his bloodshot eyes.

'You may go now,' she says, sweetly. 'I wish to speak to my guest alone. Leave Ssu-Ba-Loh to guard me, there's a good fellow. And if you are worried about the propriety of the matter, look at his grey hair.'

The Head Eunuch hovers, evidently in some distress.

'I should tell you, Lord Yun Cai, that the Head Eunuch does not approve of your presence in my chambers. After all, you are still a man. He seems to think he understands His Highness's wishes better than myself.'

He is about to demur, then thinks better of it and leaves crawling backwards. I take note of the correct procedure for a dutiful exit. Assuming I'm not dragged out feet first by the redoubtable Ssu-Ba-Loh.

'The Head Eunuch is such an amusing fellow,' she says, still vexed. 'You wouldn't believe where we found him. . . Lord Yun Cai, I really do not mind if you look at me. Indeed, it is rather important that you do.'

I grovel at such condescension, but obey. The lady sits back on the cushions and takes a sip from a delicate cup on a lacquer table beside her. A maid rushes forward to refill it, and Lady Ta Chi waves her away.

'You're wondering why I summoned you here, aren't you?'

The spell of her beauty is fading. But only a little. It is the kind of enchantment liable to renew itself each time one glances at her. I cannot match the lady before me with the one rumoured to enjoy 'the heater'. All rulers are plagued by slander. Perhaps, as is often the way, people blame the gentle concubine for her cruel master's faults.

'I shall explain,' she says. 'My mother had a scroll of your poems when I was a little girl, and used to read or sing them to me at night. The scroll had been given to her by her first husband, my father, who died when I was very young. She always loved old-fashioned things. Her life was very sad and I shared her sadness. But your poems always lightened her mood, and sometimes made her weep. Does that not make you feel flattered?'

'Deeply, Your Highness,' I say.

Indeed I do succumb to the old vanity for a moment. But I am no youth of twenty to be captivated by unattainable beauty. I must beware.

She takes up an old, worn scroll lying on the lacquer table. With my poor eyesight, I cannot read the characters, but guess they are my own.

'Lovely poems in praise of a lovely woman,' she sighs. 'Who was the lady?'

I shrug helplessly.

'I fear she was no lady at all, Your Highness, but I was inordinately fond of her. She was a common singing girl.'

The Empress-in-waiting seems surprised.

'Really? Well, why not. It doesn't matter, I suppose. Now, I must tell you that I wish to give His Majesty more than a tiger cub when I join him in the capital. It is important that I have other gifts. How difficult it is to find something the Son of Heaven does not already possess! I'm sure you see my problem. I must give him something unique, a reminder of me, so precious he will treasure it always. Do you understand?'

'Forgive my stupidity, Your Highness, but I do not.'

'Then I'll explain. I want to give him a wonderful volume of poems all about me. Each poem is to be accompanied by a picture – I've got an artist in mind, so you needn't worry about that – poems which will summon me to his mind when we are apart.'

She clearly expects some reply. I become aware of a troubling fragrance. It hints at improbable possibilities. If I were younger, I might smell it in my dreams.

'Mere words could hardly be expected to do justice to Your Highness,' I say.

She wags a reproachful finger.

'I suspect you were a rogue in your youth, Lord Yun Cai.'

I dare to bow self-effacingly. What madness is this? I'm as giddy as a fattened puppy at her slightest smile.

'So, I take it you can provide a volume, as good as this?'

Her tone is cold now. She taps the wooden end of the scroll against the table. It rattles her wine cup.

'Your Highness, if you had asked me an hour ago, I would have said no. But having met Your Highness, I believe that given time and solitude. . . Yes, I believe so.'

'Excellent, then the matter is closed. Of course, you must come to live here in the palace. I shall instruct the Head Eunuch.'

Now I grow afraid. I lack the necessary fangs to writhe with the other flatterers. I cannot imagine the Head Eunuch would tolerate me for long. And how many days would it take to displease her? A wrong word, and I might be clutching 'the heater'. Nevertheless, I would gain the freedom to observe the prison block at close quarters. This gives me an idea.

'Your Highness,' I say. 'I fear the distractions of your court would delay my compositions. With His Majesty's victory so imminent, I must work quickly. May I beg that I remain in my current lodgings, but with the sole use of my bedchamber? Also, that I receive a passport of free travel, so I may visit such sites in the city as will aid my inspiration?'

I wait with no little trepidation. Yet I underestimate her desire for these poems. A cunning look crosses her face.

'If I agree, you must deliver fifty, no, a hundred poems in a month's time.'

Three or more a day! A ridiculous demand.

'As Your Highness wishes,' I say.

She claps her hands together with pleasure.

'Then I shall issue the necessary instructions. But first I have a little test for you. After all, old men may easily live on their past glories. Improvise a poem in praise of me right now.'

She settles back on her cushions, and takes up her wine cup from the lacquer table.

'Well,' she says, sharply. 'I await.'

My mind goes back to the day Lord Xiao asked me to improvise a verse as a test. Despite the extremity of my position, I cannot help sadness, and this usually grants me eloquence.

'Travellers are beauty's best judge,' I begin.

'Carry on,' she says, doubtfully.

I sigh. But did not the Immortal Li Po write extravagant poems for an Emperor's concubine? Although he had the advantage of drunkenness at the time. So I close my eyes:

Travellers are beauty's best judge.
Moon Goddess's fragrant light
Fills roads between heaven and earth.
The Lady Ta Chi's fragrance
Scents the Son of Heaven's palace.
He pauses before his next victory,
And sadly thinks of home.

She watches me through narrowed eyes. Is she displeased? My life depends on it. And perhaps that of my family. For all its formal correctness it is an empty verse. General An Shu is not the Son of Heaven. Neither does he possess a palace, or victory for that matter. The Empress-in-waiting frowns. She is no Moon Goddess either.

'I like it, but it is not as passionate as these,' she says, waving the scroll. 'That is what delighted me about your poems when I was a girl. My mother called them *sincere*.'

Oh, the powerful! Perhaps beauty is the ultimate delusion. Does she imagine her sight and smell alone will inspire genuine love?

'However, it does describe the situation rather well,' she continues. 'But I want more, well, *detail* about me. My eyes, my face, everything about me in fact.'

'To do you justice, Your Highness, I humbly implore you for the privacy I have requested. Every worker in jade must have a space to polish. . .'

She yawns.

'Very well, it shall be so. I suppose you are the only poet available in this pitiful hole. You need not stay in the palace. Only don't disappoint me, Yun Cai! I do not like to be disappointed.'

I take this as my cue to leave and retreat in the same manner as the Head Eunuch. Back in the corridor, I can hear her playing with the tiger cub once more. Ssu-Ba-Loh grins at me conspiratorially. I'm in the same leaky ship as him now.

A small room. Bed and desk and stool. A lantern and box of tallow candles. On the desk, dusky ink and plentiful brushes, a grinding stone and blue porcelain water jug, decorated with peonies. Sufficient paper to write a thousand commentaries on General An Shu's reign. The Lady Ta Chi has been as good as her word. Within a day of my audience with her, my room-fellows were banished to other quarters in the house.

No describing the relief of privacy. It is root-space and water for a wilting spirit. Yet I sense the other prisoners' resentment, and their fear. No one, including the guards, wants to get on the wrong side of a man who has the goodwill of the Empress-in-waiting. They cannot guess its fragility.

*

Every night I blow out my lantern and sit by the balcony-window, looking out over Chunming. The faintest breath of air cools my moist forehead. Otherwise I fan myself with a poem praising Lady Ta Chi's hair. Chunming lies silent beneath its curfew. Occasionally I hear soldiers talking as they patrol the streets. Stray night sounds: an infant crying, the ululation of owls, then silence, deep, patient silence, thick as blackest ink. Except, that is, when merriment from the Prefect's residence disturbs the city's rest.

I watch, still as a heron, shrouded by the darkness of my room, hardly daring to move in case I reveal myself. Strange things go on in the courtyard before the Prefect's residence in the dead hours of night. I witness dances scarcely decent when the General is away at the wars. One night there is a series of bare-fist boxing matches where contestants lie senseless on the ground, oblivion aided by drunken courtiers kicking their prostrate bodies to punish them for losing a bet. Perhaps they merely punish their own fears of defeat. I could tell them, fear will never be mastered by more fear.

Another time, a frantic masque where robed figures act out the roles of Immortals beneath tall, guttering candles, circling round the courtyard to the solemn beat of a drum, mournful tunes on the flute. I watch prisoners dragged from the prison into the centre of the square and set upon by youths dressed in gorgeous silks, their mistress looking on from a high-backed chair. Would she like me to write a poem about that?

Dawn comes. Its light penetrates my closed eyelids and slowly I blink myself awake. Today must not be wasted on dubious verses. The time has come for desperate risks. I dress quickly and stuff the passport Lady Ta Chi provided into my pouch. Then I ask the guard to unbar the gate, and step out into the waking city, drawn by thoughts of P'ei Ti to the courtyard before the Prefect's residence.

I show my pass to sleepy soldiers at the gate, then wander round the square as though taking my morning exercise until I reach the prison block. A folly not to be contemplated. Unreason has driven me here, but then loyalty and affection are seldom rational. The cocks are crowing all over Chunming, summoning the light of another summer dawn. Outside the prison, I stop. Should I stare at the walls, will myself into the cell where P'ei Ti languishes?

A feeble plan presents itself. I walk over to the prison gates where a night-warder drinks tea while awaiting his replacement.

'Another hot day on its way,' I grumble.

He looks at me suspiciously.

'What's your business here, sir?' asks the night-warder.

He is young and, for all his tiredness, sharp-eyed.

'No business,' I say. 'Except walking somewhere safe. Best for an old man to be up early. This heat makes me swell like a melon.'

He laughs at my joke.

Encouraged, I say, 'Hey, young fellow, where are your manners? Have you no tea for an old man?'

He brings a cup out. It steams in the cool air and I sip. His accent intrigues me.

'You're not from Chunming,' I say.

He grunts.

'Not me, sir, I'm from the mountains.'

He names a valley adjoining Wei.

'What brings you here?'

'My father sold me to a tanner in Chunming, and when my bond was up my master decided to die. A shame he couldn't do it seven years earlier! So I found myself penniless and came upon this job.'

'What's your name?'

'People call me Golden Bells because I'm a good singer at weddings.'

I hesitate. Yet I must try. For P'ei Ti's sake, I must try.

'Would you prefer to be back home, Golden Bells?'

He looks at me sadly.

'If I could afford some land, I'd be home tomorrow.'

I sip my tea.

'Are you always the night guard?' I ask. 'They should pay you more for that. Perhaps you could save up a bit.'

'Yes, I am. The Chief Warder doesn't like me because I'm not from Chunming. He pays me less than the others. The Chief Warder says its easier when the prisoners are asleep.'

So he has a grievance. I shake my head sympathetically.

'A man like you should have his own bit of land up in the hills. A house and wife. You could make a bit extra by your singing. You could grow whatever you liked and sell it at the market.'

He lowers his steaming cup of tea. Looks at me closely.

'I'd give a lot for that.'

But I have neither money to bribe him, nor a plan.

'Let's see what will happen,' I say. 'The Jade Emperor is full of surprises.'

He reaches out for my empty cup.

'I've got a cousin who lives in Wei Village, sir,' he says. 'I won't mention his name, but I've visited him a few times. You might even be a bit familiar, sir. Not that it's anyone's business but our own.'

I feel a sudden, anxious thrill.

'Who knows what will happen?' I say. 'I'll remember you, Golden Bells. One good turn deserves another.'

I leave, shuffling across the wide courtyard feeling strangely exposed. A few of the servants are awake and about their business. After so debauched a night the Empress-in-waiting's courtiers sleep late. But as I pass through the gate I glance back and see the Head Eunuch, yawning on the terrace, and watching me. Did he observe my conversation with Golden Bells or has he just emerged to examine the sky? My hands are oily with sweat.

I am not suited to intrigue. It disturbs my essential breaths. My audacity with Golden Bells amazes me. Will he report our conversation in the hope of a reward? P'ei Ti himself may have sought to appease his torturers by betraying my name and the reason for his intended visit to Wei Valley. It is painful to suspect one's friends.

I have acted out of character, like a sparrow masquerading as an eagle, and must pay the price. The boldest thing about me is a taste for unconventional rhymes! Do I underestimate myself? Though old and weak, I am still Father's son. Was I not brave when assisting the Ensign Tzi Lu to hide behind Heron Waterfall? Did I not kill a man when I was young?

I am still to be reckoned with.

Let me just find the courage to turn my conversation with Golden Bells to P'ei Ti's advantage! If only I was rich, the man drools for bribes. But I must not let desire become rashness. Every action runs the risk of confounding itself. Even if we helped P'ei Ti leave the prison block, there is nowhere to hide, no horses or other means to escape Chunming, assuming the torturers have left him capable of walking. I am learning to wait, as though patience is a weapon in itself.

Still, intrigue does not suit me. I learned this long ago when I returned to the capital from Pinang. Some say we are lucky to dwell in a floating world, for one may gather wisdom from past errors and guard against similar errors in the future. Perhaps if I think back to that time I may remember lessons to assist me now.

It is dark tonight. No moon. I close my eyes, remember a billowing cloud, a bright spring sky, drawing me to the greatest city under Heaven. That cloud was no creature of my imagination. It summoned me like a joyful voice. . .

'See, sir! See!'

I was hunched over my horse, watching the road for ruts and potholes, careful because my left arm still hung from a sling. Luckily, it was a kindly beast. I believe it sensed my weakness and tried to plod evenly. I looked up, glad to be distracted from gloomy thoughts.

Mi Feng reared his own mount, making it dance on its hind legs in a tight circle, and waved his cap in the air.

What excited him? A longed-for, improbable sight. We had crested a hill and caught our first glimpse of the capital.

Mi Feng galloped around me, whooping at some peasants who were pushing wheelbarrows of cabbage to market. They scattered like frightened birds.

'Did I not say we would come back!' he cried.

I was gazing at a cloud. Golden edges round plump silver sails. My eyes descended to the jumbled rooftops and ramparts of the capital, ten thousand kite-strings of smoke from which the blue sky hung. The wind felt fresh and cool on my cheeks. I laughed uncertainly, not quite believing what I saw.

'You did,' I said.

Mi Feng reined in beside me, frowning.

'Are you not pleased?' he said.

'I feel contradictory things at once, that is all.'

'You think too much,' he muttered. 'Sometimes it is best to be simple, sir.'

I clapped him on the shoulder with my good arm, and nearly unseated myself. He steadied me.

'Mi Feng,' I said. 'Do not call me *sir* any longer. You have saved my life too often for that. Your debt to me was long ago paid off. Though we can never be equals, from now on consider yourself my free companion. No gentleman could ask for a better.'

To my amazement, he began to cry, brushing angrily at the tears as though they were troublesome flies.

'If you say so,' he grumbled.

'That is settled,' I said, wiping the corner of my own eyes.

So we rode the last twenty *li* to the capital, drawing few glances on so crowded a highway. Wise to be inconspicuous, though I had little enough idea what, or who, awaited us.

Our journey across the Middle Kingdom had been an uncertain one. At first we limped through the mountains with hordes of survivors from Wen Po's army, and every step was misery. I was in a daze of pain from my wound. Mi Feng trudged beside me, urging me on with pleas and jibes concerning my manhood. At last we reached the nearest fortified city and found an Imperial Inn, where I waved Wen Po's letter of passport and so secured a bed. I did not move from it for a month.

Feverish days and nights. The wound became poisoned, rheumy with pus, and I was fortunate not to lose my arm to a country surgeon's cleaver. Then the sickness abated. One morning I awoke in a small room to the sound of some travelling official snoring in the cot beside me. I laughed, scarcely able to believe myself alive.

We continued on our way, trusting to the vigour of youth and the kindness of strangers. Once we begged a ride from a high official sailing through the marsh regions of Lake T'ung, known as the Desert of a Hundred *Li*, for it was infested with brigands. Everyone on the boat feared for their life. The moon was so bright it might have been day. The soldiers protecting us called out from one boat to another, bows and crossbows ready to fire at the slightest danger. As we paddled along they beat continuously on drums and small bells and at last we reached more civilised districts.

A week later we could progress by water no longer and found ourselves marooned in a wretched town so poor it did not bother to protect itself with ramparts. Mi Feng suggested I wait by the river while he 'had a nose about'. When he returned it was with two sorry-looking horses.

'Where did you get *those*?' I demanded, certain he had stolen them, possibly through violence.

'Do not ask, sir,' he said, guiltily. 'The truth is, I kept back a lot of the *cash* you gave me for food in Pinang. Don't judge me too harshly, sir. I couldn't see the sense in ruining yourself for worthless cowards like those clerks. I thought you'd need some money later on.'

Though I could hardly reproach his intentions, by any standards he had robbed me.

'Some of that was government funds,' I chided.

He shrugged. Naturally, I insisted he surrender the rest of the *cash*, fully intending to pay back the Exchequer in full. I never did. So you might call me an embezzler.

Li by *li*, village by village, we journeyed south then east. It is a miracle no bandits troubled us. After so much ill-fortune the spirits of the highway must have decided we had suffered enough. Wherever we could we joined other groups of travellers and perhaps that kept us safe.

At last we caught sight of the capital. Four whole months had passed since our flight from Pinang. Blossoms unfurled from gnarled branches. Grass sprouted green shoots, drinking sunlight. And always my left shoulder ached.

We passed through the Gate of Elegant Rectitude at sunset. I halted my horse and Mi Feng waited alongside.

'Well,' he said. 'Unless we sell something, there'll be no food tonight.'

We were penniless but not friendless. Indeed, one might call it proof of a life well-lived that I had several to approach. By any natural instinct I should have sought out Cousin Hong, for he was family. Or P'ei Ti, for he was my oldest companion. But a harsh, self-punishing desire took hold. I wished to test the woman who had caused me so much misery. If I found her wrapped in another's arms, I would know love was dark folly, illusion like everything else. Then, perhaps, I might be cured.

'We shall go to Su Lin,' I said.

Mi Feng replied cautiously: 'You might find her busy. Perhaps best not to surprise her, as it were, sir.'

'I told you not to call me that, damn you! Accompany me to her house or go to hell. For that is where I am going.'

Without grumbling, he cantered behind me down the Imperial Way. How familiar the city seemed, and strange. After so long away I felt like one traversing a dream. Face after face, each turned inward upon its business. Voices and smells mingling. Not a soul caring that we had been at the edge of the world, engaged in a desperate struggle. Wine shops were as busy as ever. Tea-houses from which a faint thread of melody unwound into the street. Did anyone recognise me? I would not have noticed if they had. I rode stiff-backed, viewing everything through the corner of my eyes, afraid tears might begin, tears I could barely explain.

We rode right through the city to the West Lake. Hundreds of craft on the water, lit by more lamps than there are stars in the sky. Gay laughter floated, then died away. I watched the scene coldly.

'This must be a happy sight!' said Mi Feng. 'Sir always loved the Lake!'

He sounded anxious that I should be happy, so I tried to smile. Soon my mouth fell.

'I thought this place loved me – no, not that, only that I loved it. But it is indifferent, Mi Feng, it does not care about us at all.'

He glanced at me, then at the West Lake.

'How can water care about anything?' he asked.

I stared at him.

'You are the true poet here,' I said.

He sighed, and would have said more, but I rode on, eager to discover what I most dreaded. We reached the cottage by the lake where Su Lin dwelt. Here came my first surprise. A strange singing girl stood outside her house, hugging a drunken suitor, evidently eager to send him on his way.

'Who are you?' I demanded. 'Where is Su Lin?'

She blinked at me artfully, and giggled. The suitor bristled, as though I was trying to steal his girl. Then he caught a glimpse of our weapons.

'Don't you know, sir?' she said. 'Su Lin doesn't live here anymore. She wouldn't dirty her slippers here now. That's where Su Lin lives.'

I followed her pointing finger. On a knoll above the lakeside, stood a fine house in its own grounds.

'Are you sure?' I asked.

The girl's laugh tinkled like ice.

'Yes, the lucky whore!'

I should have struck her for such impudence. Turning my tired horse, I cantered up the low hill to the gatehouse. A sleepy servant tried to stop me, but I brushed him aside with my good arm and marched up to the house. I wanted no announcement, I wanted to find her exactly as she was, however it pained my heart. Mi Feng hurried behind me, pausing only to intimidate the gatekeeper with a glare.

'That's right, sir,' he said. 'Catch her at it.'

I strode to the entrance and did not bother to knock. Throwing open the door, I stood for a moment, one arm in a sling, the other resting on the hilt of P'ei Ti's sword. What I saw lumped my throat.

Fear creates a thousand miseries which never occur. Longing a thousand more. I was met by a gasp. A sudden cry. Su Lin sat on a stool in the courtyard beside a small pond green with lilypads. Lanterns lit the water, softening her gentle features. In her hand, a lute; on her face, sheer consternation. She froze in midsong, for she was practising a tune. Her lifeless fingers released the instrument and it slid down her knees to the ground, clanging with a discordant sound.

Our eyes found each other's soul.

'They told me,' she cried. 'Oh, I thought!'

Her voice trailed away. Then came a flurry of silks in

motion. She was clasping me hard, hurting my injured shoulder.

'They told me you were dead,' she sobbed against my chest. 'Oh Yun Cai, you have come back.'

I peered around. No other man was visible. But I could not be sure. I held her away from me suspiciously.

'Is anyone else here?' I asked.

'What do you mean? There's just us, and the servants.'

At last, I could relax. If another man had been present I do not like to think what I would have done.

'Dearest Yun Cai, how thin you look! And your arm! What has happened to your arm?'

Like a kite abruptly falling when the wind drops, my fury became its opposite. I was myself again. We clutched each other, crying out excited questions, murmuring endearments, calling out each other's name. Yet in my soul, barely noticed, was a coldness. Though I longed for it to melt, something had frozen inside me like ice one sometimes sees, full of grit and dead leaves.

What a night followed! For all my exhaustion it continued until dawn. The finest food appeared, and wines. The more I drank the more boastful I became, for I sensed Su Lin expected me to boast. She wanted me to resemble a hero in a tale. And P'ei Ti was summoned, rushing across the city to join us. I told them stories of our journey from the frontier, joking about the rapaciousness of fleas. Su Lin sat close by, urging me to drink another cup, eat another morsel, occasionally clasping me and murmuring how thin I looked.

Finally, sitting beneath the stars in Su Lin's courtyard – I insisted we eat outside because it was what I had grown used to – P'ei Ti grew serious. He indicated to Su Lin that she should be silent, though she wanted to entertain me with a favourite song. Actually, she was drunk, in the most endearing way possible.

'Well, my old friend,' he said. 'No, not my old friend, but my dearest friend. It's obvious you've had a very bad time of it.'

I tried to shrug, drank more wine.

'How did you come by your wound?' he asked.

'An arrow,' I said.

'Ah. So you saw no, what do they call it, close quarter fighting?'

I looked at him, suddenly sober.

'Better not to mention it,' I said. 'But P'ei Ti, your sword saved my life.'

I rose, pushing Su Lin aside, and paced up and down.

'I had to kill a man,' I said, a brittle edge to my voice. 'If the Buddha is right, I am damned for torment in the next life, or even hell itself. I stabbed him in the groin and his blood sprayed all over me! But I had no choice, P'ei Ti, I was allowed no choice!'

He gripped my shaking hands.

'Do not distress yourself. You are safe among friends now.'

'It was Lord Xiao's doing!' I cried. 'He hired assassins, P'ei Ti. I had to kill one of them. Oh, it is an unpleasant story!'

Su Lin was watching me, her mouth slightly open.

'Let us talk of this tomorrow,' said P'ei Ti, soothingly. 'Lord Xiao will reap what he has sown.'

'He hates me, P'ei Ti! He will never let me be.'

'No, my friend, it is his own ignominy he despises. His pride is a kind of madness and will be his undoing. Let us talk of it tomorrow. Tonight I wish you to feel only joy.'

I sat down again, flustered beyond measure. Then a voice from the shadows spoke up. It was Mi Feng, clutching a flask which he emptied from the nape. His voice slurred.

'So what if he killed a man!' he said. 'I killed three of 'em, and they all wanted my master's head. You people are always letting others fight your wars, but he acted like a man.'

Then, as P'ei Ti and Su Lin listened, he told of Wen Po's siege works and the tunnel, our fight in Pinang and flight from the Kin. I was so befuddled by drink and exhaustion, I hardly took in half of what he said. Su Lin dragged me to my feet, and led me to bed, whispering endearments. I left P'ei Ti gazing open-mouthed at Mi Feng, encouraging him with yet more wine.

When I lay on the bed the ceiling spun. I clutched Su Lin on silken sheets, sinking my head on her breast, and never thought who had nestled there before me.

The next dawn I ignored Su Lin's plea to rest. I was like a stringed instrument unable to stop vibrating. If only painful duties would let me be! As I dressed hurriedly, Su Lin watched from the bed.

'I am surprised you rush away as soon as you have arrived,' she said, pouting. 'Dearest, you must have new clothes. It makes a poor impression to be seen in rags.'

I was barely listening. Dare I strap P'ei Ti's sword to my belt? I felt vulnerable without it. But for a civilian to carry weapons was illegal.

'Do you think a man's duty should be determined by his tailor?' I snapped.

She looked at me timidly.

'Your voice has grown so harsh,' she muttered. 'I suppose it is to be expected.'

I might have countered that courtesy is flimsy. What was it anyway, except a mask? I frowned, unable to remember how I spoke before Pinang. Less angrily, for sure. Rudeness was always a horror of mine. Now I could imagine more fundamental failings.

I sat beside her on the bed and took her soft, languid hand. My own fingers were callused, grained with dirt. Once I had been fastidious about cleanliness, too. What had happened to me?

'Forgive me if I speak a little roughly,' I said. 'But this obligation cannot be delayed. It is a family matter. I must tell Cousin Hong about his brother.'

Su Lin's fingers entwined with my own. Her warmth crept through my veins, touching my heart.

'You must not expect me to be as I was,' I said, confused. Then I added, for a glance at her face told me exactly what she expected: 'Not yet, at least.'

'Return soon,' she said, resting her head on my chest.

I embraced her tightly, all the while glancing at the door. On the way out I found Mi Feng beneath a pile of blankets in the courtyard, a broken wine cup beside his head. Two of the servants were hovering in distress, broom in hand. I could tell they wished to sweep him up, ragged clothes and all. At first, I intended to wake him, for I had grown as dependent on his presence as on my sword. Mastering myself, I walked into the city.

An hour later, I found myself in the vicinity of the Pig Market, off the broad Imperial Way. Down a narrow side street, full of wheelbarrows and butcher-boys carrying sides of pork, I reached a medium-sized wine shop adjoining the pavement. A jug festooned with gay ribbons hung above the gate. There was a sharp reek as a barrow of night soil trundled past, otherwise the district smelt pervasively of dead animals and smoke. A child played by the gate and, at the sight of me, he screamed and dashed inside. A moment later Cousin Hong appeared. His expression of amazed joy, so out of character, made me smile.

'Little General! It is you! Why are you waiting in the street? Come inside!'

He rushed forward and led me into the courtyard. Despite the early hour, or perhaps because of it, dozens of men sat drinking and breakfasting on bowls of rice fried with onions, spices and pork. The aroma of ginger and garlic made me hungry. I looked round in a daze. My sister-in-law had appeared from the kitchen where she was supervising the servants. She bowed humbly. The customers on the benches watched but did not cease to dip and scoop their chopsticks.

'Little General!' crowed Cousin Hong. 'They said you were a dead man!'

He chuckled as he hugged me, roaring for the best wine in the house. I felt tearful, for it is no small thing to re-join one's family. He was all I had left, apart from my parents and sisters in far off Wei. Separation ached in my heart like a rebuke.

'How fat you've grown!' I cried. 'I can hardly get my arms round you.'

'And how thin you are, Little General. Wife, bring food with the wine. Not another word until you've eaten. No, I won't hear a single word!'

While I swallowed strips of fatty pork and rice, slurping cups of warm wine, Cousin Hong addressed his customers:

'See here, good sirs! Didn't I tell you about my famous cousin, the poet? And not one of you believed me. He's just back from trouncing the rebels up north. Don't be fooled by his campaigning gear, this man is a gentleman. A cup of free wine for everyone to celebrate the return of the Honourable Yun Cai!'

To my surprise, a butcher wearing a blood-spattered smock began to sing one of my verses. Half the words were wrong but for the first time in months I felt elation. We could have had quite a celebration, until I remembered why I had come.

'Cousin Hong,' I said, setting aside my cup, afraid of drinking too much. 'This is not seemly behaviour, given the circumstances, though I know you mean well. I must speak with you alone.'

He lowered his own drink, for he knew when I was serious.

Sitting before the ancestral shrine in his living room where Uncle Ming's spirit and ashes resided, I told him the sad story of his brother Zhi and how he had fallen fighting the barbarous Kin. At least, I told him a story. It concerned quite a different fellow from Cousin Zhi. One who always strived for the welfare of the conscripted peasants under his care so that they nicknamed him Beloved Father. How he had heroically fought off a Jurchen warrior using a borrowed spear, enabling his men to reach the safety of the pass. Then I stopped, tears in my eyes. So strongly did I wish these things to be true that I had half-convinced myself.

Cousin Hong watched shrewdly. He seemed oddly unaffected by my tale. He stood up and re-arranged a bowl of chrysanthemum petals on the ancestral shrine, straightening the tablet bearing his father's name.

'It wasn't quite like that, Little General,' he said. 'Was it?'

I did not know how to reply.

'Never mind,' he said. 'That is how we shall tell it to the children.'

He cleared his throat hoarsely, wiping his forehead.

'No,' I insisted. 'He died well.'

'Good!' cried Cousin Hong. 'Then at least he did something well! If he had passed the examinations – and heaven knows how many tens of thousands were spent to ensure he would! If he had achieved half of what Mother and Father hoped of him, do you think I'd be running a wine shop by the Pig Market? Don't tell me he died well.'

I shrugged helplessly.

'I'm sure he tried his best,' I said.

'Do you think my wife expected to be overseeing a load of butchers' breakfasts when she married me?' he continued. 'Her family own half a million in property, not that a single string of *cash* comes our way. So Zhi has gone. Then I am alone, apart from you, Little General. Who'd have thought it when I escorted you here from Wei, all those years ago? Who'd have thought it?'

He turned his face away from me.

'Life is strange,' he sighed. 'I'm sure you think me cold and unbrotherly. Maybe I am.'

'You are a fine brother,' I protested. 'What nonsense you speak!'

Cousin Hong snorted.

'To be a fine brother you need a fine brother. Otherwise

it's like throwing gold into a well. You get nothing back.'

'Oh, Hong, I'm certain he loved you.'

'Did he? Well, I'll take your word for it. All I know is that when we were ruined, you were the only one to help us out. The only one.'

I could not meet his eye.

His response had disheartened me. I was shocked he took the loss of a brother so lightly. All my life I had longed for a brother. Indeed, I found one wherever I could, especially in P'ei Ti – and Cousin Hong himself, to a certain extent – and even, in extremity, Mi Feng. We value most what we lack. Or what we imagine we lack.

'The proper formalities of mourning must be observed,' I said.

'Don't worry about that,' said Hong, dismissively. 'My wife will tell me what rites are expected. She's good at that sort of thing. Still, I'm glad to see you back. I'll close the shop today and we can celebrate your return, and drink to poor Zhi's soul.'

So we did, sitting on a bench in his courtyard beneath a clear blue sky, reminiscing about Uncle Ming's absurd wealth, until it became something comical. Cousin Hong paraded each of his children before me, boasting of his sons' cleverness and strength, his daughters' obedience and comeliness. A longing gripped my heart to become a father, too. Nothing else made sense in such a world of change.

All afternoon I felt an invisible presence, as though Cousin Zhi's spirit fluttered in distress around us, longing to join the conversation, wondering why we did not mourn him. His opportunity for affection had scattered, like the shadow of a hungry bird, across eternity.

When I returned to Su Lin's house, she was out on an engagement. In her letter to me at the frontier, she had promised to clothe me in her limbs. That night, though she returned late from a wedding, the pledge was fulfilled. Even as I hungered for her, a stubborn corner of my spirit could not open.

The next morning P'ei Ti appeared wearing a grave face. He whispered to Su Lin and this time she made no protest about me leaving.

His carriage waited outside, the horse munching handfuls of corn fed by the coachman. I nearly insisted on riding my shaggy pony so I could gallop away at the first sign of danger, then I climbed in beside him. By now Su Lin had procured me a splendid suit of silken clothes. She watched with approval from the gatehouse as we jolted down the road, two gentlemen together.

P'ei Ti smiled and laid his hand on my arm. His touch made me uncomfortable. In a rush, I told him the tale of Cousin Zhi and my meeting with Hong.

'I was sure Zhi's ghost watched us and wept,' I concluded. 'But I do not sense him here.'

'Of course,' said P'ei Ti. 'You are safe now.'

I sat in silence, watching the city pass. Each familiar sight somehow larger than itself, and unreal.

'You are no soldier,' said P'ei Ti. 'And you were thrust into that life entirely unprepared. Little wonder it has affected you deeply.'

I bridled, suspecting a slur on my character.

'Father would have been proud of me,' I said. 'I did my best.'

'That is not in doubt. You are a hero, Yun Cai. We all honour you.'

But I did not honour myself. I could not say why, yet felt it.

We travelled right across the city, passing many eyes, and I succumbed to nervousness. Sensing this, P'ei Ti tried to distract me with amusing gossip.

'Where are we going?' I asked, at last.

'I wondered when you would come to that,' he said. 'We are to meet a friend of yours, though you do not know him. He is a notable lawyer, and will help you in your troubles with Lord Xiao.'

The name fell on my ears dully. Lord Xiao bore me ill-will. It seemed the determining fact of my life.

'You must answer his questions frankly,' said P'ei Ti. 'This is a delicate time. That is why we are meeting in secrecy.'

We reached the Altar for the Sacrifices of the Southern Suburbs, which lay beyond the ramparts on a hill overlooking the River Che, where numerous barges and junks came and went, bringing all that was necessary to sustain the city. I climbed out of the carriage in a daze. The high pyramid of the Altar climbed towards Heaven. Plumed guardsmen stood like statues at the foot of the steps.

'Look, P'ei Ti,' I said. 'The river is covered with floating gulls. There must be a storm out to sea. They remind me of floating blossom on a stream. Perhaps this is a good omen.'

He peered at the Che.

'Use that in a poem,' he advised. 'Indeed, you must.'

He looked as though he wished to say something different, but asked patiently: 'What could you make the gulls represent?'

'Souls,' I said. 'See how they ride the tidal river, restless to take flight, to return to their natural elements, sky and wave.'

'Quite so. Now let us sacrifice at the Altar. I have brought flowers and wine.'

'Yes, old friend,' I said. 'Let us petition for peace.'

We poured our libation in the prescribed manner. I presented my wish to Heaven with all the fervour of my young heart. I felt obscure hurts begin to heal, as when tears force themselves out. Hard, glittering gifts, harbingers of reconciliation. If earnestness might catch the Jade Emperor's attention then I'm sure he looked down from his audience chamber, startled by my desire. I did not pray alone. The wishes of ten thousand families mourned alongside me. Never should the loss of a son be in vain.

Afterwards, I took P'ei Ti's hand. I could not believe our

prayers were not heard, at least in part. He nodded sombrely, though I spoke no words.

'I'm glad you feel reassurance,' he said. 'But that is not why I brought you here.'

I followed him down the slope to a street where caves had been dug in the hillside. He walked moodily along until we reached a doorway. The cave houses were home to hermits and wise men. Wealthy eunuchs and gentlemen of the court often went there to seek divinations.

'P'ei Ti,' I said. 'I am confused. You mentioned a lawyer.'

'This way,' he said, gruffly.

We passed beneath a rough hemp curtain and found ourselves in a long cave-room. Niches in the walls contained skulls and bones. On a low stool, beside a table covered with neatly arranged writing materials, sat a man in sky blue silks. A lamp flickered, illuminating his lower face, otherwise the cave was dark.

The man barely blinked as he regarded us. Everything about him seemed orderly, oddly so. The way he sat still and straight, his fine clothes without a single crease. Although no more than ten years older than us, his hair was iron-grey and scrupulously combed. His saturnine face a mask of seriousness. It would have been a surprise to hear him laugh, except at someone's expense. The only animation lay in his brooding eyes, behind which one might glimpse deep calculation. In short, I didn't take to the man. P'ei Ti seemed uneasy, too.

'Yun Cai,' he said. 'I have the honour of introducing you to the Lawyer Yuan Chu-Sou.'

Our host bowed stiffly, but did not rise. As there were no seats in the cave, we were forced to stand like underlings before him.

'I must apologise for this rude setting,' he said. 'Yet I am sure you understand the need for secrecy.'

'Sir,' I said. 'I understand nothing of this.'

P'ei Ti coughed beside me, then addressed Yuan Chu-Sou.

'I thought it best not to explain until we could talk properly.'

Yuan Chu-Sou nodded like a crane slowly dipping its head.

'A wise precaution,' he said. 'Then it behoves me to explain everything. Please listen carefully, for I have much to tell you.'

I scratched my chin. The air in the cave was dusty. I had acquired an aversion to the reek of earth. It reminded me of Wen Po's tunnel into Pinang.

'Then, sir,' I replied. 'I must sit down. As you may discern from my sling, I have suffered a wound.'

The corners of Yuan Chu-Sou's mouth twitched. Whether in annoyance or amusement, I could not say. Nevertheless, he retired to the back of the cave and found two stools like his own.

'To business,' he said, once we were seated. 'First I require your undertaking that not a single word of what I say will be revealed to a third party without my express permission.'

'That is a large undertaking,' I said. 'But if honour and the law are not compromised, I may make it.'

'Good. Then first be informed who I represent.'

On hearing the name, I started, jolting my injured shoulder.

'Why, I am. . . flattered by his notice.'

His August Excellency Lu Sha was a great man indeed. He oversaw several ministries and met the Son of Heaven daily to discuss the great affairs of our Empire. If Lord Xiao had gained so formidable an enemy he would do well to look around him. Yet I was disappointed. His August Excellency had a reputation for ruthless ambition – little better than Lord Xiao. Impossible such a man would interest himself in a nobody like me, unless he sensed personal profit.

'I am at a loss,' I said, cautiously. 'How can I be of use to one so powerful and illustrious.'

Yuan Chu-Sou examined me.

'That is a pertinent point. I will explain. His August Excellency is concerned that Lord Xiao's depredations and incompetence are a danger to public safety. As you will know, there are great debates at court. Should we maintain peace with the Kin Emperor through the payment of tribute, or should we wage war? Hence His August Excellency finds himself in opposition to Lord Xiao.'

'I still do not see how I matter.'

'Of course, you do not matter,' said Yaun Chu-Sou, frankly. 'Except that the circumstances of your posting to Pinang brought a surprising discredit to Lord Xiao, solely due to the popularity of your poetry. He has lost face. But, as you imply, that is hardly fatal to Lord Xiao's influence in the court. Nevertheless, His August Excellency believes a minor case could be made against Lord Xiao for abusing his position. Now is not the time to make that case, yet it might be a useful addition to more serious charges.'

'What exactly are these charges?' I asked.

So I was to be like the cabbage leaves one finds shredded on a rich dish of meat. They hoped to poison Lord Xiao and I was to be the garnish.

'I am hardly likely to tell you that,' he replied.

I met P'ei Ti's eye. He had remained uncharacteristically silent.

'My only worry is for the Honourable Yun Cai's welfare,' broke in P'ei Ti.

He turned to me.

'That's the main thing, Yun Cai. We believe you should resign your official post at once, citing ill-health. That way you would no longer be directly employed by Lord Xiao's ministry, and his immediate power over you would cease. Yuan Chu-Sou has offered to take care of this, if you agree. But you must agree soon because Lord Xiao may already have heard about your return to the city.'

I laughed.

'I would agree with great pleasure,' I said. 'But how am I to live without a salary?'

'That is simple,' broke in Yuan Chu-Sou. 'At an appropriate

time, His August Excellency will find you another position. Alas, it would be impolitic for him to do so straight away. The hour has not arrived for openness. In any case, if you are too unwell for your current position, how might you instantly take another?'

I was sure a means might be found. Yet I said, reluctantly: 'I see.'

So on top of everything, I was to be ruined. But I could hardly return to Lord Xiao's ministry. The thought of an interview with him unnerved me.

'Then I shall return to my family in Wei Valley,' I declared.

'That is not advisable,' said Yuan Chu-Sou, sharply. 'If you did, your career would be at a definitive end.'

The threat formed unpleasant associations. I could not bear to face Father in disgrace, let alone meet the expenses of so long a journey. I was a prisoner – for now at least. Then I recalled the three scrolls my predecessor at the Bureau of Fallen Heroes had concealed in his robes.

'There may be something,' I said, tentatively.

Yuan Chu-Sou leaned forward as I explained.

'Very interesting,' he said, barely able to suppress his eagerness. 'Written in a cipher or code. . . very interesting. You see, the circumstances of your unfortunate colleague's sudden departure to Pinang are well-known to us. I would very much like to see these documents.'

So I arranged they should be collected from Su Lin's house that same day.

We left soon afterwards, jolting along in P'ei Ti's carriage. I closed my eyes, affected by a crippling weariness of soul, not unlike grief. After struggling all my life to join the Golden List, I found myself struck off, no longer an official, a mere penniless poet, my future as uncertain as next month's rain.

'P'ei Ti,' I said. 'I have become nothing.'

He patted my hand, his unhappiness plain to see.

'Be patient,' he said.

And I wondered what for.

I recalled, as if through a mist, that the Buddha urges us to become Nothing. This, he advises, is preferable to being Something, however grand, because then one lives closer to the Eternal Emptiness. After all, Nothing lies at the heart of Everything. It is odd that when one needs philosophy most, it seems feeble and distant. Distress drowns it out like a clattering gong.

After months in a bare hut bobbing on the fitful sea of the frontier, Su Lin's house floated like a lily, alive with colour and animation, soft voices and languid moods. Yet I was ill at ease. I felt that I might be tipped off the lily at any time and drown.

Although small, her house possessed many luxuries. In its grounds, a pavilion and octagonal summerhouse, perfect for moon-watching. Flower gardens and rockeries and fishponds, all over-looked by a fine belvedere.

Inside, brocade carpets covered the floors of the principle rooms. When it came to ornaments – silver vases and figurines, as well as an exquisite jade tablet decorated with hunting scenes. A dozen valuable paintings hung on the walls. I was touched to find some of the poems I had written for Su Lin among them, in pride of place. Had I really written so finely? It was many months since I had composed the simplest couplet.

A perfumed house: sandalwood and incense, flowers in extravagant number sent daily by admirers, so many they were taken for granted.

Five servants tended to her needs, aided by two musicians. Needless to say they viewed me with distrust, as somehow diminishing their mistress. Well they might, for their status depended entirely on her own and I hardly enhanced it. When I commented on her domestics, Su Lin complained that the courtesan Hsu Lau had over a dozen, as well as a small orchestra.

How swiftly riches had fallen her way! She had become one of the jewels wealthy young men found it necessary to admire – and possess, if they could. By her own account, this sudden good fortune flowed entirely from the patronage of His August Excellency, who had hired her to entertain the guests at several notable banquets. His motive was obvious. The guests could both admire her and chuckle over the fact that she had rejected Lord Xiao's advances, thus diminishing his rival's reputation. The entire fashionable world followed His August Excellency's example and one absurdly rich admirer went so far as to offer her this house. What he received in return, I did not enquire.

It was with some horror I began to recognise the same jealousy toward His August Excellency that I had felt for Lord Xiao. The futility and circularity of such feelings distressed me. Most of all, I watched her excitement at being so elevated with a thousand tangled emotions.

For a week I wandered from room to room, saying little. At night, when Su Lin returned late, I strove to captivate her with my body, pretending the pain in my shoulder was no pain, the ache in my heart for lost intimacy did not matter. Mi Feng was as uncomfortable as myself, though he had a more pressing reason. Su Lin's maid swelled with his unborn child, like a seed pod about to burst. How he regarded fatherhood he did not say, but I often saw them talking quietly to each other.

One afternoon, we retreated to the garden to escape a particularly noisy group of admirers, bearing gifts worthy of a princess for Su Lin, far beyond six months' salary when I worked at the Deer Park Library. If they had not tittered then fallen silent as I passed by, I could have pretended they did not view me as a curiosity.

By now I wore splendid silks she had provided. How heavy they weighed that hot day! By a pond full of sluggish, shining carp, Mi Feng leant forward and whispered: 'My Lord shouldn't forget he faced a man more handy than these, and could have taken his head as a trophy if he'd wanted.'

Evidently he wished me to drive my rivals away with brute force. The absurdity of such a notion made me smile.

'Different disciplines apply here,' I said.

'As you wish, sir,' he muttered.

Strangely enough, I no longer objected to him addressing me as 'sir'. Since my resignation as an official, I clung to any dignity. We looked silently out across the West Lake. Pleasure craft formed shifting patterns, like the positions of the constellations. This thought made me consider my own place. After a while, I turned to Mi Feng: 'Fetch me paper and writing materials,' I said. 'I have a message for you to take to Cousin Hong.'

That evening I could keep silent no longer. Su Lin was unengaged, a rare event. We dined alone in the summerhouse, and rather sumptuously. Despite her evident enjoyment of a moment's peace in her splendid new house, I insisted she perform a few songs for me, citing the promise she had written when I languished in Pinang. Like a child, I resented favours other men enjoyed. Had I not paid for them in ways more costly than *cash*? Finally, Su Lin laid aside her lute and sat beside me. I stared out across the lake.

'I do not like to see you unhappy,' she said. 'Do I not make you happy?'

'What makes you say that?' I asked.

'Tell me, dearest Yun Cai, then I can understand.'

I stood up, and sighed loudly. How often one resembles a poorly-trained actor when speaking from the heart.

'There are always so many fine fellows fluttering around you like moths! It is not what I expected.'

'May not a few be drawn to my flame?' she asked.

'I do not like it.'

'But that is how I make my living,' she protested. 'Would you rather we share a hovel together, glad to eat a little meat once a month?'

'Yes! So long as we are the beings in each other's eyes.'

Su Lin barely hid her exasperation.

'You are in my eyes always! Now that you have lost your position, you rarely leave the house.'

I recoiled. Even in her anger, she comprehended the cruel injustice of her words. Su Lin glanced away, ashamed.

'You might recall how that misfortune came about,' I said, quietly.

She began to cry silently.

'I did not mean that, Yun Cai! I am sorry. Your situation will mend,' she said, brushing away tears. 'His August Excellency will find you a new posting, and very soon. He has promised me! Then everything will have been worthwhile.'

She clutched my hand, and showed me her palm, where the scar she had cut before the Gate of Eternal Rectitude still lay.

'Everything I am doing is to win your revenge!' she cried. 'Why do you think I court His August Excellency so carefully? It is for your sake. Just you! Remember the poison I am preparing!'

That day Su Lin had shown me a clay pot where she had sealed a centipede, scorpion, snake, frog and gecko lizard. She intended to grind up whichever of the noxious creatures outlived the others, swollen with the essences of the four it had consumed. With this a sorcerer might cast a spell on Lord Xiao. It was the kind of dark magic Honoured Aunty had practised, and little good it had brought her.

'When Lord Xiao is crushed for what he has done, you shall be complete once more,' she said, eagerly.

I held her slender hand and smiled sadly.

'Revenge will not make us happy,' I said.

'Why must you always deny what I do for your sake?'

I sat beside her. The city darkened around us. Swallows

flitted overhead and flies made rings upon the pond, disturbing the water with tiny ripples. Stars glittered on the surface, diffused, not brilliant like bright eyes.

'Su Lin,' I said. 'Every day I stay here lessens my pride. It is no reproach on you, my love, that I would sooner be poor than live in a palace as a kept man. You cannot imagine how I admire your success! How could I not? Of all the many who court you, only I knew the poor girl from Chunming who sat in an alley, dreaming of a better life. And through your grace and hard work, that is what you have attained. I honour you for it. But I cannot stay here forever. Tomorrow I will go to live with Cousin Hong. And when my own labours win me a house of my own, however modest, I trust you will visit me there. And then we may love each other, free of worry, as we did before.'

She did not take her eyes from my face throughout this long speech.

'You want to leave me,' she said, finally.

'I must.'

'It is as the fortune-teller told me,' she said, her gaze fixed sightlessly on memories I could not share. 'After Father fell into drink and debt, he sold me to a broker with connections in the capital. Oh, Yun Cai, I can remember his putrid breath now, as though it is something I may never wash away! But that is not what I meant to say. One day he gave me a few *cash*, because I had pleased him, expecting me to spend it on sweet buns, I suppose. Instead I found a fortune-teller, and offered what little I could. The future was everything to me! And the old woman touched my eyelids with her finger, and said: "Your fate is to watch from afar. You are love's spy." And now when I have gained so much, you wish to leave me! Oh, will you not stay a little longer?'

But I could not hear of it. Not if I wished to retain a spark of pride.

'Will you come here sometimes?' she asked, timidly. 'You see, I dare not visit you, I mean, in your cousin's wine shop. . . it is just that, I cannot.'

I stopped her with a harsh laugh.

'A fine sight you'd make!' I said. 'Parading through the Pig Market on tottering heels with a train of mincing maids! What if you stepped in something unpleasant? Or one of your lofty patrons saw you?'

To my surprise, silent tears again trickled down her face and I wondered if I had spoken cruelly. She kissed my hands.

'You must not go!' she said. 'Wait another week, at least.'

We argued the point back and forth until she fell quiet. Another night passed on her soft sheets. We embraced and kissed, proving our love. Her fragrance intoxicated me. At dawn we fell apart and slept. Yet in the moment before consciousness slipped away, I recalled Lord Xiao, and the irony that his malice had separated us in ways he could not have anticipated.

By contrasts we judge places; yet between one and the next, much is often shared. Cousin Hong's tavern possessed aromas quite as intoxicating as Su Lin's perfume. Wine scented the air with a hundred variations of mood, depending on its warmth. When it was hot, heady clouds rolled round the courtyard of Hong's establishment.

Welcome has its own smell too and I was lucky to find it in every corner. Cousin Hong never flinched from paying a debt. He was well aware that by discharging one obligation, fresh advantage accrues.

'Little General,' he said, after I had explained my circumstances. 'It may be that you are offered a new position tomorrow, or maybe in six months. I don't really care. The one favour I ask is that you teach my boys how to read and write. That would be a great thing to me.'

Easy enough rent, even though his sons were dullards.

Cousin Hong found me a small room at the back of the house, overlooking Jewel Cloud Canal. I was reminded of my quarters in Uncle Ming's residence, except that now I did not occupy a whole tower and shared the room with dozens of storage jars. There was space for a narrow bed and a corner table made of planks. Pegs for my clothes. Shelves for my scrolls. The joy of being re-united with my library was quiet, yet intense. For all that, I could not stop thinking of Su Lin.

My chamber had a rectangular window barred against thieves and a square back door, opening onto narrow brick steps leading down to the canal, used for wine and vegetable deliveries. I sat on the steps often, contemplating the still waters and occasionally fishing. The fish were pampered creatures, having much effluence to feed on, but I found that a juicy maggot or plump cricket tempted them to bite. Though small and bony, they were delicious smeared with a paste of lime and crushed peppers, then barbecued, the crispier the better. Cousin Hong smacked his lips and declared they made a welcome change from pork.

Inevitably, Mi Feng accompanied me to my new home. He left Su Lin's mansion with alacrity, if for no other reason than impending fatherhood. To my surprise, Cousin Hong welcomed his arrival as warmly as my own for Mi Feng was instantly useful to him, whereas my upkeep cost hard cash. Recently Cousin Hong had been troubled by a gang of neighbourhood toughs who demanded free wine and upset the paying customers. Within hours of Mi Feng's installation they decided to frequent other wine shops. Nevertheless, dire threats were made against him and it was the kind of district where a wise man took such things seriously.

I spent many hours wandering the streets. Luckily I had money in my purse. The Lawyer Yuan Chu-Sou had tendered my resignation from government service as promised and insisted that I receive back-pay for my months in Pinang. A sum amounting to several thousand *cash*. So I could afford to while away an hour in a humble tea shop or outside a noodle stall, listening to the conversations as a man of leisure in the countryside listens to the birds. It is a fine thing not to be ashamed of modest pleasures. Around the Pig Market a few *cash* made me rich.

Sometimes when I could not sleep I left Cousin Hong's house in the hour before dawn, driven by restlessness and bad dreams. While the city slept the Pig Market was full of noise and bustle. Hundreds of squealing swine, their legs bound, were unloaded from barges on the East Canal and carried by porters to pens where each beast was purchased after a careful examination. Bald pigs, hairy pigs, some speckled, others albino with feverish pink eyes. All were judged, and weighed, and paid for in double quick time. Dawn was already splitting the sky with slivers of golden light and everything had to be ready for the first customers.

The market was divided by two broad lanes, each subdivided further by a hundred butchers' stalls, behind which the beasts were slaughtered. At this hour I was reminded of a battlefield. Did the pigs squeal for mercy? We could not, or did not care to, understand their voices. Ribaldry and shouts from the assembled butchers, blood trickling in red, bubbly streams down channels lined with stone into the nearby canal. Naturally, small fish thronged in the waters and poor fishermen followed suit, singing as they cast and hauled in their nets.

Once dead, the pigs were hoisted onto thick wooden tables. Skilled men plied knives and cleavers shining dully in the lamplight, apportioning sections of the animals to slippery wooden trays. From there they were carried to the stall itself. Pyramids of kidneys and lungs, sides of best flesh alongside piles of legs. Meat possesses a peculiar smell before it decays, as though clinging to life.

The butchers were tired by then. Wine sellers specialising in a thin, watery brew filled jugs and wide-brimmed cups, for this was thirsty work. By sunrise, all was in readiness. Noodle merchants seeking ribs or offal arrived first, each competing to attract the breakfast trade, followed by buyers from wine shops, tea-houses, pickled pork shops and the humblest street vendors hoping to pick up a bargain which they would cook at noon and serve until dusk. By early afternoon the market had been stripped bare and officials wheeled vats of water across the huge square, washing the stones clean, ready for the next night.

So I wandered, thinking sparse thoughts. How people will laugh as they work, making the best of whatever fate or chance has cast their way. How the sky changes shape and colour, indifferent to the bustle it provokes. How men and swine share similar destinies, though the former are not generally eaten, except by weariness and worms.

Those were years when, for many, not enough was eaten. The capital thronged with peasants driven by ruin in the countryside to try their chances in the city. Rickety buildings several stories high might contain a dozen families, three generations in every room, countless more if you included the dead lurking in the tablets of their ancestral shrines. All this I observed with a mixture of guilt and anger. To see a child begging, her eager, hopeful face already lined by hunger and humiliation. Oh, then you begin to doubt whether the Mandate of Heaven truly belongs to those in authority.

By now almost a year had passed since I last took up brush and ink to compose. That gift – for it is a gift, though nourished by intense labour – had withered within me. One evening, subdued by care, I retreated to my room, listening to sounds of merriment in Cousin Hong's courtyard.

The lamp flickered on the table. I lay on the bed, watching a moth's fluttering progress round the room. Then I rose and ladled myself a cup of cheap wine from one of the storage jars in my chamber. Opening the back door, I sat on the steps, sipping and noting patterns of shadow on the dark waters of Jewel Cloud Canal. Stars glittered. Voices scented the night with sound. Within the radius of a single *li*, a thousand feelings and perceptions contended in as many breasts, fleeting streams of life. And the dark canal slowly drifted beneath me, its waters speckled with disappointment and joy, all flowing in accordance with the Way.

I remembered moments of friendship, shifting terrains of mind, until the world is freshly perceived. One longs to hold onto what is good, just for a while, aware of hours seeping like wind through your fingers. The rich must endure this ceaseless transience as well as the poor.

Then I knew I must write again, if only to hold still a floating life, my words already fading as soon as set down. Just thoughts. And thoughts re-shape themselves with each succeeding generation.

Without fuss, as though undertaking the most natural thing in the world, I mixed ink, poured another cup of wine and wrote poem after poem until dawn shone through the open doorway. That night was among the best of my life.

I wrote of slipping love, tears filling my eyes. Then satires questioning the abuses endured by the poor. Again of how feelings find an hour and drift away, though one clutches to hold them. Finally, for I had begun to think of breakfast, a poem entitled 'Fish Caught in the Jewel Cloud Canal':

Thin, bony fish caught from brick steps.
Do not say they are less than carp.
Lure and hook whatever swims your way,
Hold slippery, drowning mouths,
Scales crusting hands like moonshine.
Finest foods are a matter of taste.
Once eaten, any fish becomes you.

I received a summons in the form of a letter delivered by one of P'ei Ti's servants. It read simply: *Be on the brick steps you told me about at the back of your cousin's shop when the second bell*

of night is sounded. Tell no one of this. I anticipate a meeting to your advantage.

Why he chose such a rendezvous, I had no idea, but I sensed unpleasantness. The evening passed slowly. I debated whether to take my sword, or even Mi Feng along, all the while considering P'ei Ti's injunction to tell no one. At last the watchmen could be heard on the street, beating their wooden drums and calling the second hour. I opened the back door and stepped outside.

All was in darkness, even the stars obscured by sluggish clouds. A scent of rain and earth in the air. Drips broke the silence at irregular intervals. I could hear rats scurrying in the eaves of the opposite house. Somewhere a man bellowed in anguish. Rowdy voices sang, then dwindled.

Once my eyes had accustomed themselves to the night, I sat on the steps, staring at faint tendrils of mist as they curled across the canal. Minutes passed. The night was cool and I would have found it pleasant if not for the anxious fluttering in my heart. I flexed my shoulder muscles. They were gaining strength and might be needed that night.

A gentle splash of oars made me alert. The sound grew steadily. A long, narrow boat appeared through the fog and I rose. The boat paused at the foot of the steps, a white face peering up at me. I caught a flash of eyes.

'Yun Cai!' whispered a familiar voice.

I relaxed, and climbed gingerly on board. P'ei Ti was out of uniform for once, dressed in a merchant's plain robes. I sat heavily beside him so that the boat wobbled.

'Why have you brought that damn sword?' he hissed.

I could hardly admit that fear had armed me.

'Where are we going?' I whispered back.

'Shhh!'

He lay his hand on my arm.

'It will become clear.'

The boatman pushed off and propelled us forward, working the oar at the back with his feet. We moved quietly through a maze of canals. Most of the houses we passed were silent. A few showed lights behind bamboo curtains. We drifted under high, hump-backed bridges where impoverished peasants sheltered. Often there were watchtowers, containing soldiers of the City Guard.

'Hide your sword at the bottom of the boat,' muttered P'ei Ti. 'You will bring ruin on us all.'

I took his point. Armed men arrested at night were automatically guilty. A few guardsmen watched us paddle by, but we received no challenge. Finally I recognised the North Eastern Ramparts rising on our right. In that district, wealthy courtiers and officials, especially the Son of Heaven's eunuchs, had constructed stone warehouses, surrounded by a network of canals. Merchants hired space within them at exorbitant prices, safe in the knowledge that the frequent fires vexing the city could not destroy their goods. I thought of Uncle Ming then. He would have done well to store his wine in such a warehouse. The Great Fire would not have ruined him.

I turned to P'ei Ti.

'Who are we meeting?' I asked.

He glanced at the boatman.

'Someone you once met in a cave,' he said.

So it was the Lawyer Yuan Chu-Sou. I should have guessed. Such secrecy implied grave interests.

The boatman guided us to a jetty beside a towering warehouse. A watchman waited on the steps, holding a pole from which hung a lamp. He seemed to be expecting us.

'What is the colour?' he asked.

The clouds above parted for a moment and I glimpsed stars.

'Vermilion is the colour,' said P'ei Ti.

The watchman grunted.

'Then follow me, sirs.'

As we climbed ashore, leaving the boatman to wait for us, I said to P'ei Ti: 'I take it this warehouse belongs to a certain August Excellency?'

'Of course,' he replied.

I had rarely seen him so tense.

We were led to a heavy wooden door, studded with iron. Another watchman waited. Both looked us over suspiciously.

'No sword!' called out the eldest.

I had concealed it under my cloak as we left the boat. At once I sensed danger.

'We are entering a trap!' I whispered in P'ei Ti's ear. 'We must not go in there!'

He shook himself free.

'I beg you to trust me,' he said.

'I will not leave my sword!'

P'ei Ti turned to the eldest watchman.

'I have told you the password,' he said, harshly. 'Now let us in!'

The man glanced uncertainly at his colleague, then shrugged. We were led into a huge, darkened space, filled with bales and boxes and casks. The tramp of our feet echoed on the earth floor. A glow of lamps lit one corner of the warehouse. As we approached, I saw two men whispering together at a long table. Papers and writing materials covered the boards, including the scrolls I had recovered from Pinang. The first man was the Lawyer Yuan Chu-Sou, but the second had his back to me. When he turned, I gasped.

In a moment, my sword was drawn. The watchmen leapt back, fumbling for weapons.

That second man was Lord Xiao's secretary, complete with his customary, supercilious smile.

'What treachery is this?' I cried. 'P'ei Ti, stand behind me! I will protect you.'

Surely it is something when a peaceable man like myself is enraged.

The watchmen hung back, staring at my sword. Even P'ei Ti was looking round for a means of escape. If I was to die here, I had already determined that Lord Xiao's secretary would perish with me.

Yuan Chu-Sou stepped forward, unruffled as ever, yet his brooding eyes suggested darker feelings.

'Gentlemen!' he said. 'Honourable Yun Cai, do put away that sword! You are in no danger, sir.'

'What is *he* doing here?' I said, reluctant to lower my weapon. Part of me wished to use it. The contempt I felt for Secretary Wen can scarcely be imagined. He had been party to every humiliation I had suffered at Lord Xiao's hands. To me, at that moment, he was Lord Xiao. I noted with relish that his smile had vanished. He looked nervously to the Lawyer Yuan Chu-Sou for protection.

'Enough of this,' said the latter. 'If we desired your life, Yun Cai, I'm sure a simpler means could be found than this. Do you not think?'

P'ei Ti turned to me eagerly. I did not like to witness his loss of nerve. Such moods are infectious.

'That is true, Yun Cai. I beg you, put it away.'

So I did, glaring at my enemy. The secretary's smile returned, except now it was less certain.

'You have certainly changed,' he muttered.

Then he added: 'After all the wrongs you have suffered.'

Yuan Chu-Sou stepped between us.

'It is natural you should be suspicious,' he said. 'But I would prefer it if we got straight to business.'

So I found myself at the table, P'ei Ti by my side. Yuan Chu-Sou stiff in his chair, like a merciless judge.

'I wish this meeting to be brief,' he said. 'I have gone to great lengths to ensure its privacy. First of all, Yun Cai deserves an explanation for Secretary Wen's presence. You need know only this: he is working for His August Excellency now.'

I met Secretary Wen's eye.

'I take it Lord Xiao is unaware of your shifting loyalties? How filial!'

The Lawyer Yuan Chu-Sou answered for him.

'Quite so. The good secretary is demonstrating his filial loyalty to the Son of Heaven, by acting as a kind of. . . a kind of. . .'

'Spy?' I suggested.

'Quite so. For which His August Excellency will proffer an inestimable reward.'

Secretary Wen wasn't grinning now. I could not help goading the man.

'Lord Xiao will be offended,' I said. 'And understandably.'

'Never mind that,' said Yuan Chu-Sou, sharply. 'Time is short. Now, Yun Cai, to the matter of the scrolls you provided. They made most interesting reading. Indeed, they prove conclusively that Lord Xiao has been transferring large sums from the public exchequer for his personal use. As such they are evidence. Secretary Wen here can provide further evidence, to corroborate your own. In short, it transpires there is a strong case against Lord Xiao. It seems that his tastes are extravagant, as are those of his wife, and that he has resorted to peculation in order to satisfy them.'

'Such practices are generally winked at,' I said, mildly.

P'ei Ti fluttered beside me.

'Not so, Yun Cai. I speak as an official of the Bureau of Censors and, believe me, if this can be proved Lord Xiao has committed a capital crime.'

'My point,' I said. 'Is that it is unusual for anyone to bother to prove it.'

The Lawyer Yuan Chu-Sou gestured airily.

'That is true. But it is our intention to prosecute this case.'

I sat back. So Lord Xiao's enemies had decided to act. Certainly the time was favourable. He had always been among those advocating war against the Kin barbarians instead of the payment of tribute, perhaps because his wife's family not only held several generalships but had important interests when it came to military supplies. A few years ago such a policy had attracted His Imperial Highness. It seemed that, given recent reverses, the Son of Heaven now thought differently and was happy to buy peace. If His August Excellency wished to bring Lord Xiao down, he had to be bold. After all, his old rival might declare himself a convert to the peace party at any time and then the opportunity would be lost.

'How does this involve me?' I asked.

The Lawyer Yuan Chu-Sou leant forward.

'That is obvious. You are our sole witness to the provenance of the scrolls confirming Lord Xiao's corruption. You, Yun Cai, can prove that you found them in Pinang and that they belonged to an official, unfortunately deceased, who was privy to all Lord Xiao's tricks. In short, you can testify to the scrolls' authenticity. I should say you represent one element of the case I am preparing. That is how you are involved.'

'I see.'

'Witnesses can be decisive in these affairs,' declared the Lawyer Yuan Chu-Sou, airily. 'For example, it seems one of the clerks from your mission in Pinang managed to survive the debacle there. I should tell you that I have arranged for him to be imprisoned on various charges, so he is out of the way. It would not do for an employee of Lord Xiao's ministry, however humble, to contradict our evidence.'

'Do you mean he has been imprisoned on false charges?'

Yuan Chu-Sou raised an eyebrow.

'When one's case hangs in the balance, such measures are sometimes necessary.'

I did not like this. I had been my clerks' protector and father. Was I to betray that trust now?

'He is guilty of no crime!' I protested.

'That is irrelevant,' snapped Yuan Chu-Sou. 'I want him out of the way.'

I looked from face to face. Ruthless men. They would stop at nothing. At last I understood my role as pawn.

'It is my intention to return to my family in Chunming Province,' I declared, dully.

I turned to P'ei Ti, showing my distress. His expression hardened.

Yuan Chu-Sou leant forward.

'As I have had occasion to mention before, that would be a most unfortunate event for you. There is no avoiding one's destiny.'

P'ei Ti nodded.

'Now is not the right moment to visit your family,' he said.

Unexpectedly, he tapped the table three times. Everyone turned to him. P'ei Ti was young then; the noble positions he later attained as yet unwon. But he possessed a strength, flowing from his essential virtue, an authority lesser men were forced to acknowledge. When he glared at the Lawyer Yuan Chu-Sou and Secretary Wen they both glanced away.

'Prosecuting corruption is all very well,' he said. 'And as an official of the Censor's Office, I share your desire that Lord Xiao should be punished for his crimes. But if one of Yun Cai's former clerks is to be falsely imprisoned as a consequence, I cannot tolerate it. Justice will never be served by injustice.'

Yuan Chu-Sou frowned.

'Young man. . .' he began, menacingly.

'No!' interrupted P'ei Ti. 'I insist that clerk is released! Have him posted to a distant province, by all means, if you want him far away. Only make sure his new position is not dangerous or ignoble. If this does not happen, I shall use my influence as Censor to ensure the innocent do not suffer unduly.'

It was a pleasure to see the Lawyer Yuan Chu-Sou lick his lips, calculating the limits of P'ei Ti's power.

'Very well,' he said.

'Naturally, I require written confirmation of the man's release and transfer,' said P'ei Ti.

I could have embraced him. He risked much by his stand on behalf of a nobody.

'There is another matter we have not touched upon,' said P'ei Ti, agreeably. 'The Honourable Yun Cai is currently without a position. When is it His August Excellency's desire that a suitable posting shall be found?'

Now the Lawyer Yuan Chu-Sou was on safer ground. He tutted.

'That depends on the successful prosecution of Lord Xiao,' he said.

'Not before?' asked P'ei Ti.

'Under no circumstances.'

His reasoning was obvious. They wished to dangle me like a puppet, my limbs twitched by their strings, my voice used to speak words they had chosen. Only through renouncing ambition could I deny their power over me.

As we paddled away, dawn mists thickened over the canal and P'ei Ti hugged his cloak for warmth.

'A most unsatisfactory meeting,' he said, at last.

I raised an eyebrow.

'His August Excellency and Lord Xiao seem much the same.'

'One foot cannot stand on two ships,' he countered.

'Water can both sustain and sink a ship,' I replied.

He burrowed himself deeper in his cloak. Was that the splash of oars behind us, hidden by the fog? A dark foreboding that Lord Xiao was following our progress made me grip the side of the boat.

Then I remembered brandishing my sword in the warehouse and felt uneasy. I had been quite prepared to kill Secretary Wen. Dark promptings had entered my soul and, worse, they excited me. Secretary Wen was right, I had changed. I could not imagine it was for the better.

A day or so later, I found myself on the Imperial Way. It ran the whole length of the city, sixty yards wide, paved in stone and brick, except for a central road covered with fine white sand reserved for the Emperor's use. A good place to be alone, for tens of thousands thronged there and dense crowds make one inconspicuous. Merchants' arcades, temples and mansions lined the Imperial Way. Every *li* or so there were tea-houses where a single scented cup cost a labouring man's wages for the week. It was to just such an establishment I headed.

Needless to say I had no prospect of settling the bill. Su Lin had invited me to drink tea with her, perhaps expecting me to be pleased by a little luxury. This thought rankled as I trudged along. My clothes glinted and rustled. Bright new silks sent to me that morning with a note from Su Lin claiming they suited my complexion.

I feared being dressed up like a doll. You would expect the owner of such silks to travel by litter or carriage, not walk under the blazing noon sun without even an umbrella for shade. My clothes were a fraud: I was not the worthy man they declared but someone obliged to his mistress for a little tea.

The Imperial Way seemed full of staring eyes, the sense that behind each floating face lurked scorn, animosity. I could not explain such feelings. Discomfort in every pore, a sweat of fear, as though the city was an endless maze. I hurried onwards through the crowd and had never felt so friendless.

Above all, I was obsessed with meeting Lord Xiao. Once reminded of my existence, he would hatch a thousand cruel troubles. The sides of the Imperial Way were green with fruit trees, plum, peach, pear and apricot, some still showing a blush of blossom. But I did not notice. My thoughts were a swirl of imagined enemies and failures. I was entirely turned inwards – and that is blindness, unless one seeks acceptance of the Way.

The carriage of a high official approached through the crowd. Was it Lord Xiao? At once I sought a place to hide, hurrying into a girdle merchant's arcade. I did not listen as the fellow jabbered at me, holding out costly belts, and soon he fell silent, eyeing me curiously. I was finding it hard to breathe. My heart raced painfully.

At last I judged the danger past and emerged in time to see the carriage turning into the gateway of the Jade Disk Tea-House. My fears instantly doubled. I felt certain it contained Lord Xiao and his mocking cronies.

For a moment I considered turning back. But Su Lin was waiting in there. What would she think if I failed to arrive? And the carriage might be carrying anyone. However hard or far I fled, I would never outrun fear. Light-headed, I walked over to the gatehouse.

The Jade Disk Tea-House was like all such places. No doubt it exists still. Around a central courtyard were dozens of sumptuous rooms, red and green stairways, painted blinds to ensure privacy when conducting a liaison or shady business deal. These curtains were seldom lowered, as the main reason for visiting the Jade Disk Tea-House was merely to be seen there. Miniature pines and vases of flowers stood in tasteful locations. Waiters flowed round elegant chairs with trays of rarest tea, or aniseed cakes, or health-giving cordials. An atmosphere of constant chatter, punctuated by the melodies of singing girls. I stood awkwardly by the entrance until a waiter rushed over. My forehead and hair were damp with sweat. He examined me, assessing my potential for tips.

'I am here to meet a lady,' I said, as haughtily as I could. 'Miss Su Lin.'

At once his eyes brightened. He led me to a long private room on the first floor. Here sat Su Lin, fanning herself and chattering gaily to a man in the uniform of a viscount.

She had dressed exquisitely for the occasion. Her silks shimmered, as did her coiled hair. The official smiled politely as I arrived.

'Well, well,' said the fellow. 'It seems an honoured guest has displaced me.'

I said nothing. Perhaps strain showed on my face. Perhaps I was a trifle grim. Certainly I felt that way. He excused himself and I nodded curtly as he left.

'You could have shown a little more courtesy to Viscount Shao,' she said, pouting humorously though I could tell she was troubled. 'A man like that is not without influence.'

I sat beside her, taken aback by such a greeting.

'Really?' I said.

'Of course.'

Then she explained his offices and friends in a gay, playful tone as though it was all a wonderful game. I barely listened.

'You are the reason I am here,' I replied. 'No one else, whatever strings they can pull.'

She bit her plump, carmine lip. A waiter brought me a cup of tea and hovered expectantly. I waved him away. Su Lin nodded to one of her serving women who promptly tipped him. It was all very smooth and designed in advance not to embarrass me.

'You seem uncomfortable,' she said, in a low voice. 'Are you unwell?'

For once her disappointment did not affect me. In fact I found it curious.

'Perhaps I am,' I said. 'This is a strange place to meet.'

'Why? I come here often.'

'But I do not. And that is why it is a strange place to meet.'

She sighed, and sipped a cup of jasmine tea. One of the leaves stuck to her upper lip. She brushed it away delicately. Then she asked her maids to wait outside. No doubt they listened by the door.

'You have not visited me for a whole week,' she whispered. 'I do not know what to think.'

'I have been composing poems. Besides, how am I to know when you are free or engaged?'

Su Lin had developed a particular way of expressing frustration. It was confined to the angle of her eyebrows. When we first met her emotions had been more obvious and natural. Still the changes of her face fascinated me.

'I have heard such delightful news,' she announced. 'Can you guess what it is?'

'Probably not.'

'Then I shall tell you. A certain person – I mean the one who has promised to help you – has hinted that he will use his influence to have me play at the Feast of Lanterns. Before the Son of Heaven himself!'

Now I understood her brittle gaiety. Such a prospect was worth a year's anxiety.

'I am pleased for you,' I said.

She pouted again. Her eyes reached for my own but I glanced away.

'Oh, Yun Cai,' she whispered. 'What is wrong? I thought we would have such a gay celebration! And surely there is much to celebrate.'

I held out my hands helplessly. Any reply resembling the truth would suggest self-pity. How I longed for her to respect me.

'I know what it is,' she said in a low voice. 'You feel restless because you do not have a position worthy of your talent. No wonder you feel strange when you cannot be yourself. And having to live in the backroom of a wine shop by the Pig Market! The whole situation is absurd.'

I shook my head.

'Please do not condemn Cousin Hong for poverty. He is very good to me. Besides, I am poor myself.'

'That is the problem,' she said, eagerly. 'How glad I am that you mention it! I have been thinking. Will you listen if I tell you some of my thoughts?'

'I always love to hear you talk,' I said.

This seemed to relieve her.

'I have had the most wonderful idea. In a few months the Imperial examinations are to be held. You are so clever. And I thought, why should not my Yun Cai enter when he is far more worthy than all the others. If you passed, which I am sure you will, you'd be granted a fine posting. And anyway, the gentleman of whom we spoke has promised to support your candidature.'

I looked at her in surprise. She had been canvassing my interests in a way which surely proved love. The Imperial examinations were the highest test, overseen by the Son of Heaven himself. Those who succeeded were guaranteed prosperity – assuming they did not displease His Highness. Even P'ei Ti had not yet gained such honour, though he planned to sit the examination that autumn.

'Do you really think I could pass through the Vermilion Doors?' I asked. 'In my current situation? And His August Excellency will really act as my sponsor?'

'Of course! You must believe in yourself and stop dreaming your life away. Then you will be free and depend on no one. I beg you to at least consider it.'

I sipped my tea while she watched. Suddenly it tasted less watery.

'If I studied hard, who knows?' I said, thinking aloud. 'The worst is that I should fail. Better men than I have failed.'

'So you will enter?' she asked, eagerly.

I met her deep, almond eyes. Could she not love me as I was? I let the question float, like wisps of steam.

'Yes,' I said. 'I'll try, at least.'

Su Lin took my hand.

'Now you are yourself,' she murmured.

'Oh, I'm always myself,' I said.

We were interrupted by a young woman entering the room, bowing as she came. It was one of the tea-house's singing girls. Her lowered eyes evaded Su Lin, evidently paying dutiful homage to a superior. Then I understood how high Su Lin had risen in her profession. A compulsion to prove myself her equal – no, her superior – made me affect a yawn. I remembered the proverb: *Why should not sparrows possess the dreams of swans?*

Su Lin flushed with pleasure. When the singing girl had gone I squeezed her hand.

'A proud moment for you,' I said, mastering envy.

She fanned herself, cooling hot cheeks. The glow beneath her make-up reminded me of other times, when that warmth had been for my sake alone. I longed for her to desire me.

'Are you engaged this evening?' I asked.

'Well, yes. But no, if you want. It is not someone important. I could always be ill.'

'Then be ill with me,' I said. 'I could make you better. And in the morning I'll begin my studies.'

She met my glance in her old, frank way.

'Must my success come between us?' she asked. 'It would make me so unhappy.'

Her honesty, vulnerable and well-meant, brought tears to us both.

'I was jealous for a moment,' I said. 'That is a trifle. It changes nothing between us. Sometimes clouds cover the sun, but they always blow away for us. Then our day is bright.'

Our tension dissipated into nervous laughter, eye-dabbing and smiles.

'What a fool I am, always hanging on your clever talk,' she said, in her thickest Chunming accent.

We left without bothering to finish our tea. That evening I begged her to lie on the bed naked, white jade softened by lamp light, while I lay beside her in my clothes, delighting in the warm, fragranced places of her body. Fully provoked by touch and taste, she pulled off my silk robes and we loved each other. I cradled her head on my chest as she slept, thinking of the texts I must learn by heart, thinking until sick of thought. Hope and depression, light and shadow. Was that our last night of untainted joy? There must have been others. How long ago it seems and far away, like a ship of many lanterns dwindling.

It was a time for love, if marriage may be called love. On a bright, summer morning, before the first hints of autumn, a sedan chair carried by two sweating porters arrived outside Cousin Hong's wine shop. People leant from windows to watch as a plain-faced girl in second-hand silks climbed out, carrying a baby wrapped in hemp. She looked round in a daze at her new home.

By the gatehouse stood three men awaiting her impatiently: Hong, myself, and the bridegroom. My cousin's children threw handfuls of rice and seeds and shiny *cash* coins onto the street as she stepped towards us, her head lowered modestly – though the babe in her arms suggested it was a little late for that. I could not help smiling at the strained dignity of the bridegroom beside me.

'Mi Feng,' I whispered. 'Go inside. We will lead her to where you sit.'

The bride, Su Lin's former maid, reluctantly passed her infant son to Cousin Hong's wife for safe-keeping, then was escorted to the courtyard where cups and wine were laid out. The couple knelt and faced each other, drinking in turn from the same bowl, while a small crowd of well-wishers murmured and joked. It did not do to joke too loudly. One could never be sure how Mi Feng might take it.

The bride came with a small dowry of *cash* and household necessities provided by Su Lin who had chosen not to join our celebration. Her absence grieved me. Within less than a year she had grown too good for us. I grieved, too, that I had not been able to afford a banquet for my loyal servant on his wedding day, the man who had saved my life a dozen times over. So it was. I could only show my goodwill through petty presents. Cousin Hong paid for the wine we drank, the food we ate. Once again I was the poor relation.

Perhaps my shame showed for Mi Feng took me to one side.

'Well, my Lord,' he said. 'It's you I should thank for all this.'

I stiffened.

'If I could have afforded more, I would have gladly given it,' I replied. 'It is Hong you should thank.'

He laughed in a way I had not heard before, without a trace of harshness. It made me wonder to see him softening.

'He wouldn't own this place if you hadn't given him the money. But I don't mean that, sir. It's time to settle down. I'm contented enough.'

'Then I am contented, too.'

He seemed embarrassed to have said so much.

'And you have a fine son,' I said.

A son seemed the finest thing in the world, if for no other reason than a man could encourage him to succeed where he had not.

Cousin Hong bustled over.

'What are these long faces for? Little General, you are always frowning these days.'

The way Mi Feng's eyes lit up at the sight of his new employer made me jealous. No doubt that was a fault in me.

So Mi Feng and his family took up residence in a tiny room beside the gatehouse and the wine shop rang with a baby's cries. His wife helped in the kitchen and everyone seemed happy except me.

Ambition swelled and tormented me. Day by day the Imperial Examinations approached. Whenever I saw Su Lin or P'ei Ti they talked eagerly of my fine prospects until I dreaded disappointing them. They urged me to attend the Society of the Western Lake and enter my poems for the monthly competition. I did go, though only to watch and renew old acquaintances. I felt too tender to risk failure in the poetry competition. Besides, I dreaded attracting the jealousy of Lord Xiao by winning. Nevertheless, my most recent verses found an eager audience, thousands of copies circulating through cheap wood-cut prints. Needless to say, none of the profits came my way.

I decided enough was enough.

Mi Feng was arguing with his wife in the kitchen of Hong's wine shop and, though I carried an armful of books to the brick steps overlooking Jewel Cloud Canal, their voices disturbed my concentration. It was strange to witness so masterful a man as Mi Feng being shaped by his new wife, yet part of him evidently welcomed the change. As we all did.

She cooked meals of such flavour that Cousin Hong gained dozens of new customers. Spicy dishes, warming the blood with ginger, a dozen herbs turning plain ingredients into a banquet. And she could be tender with her husband, if patience is tenderness, listening for hours while he boasted and talked about his life. I believe this talk was a great unburdening. The exact details were kept from me. He was always reluctant to show weakness when I was around. With his wife he felt no such inhibition.

At first I felt offended to be denied the truth about his past. Yet I owed him too much to sustain a resentment. There are limits to the frankness between master and servant; and he was no longer even my servant.

But, for all the goodwill surrounding me in Hong's establishment, I'd had enough.

'You wish to say something but don't know how,' Su Lin commented one night in the plain way she reserved for me.

We lay in each other's arms, my head upon her breast. Fragrance of perfume and musky sweat. Her silken sheets moulded round my skin.

'You are so distant,' she coaxed. 'If you shared your burden it would be lighter.'

I rolled over and stared at the ceiling, unable to express what did not make sense.

'Are you trying to punish me for some fault?' she asked. 'You are cruel not to explain.'

That word opened the cage where I'd imprisoned my thoughts.

'Cruel people take pleasure in another's misery,' I said.

She considered this. In the close air of a hot summer night, our breath rose and fell.

'You make me miserable when you hide yourself away,' she said. 'What have I done to make you withdraw from me? Ten days have passed since you last visited.'

I rolled over on the bed until I lay on my front.

'Not everything I feel relates to you,' I said.

She stiffened beside me.

'Do I bore you, is that it?'

'Oh, Su Lin,' I said. 'When you talk like that it is just a kind of game!'

'Then what troubles you?' she asked. 'Am I not enough for you?'

How could I answer without hurting her? But I tried.

'I'm sick of the city,' I said. 'I cannot study for the Imperial examinations in these conditions. If I am to succeed, as everyone seems to believe I must, I require space to think. The city is wasting my essential breaths.'

She pulled me over to face her.

'What are you saying?'

'I must go away for a while. That is all.'

It was dark, yet light enough to find each others' eyes.

'I remember the first time my broker ordered me to sing,' she said. 'It was a few weeks after Father sold me, as we travelled to the capital. My broker wished to make a little money by parading me in a roadside wine shop. Of course, everyone knew I had a fine voice, but that was beside the point. Singing for strangers is not the same as for loved ones, especially if one is shy. My broker – or should I say, owner, for he seemed to own everything I was – shook me until my teeth rattled. "Sing!" he commanded. So I did, my voice broken by sobbing. Then he beat me and said again: "Sing!" This time I did not sob, all my notes were pure. So you see, Yun Cai,' she said, sadly. 'I know what it is to study under hungry eyes. And I hope you do not think I encourage you to sing in the examinations in the way that horrible man did me.'

I replied with all my tenderness and ardour. Afterwards, we both pretended to sleep.

The next day I set my affairs in order and left Cousin Hong's house followed by a youth hired to carry my bags of scrolls.

'Take this message to P'ei Ti,' I told Hong. 'I'll send the boy back with news of where I may be found should it be necessary to summon me in a hurry. P'ei Ti will know exactly what I mean.'

Many roads lead to and from the capital and I could have taken any of them. I picked the Western Highway, the one heading toward Wei Valley, because just as the compass always points north, so the heart points home. In truth, I had no idea where I was heading.

Li after *li* passed beneath our feet. We slept in villages where gibbons cried mournfully all night. Hill country, wooded country. At once I felt at home. On the fifth day I came across a small monastery overlooking a narrow lake surrounded by steep hills. I knew at once, here was the place I sought. A passing peasant told me I had arrived at Five Gong Monastery.

'Is it Daoist or Buddhist?' I asked.

That peasant must have been an Immortal in disguise. He took one look at me and said, 'Does it matter to you, sir?'

So I proceeded up the hill to the monastery gate and begged an audience with the abbot. A crowd of monks followed curiously and I guessed they received few visitors. We bowed respectfully to each other.

'Reverend Sir,' I said. 'I am a humble seeker after the Way. I beg that I should be allowed to stay in this holy place for a few weeks in order to contemplate and study.'

He looked me over shrewdly. I sensed he was a grasping kind of fellow as his reply soon made plain:

'Sir,' he said. 'We welcome any who wish to study the Way. Our doors lie open. But, of course, we cannot live on lofty thoughts alone.'

A few hundred *cash* satisfied him. It represented almost the last of my wealth. I wished only to inhabit the moments flowing through me, and something about Five Gong Monastery encouraged lofty thoughts. Perhaps the view of the hills and mountains reminded me of my earliest dreams.

The monks led me to the main hall where candles cast dancing shadows, illuminating frescoes of the Seven Daoist Immortals. The five gongs of the monastery were sounded, each five times. As the last reverberation faded, I was washed with holy water poured from a sacred lacquer bucket once used by a hermit who had lived for two hundred and fifty-three years. The abbot intoned that I was now 'spotless as from the first', and indeed I felt cleansed.

I believe this purifying of my essential breaths saved me during the weeks of trial and constant fear that followed.

It might seem strange that I forgot the intrigues concerning Lord Xiao so easily. Of course, I did not. He hid beneath the surface of my thoughts, troubling my dreams. Often I deliberately emptied my mind, counting breaths to find the infinite doorway between each intake and expiration. Then I regained balance – for a while at least. Yet I could not stay there forever. And though I did not know it, events in the city were preparing to drag me back.

The five gongs resounded at dawn, noon and dusk, echoing across the valley. When they called even birds paused in their endless tasks of feeding and mating. Dull, deep, sonorous tones, rich with vibration, perfect echoes of the Way. I could not listen to them forever. I was no Immortal, just a visitor.

One afternoon the restless world summoned me back. I was fishing when a unit of horsemen wearing the uniform of the

Imperial Guard galloped up the road and entered Five Gong Monastery. A few minutes later, the abbot appeared by the gate, and I could see him pointing to where I sat on a large boulder, fishing rod in hand. They trotted down the path to where I sat.

'Yun Cai?' called out a grizzled-looking sergeant. 'Are you Yun Cai?'

I lowered my fishing rod, and pulled in the line.

'You are summoned to the capital at once,' he said, curtly. 'From henceforth, consider yourself under close arrest, on the orders of the Chief Censor.'

I did not question his authority to cancel my freedom. When four guardsmen are glowering at you, silence is advisable.

'There's a spare mount waiting for you up at the monastery,' the sergeant continued. 'I'll give you half an hour to pack, then we leave.'

I nodded. The end was beginning. I anticipated a trumped-up charge from Lord Xiao, most likely a capital charge. There could be no escaping it.

I threw the single fish I had caught back into the lake and washed my hands in the pure water. It floated belly side up, a bad omen. Then I turned. The sergeant stood before me on the lakeside, holding out a pair of iron manacles.

eight

'. . . Your fragrance left my being
so long ago.
                    Yet scent lingers in dreams
and each night I assure myself it means nothing.
I shall forget, in time, surely as morning.

Then your fragrance – honey, sweat-musk, elusive
  dew – revives
a desire never wholly forsaken.

When I clear my nose, this curtained room
reeks of musty pain. . .'

The rains are distressingly late. A fresh edict posted on the street corners of Chunming claims the monsoon has been delayed by a black alliance between the Emperor and demons. A strange document, I must say. It also states that anyone failing to refer to the Emperor as 'The Vile Usurper' is guilty of treason and liable for the Four Punishments 'or other just measures'.

The Empress-in-waiting issues edicts of this kind every few

days. One struggles to remember them all, as dozens have found to their cost. Chunming has become a fine place for settling grudges by laying false charges. Each morning the square before the Prefect's residence resounds with screams and a large pit has been dug beyond the ramparts to hold all the corpses.

Of course, we have experienced late rains before. One year the monsoon never came at all and the famine was severe. In Chunming it is safer not to recollect awkward truths. Even thoughts fall under the new edicts; thus anyone capable of doubt becomes a traitor.

A knock at the door, and a guard enters. He speaks respectfully, as all do, since the Empress-in-waiting showed me favour.

'I have a message here, sir,' he says. 'A boy delivered it at the gate and went away.'

'Lay it on the desk.'

Once unfolded, the message is absurd. The characters are wild and flowing:

I have seen Lord Yun Cai in the streets but he hasn't seen me. Come to the house of Shih-kao in the Fourth Ward this afternoon to pray for rain.

It is not signed. The paper is cheap and mottled by mould. The ink has been badly mixed. Such a summons should be ignored.

I pace the room. Can it have come from the night warder, Golden Bells? But surely he is illiterate, and only my dream of freeing P'ei Ti makes me think of him. There is a single way to discover the truth. I must be bold for P'ei Ti's sake.

Someone is following me. I am sure of it. But when I glance back the street seems ordinary, full of guileless faces. I pause at a public well and look round for suspicious loiterers. No one. So why does my back itch?

I press on, thinking only of P'ei Ti. Never mind the possibility of Eldest Son clutching the 'heater' or Three-Step-House burning. Duty is both ordained and indistinct. So I wander further into the Fourth Ward.

A group of drunken officers are watching a troupe of acrobats who tumble and leap then walk around on their hands. The officers throw coins and the acrobats scrabble in the dirt to seize them before the street urchins. There are many orphans in Chunming these days, many stunted little bodies. I slip by unnoticed.

'Where may one find the house of Shih-kao?' I ask a passer by. 'I am told it is in this district.'

He looks at me curiously.

'The house of Shih-kao?' he says.

'Yes.'

He shrugs and points down a side street descending to the gorge where the river flows.

'It is not exactly a house,' he says. 'But there you may find him, watching the waters.'

I nod gratefully. As I enter the side street I glimpse movement from the corner of my eye. Someone behind me. When I turn, a young man and his wife are following. They ignore me as they pass. Chunming has always been a city lacking in courtesy. For a moment I pause. They enter a low doorway and disappear, the man glancing back sharply at me. What does that look mean? Nothing, probably. Just that I am a stranger.

The street becomes a series of broad steps climbing down to the river. Here the gorge echoes with water voices. A boat slides past, carrying firewood and supplies to General An-Shu's army further downstream.

Now I am perplexed. There is no sign of a house. Foam gathers around rocks. Moss and dwarf ferns cling to the stone. Then I notice a small statue of an Immortal grinning at me from a narrow walkway over the river. Perhaps this is Shih-kao.

I sidle over slippery boulders and find a hidden entrance. Darkness within. I clear my throat noisily. No one invites me to enter. Feeling a way down clammy walls, I step into a cave lit feebly by such daylight as seeps through the entrance. My feet crunch gravel and sand. Slowly my eyes accustom themselves to the dark until I realise I am not alone.

'You!'

My voice echoes from wall to wall.

'I hope you have an explanation for this,' I say.

For a moment I wonder if he will devour one of his ridiculous insects. He sounds almost sober when he replies.

'Lord Yun Cai requires an explanation!' he chuckles. 'Not that so wise a gentleman will believe one like Thousand-*li*-drunk.'

'Why should I? Since you always talk nonsense.'

His face is in shadow. I cannot see if he is stung by my words.

'No time for that now,' he says. 'You need to know that Thousand-*li*-drunk desires the same as you. He is here to free His Excellency P'ei Ti.'

I start at the name.

'Who?' I ask.

He chuckles again.

'Very good to be cautious! What of another name, that of Ensign Tzi-Lu?'

'Never heard of him,' I declare, flatly.

Does he mean to blackmail me? If I were young again, I could drown him in the river.

'How strange,' says Thousand-*li*-drunk. 'The Ensign remembers you.'

We wait for each other to speak. A drip falls. Then another.

'I prefer you drunk to sober,' I say.

He bows and grins.

'That way you feel superior?' he suggests.

I gain nothing from provoking him, so I ask: 'Who are you?'

'Content yourself with this: Thousand-*li*-drunk is a spy. But here in Chunming I must do more than spy. Tell me, what are you willing to do to save your friend? We know you have access to the Prefect's residence. And we know that the Empress-in-waiting has honoured you with a commission.'

I do not enquire how he has learned these things. Now is the moment of decision. Either I trust him or scurry back to my room.

'Tell me what you know about P'ei Ti,' I say.

'Only that he is in the prison attached to the Prefect's residence.'

I hesitate for a moment. Everyone knows that. Once I have spoken my life is in his grimy hands.

'Then you need to hear this,' I say.

I tell him of Golden Bells, his potential for bribery, and that if I had the money I would have propositioned him myself. I describe P'ei Ti's prison, the unguarded side gate and how one might use it to enter and leave the gaol unobserved. Thousand-*li*-drunk's eyes gleam in the dark.

'Do you know where this gaoler lives?' he asks.

'I don't.'

'No matter. That can be found out.'

'Do you have the money to bribe him?' I ask, doubtfully. 'Assuming you are what you claim.'

'It can be provided,' he says.

'And who will approach the fellow? Really, the matter is more complicated than you seem to imagine.'

'You will approach him, Lord Yun Cai.'

His confidence unnerves me. Never has he seemed more like an Immortal.

'I would not know what to say,' I protest.

'Tell him, ten thousand in *cash*. That is what you will offer this Golden Bells.'

I am taken aback by such a sum and begin to wonder if he is mad after all.

'He will not believe me,' I say.

'He will when you give him this.'

Thousand-*li*-drunk smiles without revealing his teeth. He reaches into the basket where he keeps his food. Several crickets try to escape. Cursing, he stuffs them back. Then he lifts a secret flap and pulls out a bar of glinting silver.

'This will persuade him,' he says.

I shake my head.

'But my family. . . You know quite well. . . No, I cannot risk it.'

'Do you wish to save His Excellency P'ei Ti?' he demands, angrily. 'There is no other way. Remember, the Mandate of Heaven has not been withdrawn from His Imperial Highness. Hah! I told you that once before. General An-Shu will be crushed. That is his fate.'

'If I do as you say, how will you learn whether Golden Bells has agreed?'

He thinks for a moment.

'Hang a white garment in your window. After that you must not contact him again. Tell Golden Bells that a stranger will approach him. We will do the rest.'

I nod. All this is sensible.

'I don't trust you,' I say, examining him closely. 'You wear too many faces.'

He nibbles his thumb but does not reply.

'I agree,' I say. 'For P'ei Ti's sake. But if you betray me, I will haunt you in this life and the next. I shall clutch your spirit and never let go.'

An empty threat. I rise, hiding the bar of silver in my tunic. It is heavy and cold. We bow slowly to each other. Without blinking or removing his gaze from my own he reaches into his basket for a fluttering cricket and pops it in his mouth. I look away as he crunches. This cave reminds me of Wen Po's tunnel into Pinang. The same stench of graves.

When I return to the house by the ramparts a crowd has gathered. Wagon after wagon of wounded men, many groaning pitifully, rolls through the street. I search the wagons for Youngest Son's face, but recognise no one.

The fighting to the east must be severe and I feel a strange confusion, longing for the Son of Heaven's victory yet hopeful my son will survive. I fear these desires are incompatible.

Tomorrow or the next day I must seek out Golden Bells and, once I have spoken, I will be entirely in his power. I stand by the balcony-window. To the east, darkness fills the sky. The air is tense and hot. The very walls seem to sweat. Perhaps demons are indeed delaying the monsoon.

At last, black clouds fill the horizon and the air shimmers with constant rain. We hurry into the garden, cooling ourselves in the downpour until water drips from nose and chin. Our clothes become wet rags and our spirits embrace the clouds. Even the guards do not hide their delight, all differences between us washed away.

'May the wells be full for a thousand years!' we cry.

Perhaps the sky appreciates our gratitude. Thunderclaps echo round the hills, hearty and profound. For a whole day nothing but delightful rain forming streams and trickles, an opera of click, splash, sigh. Pools take shape in the street outside and urchins kick water at each other, laughing all the while.

With the monsoon comes news from the front. I learn that the rains broke there three days before they reached Chunming, halting all fighting. A happy occurrence for General An-Shu. His forces have fought an inconclusive battle. Suffering dreadful losses, he has been obliged to stage a costly withdrawal.

Any advantage the Son of Heaven may have gained has been washed away by the monsoon. Roads and rivers are impassable quagmires. Floods have broken a key bridge, allowing General An-Shu time to lick his wounds. Though I ask after the Winged Tigers Regiment, no one has reliable news. I am told only that many perished. Does that mean Youngest Son is dead or wounded? Or captured, which surely amounts to his death? No one knows. A true father might sense the truth without the need for words. I feel only trickling fear, just as the monsoon whispers and splashes, from dawn until dusk.

It is said the Imperial forces are a mere ten days from Chunming. Of course, General An-Shu's remaining troops block their way. History is full of generals who turned disadvantage to victory. He may yet drive back the Imperial army and re-commence his march on the capital.

Chunming swirls with rumours that the city will go to the sword if General An-Shu fails, and that a plan exists to forestall this event by driving out the Lady Ta Chi and declaring Chunming loyal to the Emperor. It says much about her authority that such things are whispered openly.

Now I must approach the night warder, Golden Bells, and seek to buy him. Time is running short. I must act soon. If the Imperial army draws near, it is likely that all prisoners will be executed in a final act of revenge or despair. Yet I am paralysed by unease, full of plausible reasons for delaying another day, then another.

When I lie on my bed the bar of silver reproaches me. It is hidden within my mattress and I feel its hard, rectangular shape pressing against my back.

At sunrise I am woken by shouts and cries of alarm. I sit bolt upright in bed. The room is full of shadows. Heavy feet pound the stairs. Have they come for me so soon? Perhaps Thousand-*li*-drunk has betrayed me. I hear doors being kicked open, men protesting as they are dragged from their beds. Voices fill the tall, narrow house.

'Quickly! Everyone outside! All prisoners outside!'

I barely have time to dress before my own door is flung open by the sergeant, looking wild-eyed.

'Outside!' he barks. 'Quickly!'

I find myself in the water-logged street. Mud covers my shoes. Fortunately the rain has faltered. Between downpours the air grows humid and the puddles steam.

The soldiers strut up and down, marshalling us into a column. In silence we march toward the South Gate. A short distance, yet the streets are clogged with soldiers and streams of prisoners. I can sense the guards' fear. They are outnumbered by those they are supposed to hold captive, a dangerous, foolish occurrence. I wonder how it has come about.

The explanation is revealed as soon as we leave the city gates and form up on a strip of levelled ground before the ramparts. There a strange sight awaits.

The Empress-in-waiting sits stiffly on a platform twenty steps high, shaded by awnings of silk. Her painted throne is surrounded by smoking censers, scenting the air with perfume, to spare her nostrils from the reek of the prisoners. General An-Shu's banners decorate the platform.

Lines of troops and armed eunuchs protect her throne, weapons drawn, crossbows cocked. My eye is drawn to a rectangular pit, twenty paces long and a dozen wide. Burning coals and charcoal may be glimpsed within the pit, covered by a grid of iron bars. A heat haze rises, so that the Lady Ta Chi seems to float as she sits in state, her august presence distorted by veils of swirling air.

The man beside me mutters: 'May the Jade Emperor bring judgement soon.'

Do they know what this pit portends, as I do? Or how the original Lady Ta Chi, long ago, devised a new punishment for those who displeased her. Something worse than the 'heater', because it had grown tedious. She called it 'roasting'. It is recorded that she would laugh at the capering antics of those she punished.

Two officers from the Penal Battalion confer with the sergeant guarding us. He glances in my direction and nods.

The sergeant leads the officers over to where I kneel. I close my eyes. So this is my fate. Thousand-*li*-drunk has reported me as a traitor. A blow forces me into the mud and I cry out. Voices rise in fear. I wait for harsh hands but they do not come. When

I look again, the man beside me is being dragged away to join a huddle of prisoners by the burning pit. He bellows like a hog, and I think of the Pig Market, far away in the capital.

The Head Eunuch steps onto a podium at the foot of his mistress's throne. The crowd before him is silent. Occasionally one hears the whimper of prisoners, the crack of a coal consuming itself.

'Hear the will of the Empress-in-waiting!' roars her Head Eunuch. 'It has become known that vile traitors are plotting against the eternal rule of the Son of Heaven, Tiger of the West. . .'

General An-Shu's titles are lost in a sudden commotion. One of the prisoners has grown hysterical. The Head Eunuch carries on, apparently unperturbed, while the man is beaten.

'. . . Ineffable Dragon of the Four Winds. May he live ten thousand years! See now what befalls those who follow the Vile Usurper!'

The Lady Ta Chi leans forward on her throne. We all watch expectantly.

The first prisoner is dragged barefoot to the burning coals. Heat waves envelope him. Guards using long poles thrust him forward. He emits a single, piercing shriek. Once more, I close my eyes, sickened by such scenes. Why can't the authorities execute their enemies with more decorum? Then a shout goes up among the assembled prisoners and hostages.

'Abbot Ssu-Ma! They've got Abbot Ssu-Ma!'

The abbot is popular in the city, a holy man, guardian of the Golden Lotus Monastery. At once men are on their feet shouting and gesticulating. An old fellow wearing a monk's robe steps forward.

'This is not the Mandate of Heaven!' he cries.

That old monk is the spark igniting the crowd. The punishment meant to cow those who defy the Empress-in-waiting becomes its opposite. In moments all is chaos. Prisoners grapple with their guards. The loud click and rattle of many crossbows being discharged reaches us through the screams and curses. Bolts darken the sky in front of the Lady Ta Chi's throne then fall upon us in a shower. One lands near my feet and I grow stiff with fear, unable to stir or save myself.

A group of unarmed prisoners wrestle a tall guardsman to the ground, tearing at his armour, pummelling, biting, kicking, until dust rises and he lies still. Others rush back and forth waving weapons captured from the soldiers. The air is thick with the noise of battle. I lurch as a prisoner clutching a crossbow bolt in his belly careers into me then staggers away, shrieking for relief. At last my limbs unfreeze and I join a stream of men fleeing toward the city walls. All around us groups of soldiers from the Penal Battalion hack indiscriminately with broad-bladed halberds, desperate to quell the mob. Too late to intimidate men provoked beyond all forbearance, they must depend on superior weaponry and discipline now.

I am swept by the crowd into the city and stumble back to the dubious safety of the house by the ramparts. Some of the rioters are gathering on street corners, knives and bamboo staves in their hands. Once in my room I cower, the door bolted and wedged, until night falls. All day sounds of fighting drift through the window, mingled with the steady whisper of a fresh downpour. Thankfully the monsoon has resumed, dousing those buildings set alight by the rioters.

In the midst of fear I discover the resolve needed to free P'ei Ti. Such rulers as General An-Shu and his queen do not warrant the Mandate of Heaven. My thoughts gather round a young man's face: Golden Bells.

I acquire an umbrella and before dawn I walk out, telling the guards I cannot sleep and that I desire a morning stroll. My destination is the square before the Prefect's residence. Truly, I must make an odd sight, occasionally pausing as though contemplating my poetic labours. Yet even the most outlandish can become familiar and the guards are used to my morning walks; they allow me entry without comment.

As I totter about, exaggerating the need for my stick, I pause outside the prison where Golden Bells can invariably be found awaiting his replacement. There are half a dozen other night warders but they drink their morning tea in the guardroom while he is banished to the entrance.

Today, after polite greetings, I mention yesterday's riot and the fighting in the east. Each day more wagonloads of wounded return from the front. I tell him General An-Shu is said to have retreated to higher ground, bringing the Imperial army another day closer. Golden Bells watches me shrewdly. I sense he is waiting, as I am waiting, for a sign that we might unravel our intentions.

'Golden Bells,' I say. 'I had a dream last night that the Vile Usurper's forces were camped outside Chunming. Does that seem likely to come about?'

He drinks his cup of cheap, bitter tea.

'From what I hear, sir,' he says. 'Yes.'

We assess each other's reaction then glance round the square. We have both said much.

'It also seems likely to me,' I say. 'When it happens, a wise man would prefer to be snug in the mountains, his pouch weighed down with *cash*.'

My heart is fluttering. A servant boy walks from the Prefect's residence and relieves himself against a pillar. Red strands of dawn pierce the dark clouds.

'A man must be loyal to himself and his family,' I declare. 'It is said that danger brings silver. Have you ever heard that, Golden Bells?'

'No, sir, I haven't.'

'Do you have the courage to take an opportunity? One which might set you up for life, so you could drink wine and eat the best rice every day? Would you have the courage for that?'

The strain of not speaking openly is unbearable. I sense that now is the time, or never. The bar of silver in my pouch weighs heavy.

'I'm just a simple man,' he says, evidently distressed. 'If Lord Yun Cai has something to offer, speak it quickly before the next watch arrives.'

'Golden Bells,' I say, quietly. 'I have a bar of silver in my pouch worth a thousand *cash*. If, when the time is right, you can help me, you'll receive ten times that amount.'

He licks his lips.

'What help would you want?'

'That a certain prisoner should escape.'

It is done. Or I am. I wait, my life hanging on his next word.

'What proof do I have of your goodwill?' he asks, breathing heavily.

'Give me your word, then comes the silver.'

He squeezes his empty cup.

'I'd do pretty much anything for the sum you mention,' he says. 'If the plan was right.'

'It will be right. First hear the name of the prisoner.'

I whisper and pretend to fuss over my drink. His breath hisses.

'Now I see why you offer so much.'

His glance flickers fearfully round the square, as does my own.

'You agree?'

'Yes, but how do I know. . .'

'That I am serious? When you take back the empty cup, I shall pass the silver. Take it quickly and hide it in your sleeve.'

His eyes signify agreement.

'Golden Bells, you won't see me again. A stranger will contact you with further proof of your reward.'

Somewhere within the prison a door slams.

'Take the cup,' I say. 'And do not be so foolish as to sell the silver. Patience will make you a great man. Impatience will bring you a bad end.'

I slip the silver from my pouch and pass it over. It disappears into his sleeve.

'Remember this,' I say, nodding agreeably, as though thanking him for his tea. 'The Son of Heaven's army is only a few days away. Do what you're told.'

He bows, and turns without a word, carrying the cup inside. It is over. I hobble round the square, greeting the guards as I leave. They do not seem to notice my anxiety.

There are countless agonies of mind and over a long life I have endured many. But the hour after my conversation with Golden Bells is among the worst. This is the decisive time. If he has chosen to betray me, to forego his bar of silver and a promised reward for immediate gain, then disaster is certain.

I pace the narrow room. Another hour passes. Still I am not secure. Perhaps the Head Eunuch is merely debating the best way to apprehend me so that I will lead him to my fellow conspirators. I lie on the bed and strive to meditate. Time flows slowly. I cannot clear my mind.

The watchman in the street announces the third hour after dawn. Still no vengeful feet pound on the stairs. For a terrible while I imagine the disgrace and agony of the 'heater', clasping a burning ingot of iron until my fingers are withered to stumps. Perhaps they will heat the bar of silver instead. That might be considered a fitting punishment. How I love my fingers. Once they played the lute with delicate fluency and balanced a writing brush, my calligraphy delighting every eye. I listen to the rain outside and count ten breaths at a time.

A fourth hour passes, then a fifth. I dare not descend to collect my ration of steamed vegetables and rice, all appetite lost.

By the seventh hour I fall into a distressed doze. When I awake it has grown dark. So I have survived. Golden Bells has evidently decided to profit by me – unless he loses his nerve and makes a late confession. Though I am steeped in fear, this seems unlikely. The authorities would enquire why he delayed and their style of questioning would deter anyone.

I take a pitcher of water and pour it into a bowl. Then I wash my white shirt and hang it from the window-balcony. Rain fills the night with whispers and chuckles. At dawn, Thousand-*li*-drunk will see my sign. I have done all I can for P'ei Ti.

At last I fall into an exhausted sleep, haunted by the thought that on the morrow I must compose more poems praising the Lady Ta Chi. She enters my dreams, leading a huge tiger by a silken leash. The beast snarls as it advances towards me. Then the dream changes and I gaze at my wife's patient face. She shakes her head sadly, saying, 'Why do you never think of me?' I am filled with a desire to justify myself until she fades too. And sleep becomes oblivion.

Distraction arrives in the shape of a palace servant. He appears in my doorway with a letter, an ornate box and a large jar. My nostrils twitch. The jar contains wine.

I greet him in the doorway. The stairwell behind is dark but I hear the voices of my fellow prisoners, joking as they dress.

'Who may I thank?' I ask.

'Why, the Empress-in-waiting,' replies the servant.

He bows once more and leaves.

The letter reads: *I would summon you before me but I am at present indisposed. Ensure the poems owed to me are delivered at sunset.*

So she wants the poems a dozen days before they fall due. One may read her command in several ways. Perhaps her illness is related to the riot sparked by 'roasting' the Abbot Ssu-Ma – certainly there have been no more oppressive edicts since then.

But her haste also intrigues me. She requires these poems as a present for General An-Shu and it is reported he is eight or nine days' march from Chunming. A swift rider could accomplish the journey in a quarter of that time. Does that mean she expects him imminently and wishes to have her gift ready? With such a woman it is unwise to assume anything.

The lacquered box contains a thick wad of paper and several ink cakes. Such paper! When I rub it between finger and thumb, it is thick as bean curd and as porously smooth. A delight to write upon, pure and unspoilt as a young woman's thighs. The ink is finer than anything I have possessed since my banishment from the capital. The kind of ink one uses to write missives to distant kingdoms. A magisterial ink for impressing one's enemies or friends. Capable of subtlety, yet imbued with force. My calligrapher's instinct revels in such ink, and such paper.

All day I copy out my praise-poems, improving them as I go along. By late afternoon I have finished. May she appreciate them! They do her more honour than she deserves. Indeed, I am proud. I have excelled myself.

Exhausted, I carry them in the box, step by step, down the narrow wooden stairs to the guardroom.

'Sergeant,' I say. 'This must be delivered to the palace at once!'

Back in my room, I pace about, circling the wine jar like a stalking cat. Anticipation is a pleasure in itself. Never mind that I have been sent this gift while plotting to betray its giver. When I pour the first cup, its very smell intoxicates me and I raise it with shaking hands. The taste lingers on lip and tongue. I drain the cup in one.

A few hours later I'm on my back. The low ceiling of the room swirls. I cannot marshal my thoughts. One moment I'm old and tired, my mind swarming with a lifetime of failure. Then I'm young again, back in the darkest hour, drunk on remembered youth, beating off a hundred blows.

I laugh senselessly. A drunkard's loud, inconsolable laugh. My arrest outside Five Gong Monastery nearly ended my life! Cold, heavy, remorseless manacles round my wrists. Those iron manacles chafed my soul.

A wise man lives his whole life trying to avoid judicial proceedings. Accusations are dangerous. Who knows which way the judge will lean? The accuser may become the accused in a moment. If nothing else, he is guilty of disturbing the judge's equanimity.

It took a single day to reach the capital from Five Gong Monastery, for we rode hard. My wrists were bleeding from the manacles, but the worst pain I suffered was loss of face. To travel like a common criminal, exposed to every eye, shamed me indelibly.

On arrival in the city I was taken straight to the Palace, and thence to the Prison of the High Censor. Only then did I realise the gravity of my situation.

The Censor's gaol was reserved for officials in disgrace. Common criminals rotted elsewhere. Though not a large building it was dismal, as befitted its purpose. I was led through the courtyard and flung into a lightless cell, so small I could touch all four walls and ceiling when I stood in the middle. The door clanged with a grinding of bolts. Within the space of a few minutes I passed from incredulity at my situation to outrage, then numb dread. By groping in the dark on all fours like an animal I discovered my prison's only amenity: a chipped bowl half full of decaying human waste. The stench made me retch uncontrollably. There was not even a jug of water, though I was parched. I slumped on the cool earthen floor and trembled.

Hours passed. Perhaps many hours. Without light it is hard to measure time. Then a tiny glow, no longer than a finger, appeared in the wall above the door. By this means I knew it must be day. Only with the proof that light still existed, out there beyond my reach, did I find the hope required for sleep.

A scraping of bolts woke me from my slumber. At once I was

alert. With consciousness came thirst, and terrible hunger. The door creaked and I shielded my eyes. Two figures were silhouetted by the brightness of day. One was a gaoler, keys hanging from his belt, a leaden cudgel in his hand. The other's silks glinted as they caught the light. His expression was grim. Implacable. Yet I cried out for sheer joy at the sight of him. It was the Lawyer Yuan Chu-Sou. He regarded me silently for a moment, then gestured to the gaoler.

'Release him,' he said, curtly.

Tears filled my eyes.

'Say nothing!' he cautioned. 'Follow me.'

I would have followed him to hell itself as long as he took me away from that noxious hole.

They led me past door after door, beyond which I could hear men muttering or screaming pitiful self-justifications at imagined accusers. Some sang strange, keening melodies to comfort themselves. Most doors were silent. One could only speculate what misery they contained. But I was free. Temporarily at least. I strove to control the hysterical laughter rising from my soul.

I was shown to a plain chamber, its barred windows overlooking a courtyard. Throughout the interview that followed, I had ample opportunity to witness a prisoner strapped to a pole, being whipped by a disgruntled guard. The warder was a palace eunuch, flabby and bare-chested. Though the prisoner winced and cried out the guard could not stop yawning. His boredom affected me deeply.

The lawyer Yuan Chu-Sou gestured at a jug of water on the table. I drained it in long gulps, my throat working furiously. After that I felt more myself. It is strange how dignity depends on essential needs. When I sat back, gasping with relief, I found him watching me. As always, his expression was unreadable.

'Matters are proceeding according to my plans,' he announced, with quiet satisfaction.

I was still too close to that vile cell to respond as such a comment deserved.

'You appear shaken, Yun Cai,' he said. 'Perhaps it is because you do not have a sword to lend you courage.'

I might have guessed he had not liked me waving my sword around.

'What is the accusation against me?' I croaked.

He blinked.

'There is no accusation,' he said.

'Then why am I. . . Why am I *here*?'

'Because you are a witness. I can hardly be expected to protect you from ordinary procedures.'

Assuming he wanted to. I waited sullenly.

'I'm glad your fiery loquaciousness has been dampened for once,' he said.

It was only then I understood how much he disliked me. 'It means we can get straight to business. So listen carefully. Lord Xiao has been arraigned as I predicted. Indeed, he is being held in this very prison. Naturally, his quarters are more salubrious than your own. Nevertheless he is a prisoner and stands accused.'

I nodded.

'Of what?'

'Many charges,' said the Lawyer Yuan Chu-Sou regretfully. 'All serious. You need not concern yourself with them. Your sole purpose is to confirm the provenance of the three scrolls you found in Pinang. All I require of you is that you tell the truth when you are called before the judges. That you found them in your predecessor's robes, that his name was Lu Sung, that you inherited his position as Chief of the Bureau of Fallen Heroes. Do not speculate, do not utter a single opinion. State only the facts. I assume that is not too difficult?'

I licked my lips.

'Will I have to return to that cell?' I asked.

'Of course.'

'For how long?'

'Not long, the trial is imminent.'

'I cannot go back there. I will make a shabby witness if I go back there. That cell might send me mad.'

He seemed to consider this.

'Well, we don't want that,' he said, at last. 'I shall arrange for you to be held in more congenial surroundings.'

'Will those surroundings contain food?' I asked.

'If you like,' he said, impatiently. 'Why not?'

My eyes flickered to the prisoner being whipped outside. He was unconscious. I almost envied his insensibility.

Yuan Chu-Sou was as good as his word. I was taken under guard through the palace grounds, passing the Deer Park Library where I had spent so many delightful hours. Finally I reached a small temple capped by a four-storey pagoda near the palace walls.

The Temple of Flying Petals was used once every five years to applaud the Son of Heaven's ancestors and their gift of blossom. This was to be my new prison until the trial of which Yuan Chu-Sou had spoken.

You might say I was lucky. No, I *was* lucky. My lenient treatment showed how badly Lord Xiao's case stood, though I scarcely realised it at the time. Yet before we parted, the Lawyer Yuan Chu-Sou had whispered to me, 'You know that Lord Xiao has been scheduled for torture, don't you?'

I looked at him as though he was deranged.

'Such a man is not liable for torture,' I replied. 'He is not like other men.'

Yuan Chu-Sou seemed delighted by my reply.

'But he is, Yun Cai! Step by step, he descends to the level of you and I. Though I suspect you lack the wit to appreciate it.'

Such certainty of his power over me! He felt he could insult me at will. Yet I retained a few stings.

'Lord Xiao might fall,' I said. 'But if I was ambitious for high office, which I am not, I would be wary of offending his friends.'

His eyes narrowed.

'Make sure you deliver the testimony I have taught you,' he said.

I pretended not to hear his interruption.

'I wouldn't be surprised,' I said, as though thinking aloud. 'If those who are so eager to bring about Lord Xiao's destruction, distanced themselves from the means by which their enemy had been brought low, as soon as his fall was accomplished. Surely, that is mere prudence.'

He took my meaning all right. When young, it was always my destiny to speak rashly and regret it later.

'That will not occur in this case,' he muttered.

But the doubt had been planted. As I was escorted to the Temple of Flying Petals, it afforded me a slight satisfaction. After all, what applied to him was equally true for myself.

The Temple of Flying Petals was overseen by a single monk, so old that I believed he would not witness the Son of Heaven's next sacrifice there. The temple was the size of a long pavilion, its pagoda attached to the side of the building. It possessed a single entrance, easily guarded. The monk slept and ate in a room behind the altar, passing his days in rituals no one bothered to witness, except perhaps the gods. Certainly he was diligent in his duties, as I saw with my own eyes for I was forbidden to leave the place except to relieve myself behind a stand of bamboo adjoining the palace walls. Twice a day meals were brought to me, simple dishes of rice and vegetables, cold by the time they had made their long journey from the nearest kitchen. Anxious thoughts, often concerning Su Lin, filled each wakeful moment. We had no means of communication. I could neither receive nor send the simplest letter unless it passed through the Office of the Censor. At night I slept beside the altar on a pile of blankets provided by the monk.

Each day my trepidation grew. The old monk would come upon me as I sat hugging my knees on the altar steps. He would lay his withered hand on my shoulder, his touch as light as paper.

'I have prayed and received a favourable sign,' he said. 'Soon you will be reborn as blossom, which is to say, as a cloud.'

Though I tried to appear grateful everyone knows that, to be reborn, first one must die.

That same day, the threads of my destiny tightened. The doors of the temple were flung open and there, splendidly robed, stood the Lawyer Yuan Chu-Sou. He swept past the guards with their plumed helmets and halberds, clanging the double doors behind him. Echoes filled the dark altar-room. I rose tentatively. His scowl alerted me that all was not well.

He did not bother to bow before the image of the Blossom God and I had no doubt bad luck must follow.

'It is usual to make three prostrations before the holy image,' I said, hoping the god heard me. 'Even the Son of Heaven does as much.'

The old monk sat beside me, nodding his approval, but the Lawyer Yuan Chu-Sou glared at him.

'I wish to speak to Yun Cai alone,' he said. 'And at once.'

Grumbling, the monk retired to his private chamber. Yuan Chu-Sou looked around for somewhere to sit. Finding nowhere, he stood before me while I lounged on the altar steps.

'You seem at home,' he said, sarcastically.

I did not reply, but waited.

'You may wonder why I have come to see you so soon after our last meeting,' he said, in a brittle voice.

'I can guess the reason.'

He sniffed.

'I suspect not,' he replied. 'You should know that your importance in the proceedings against Lord Xiao has increased. Do you remember Secretary Wen?'

How could I forget him?

'Only too well,' I said.

'Your habitual flippancy is misplaced,' he said. 'I must inform you that Secretary Wen has been found hanging from his feet beneath Blue Peony Bridge. Not only was his throat cut but many burns on his body indicate that he was tortured before he died.'

I blinked at him.

'But who . . ?'

'We must assume friends of Lord Xiao,' said Yuan Chu-Sou, evidently flustered. 'We must also assume he talked before he died. I bitterly regret telling such a fool the details of our case. It is very unfortunate.'

Particularly for Secretary Wen. I did not speak my thought.

'That means,' he continued. 'You are now my principle witness. The scrolls you found have become ever more important and, with them, your testimony.'

He had my entire attention now. I was alarmed to see so still a man pace up and down.

'Surely Lord Xiao has confessed under torture,' I said. 'You told me he has been tortured.'

Yuan Chu-Sou stopped pacing. His eyes glinted red in the guttering candle light.

'Either the torturer was incompetent, or bribed, or Lord Xiao is a man of peculiar fortitude. For he has not confessed.'

It was no good to wish myself a thousand *li* distant.

'I'm sure you realise the implications for your own position,' he said.

I shook my head, pretending naivety.

'Then I will explain. Firstly, should Lord Xiao be acquitted, your role as witness will become a crime in itself. Secondly, those who decided that Secretary Wen should be removed may reach the same conclusion concerning yourself. Do I make myself clear?'

'Very,' I said.

He resumed his pacing, apparently lost in thought.

'So you came here to warn me to be on my guard?' I said.

He did not deign to reply.

'When will the trial take place?' I asked.

'Soon. Lord Xiao's supporters will seek a swift trial before fresh charges can be gathered.'

'And what of His August Excellency? Can he not influence the judges in our favour?'

Again the Lawyer Yuan Chu-Sou glared at me.

'His August Excellency has nothing to do with this prosecution,' he said. 'You would be well-advised to remember that at all times.'

Then I understood the precariousness of our position. We were husks caught between the grinding stones of two great men.

'I would strongly suggest that you take care what you eat,' he said. 'Even in the palace, no, *especially* in the palace. Poison has a habit of silencing unwelcome tongues.'

After he had gone, I climbed the spiral stairs of the pagoda until I reached the topmost storey. From there I could look out across the palace grounds. A small herd of deer stood beneath a clump of elegant pines. Buildings rose, filling the sky with soaring roofs and gatehouses. I could see the guardsmen assigned to keep me captive conferring on the gravel path below. They, at least, seemed contented. They would draw their rations each day and fear nothing much, protected by their lowly position from dangerous choice.

When I turned to the south I could see the countryside beyond the River Che, coloured hills and monkey-haunted woods, villages where a man might learn peace. And elsewhere I could see the rooftops of the city, the West Lake glinting, aware Su Lin might be walking in her garden, perhaps thinking of me, perhaps not. P'ei Ti would be at his desk, his fingers black with ink, while I waited like a lonely ghost.

I noticed a pair of carriages crossing the Imperial Deer Park, their occupants hidden by large, gaudy umbrellas. Beside them rode an escort of soldiers, red pennants fluttering in the autumn breeze.

The carriages neared the Temple of Flying Petals and halted a little way off. I craned from the window in the pagoda but could not identify my visitors. A familiar, coiffed head of black hair peeped out. Then I was running down the spiral steps, two at a time until I reached the temple entrance. Pulling open the heavy doors I surprised my guards, who at once blocked the way with their halberds.

Before me, just beyond the limits of the courtyard, was a sight to make me reckless. In the first carriage, reclining against a cushion, was Su Lin, evidently distressed, her face hidden by a sumptuous pink fan. Stern and upright in the second carriage sat P'ei Ti. I called out in pleasure, certain my liberty had come. The presence of friends dispelled all the shadows cast by the Lawyer Yuan Chu-Sou.

P'ei Ti climbed down stiffly and saw me in the doorway. He waved impatiently to the guards that I should be allowed to pass. I rushed out to greet him. We did not speak, but embraced. Then he nodded towards the carriage where Su Lin leant out, beseeching me to come to her with eloquent eyes.

'We can only risk a brief meeting,' muttered P'ei Ti. 'Even that is too much, though she insisted on it. Remember, you do not wish to implicate her.'

I walked over and stood beside the carriage. She held out her hand and I clasped it feverishly. Its softness revived hope.

'You are the being in my eyes,' I said – though, in truth, they were full of tears.

Her own glistened.

'We do not have long,' she whispered.

'One moment is a hundred years,' I said.

She shook her head though I could tell my words pleased her. They were all I had to offer.

'I hear bad things,' she said, peering at my prison. 'Do they treat you well here? This is a strange kind of gaol.'

'It is a holy place,' I said. 'So I am quite comfortable. But it is you I wish to hear about. Are you well? Do you suffer any annoyance from those who mean us harm? You must tell me quickly.'

'No, nothing. My life continues as before.'

'You are not threatened or harassed?'

She smiled at me uncertainly.

'I have regular engagements. His August Excellency ensures that I do not suffer. His generosity towards me does not flag.'

At this my jealousy rose. How such passions demean a man! She must have sensed my doubt, for a look of concern crossed her beautiful face.

'He is everything we rely on,' she pleaded. 'You must trust me! I will not draw him forward too far. Our only thought must be to please him.'

'So long as, through doing so, we please ourselves,' I said, doggedly. 'You must beware that man. He is no better than Lord Xiao!'

'Oh, Yun Cai, I am not a fool!'

She subsided in confusion. It was hard to read her true thoughts, masked by layers of white powder, like an actress in a play. I pored over that face for a sign of tenderness, as one studies a beloved book. All I craved was a simple sign of affection. Then my trial would seem bearable.

'Do you ever look out over the West Lake and remember how we sailed there?' I said, softly. 'Every time I dipped the oar silver and gold droplets scattered behind us.'

She looked at me, perplexed and helpless.

'I do,' she said.

'And when we embraced,' I continued, eagerly. 'You filled more than my arms. You filled every part of me that is good.'

She laughed, dabbing her eyes.

'I liked that,' she said.

And I could not help laughing, too.

'That is what matters,' I said.

Abruptly her smile became strained.

'It is Lord Xiao who took that from us,' she said. 'I could tear out his heart!'

'Let us not talk of him,' I said.

'How can we not? Yun Cai, you must fix your mind on your situation. It is hardly pleasant.'

I chuckled.

'It seems pleasant as I gaze at you.'

She squeezed my hand so that her long nails dug in and I recoiled in surprise.

'You must stop this!' she cried, in distress. 'Vengeance against your enemy, only that will save you! Have you not heard about Secretary Wen?'

P'ei Ti appeared at my elbow. His intention was clear. We had conversed too long. Yet nothing had been said. At least, not the words I desired. He fluttered his hands at her, evidently a prearranged signal, for she withdrew tearfully into the carriage.

'Ride on!' he barked at the coachman, who at once twitched his reins.

The wheels of the carriage crunched over the gravel path. Then it was turning, crossing the Deer Park at speed. I watched helplessly, consumed by grief. In her frustration she had not even said farewell. P'ei Ti's hand clasped my elbow and I shook it off.

'Come inside the temple,' he said. 'I too have little time. We must talk frankly.'

I allowed him to lead me inside. We sat upon the altar steps. P'ei Ti tugged at his collar. He was sweating, despite the coolness of the temple. As always it was my weakness to sympathise with others better than myself. Or what is more dangerous, believe I did. Despite the extremity of my position I wished to comfort him, with lies if necessary.

'The Lawyer Yuan Chu-Sou has visited me and says all goes well,' I said, brightly.

'Then he speaks a shameful untruth,' said P'ei Ti.

I patted his arm. His gravity and barely concealed fear began to infect me.

'Tell me what is on your mind,' I said. 'Then my dear friend will feel better.'

He pushed me aside and rose quivering. 'Why must you be so infuriating?'

I watched him in alarm.

'Yun Cai,' he said, carefully. 'I beg you to listen. I am at fault. I am at grave fault. I am like a father who has advised his child badly.'

'Do you mean to call me a child?' I said, smiling.

'In these matters, yes! Yes! The prosecution against Lord Xiao is flawed. Terribly flawed. They have allowed their chief witness to be murdered, an astonishing oversight. I placed too much trust in the Lawyer Yuan Chu-Sou and taught you to do the same. But I begin to fear the man is a leaking cup. I am to blame.'

We were disturbed by one of the guards peering in through the temple doors.

'Get out!' bellowed P'ei Ti.

The door closed.

'Damn those guards,' he said. 'Who knows what bribes they receive. Now listen, Yun Cai, you must keep a steady nerve. Soon you will stand before the judges. I am assured it will be soon. Of the hearing itself and how you should behave I shall not speak, for your honest heart must convince them, if nothing else does. This is what I have come to say. As soon as the trial is adjourned, or you regain even a little liberty, you must flee the capital. I have a horse prepared, and money. As soon as you are able you must go.'

'Are things so bad?' I asked, reluctant to believe him.

'They are.'

I sighed. Squeezed my own hands for comfort.

'What of the Imperial examinations?' I asked, defiantly. 'They fall due in a few weeks' time. You know how I have studied for them.'

It was his turn to sigh. 'You must forget the examinations.'

Suddenly I flushed.

'You intend to sit them, don't you?' I demanded. 'Why should I not take my chance? Am I so accursed?'

He held out his hands miserably.

'You must preserve your life. That is your true duty now.'

I shrank into myself. Yet a corner of my soul felt no distress. That corner was a door through which the Way poured, teaching acceptance. Through that doorway I glimpsed an eternity free from vile pettiness.

'Where is this horse you speak of?' I asked.

'At my parents' house. Yun Cai, wait here one moment.'

He went to his carriage and returned with two parcels. One was long and thin, the other small and squat as a toad.

'Take these,' he said. 'The bag contains two thousand in *cash*. Use it to bribe the guards if you must. The other, well, it is an old ally. I collected it from your room in Cousin Hong's wine shop. He asks after you, by the way. Your old servant, Mi Feng, also urges you to remember him. He said you must not hesitate to call on him if you require a certain kind of help.'

No need to explain the kind of help he had in mind. I loosened the hemp wrappings of the package. It contained my sword, the same weapon I had used to kill a man.

'So that is how things stand,' I said, dully.

'Forgive me,' he muttered.

'What nonsense! Forgive you for what?'

The temple doors opened again. I made sure the guards caught no glimpse of my sword. P'ei Ti was obliged to leave under their watchful gaze. When he had gone, I sat for a long while, the sword across my lap. The old monk shuffled from his private chambers and shook his head. Somewhere in the palace, across the Imperial Deer Park, a gong tolled out the hour.

That night, I begged ink and paper from the monk and wrote a short poem. Its characters have never left me:

To the tune of 'Wind-Washed Sand'

Climb pagoda steps, gaze across the lands.
Stars hang motionless, night is numb.
Old friends offer what comfort they can.
Lonely shadow, do not imagine
Daybreak will scatter you forever.
Do not forget kind words said in parting.
In pools of darkness, jade faces glow.

I was granted another day before the assassins came. Another day of pacing and pointless misery.

At last, evening chill settled on the Temple of Flying Petals. My dinner had not arrived by dusk and perhaps that saved me. Perhaps that was why, though hungry, I climbed the pagoda and lolled on a step half-way up, P'ei Ti's sword across my lap, and fell into a doze.

When I descended, a strange scent filled the air. The temple was full of delicious aromas. Ginger, certainly, and aniseed, as well as something cloying. I stepped into the temple and sensed an unnatural stillness. I made my way warily to the altar of the Blossom God.

There I found a reason to pause. The old monk slumped on the steps, beside a basket of coloured rice and spiced meat. Two chopsticks lay by his lifeless hand, oily with sauce. We had got into the habit of sharing our rations, which in any case came from the same kitchen. Now I bitterly reproached myself for not warning him that I feared poison. His head was twisted in a strange angle. Foam flecked his mouth. The whites of his eyes stared into nothingness.

'Father!' I cried.

Though I shook him vigorously he gave no sign of life. Gently, I let his grizzled head fall back.

The temple doors were customarily locked by my guards at night, but when I tried them they opened easily. I intended to summon the soldiers and tell them the guardian of the temple had been taken ill.

'Guards!' I shouted into the dusk. 'Come quickly!'

My voice echoed round the courtyard. No one replied. I had been abandoned. The temple lay open to any who would enter.

Of course I should have fled at once and hidden in the darkness of the Deer Park undergrowth. Or ran to the nearest building and sought the protection of whoever lived or served there. More guards could have been summoned. It would have been sensible. Instead I hurried back to the old monk and slapped his face. To my relief he stirred. I realised that the poison must not be lethal, merely enough to cause unconsciousness. But why drug a man into sleep when you can silence him for, good with something stronger?

Oh, I should have run like a deer that has heard distant hounds and knows what to expect when they burst into view! Instead I went to the old monk's quarters and fetched a bowl of water. Using a small cup, I dribbled some onto his wrinkled lips. Then I opened his mouth gently and was relieved to see his tongue take a drop. I was about to try again when I heard someone testing the temple door.

At once I understood why the poisoned food brought sleep rather than death. Men had been sent for me at a time when the guards had conveniently disappeared. Perhaps they wished to question me before I died, as had happened to Secretary Wen. Perhaps they would torture me as they had him. I was certain no one would hear my screams or cries for help. The Temple of Flying Petals stood well away from the nearest dwelling. And even if someone did hear, those who dwelt in the Son of Heaven's palace were accustomed to minding their own business.

The door creaked. The temple was dark, except for a small lamp on the Blossom God's altar. I retreated to the stairwell at the bottom of the pagoda and waited, concealed by deep shadows. With a clawing sensation, I realised that P'ei Ti's sword remained in its hemp wrappings beside the old monk. I was defenceless.

As the temple door opened, I almost darted forward to snatch up my sword. If I had, they would have seen me at once. No doubt I would have fought. Perhaps I might even have managed to wound one of them until they cut me down, like a hero from an old story. Thankfully, I hesitated. My true nature saved me for, despite Father's trade, I was no soldier.

Three men dressed in black robes glided into the temple. I hardly dared breathe, let alone move. They looked around wordlessly. Each carried a drawn sword in his hand. One of them held a lamp.

Yet they could not see me peering from the stairwell. In a strange way, though unarmed, I had an advantage. I had grown used to wandering round the temple at night, whereas for them it was a strange place. Yet I hardly doubted those black-clad men would end my life quite efficiently, perhaps even courteously, within moments of finding me.

So I made no noise as I climbed the pagoda stairs. Half way up I paused.

'This isn't him,' came a distant voice.

How confident the man sounded! He spoke as though there was no need for caution. Perhaps he wanted me to hear so I might panic and betray my presence. I heard the thud of a boot. A faint groan.

'Leave him,' commanded the first voice.

'We were told he would be asleep!'

This second was as nervous as the first was nonchalant.

'It does not matter.'

After that they did not speak. The hunt had commenced and I was the quarry. Every scrape of my feet on the stairs as I ascended brought terror.

Was I weak? Was I less than a true man to offer no resistance?

Perhaps. Perhaps.

My one refuge lay further up the stairs. It was not long before I heard them below. After all, the temple was small and could be searched quickly. At last I saw a faint glow from their lamp. I climbed further. Did they hear me? No shout broke the silence. Now I was at the top. The stairs had run out. I was trapped.

They say one's life passes before one's eyes in the moment before death. If so, I must have possessed a peculiar mind. For I did not glimpse my whole life but an hour of it. Long ago, when I was eight years old, Little Wudi beside me, hunting a fat, noisy cricket. It had retreated to the roof of Three-Step-House and, in a rush of bravado, I had climbed after it, clinging like a spider to the roof tiles. . .

Now I could hear them on the stairs quite clearly. I knew what I must do. I dared not. If I hesitated a moment longer they would catch me. Trembling, I climbed onto the window frame and seized the roof tiles. Some instinct kept me from looking down. Now I was outside and the cold night wind ruffled my hair. Then, taking a firm hold of the wooden frame, I hauled myself up.

Suddenly, the silence was broken by the rolling, mournful echo of a great ceremonial gong from within the palace: *Deng deng deng deng. . .* So loud and entirely unexpected that I almost lost my grip. Somehow I held on and managed to swing my legs onto the sloping roof, while the gong beat repeatedly. I believe that gong saved my life for it covered the sound of my passage.

I lay face down, gripping the tiles with a desperate strength. Every portion of my body except my breath froze. I glanced once at the sky beyond the roof-ridge, then squeezed my eyes shut. I willed myself into thoughtlessness. Hold on, that was all, that was everything, hold on lest they discover me, seize my ankles and drag me off the roof, hold on lest my slow, twisting fall ended in a dull crump as I hit the ground.

How long did it take them to reach the top of the pagoda? When they arrived I could hear their conversation clearly for the tolling of the great gong had died away.

'Did you hear a noise?'

'Apart from the bell?'

'Yes. Hush, you fools!'

Hush. The sound of the wind.

'He's not in the temple.'

'Where is he?'

'I swear I heard something.'

'It must have been the bell.'

'He has been warned. That's why he's not here.'

'I'm not giving up so quickly.'

'Hush, you fools!'

Hush. Somewhere far away, a faint wisp of music.

'He must still be in the temple.'

'But we've searched there.'

'We will search again.'

The quiet padding of feet. They were descending. I clung on, eyes closed, gripping the roof tiles. At last I heard the temple doors slam. Still I dared not move. Hours passed and dawn brought colour to the sky. I had to assume the assassins had gone; it was impossible to hold on any longer. Hand by hand, I lowered myself down the roof and swung my legs inside the pagoda. I landed with a heavy crash on the floor and lay gasping and shivering. There was no one to hear. My murderers had gone. I had survived.

At daybreak I heard marching feet. The guards were returning.

A fierce, perverse desire took hold and, exhausted though I was, hungry and thirsty though I was, I stumbled down the pagoda steps to the temple doors, passing the old monk as he clutched his stomach. Flinging open the golden doors, I blinked in the light of a new day. The guards' faces froze.

Then it occurred to me that they might finish the assassins' work in order to conceal their treacherous negligence. So I slammed the doors shut and retreated to my friend, the old monk. Now they would have to do away with both of us. Who knew what the guards had been paid to allow the murderers access? No one will ever know. Yet they had fulfilled their part of the bargain, whether I lived or died. It happened that I lived.

After I had given the monk a cup of water he retched out the poison. His drugged sleep of the previous night had been replaced by nothing worse than a griping belly. I knelt before the altar and prayed to the Blossom God, whispering: 'I have been reborn as blossom, which is to say, a cloud.'

And I meant it with a whole heart.

So when the official from the Censor's Bureau arrived that same morning I floated to Lord Xiao's trial. I was still a cloud. A dark cloud for him. Purity lit my soul, the purity of one who has survived improbable odds. I feared nothing because I had outlived fear. Drunk on unexpected life, I made my way across the Deer Park to the palace and forgot the trial before me. Each nuance of sky a delight, the chorus of birds, the sheen of dew on bladed grass. . . All strengthened me.

I was escorted through towering gatehouses, wide courtyards lined with shrines and statues, into the heart of the palace. A fitting place for Lord Xiao's trial.

All his life he had fluttered like a moth round the Son of Heaven. A gorgeous, powerful moth, his wings purest vermilion, his appetites intense. Here he had advocated a hundred policies, whispering and cajoling, tempting fate in order to fashion fate. He was a man who came alive among the great and barely noticed his inferiors at all, for they did not matter.

No doubt I oversimplify him. It was said that he was tender and indulgent to his children. The rest of mankind were a passing show of utility. One might stand in a field of flowers and be pleased by what one smells and sees. He considered only what he chose to pluck. In that, for all his dreams of power, he was a type.

And I was another type. One who stared in awe as I entered the inner precincts of His Majesty, while part of me remained aloof. So you might call me as arrogant as Lord Xiao, merely in a different way.

Finally we reached an inner courtyard and my escort presented arms before a surly officer.

'I'll conduct him from here,' he said.

Evidently I was anticipated. He led me to an antechamber before a pair of ebony doors carved with phoenixes. There I found the Lawyer Yuan Chu-Sou, attired in a splendid court uniform. He did not look happy.

'Sit down.'

I did so with relief. My night on the pagoda-roof had exhausted me.

'Are you unwell?' he asked, sharply.

I laughed mirthlessly.

'You might say that.'

Then I whispered how the previous evening had gone. He retained a fixed, unnatural grin as he listened.

'You are lucky to be alive,' he said. 'Though right now I would trade you for Secretary Wen. His testimony is dearly missed.'

This impudence revived my pride. Perhaps I should have thanked him for that, seeing what followed.

'You won't even have me,' I said, loudly. 'Unless I get something to eat. It is likely I'll faint in front of the judges.'

The clerks and hangers-on in the antechamber looked up in surprise. Everyone was whispering in that long room. Yuan Chu-Sou glanced round nervously. No doubt he feared I would let slip an indiscretion.

'Very well.'

He set about it and I slumped against the wall, listening to voices droning in the courtroom beyond the double doors. At last he led a serving eunuch to me who carried a tray of steamed buns.

'I hope you realise that meal cost three-hundred *cash* in bribes.'

I ignored him and ate my fill. When I looked up again, I felt more myself.

'What am I to expect?' I asked.

He re-arranged his silks.

'Questions. Simply answer as I have taught you.'

A hundred questions of my own concerning the prosperity of our case crowded my mind, yet I dared not ask them in this room full of spies. I suspected Yuan Chu-Sou's grim face answered them anyway. We subsided into silence.

'You had better spend a few more strings of *cash* on some water,' I said, finally. 'For I am parched.'

Then I fell into a restless doze.

Hours later the double doors opened and an official, dressed more like a peacock than a man, bellowed: 'The Most Ineffable Judges require Yun Cai of Wei District!'

The Lawyer Yuan Chu-Sou was on his feet in a flash.

'None of your insolence now. Make sure you show the proper respect or they might decide to use the implements on you.'

We were led into an octagonal chamber lined with stone benches. High windows filled every angle of the room so that a circle in the centre was brightly lit. Officials in uniform sat patiently on the benches, for this was a very public trial. Of Lord Xiao himself there was no sign.

Three carved chairs on a platform filled one end of the room. Here the judges sat in grey robes, undecided between the black of happiness and white of death. I advanced slowly, copying the Lawyer Yuan Chu-Sou's diffident shuffle, then prostrated myself before the judges as he did. So nervous was I that I struggled with the need to pass wind. That would have been fatal to our case. I clenched my buttocks tightly and the effort helped me forget some of the peril I faced.

'I see you have another witness,' said the Chief Judge, in a bored tone. 'Both of you may look up. We need to read your faces.'

I did so, and almost met his eye.

'Explain your propositions,' commanded the judge.

I waited while Yuan Chu-Sou recommended the scrolls I had found in Pinang, reminding everyone present that they had already been scrutinised by the court. It became obvious those scrolls were the beating heart of the case against Lord Xiao. Yet I sensed that heart was weakening.

'You have claimed the scrolls reveal Lord Xiao's corruption,' said the judge. 'And indeed, if one accepts they are genuine, matters stand badly for the accused. The question is, are they genuine?'

Yuan Chu-Sou was instantly voluble.

'Ten thousand times genuine!' he cried. 'As I will prove.'

'Then prove it,' said another of the judges.

I realised the judges liked this trial even less than I. What could they gain from it, after all? Nothing but enemies. And Lord Xiao had powerful friends.

'Yun Cai is the gentleman who discovered the scrolls,' replied Yuan Chu-Sou. 'As he will be glad to attest.'

All eyes in the court were upon me.

'Stand up,' barked the judge.

I did so.

'Well then, tell your story.'

So I told it in simple terms, for indeed there wasn't much to say, explaining how I found the scrolls, preserved them, then gave them to the Lawyer Yuan Chu-Sou without understanding their contents.

'Do you claim not to know what the scrolls allege?' asked the third judge.

'Ineffable Sir, they seem to be written in some kind of code. I must confess that I have had too many things on my mind to wish to decipher that code.'

The court rippled with amusement. I heard Yuan Chu-Sou wince beside me.

'Too many things on your mind! What arrogance is this?' demanded the judge.

'Not arrogance, sir, just honesty.'

'Yet you thought it worth your while to preserve them and pass them to one who wished to make use of them?'

'Ineffable Sir,' I said. 'That is merely because I sensed they might be important. But, as I say, even now I have no detailed knowledge what they contain.'

'Ah, you are like an innocent child,' said the judge, sarcastically. 'Who finds a murderer's dagger in a dead man's robes, without understanding a thing about it! As the proverb says: *When the map is unrolled the dagger is revealed*!'

His colleagues chuckled at his wit.

'Come now,' he added. 'Admit you bear Lord Xiao a deep-seated grudge.'

'Sir, let the clerks record my words, when I say that I do bear Lord Xiao a deep grudge.'

The court murmured.

'Silence!' bellowed the Chief Judge. 'Witness, explain yourself.'

I did so, in a steady flow of words. How my appointment as Chief of the Bureau of Fallen Heroes had come about. How I had been ordered into perilous siege works through letters sent to Lord Xiao's cousin, His Excellency Wen Po. How that same illustrious general had commanded that I crawl through a noisome tunnel into the rebel stronghold, and how I had been set upon by men hired to kill me. How my own cousin, hoping to gain a Sub-prefect's position through pleasing Lord Xiao, had assigned the murderers to be my bodyguard. My own cousin! How I had striven all my young life to make my father proud by passing His Majesty's examinations, and that now I had nothing to show for it. How I had been obliged to resign my humble office for the sake of a great man's jealousy and pride, for there was no other explanation for the misfortunes I had suffered. So that, yes, I bore a grudge, because I would not be made of flesh if I did not.

But that grudge did not make me a liar. And that grudge did not make me claim anything false about the scrolls and how I had found them. For all I cared, Lord Xiao could continue as always, so long as he left me in peace. I had nothing to reproach myself with, except too much fondness for a captivating woman and that, ridiculous as it seemed, was the sole reason I was sent to Pinang. That was how I discovered those tightly-rolled scrolls in a dead man's robes. Because of folly and absurd pride. And that was why I held a grudge, more against the vice itself, than the great man who had demeaned himself by exerting his power to crush a butterfly like myself. And, if that was not all, I had no illusions that Lord Xiao's friends would forgive me for standing as a witness against him, and yet it was the last thing I wanted in all the world.

I trembled as I finished. The court heard me in silence, apart from low chuckles when I alluded to Lord Xiao's jealousy over Su Lin, for everyone in the city knew that old story. Long moments passed. The Chief Judge turned to his fellows.

'Yun Cai is either very honest or exceedingly false,' he said.

A second judge said shrewdly: 'Yet there can be little doubt he will be rewarded for his testimony by those who hate Lord Xiao.'

The third opined: 'Beguiling women have brought down dynasties before now. One may think of many examples.'

I could sense Yuan Chu-Sou's excitement as he stood beside

me. Then a loud voice spoke out. It was another lawyer, the counterpart to Yuan Chu-Sou, acting on Lord Xiao's behalf.

'Ineffable Sirs,' began the rival lawyer. 'Let us not be swayed by Yun Cai's eloquence. After all, he is well-known as a poet. This is a man to whom words come all too easily. I beg you, do not trust his words unless they are properly tested. Surely this witness's testimony should be proved by torture?'

I looked at him dully. My head swam. His final word echoed in the huge room. The judges looked among themselves.

'Besides,' continued the lawyer. 'Yun Cai is not as he presents himself. I have a witness, Ineffable Sirs, a noble witness, to contradict his testimony. I beg to bring before the court His Excellency Wen Po, he who led our glorious forces against the rebels in Pinang.'

So that was how it would end. Just as generals of old saved their best charioteers for when the battle was most desperate, they had decided to wheel out Wen Po. I had last seen him in the mountains after we fled the stricken city of Pinang. He had given me a letter of free passage then. But he was Lord Xiao's cousin, and family is everything. Who would believe a nobody like me against a hero of the Empire, even one besmirched by failure? I shook my head sadly. It may seem a strange thing, but I feared most of all that Father would believe my accusers when news of my disgrace reached him.

His Excellency Wen Po was helped into the court. He had been plump when I last saw him. Now he was bloated. And if I looked uncomfortable he seemed doubly so. Since the debacle at Pinang he had confined himself to his estates north of the capital, lucky to have escaped a command to commit suicide from the Son of Heaven.

I was left standing in the illuminated centre of the room, while His Excellency Wen Po was immediately granted a high-backed chair at the side of the judges. I had nothing to lose. Indeed the outcome was certain. So I turned to meet his eye and, to my surprise, he glanced away.

After the formalities, the judges began their questioning.

'Your Excellency,' said one. 'It is a privilege to behold you.'

Wen Po nodded a slow acknowledgement.

'We believe you have come here to speak against this last witness, Yun Cai of Wei, is that correct?'

Again Wen Po nodded. His face was puffy, strained by illness. Then the judges ordered the scribes to read out my testimony. His Excellency Wen Po listened impassively. After they had finished, Lord Xiao's lawyer rose to his feet.

'We have heard the calumny and lies of Yun Cai for a second time. I beg our Ineffable Judges to settle the matter. His Excellency Wen Po will be heaven's witness.'

'As you say,' said the Chief Judge.

Emboldened the lawyer asked: 'Your Excellency, do you know this Yun Cai of Wei?'

'I do.'

'You know him as a notorious scoundrel and liar, do you not?'

Wen Po frowned, seemed about to speak, then thought better of it.

'This Yun Cai was notorious as a coward and slanderer in Pinang, was he not?' repeated the lawyer.

I glanced at Wen Po's unhealthy face. To my surprise, his eyes had turned my way and met my own. For a long second we surveyed each other.

'I could not call him a coward,' he said, reluctantly.

'But a scoundrel, yes?' demanded the lawyer, quickly. 'Whose malicious testimony bears no more weight than a flickering adder's tongue? A jealous, malicious man only concerned with furthering his own interests. So much so that he has constructed a false tale of finding certain scrolls in Pinang. A proven liar, is it not so, sir?'

Wen Po shrugged.

'He may have found some scrolls for all I know. I did not keep watch on him from dawn till dusk.'

The court murmured. Lord Xiao's lawyer narrowed his eyes.

'Sir, he is saying you ordered him into dangerous places at your revered cousin's behest. The court would welcome your confirmation that he lies.'

Wen Po sighed.

'Everywhere is dangerous during a battle,' he said. 'I must say that Yun Cai did not act like a coward. Perhaps he was a coward inside. I cannot say whether that is true. How may one read a man's heart except by his actions?'

Suddenly the Lawyer Yuan Chu-Sou was on his feet.

'Your Excellency,' he said. 'One might almost conclude from your words that Yun Cai was, how can I put it, *brave*?'

Wen Po licked his lips, cornered by questions.

'I cannot call him a coward,' he repeated, doggedly.

Yuan Chu-Sou seized the advantage.

'Why do you say so, sir? I beg you to explain.'

'Because,' replied Wen Po. 'Because he acquitted himself well. Damn it! He showed more spirit than some of my officers.'

Again the on-lookers muttered amongst themselves. This time the judges did not stop them.

'A brave man may still be a scandalous liar,' interjected Lord Xiao's lawyer. 'There are countless precedents.'

'Of course, of course,' replied Wen Po.

'And that is true of Yun Cai, is it not?'

Again his witness looked uncomfortable.

'It depends what you refer to,' he said. 'If you mean, did Yun Cai tell me lies, I have to say, I do not know of any. But that does not mean he did not tell lies.'

'We can be sure he is telling a lie when he says he found the scrolls in Pinang, can we not?' insisted the lawyer, desperately.

It was strange to hear an advocate berating his own witness, almost embarrassing, like watching an honourable man lose face. The Chief Judge raised his hand. Perhaps he, too, found the exchange uncomfortable.

'What's your point? Be quick with it.'

The lawyer flushed.

'My point, Ineffable Sirs, is that His Excellency has come here, despite grievous ill-health, to contradict Yun Cai's claim that the scrolls are genuine documents.'

The Chief Judge looked across at Wen Po.

'Tell me,' he said. 'We've known each other a long time. Did we not enter the Vermilion Gates together when we were both young men? Wen Po, I ask you, is that why you are here?'

The old general seemed oddly relieved by this question.

'I must tell you, since you ask,' he said. He fell silent. Then he added quietly: 'My family assure me that Yun Cai is a liar, and that he could not have found these scrolls in Pinang as he has described. They swear that he has devised these lies to revenge himself upon my cousin, Lord Xiao. For my part, I say what I have already said. I have nothing more to add.'

The judge nodded solemnly.

'I understand. His Excellency may withdraw. I have heard enough.'

I was alone in the centre of the court.

Lord Xiao's lawyer stepped forward. He was like one of those game fighting cocks which always return to the fight, even with a wing torn off.

'Only torture will settle the question of Yun Cai's testimony!' he cried. 'Rigorous, probing use of the implements! I insist that this false witness should be tested under torture!'

The three judges regarded him.

'You, sir, may not *insist* on anything,' said the Chief Judge. 'We will consider your request. For now, today's hearing is over.'

Suddenly, the wide room, so long repressed, was full of voices. In a daze I felt the Lawyer Yuan Chu-Sou lead me outside. As he conducted me to the soldiers waiting by the gate, he gripped my arm. I swear there was approval in the gesture.

'We must see whether they decide you should be tortured,' he whispered. 'When you go under the implements, for heaven's sake stand firm, or we will lose all our advantage. I must report what has happened to our great sponsor – you did well not to mention his name, by the way. Who knows, he may be able to influence what implements are used.'

Then he delivered me to a waiting escort of soldiers.

Four guardsmen marched me back to the Temple of Flying Petals. I kept my eyes to the ground, ignoring the courtiers and officials we passed on the way. My undergarments were clammy with sweat, my face chilled by a dry wind. Words and faces, snatches of phrases from the trial, all blew round my mind so that half my spirit remained in that perilous room. Nothing had been resolved for me there except that I must endure a night of dreadful uncertainty.

I no longer cared whether Lord Xiao would be found guilty. All that mattered was the prospect of torture.

Torture! You could say everyone is tortured during life, through malicious gossip or unkind acts, sometimes one's own. Through love becoming its opposite, step by step, until one is alone and forlorn. But the prospect of a practised hand testing weakness through gradations of pain, studied blows to soles or genitals, perhaps a little judicious fire, or red-hot tongs delicately applied to one's nose, or a simple old-fashioned whipping. . . Oh, I could not think of it. Or stop thinking of it. Imagined agonies so unbearable I almost wished they would set about me at once, just to get it over with.

By the time I reached the Temple I was losing my balance. I found my friend, the old monk, waiting by the doors. He began to chant a low, mournful sutra as my guards thrust me through the portal. Scooping handfuls of dried petals from a bronze bowl, he scattered them upon me, as blossom graces the earth. I staggered and he led me to his private chamber. There a basket of rice balls lay on the table beside a flask of wine.

'Eat!' he commanded.

My stomach revolted at the thought of food. I slumped on his low cot, burying my head in my hands.

'Eat,' he said again, more gently.

I managed a gulp of rice-ball, then another. Soon I had emptied the basket.

'Drink,' he said. 'Do not fear. The wine is good.'

With shaking hands I drained a large cup.

'Now sleep,' he said, softly. 'Whatever will happen has already occurred. Who knows how many lifetimes you have endured? Sleep. And perhaps the Blossom God will comfort your dream.'

I lay on the cot like an exhausted child and felt a rough blanket thrown over me.

Perhaps the Blossom God did visit my dreams. I do not remember. When I awoke it was bright morning and a short, pot-bellied man shook my arm.

'Hey, you! Wake up!'

He wore the uniform of a eunuch serving the Censor's Bureau. I recognised him as an official from the trial. I swung my legs to the floor. So they had come for me.

'They say a man with a clean conscience sleeps well,' he chuckled. 'But I say, everyone is guilty of something.'

I waited.

'You are free to go,' he said. 'The judges have no further use for you.'

My puzzlement must have shown.

'On your way! Go!'

'Where must I go?'

He tutted, then laughed heartily.

'Anywhere that will have you.'

At once I understood whom I should thank for my release. The last person I might ever have imagined. His Excellency Wen Po's refusal to condemn my character or the provenance of the scrolls had swung the judges behind my testimony. To this day I do not know why he defied his family and refused to brand me a liar. Perhaps he resented being dragged from his final sickbed. Perhaps he sensed death was near, indeed he was buried a month later, and feared to tell a lie lest he pay for it before the infernal judges in Hell. Perhaps he simply hated his cousin, or even liked me and, being a soldier, a plain man at heart, that was enough. No one can ask him now.

I stood outside the Temple of Flying Petals staring up at a blue sky ribboned with clouds, a bundle at my feet containing P'ei Ti's sword and his gift of money. The old monk stood beside me. After I had thanked him, bowing as low as I ever did for Father, he said: 'You have forgotten someone, young man.'

Indeed I had. I prostrated myself nine times before the image of the Blossom God but he granted me no sign. Why should he? He had granted me his greatest favour, another cycle of life.

'Little General, can that be you?'

Cousin Hong rose hurriedly as I stepped into the courtyard of his wine shop. The customers looked up curiously, then returned to their conversations. Without replying I accepted his embrace. Perhaps he read my mood for he asked no questions.

'This house is your own,' he said, simply. 'You are safe here.'

Once again I found myself in the storeroom overlooking Jade Cloud Canal. Again, all I could do was wait. If the judges decided in Lord Xiao's favour I must flee the city, though a thousand *li* could hardly be expected to protect me. Sooner or later his anger would find me out.

But if he fell, if he was banished or stripped of office and His August Excellency continued to protect me; if Lord Xiao's family and friends decided I was not worth ruining for revenge's sake; and if I passed the Imperial Examination with honour and was appointed to the Son of Heaven's service; then perhaps, just maybe, I might face the future with a light heart.

Hours spent alone in the storeroom at the back of Cousin Hong's wine shop, watching light change into night. I dared not visit P'ei Ti or Su Lin, in case my company infected them. Yet I longed for their fellowship, and letters passed between us, though neither found the courage to meet me in the days leading up to Lord Xiao's verdict. All the while, I secretly resented their prudence. Especially Su Lin. I had risked so much for her. Could she not do the same for me?

We were all waiting. It was a bitter time. And it exposed our frailties, and strengths.

After two days of seclusion, I'd had a bellyful of Cousin Hong's storeroom. Instead of skulking like a brigand in a cave, I stepped out into the courtyard wearing my brightest silks. There I surprised Mi Feng and Cousin Hong in earnest conversation.

'Little General, you look pale as a ghost,' exclaimed my cousin.

They seemed in high spirits.

'I have a request,' I said.

They watched me. Two shrewd men. Cousin Hong sighed, and I knew him well enough to read his mind. He was afraid I needed a loan.

'It's not that,' I interrupted. 'Can you spare Mi Feng for the day?' I asked.

'Of course! I must tell you, he has become my business partner now. In fact we were just discussing my plan to buy another small wine shop.'

When they turned to each other I noted the affection between them and felt a pang of jealousy. How I envied their ability to prepare a brighter future! Yet I was not without plans of my own.

'May the venture bring great profit to you both,' I said.

'If you want me,' declared Mi Feng. 'Then I'm your servant once more.'

Before we left I whispered that he should carry his knife and I would take my sword. If he expected a wild escapade I soon disappointed him. All I intended was to cross the city. Given my brush with Lord Xiao's assassins in the Temple of Flying Petals and the fate of Secretary Wen, that seemed dangerous enough. It was quite possible spies observed the wine shop waiting for me to emerge. In fact my plan was hazardous in other ways. At the very least, I intended to compromise my reputation as a gentleman. I might even provoke Father's utter rejection.

We left by a side door and, after weaving through alleyways, walked long miles through the city, wary of faces following us among the crowds. It was a grimmer, less gay place than the city of my youth. Soldiers recalled from the frontier were everywhere, as were drifting groups of peasants driven out of the countryside by famine. Each fresh proof of destitution confirmed my sense that the Way did not flow well through our Empire. Yet I wore splendid silks, costly enough to feed dozens of families. Was I not complicit?

Finally, we reached the West Lake. The sight of a hundred pleasure craft weaving round each other did not bring the gladness I expected. I felt, like one who has watched a delightful play too many times.

I hired a boatman and half an hour later disembarked further up the lakeside. A low hill rose capped by Su Lin's house and gardens. Mi Feng turned to me.

'Should you be coming here?' he asked, quietly.

'No. And because of that, yes.'

I felt his hand on my arm and met his cold eyes.

'Remember what she owes to you,' he said.

He was right, but the memory did not smooth my anxious heart as I approached her gates. Perhaps she would not be at home. Should I wait like a common suitor or messenger for her return? The porter took one look at us and scowled. It was the same cocky fellow Mi Feng had threatened when we returned from Pinang.

'You need not announce us,' I said.

Mi Feng raised a finger and pointed at the door. The porter bowed nervously and ushered us through.

I walked into the house and paused. Then I heard her light, indifferent laugh. A taunting, playful laugh guaranteed to provoke a reaction. A man's voice rose in mock protest. I froze. Mi Feng halted beside me. If not for his presence I might have turned back, afraid of shame. Instead we entered the courtyard and silently watched four or five young men, gathered around her as she lolled on the low wall of the fishpond. Several were painting her portrait as she reclined. One by one they became aware of us and their brushes went still.

Su Lin's eyes met mine. Her expression passed rapidly from surprise to alarm.

'Yun Cai!' she cried, rising hurriedly.

The gaily-dressed young men rose with her in a loud rustle of silks. Her voice faltered. I examined my rivals and they returned my gaze curiously. Everyone knew about the trial of Lord Xiao and my own part in it.

'How remiss of me, gentlemen!' she cried. 'It quite fled my mind that the Honourable Yun Cai had arranged to visit me today! I must beg your deepest pardon, gentlemen, for I fear your delightful portraits must wait until another day.'

They muttered amongst themselves. No doubt they had paid for her company with splendid gifts. They left after several pretty speeches and I found myself alone with her. Mi Feng withdrew to the shadows. She stepped forward eagerly. I could see golden carp swimming in the fishpond behind her as we talked.

'Have they reached a verdict. . . Yun Cai, are you safe?'

She was trembling.

'For now I am quite safe. The verdict is still not known.'

'But what of Lord. . .'

She hesitated before naming him.

'We can speak Lord Xiao's name if we like,' I said. 'It will hardly offend the judges. Sit down beside me, Su Lin, you make me nervous standing there.'

We sat beside the fishpond and I explained all that had happened: my night on the roof of the Temple of Flying Petals; how I had barely escaped torture as a consequence of my testimony at Lord Xiao's trial. Even as I spoke I sensed something base behind my words. I wanted her to feel an obligation to love me.

'You have suffered,' she said. 'Poor Yun Cai!'

And that was my reward: pity.

'I came here,' I said. 'Not just for the pleasure of your company.'

For the first time in the long years we had danced around each other conversation failed us. Perhaps she anticipated what I would ask. Silence grew like a shadow.

'I need to know where I stand,' I said. 'Surely that is natural.'

'Of course!' she cried, with brittle gaiety.

I longed for her to reach out, enfold me in her arms. Yet her hands lay modestly on her lap. When I looked into her face I noticed the first signs of tiny lines round her eyes. It was a guarded face. She seemed almost afraid. So I tried again.

'Are your feelings unchanged?' I asked. 'That is why I have risked coming here. Because I must know how deeply you love me.'

She reached to her broad girdle for a fan to flutter, but none hung there.

'I am happy,' she said, with false brightness. 'It is kind of you to enquire.'

'Su Lin, you speak so strangely! Is something wrong? That does not answer my question.'

To my surprise, she stood up and stared mournfully into the pond of golden, circling carp.

'How hard this is,' she said. 'You really shouldn't have come like this. I do not know how to answer. You see, my feelings are one thing, my situation quite another. Everything has happened so fast! Things I did not anticipate.'

I waited for her to say more. Her words were a kind of destiny, one I had long foreseen. For the last year, Su Lin had been the foremost singing girl in the capital, an object of universal admiration. She had become the season's brightest ornament and the whole giddy world of the rich and idle lived for such fashions. This was her hour, a time I could not share. No doubt she understood better than I that she must reap while she could before a younger woman supplanted her. It had always been thus. And so I believed that I might offer her a future.

'Su Lin,' I said. 'Will you marry me? It is time to banish the uncertainty between us.'

Her hand flew to her mouth. It was as though I had struck her across the face.

'Oh, Yun Cai,' she whispered.

'I wish you to become my wife,' I said, stoutly. 'Let all the demons in hell take the consequences!'

'Your father would never approve. This is. . . You have not thought through what you are saying.'

I shook my head.

'I know exactly what I am saying. We shall find a way to live and have many sons to make us proud. My father will learn to respect you for what you are. Who could do otherwise? Marry me, Su Lin, and I promise you my affection will not wane until the day I die. And that is worth more than a fine house or clothes. Love is the finest house imaginable and its rooms are never bare.'

I knew it must be so. Our children seemed something destined. I knew we would be contented together. She stood, her head downcast.

'Oh, Yun Cai,' she repeated.

'Then you agree?' I asked, eagerly. 'We will live in the country if necessary, and all our neighbours will envy us.'

Still she stood silently.

'Why do you not speak?' I asked.

Her kohl-lined eyes were wet with tears.

'I cannot agree to this,' she said. 'It is more tangled than you imagine. His August Excellency has. . . No, I cannot agree.'

That man's name was like a cuff to my forehead.

'He is an old, avaricious goat!' I cried. 'He has nothing to do with us! Marry me and be happy.'

She shook her head miserably.

'I am honoured. You cannot imagine how I am honoured. But I dare not live the life of a poor woman. I have always wanted more. Yet I want to say yes with all my heart!'

A minute passed. We were too distressed to speak.

'And it is not so easy to dismiss His August Excellency as you believe,' she continued. 'I sometimes fear he has grown too fond of me, and then I'm afraid.'

Now in my desperation I laughed scornfully.

'Pay him no regard, I beg you.'

'But I must! It is not so. . . And there is more. You see, if I carry on as I am for a few more seasons, I could offer you a dowry. I could sell this house, even some of my jewels and silks. We might leave the capital together, live as man and wife. But dearest Yun Cai, do not ask me to become poor or ordinary. I have known poverty. You must not ask that.'

'When I pass the Imperial examinations,' I said, stoutly, 'we will live on my salary, however humble at first, until I am promoted. Then I will earn enough for you to fill whole carriages with jade!'

'If you anger His August Excellency there shall be no promotion,' she countered. 'Is he not your sponsor in the examinations?'

'Then he must smile benignly upon us,' I retorted. 'And send a wedding gift.'

'He frightens me sometimes,' she said, as though thinking aloud. 'More than Lord Xiao did. He reminds me of the broker who. . . but that is foolishness. He is quite, quite kind. And noble, too.'

I took her soft hands in my own and lifted them to my lips.

'I know you too well, Su Lin,' I said, rising. 'You could not be happy without love. And I have proved myself a thousand times over in that regard.'

She nodded unhappily, and I left with what dignity I could muster. Her sobs followed me to the door. How I raged inside to prove myself worthy of her devotion! They say that the man in the moon ties a magical and invisible red thread around the ankles of all newborn girls and boys. When they grow up, that thread draws them closer, closer and, should they meet, marriage is inevitable. I believed that red thread tied Su Lin to me.

Mi Feng followed at a trot as I swept out of Su Lin's house. He had too great a regard for my dignity to discuss what had happened. If Lord Xiao's assassins had accosted us then, I would have gladly fought. Such contests are simple. One falls or walks away. But my struggle for Su Lin's love had disarmed me completely. How does one subdue one's own heart? I could almost feel the man in the moon's red thread dragging our ankles together.

When I was a boy, a plum tree stood in the small orchard at the back of Three-Step-House. A twisted, wizened kind of tree. No one knew its age for sure. Instead of branches heavy with fruit, it blossomed reluctantly, producing a mere hatful of plums each season. Yet of all the trees in the orchard I longed for it to surprise us, to bring forth a miraculous crop. Year after year I waited. Then, one autumn, my games with Little Wudi took me to the orchard and I found the plum tree on its side. Father had decided it was no good. Now it was firewood. When I protested to the servant who stood beside it, axe in hand, he laughed.

'Why waste good soil, Little Master? No one likes sour plums.'

Was Lord Xiao a waste of good soil? Certainly he had borne fine, healthy fruit for the Son of Heaven in his younger days. Is a man's early good cancelled by later failure? The philosopher Shao Yung used plum-blossom to foretell human fate. But no one could have foretold Lord Xiao's destiny, least of all himself.

I was dreaming of that plum tree at dawn, when Mi Feng's gruff voice stirred me.

'You have a visitor,' he said, urgently. 'He says you must dress in your very best clothes.'

I could not shake the plum tree from my sleepy mind. Somehow, in the strange way of dreams, I thought of Su Lin.

'You must hurry,' he said.

'Have they come for me?' I asked.

But he did not reply.

P'ei Ti was waiting in the courtyard, among a crowd of blood-spattered butchers. Like them, he was bolting down a large cup of wine. Unlike them, he wore a fine uniform. A strange smile played across his lips, as though he relished the absurdity of being seen in so low a haunt. I fastened my broad silken girdle hastily.

'Did you expect soldiers to arrest you?' he asked. 'Well, it's only me. The time for such fears is past.'

I looked at him sharply.

'Do you mean . . ?'

'After winter the fruit appears,' he intoned.

This reference to my dream startled me. It was as though he had turned sorcerer.

'Why do you mention it?' I asked.

He looked puzzled.

'No reason. It is just a saying. Surely you have heard it before.'

But I thought of the Blossom God and the Temple of Flying Petals.

'You have come here to tell me I am reborn,' I muttered, in amazement.

'How obscurely you speak, Yun Cai! But yes, in a sense, that is why I have come. And to take you to witness something none of us dared expect. My carriage is waiting on the Imperial Way. We must hurry.'

Once we were seated and jolting in the direction of the Palace, he told his story. Perhaps I had been reborn. For, as I had sensed when a prisoner in the temple, to be reborn required a death. His was a story soon told. Lord Xiao had been found guilty of a capital crime and his execution was scheduled for that very morning.

'You are mistaken,' I said. 'A great man like Lord Xiao... One would expect banishment, certainly deep disgrace, but not execution. You must be mistaken.'

P'ei Ti shrugged.

'There are precedents,' he said.

'Was his crime so great?'

'He embezzled a great revenue from Chi Province intended to finance the very war he supported. And all to maintain his wife's pretensions! And his own, of course, one can hardly blame her for everything.'

'So the scrolls were the key to his downfall,' I said.

'Partly the scrolls,' replied P'ei Ti. 'But I suspect his fall may be attributed to backing the wrong party in court. You see, ever since the Kin Emperor's capture of Pinang, the Son of Heaven has turned his back on the policy of trying to regain our lost lands. As you know, Lord Xiao was the foremost advocate of that policy. So I read his execution as a kind of warning. Times have changed, and all our opinions must change accordingly.'

We entered the district near the palace. Hundreds of officials in their uniforms, from lowly clerks to Prefects in gilded carriages were travelling the same way.

'There is another reason, of course,' said P'ei Ti. 'The current famine is the worst for thirty years. The people are angry, and

Lord Xiao's policy of efficient taxation has ruined countless peasants. By holding up the Finance Minister's head for all to see, the Son of Heaven is demonstrating that he feels for the people's sufferings.'

'Beheading Lord Xiao will not fill a single belly,' I said.

'Perhaps,' he replied. 'There is one final point. Tomorrow is the day of the Imperial Examinations. By executing Lord Xiao today His Majesty sends out a strong signal concerning the probity he expects from all his officials, even the very highest.'

'I see. You still have not explained where we are going.'

'Isn't that obvious? To the palace.'

'But why?'

'So you shall witness with your own eyes that your bad dream is over.'

An hour later we found ourselves in a great courtyard before the Temple of Inextinguishable Light amidst a crowd of officials, thousands strong. I thought then of Father's orchard above Three-Step-House at blossom time. So many gorgeous, resplendent uniforms! Every colour in the Empire, turquoise and pink, yellow and green jade.

A huge eunuch in white robes led Lord Xiao to the block. From our position in the crowd I could not see his expression. I was glad of that. I later heard he died calling for the Son of Heaven to live a thousand years. Perhaps his death brought some good to the Empire, though I am not convinced. In truth, nearly every tree in that orchard bore sour plums and corruption did not end with him. Over my long lifetime, it has grown ever more blatant.

Yet I was rid of Lord Xiao's spite! I need no longer fear a powerful man's malice. Su Lin and I were free to marry and be happy, for now I might even regain my former position. I had received a letter from her the previous evening and gained great reassurance from it. She wrote:

Dearest Incorrigible Friend,
You must believe that I am thinking and striving to find a means so we can live together in dignity and comfort. I beg you to ignore malicious rumours. Wait for me to contact you when I have more definite news. I enclose an amulet to bring you luck in the examination. It seems you and I have been sharing doorsteps – and jetties – for as long as I can remember. We have also shared our dreams.
Your dear friend across the lake, Su Lin.

'Will you go to her tonight?' asked P'ei Ti, as though reading my thought.

'Tomorrow is the day of the Imperial examinations,' I said. 'And I must prepare myself.'

'Then you still mean to take your chance?' he asked, eagerly.

'Yes!'

He seized my hands.

'I honour your strength!' he cried. 'You are bamboo! To have suffered as you have over the last month and still brave the hardest test! You constantly surprise me, Yun Cai. Why, I am speechless.'

'Now *that* surprises me,' I said.

'Meet me at the Examination Enclosure and we will enter together, arm-in-arm!' he said. 'You and I shall serve the Son of Heaven as equals. Just think of it!'

I tried to share P'ei Ti's joy. But as his carriage rolled away from the palace, we passed roadsides where landless peasants huddled, begging openly without a licence. Children with bellies swollen by hunger, their eyes huge and strangely bright. I witnessed a group of soldiers beating a peasant with the butts of their spears.

'If we pass the examination,' I said, gesturing at a family sheltering beneath a bridge. 'Is it to help these wretches?'

'Of course,' said P'ei Ti. 'Of course.'

He did not explain how. And doing just that, I felt, was where true duty lay.

I stood outside the Examination Enclosure like a soldier in the foremost line of battle. Never had I been more like Father, or how I imagined him. For he feared only disgrace. And I had armed myself with many weapons. My youthful heart rejected all shades of grey. Instead of a sword, I carried brushes of tapered horsehair. My armour was ink. My shield was the dawn sky, redolent with the Way. My quiver was crammed with earnest conceptions of truth.

A fierce wind blew dust round the square. Of all the candidates that autumn morning, of all the hundreds gathered for the test, only I was not accompanied by influential relatives or wealthy sponsors hoping to gain from my success. I had just Cousin Hong and Mi Feng, awed by the nobility around them. Yet I did not lack a patron, albeit a hidden one. His August Excellency had pledged to support my candidature as a reward for testifying against his enemy.

My intention was to answer the question set by the Son of Heaven with integrity, as Confucius says all honest officials must do, whatever the consequences for themselves. It seemed to me the dismal state of our Empire demanded nothing less. Now was the time to speak. Perhaps I secretly hoped to claim Su Lin's admiration through a noble gesture. Cousin Hong shook me out of my reverie.

'Little General, I hope you've brought everything you need this time.'

'What?'

'Never mind.'

Though it was cold, Cousin Hong mopped his brow.

'Eat another dumpling,' he said. 'I know they're your favourite.'

I did, chewing slowly and deliberately. Tension turned the dough to clay in my mouth. The crowd shuffled restlessly towards the huge, closed doors of the Examination Enclosure. Fire crackers were set off to scare away demons. To the east, day tinted the cloudless sky. Gold and swelling red, orange and dull silver. I saw P'ei Ti surrounded by relatives and well-wishers. When he met my eye, his face lit like the dawn. This was the moment for which he had proffered his entire life. The doubts I suffered concerning the Son of Heaven's legitimacy were alien to him. This examination was his birthright; he could not conceive of failure. I sensed he would have come to me, so that we could enter arm-in-arm as he had promised, but for the people around him. Then the gong sounded. One by one we passed through the Phoenix Gates to be assigned our huts.

Words on plain paper can make or condemn a man. So it was for me. The question, set by His Imperial Majesty himself, was a delicate one. It concerned the famine threatening to unbalance the Empire and asked how it might be ameliorated. A broad question. A needful question. My heart swelled with love of our sovereign as I read it. Here was proof he cared like a father for his people!

At once a safe answer filled my mind. Firstly, the peasants should be obliged to work harder. Secondly, supported by choice references to the *Book of Rites* – all memorised in advance – that more effective supplications to the Jade Emperor in Heaven would ensure better harvests. Thirdly, the merchants should pay higher taxes in order to. . . one could go on.

I read the question several times. The need to pass at any cost, so I might support Su Lin when we were married, fled my mind. I planned my answer paying scant regard to the sensitivities of the Imperial Examiners. Such was my zeal I forgot their distaste for any form of original thought:

The Son of Heaven is badly advised... Better administrators must be selected, the inept must be demoted. . . Revenue should be diverted from the court to pay for famine relief. . . The great landowners should pay a special tax. . . The army, currently idle, should be employed in irrigation and flood control. . . The boarding of grain to artificially raise prices should be viewed as treason. . . A system of fixed prices for basic foodstuffs should be introduced. . .

Every brush stroke mired me deeper in controversy. The narrow walls of my hut, sealed from the vile world of compromise and greed, injustice and indifference, seemed a safe place where commonsense might reign.

How foolish I was! What did I truly expect? Yet I felt justified in every essential breath, as though the elegant sentences flowing from my pen might feed our Empire. And those hours of enthusiasm, confined in a wooden hut six feet square, determined the course of my life.

It was customary for candidates to seclude themselves during the period of waiting for the Imperial Examiners' verdict. Many made daily offerings to their ancestors and the Imperial Family. Less scrupulous candidates were known to seek the aid of demons. P'ei Ti buried himself in papers from the Censor's Bureau. Perhaps official duties were his true demons. They tormented and beguiled him.

As for me, I spent the time in Cousin Hong's wine shop, writing poems and consuming large amounts of pork. Wine diverted me frequently. In truth I had little certainty of passing. Some of the things I had written made me wince inwardly. It was not that they were treasonous ideas, for I had uttered no criticism of the Emperor. Indeed, some of my suggestions were stolen from a previous First Minister, Wang Shi, and I had heard the rest discussed quite openly. No, my fault, if there was one, lay in taking the question too seriously, in proposing too practical a solution to the famine. That alone made me an oddity. Only a brave Examiner would grant the prize to a maverick, lest he later prove an embarrassment and so diminish the Examiner's own reputation. But what did it matter? I had been promised a position by His August Excellency and expected it any day.

My real worry was quite different. Would Su Lin consent to be my wife when I was posted to some obscure province to take up a lowly office? Did she love me enough for that?

Days passed. A week. Still I did not hear from her. I convinced myself that her silence was mere prudence. After all, any woman would want to know whether I had entered the Vermilion Doors before binding her destiny to my own. Inner struggles restrained me from writing a letter, though many were composed in my imagination. In one, my tone was peremptory. In the next, pleading. In a third, reasonable and kind, while the fourth considered the matter entirely from her own perspective, anticipating any objections she might deploy against my proposal, point by point. That letter ran to a hundred pages. I am glad I did not write or send it.

However, it turned out that the letter came from her. She wrote:

Dearest Yun Cai,
You must be surprised at my silence this last week. I beg you to be patient. Once, when we first met, you told me that without knowledge we are dust blown from one street to another. Oh, my dearest, if only I was wise! Perhaps I would see a clear answer to our dilemmas. You must believe that I seek it always.

How mysterious I sound! I do not mean to be. One day, perhaps, when we are old and grey together, I shall explain, and then we will laugh at the foolish alarms of today. For now, I beg you to stay away from my house until I send word otherwise. Do not fail me in this, dearest. I shall explain all when I can.

Your Su Lin

My first instinct was to hurry at once to her house by the West Lake. Instead, I called upon P'ei Ti in his office. He was surrounded by mounds of ledgers and seemed quite dull-spirited. At the sight of me he brightened until I showed him Su Lin's letter and asked if he could explain it.

'Most mysterious,' he muttered, avoiding my eye.

'P'ei Ti! I believe you know more than you say!'

'No,' he replied. 'Nothing certain. Go home, Yun Cai. Drink some of your cousin's wine and write a tender poem. The verdict of the Examiner will come soon. Then you will not care about wretched letters. All that will matter to you will be your new, noble position!'

I left P'ei Ti's bureau, threading a complicated way through narrow alleys and broad streets until I entered the Pig Market. When I reached Cousin Hong's shop, weary and hungry, another letter awaited me. It was an official note sent to me under the authority of the Chief Examiner. I have it still in one of my chests at Three-Step-House.

Yun Cai of Wei is informed that his answer to the Son of Heaven's question set to the Vermillion Candidates on the 6th Day of the 9th Month during the Year of the Snake has proved most unsatisfactory, wherefore the Honoured Examiners have consulted Yun Cai's sponsor in the Examinations, His August Excellency Lu Sha, wherefore His August Excellency has expressed great dissatisfaction with the tone and tenor and tendency of Yun Cai's submitted answer which, though not immediately treasonable in itself, is without doubt disrespectful in sundry degrees to the spirit of His Highness's question. Wherefore, considering His August Excellency's plea for clemency on Yun Cai's behalf, it has been decided that this same Yun Cai must proceed to his family's home in Chunming Province within two dawns of this letter's receipt, on pain of a frank and scathing enquiry as to possible treasonous implications and utterances within his answer to the Son of Heaven's examination question on the 6th Day of the 9th Month during the Year of the Snake. It is further decided that Yun Cai should not return to the capital unless expressly summoned by the Minister of Justice, His August Excellency Lu Sha. Should Yun Cai of Wei disregard these injunctions in any manner whatsoever, he shall become subject to harsh admonishment.

I read and re-read. Scarcely believed it. The meaning was obvious and beyond credibility. His August Excellency was doing exactly the same as Lord Xiao had done, and for the same reason! He was getting me out of the way. Only my banishment was not to war and an unpleasant death but to certain exile. An exile which might last forever, if he so chose.

An hour later I stood beside P'ei Ti while he read the letter. He lowered it to his knees with trembling hands and glared at me accusingly.

'What nonsense did you write in the examination to provoke this?' he demanded.

I stammered like a boy rebuked by his father. Indeed I was too deep in shock to be myself.

'Nothing, I swear. Only what is said every day, though some might not like the ideas. Indeed, I have heard you profess some of them many times.'

P'ei Ti shook his head in disbelief.

'Why must you always act differently from other men? Why can you never place your head beneath the yoke without some murmur or sardonic comment?'

At this jibe I regained my pride.

'So you take His August Excellency's side?'

P'ei Ti rose angrily.

'It is not about sides.'

'You know very well why this has happened to me,' I said.

'And it has nothing to do with my loyalty to the Son of Heaven. As ever, it is my loyalty to another that has caused the mischief.'

P'ei Ti twisted the letter in his hands.

'I'm sure His August Excellency will recall you from Wei very soon,' he said. 'You must not offend such a man.'

I laughed bitterly.

'Oh, I have every intention of offending him! Not through appealing against his decision, there is no point. To Wei I must go, that is certain. What he does not realise is that I shall take Su Lin with me as my wife. That *will* offend him. For we both know that he has grown besotted with her, as Lord Xiao did before. What is it with these great men? They think everyone in the world is a trinket to dangle from their girdles. But Su Lin and I will prove them all wrong!'

I turned to leave. P'ei Ti blocked my way.

'Has she agreed to marry you?' he asked, in amazement.

'Not exactly,' I said. 'But there is no avoiding one's destiny, P'ei Ti, whether it is mine or hers.'

His face contorted with genuine distress.

'Don't rush to her! I beg you! Think, she urged you not to visit her house. Do not throw yourself into the flame!'

I tried to step round him but still he barred the way.

'I have heard things, Yun Cai. No doubt, in your present mood, you'd just call them rumours. Oh, do not go to her! This is more delicate than you imagine.'

I swept past him, deaf to his cries that I should return.

As he had anticipated, my way took me straight to Su Lin's house. I was full of plans. We could marry on the road. Naturally, she would need to sell most of her possessions and this would be a great hardship to her. Yet I was sure she would undertake such a sacrifice. I was like a drunken man who can conceive no other way of thinking than his own. Most of all I dreaded Father's reaction when he met her. But surely he must come to admire what all men admired? Her elegant charm would win him over. Perhaps she could sing a few songs. He had always loved music.

But when I reached her house, when I reached her gate, I found her leaving in a splendid carriage pulled by two fat palfreys, followed by another full of servants and musicians playing lutes and finger cymbals. She looked nervous but was laughing gaily with a man dressed in badges of high office and dazzling silks. A man more than twice her age. And at last I understood her letter.

I stood at the roadside and called out her name as the carriage rolled towards the city. At once, Su Lin and His August Excellency recognised me. Their conversation faltered. He frowned, turning to note her reaction. For a fleeting, fluttering moment she seemed distressed.

I stepped forward eagerly. Her eyes blinked as they met my incredulous gaze. Her plump lips, so often adored and kissed, parted as though about to speak. I reached up my hand, as though to take her own and help her down from the carriage. But her hands remained on her lap.

Then, with great effort, she smiled stiffly at His August Excellency and spoke quiet words. How he roared with exaggerated laughter! Yet for all his mirth, his sideways glance at me expressed pure menace.

'Su Lin!' I cried, desperately.

She ignored me. I might as well have been a peddler on the street, crying out wares she could not afford to buy.

'Su Lin! You must not do this!'

The carriage gathered pace. She did not look back. Perhaps she did not dare.

I stood alone on the busy, dusty road for a long while, jostled by people flowing round me. For a long while on that busy dusty road.

I left the capital at dawn the next day. P'ei Ti, Mi Feng and Cousin Hong accompanied me to the dockside. None of us wept. My entire worldly goods were loaded into the riverboat, three chests and a few bags, and while the oarsmen ate bowls of lucky coloured rice in preparation for the long journey upstream, we shared a flask of wine provided by Cousin Hong.

'I will write as often as I can,' said P'ei Ti, anxiously filling the silence. 'Whenever I hear of messages being sent to Chunming Province I shall enclose a letter. And you must know that I will seek an opportunity to petition on your behalf. But a suspicion of treason is no light thing, Yun Cai. It will follow you around.'

I clasped his hand.

'You have done enough for me already. Why put yourself at risk? My dear friend, you must see that my main reason for wishing to stay here has gone. It has floated away, like those clouds above our heads.'

And they were fine, billowing white clouds. I remember them still.

I did not need to mention her name. It filled all our minds.

'She was wrong to ignore you,' he said. 'I believe she did so for your own safety. I am sure she was simply afraid to do otherwise. How else could she divert His August Excellency's ill will? Think kindly of her, Yun Cai, for your own peace of mind.'

I shrugged.

'She has chosen. Let us not talk of her. At least I will see my family. That is something.'

Brave words could not mask the desolation I felt. To return without wealth or position or honour, except perhaps among those who sang my poems. I knew Father well enough to anticipate his respect for poems sung on the street.

'I will write often,' he pleaded. 'We will never be parted if we write.'

'P'ei Ti,' I said. 'Was there ever a friend like you? You are the brother I never had.'

I turned to Mi Feng and Cousin Hong. They embraced me in turn. Mi Feng suddenly flushed.

'Forget that whore!' he cried. 'I'll kill her for you if you ask. I swear it.'

A silence fell among us. We all knew he meant his threat. Indeed, for a man with his conception of honour, he had uttered a kind of oath. I understood his reasoning well. I had been wronged. She should pay.

Shaking my head, I clasped his hands, for he had offered the greatest sacrifice, trading his happiness for the cold logic of revenge.

'Mi Feng,' I said. 'Just think, if I had not courted that lady, you would never have met your wife. So perhaps you should thank her. Or thank our intermingled fates. For my sake, enjoy your woman and child. Forget ill will, which is a slow poison. That way, my honour will prosper alongside your own.'

He sighed. I could tell he was relieved.

'You're too soft, sir. You always have been.'

'Perhaps that is my strength,' I said.

'Find yourself a good, honest wife,' broke in Cousin Hong. 'Have a dozen sons and name one of them after me!'

We all laughed. I slapped his back as though he had read my dearest wish, but such a prospect filled me with revulsion. There could only be one woman, one love, for me. Her betrayal had shaken my capacity for affection, just as a rockslide in the mountains undermines a once secure house, so that no one dare live there again. And it was to the mountains I must go.

The ship's captain summoned me aboard. Oars rose and fell in obedience to the drum's rhythm. Water churned. The capital and my hopes and dreams fell behind, until with a bend in the river, the City of Heaven was lost from view.

nine

'. . . The Provincial Capital echoes
with disorder.

Armies prowl the five directions
gorging on tattered villages that survive. . .'

It is the Festival of Ghosts. Only the foolish are unwary. On the fifth day of the fifth month the summer solstice marks a decline. The sun is already dwindling and dark spirits lie in wait.

Throughout Chunming, I observe people taking the usual precautions. No one hangs clothes out to dry in case ghosts infect the garments and their children are taken ill. Talismans are fixed to doors and windows. Bottle-gourds made of paper flutter on lintels so that Li Tie-guai may fend off encroaching demons.

Now is the time when hungry spirits seek revenge for neglect or insult and I grow restless thinking of Cousin Zhi. What of Honoured Aunty or the man I killed? Those who died in remote parts, far from their families, unappeased by sacrifices, will be busy tonight. Their coats are without hems, and when they speak their voices sound strange to us. We may only see them as dark clouds. Yet they are notoriously short-sighted, seeing the world as a red glow, so perhaps I will not be found out. I hang up two bottle-gourds to make sure and wait for what night brings.

The moon forms a bright sickle in the sky. Its radiance finds gaps between clouds. Then the moon's grinning face is obscured once more. I am back on earth. Back in my narrow attic room. Back in doleful Chunming.

So my thoughts. . .

A white cloth hangs from the window, signalling to Thousand-*li*-drunk that Golden Bells has been bought. For several days it has hung like a flag while the hours have alternated between rain and stifling heat. Still I hear no word from him. I must assume he has reasons for silence, that he is busily seeking P'ei Ti's release. Perhaps he has been captured.

Tonight I am just a fearful old man. Slowly, slowly the moon reappears until it, at least, is brave. The Festival of Ghosts swirls towards dawn.

In the depth of night, one must find comfort where one can. I lie on my bed meditating upon a spider's web as it catches the moon glow. Always thought intrudes. Feelings are caught in its sticky strands like helpless flies. Youngest Son's face is trapped there. I do not recollect him as he is now, a stern officer in a doomed army, but as a boy, often beside his mother. And it is strange to remember her.

Unwelcome thoughts. I recall returning from a week of carousing and fitful piety in a nearby monastery. It was morning, all the servants busy about their business. But Youngest Son sat patiently in the gatehouse. He must have been eight years old. I sensed he had been waiting for days. He regarded me with up-turned eyes.

'Little cub,' I said. 'Have you become a gate god?'

He looked away. Bit his lip.

'Is something on your mind, little fellow?' I asked.

Perhaps I felt guilty. Perhaps not.

'You do not love us, Father,' he muttered.

Of course, I should have beaten him soundly for such impudence. Most men would. A hot breath filled my spirit. I lifted my arm. Then I saw the cringing defiance in his eyes. My arm fell. I sat beside him on the bench lining one wall of the gatehouse, throwing to the floor a bundle of poems I had written during my stay at Whale Rocks Monastery. I could feel his warmth against my own.

'You are wrong,' I said, shaking my head. 'Quite wrong.'

He bristled, as a boy will. How eager he was to amend my faults! Had no one told him a father has no failings, only oddities?

'Father, why do you stay away so often? Mother is sad when you are away.'

'Is that why you are angry?' I asked.

'Yes.'

I held out helpless hands.

'It is just that, sometimes, I need fresh winds on my face.'

He watched me intently. Every shred of his being contended to understand what I barely understood myself.

'You go away as often as you can,' he said, finally.

One should not deny the truth. Especially to a child. Especially to one's son. Your whole duty is to bring him up well, so he despises a lie.

'I will spend more time with you,' I muttered. 'Yes, I will.'

For all my promise, I didn't. Or not enough. That night I railed at my wife, drunk again, reproaching her for turning my own sons against me.

My wife. Why is it hard to remember a familiar face? Though she knew me better than anyone in Wei, except perhaps Wudi, she eludes me.

Her breasts were firm and large, though sagging in later years. Her thighs were broad and strong from climbing steep hillsides. And, of course, she relished every kind of food and so did not resemble a willow.

My wife maintained a comfortable home for me and perhaps I did not deserve her labours. Nevertheless, she gave them dutifully. Not for my sake, I always thought, but for our children. Certainly she gained much through our marriage. I have no reason to reproach myself. If I barely recollected her for years, why think of her now?

Oh, my longings were elevated and far away, fixed on a woman who never aged as we did, one forever lithe and beautiful. Beloved, immaculate Su Lin. Every day of exile painted a fresh layer of lacquer on my disappointment.

I rise. Splash my face. The night is full of rain-sounds. When I return to the bed, my wife's image is not washed away. A plump face, inclined to happiness, easily delighted by small things: a pleasant gossip with one of the servants, or a good meal, or singing a mountain song with the other women as they sewed. I greet the dawn with a strange thought. Men are lessened by too much rule over their wives. That, too, is nonsense. One often thinks foolishly between sleep and wakefulness, especially on a night like this.

Light creeps into the room and I am glad of day. My wife and son will leave me now. She had a beautiful name: Fragrant Dawn. A name to set day ablaze, though her face could resemble a stubborn mare, its jaw thrust forward. And her fragrance was variable, too.

Let her be. Let her rest. In the past I did not honour her spirit enough and that is why she haunts me. Remembering is a kind of punishment. If I ever return to Three-Step-House I shall sacrifice a dozen scented dishes to her memory on the ancestral shrine. Then the outer will match the inner and harmony will be achieved. It was simply not our destiny to grow old together.

I am quite resolved to cease brooding over Fragrant Dawn. She has gone. Those years and all I might have enjoyed through them are gone. Now I have a new duty to justify my life, a noble endeavour. Freeing P'ei Ti might vindicate every failure.

'Venerable Sir! Venerable Sir! See these plums! Such fruit will gladden your family!'

I brush the man aside. What use have I for plums when anxiety is giving me indigestion?

Another fellow appears at my elbow.

'Bronze tripods! Urns for your ashes so splendid that your descendents will honour you like a prince!'

Walk deeper into the market. Ignore him. All this talk of urns may be a bad omen.

The entire contents of houses are spread out on the moist earth. Those impoverished by war or the families of those executed as traitors by the Empress-in-waiting must sell all they possess for a little food. Respectable people, parting with dearest heirlooms for a few *cash*. One cannot eat an ornament one's grandfather scrimped to buy. General An-Shu's rule has carved a thousand cuts on the body of Chunming, so the city bleeds out its wealth, gash by gash.

'You have a kind face, sir! Pity a poor widow. Buy my dumplings and luck will serve you forever!'

This makes me pause. I need luck. And I need pity, if for no other reason than to feel superior. Besides, dumplings are my favourite. So I buy a handful and eat one while the wretched woman screams to heaven itself that I should be blessed with a thousand grandsons. Will the Jade Emperor hear her among this babble of voices? It seems unlikely. And her dumplings are stale. I move on.

A message reached me this morning, summoning me to a

certain shop in the South Market. From its crazy style I believe it was sent by Thousand-*li*-drunk. Yet I have no proof. It might well be a snare, a means of confirming my guilt. And in times like these, in a desperate city like Chunming, guilt comes easily.

At last I find my destination. The message instructed me to seek out the Astrologer Mu behind a shop selling caged birds. I hear the establishment before I see it. Even in an uproar such as this the sweet, pure trill of songbirds pierces through. The merchant lolls in his doorway. He has a curved nose and expressionless, flickering eyes. He bows and gestures me inside. I follow, glancing round nervously for a sign that I am being watched. In such a crowd, who may tell?

His shop consists of a narrow, rectangular room. Dozens of bamboo cages hang on the walls and the air is full of cheeping. Thrush and sparrow, oriole and swallow. A man who can understand the language of birds may learn enough to avoid danger. But who is to say bird-demons do not watch from these cages? If so, their situation is precarious. A brace of thrushes is a feast to many in Chunming.

'Ah, sweet music!' I remark.

He nods. To grin so steadily would hurt most men's mouths.

'Perhaps I will consider a purchase after I have consulted the Astrologer Mu,' I say. 'He is available for a consultation, I take it?'

He points to a curtained entrance at the rear of the shop.

'Through here?' I ask, determined to provoke a reply.

But he is back at his perch in the doorway, scanning the crowd for customers.

The curtain he indicated is tattered and made of the coarsest hemp. I step through and at once someone is beside me. A glitter of metal catches my eye. I cry out. A rough hand grips my arm. A blade forces up my chin.

There are two of them in the darkened room. One on a low bench: Thousand-*li*-drunk, complete with his basket of crickets. The armed man is the Ensign Tzi-Lu. He appears to have recovered from his day beneath the privy in Three-Step-House and bows gracefully as he lowers his knife. I have no doubt he would have cut my throat quite as nimbly.

Thousand-*li*-drunk motions that I should sit beside him on the bench. There is nowhere else to sit.

'I take it you are the Astrologer Mu?' I ask.

'Sometimes,' he admits.

'Please remove your basket of insects,' I say. 'I would prefer it if you did not dine right now.'

His eyes widen a little.

'Lord Yun Cai is displeased?'

'How could I be otherwise? It seems strange you did not contact me earlier. A white cloth has hung from my window for several days. Considering the risks I have taken, I expected some word.'

'About what?' asks Thousand-*li*-drunk.

'Whether you have conversed with Golden Bells.'

'Oh, we've done that.'

'And?'

'He is pliable,' says Thousand-*li*-drunk. 'You did well.'

I settle back on the bench. The Ensign Tzi-Lu stands guard, listening by the door with the utmost attention.

'So Golden Bells has been purchased?' I remark.

'Indeed he has,' breaks in the gallant Ensign. 'But that is nothing, unless we have a plan for freeing His Excellency P'ei Ti.'

'Do not utter that name aloud!' hisses Thousand-*li*-drunk.

I glance between their taut faces.

'Do you possess such a plan?' I ask.

Thousand-*li*-drunk glowers at his basket of crickets.

'A delicate question,' he says.

'One may say that,' snorts Ensign Tzi-Lu. 'Days pass and still we are no nearer our goal. Who knows what they are doing to His Excellency? As for me, I do not like to think of it.'

I watch them shrewdly, reminded of debates between Wudi

and Eldest Son about managing the estate. It is my habit to remain silent.

'We should act at once,' declares Ensign Tzi-Lu. 'Delay plays into the hands of the enemy.'

'You are too hot,' replies Thousand-*li*-drunk. 'Even if we gain entry to the prison through the side door, kill the guards and release His Excellency from the cell; even if we escape through the same side door, where do we take him from there?'

The Ensign Tzi-Lu brushes aside this objection with a contemptuous hand.

'We hide him in the city.'

'But where? You are too hot, my young friend.'

I raise a finger. Both fall silent.

'If one is to judge the harvest,' I say. 'One must consider the weather. How does the wind blow?'

'His Majesty's forces draw closer and closer,' says Thousand-*li*-drunk.

'How close?'

'From the word I receive, a few days at most.'

'What of it?' protests the Ensign. 'One day or ten, we must brave the prison and I say sooner rather than later.'

I cough politely.

'Let us consider this from General An-Shu's position. Or that of his advisers. Firstly, His Excellency P'ei Ti is a great prize. He must not be squandered. But how is one to use him? That is the question. How?'

The Ensign shrugs.

'Who knows how traitors think?' he says.

'Young man, they think mostly like you and I. Now, His Excellency may be useful as a hostage,' I continue. 'But they will know very well that the Son of Heaven would sacrifice him if need be. Or he may be used for other purposes. What might those purposes be?'

Thousand-*li*-drunk mops his brow. Certainly it is close in the room. He is out of his depth, and I sympathise. Playing the madman is one thing, a desperate venture like this quite another.

'We need confusion to aid us,' he says. 'Remember, while the snipe and mussel were fighting, the fisherman caught them both.'

'You've lost your nerve, old man!' jeers Ensign Tzi-Lu. 'I say, we get him out and then see how things stand.'

I sigh. In so small a room, so hot and unpleasant a room, a sigh can be loud.

'Why exactly have you summoned me here?' I ask.

Thousand-*li*-drunk examines me sharply.

'We need to know whether anyone has questioned you concerning His Excellency.'

Then I understand. If P'ei Ti has mentioned my name, I might already have been interrogated. If they believe this, I will never leave the bird seller's shop. It says much about their incompetence that they took the risk of drawing me here. After all, I now know their hiding place. And who is to say I did not bring spies with me.

'No one has uttered P'ei Ti's name in my presence,' I say.

They regard me silently. For a moment Thousand-*li*-drunk seems about to speak.

'That at least is settled,' breaks in the Ensign Tzi-Lu, evidently relieved. After all, he owes me his life. 'Your loyalty was never doubted.'

My faith in them, hardly high, descends another rung. The morning is passing; perhaps all hope of releasing P'ei Ti is passing. I rise and bow. They say nothing as I leave. My disquiet can scarcely be expressed. Success lies beyond too many locked doors.

When I step into the market square, stallholders are frantically gathering their goods and everyone is in a hurry to leave. I chance upon the widow who sold me a handful of dumplings.

'What is happening?' I ask.

She replies with the whites of her eyes and I am none the wiser. Families bustle away. Two wheelbarrows collide and the merchants loudly abuse each other. I clutch a stranger's arm.

'What is happening?'

'Get yourself home, old sir,' he says. 'The General is returning. Best not to be on the streets today.'

With the aid of my stick, I shuffle towards the house by the ramparts. Yet prudence must not always rule a man. There are things I would know and that entails risk. Most of all I long to see Youngest Son's face. So at the crossroad I turn toward the East Gate, joining a crowd of merchants and streetwalkers, beggars and urchins, eager to witness the entrance of the army. I arrive just as the first soldiers appear and take up position beneath a tattered awning, jostled by idlers.

The air fills with a triumphant blare of trumpets and drums. One might think General An-Shu was returning in glory rather than scuttling back to Chunming like a wounded fox to its lair. He rides at the head of his elite guard. The General's back is straight, his face resolute. He is remorseless, a beacon of discipline. Others in the crowd sense it too and some even manage a ragged cheer.

General An-Shu only holds my attention for a moment. I am drawn to the carriages that follow, filled by his closest advisers. Then I shrink back. The occupant of one carriage is familiar, yet strange with age. The years between our last meeting melt. Beneath his grizzled features lies a discarded face. I remember a young man consumed by purpose and ambition, dressed in an advocate's gaudy silks. Over thirty years ago when he was the Lawyer Yuan Chu-Sou.

I hide, pretending to fuss over my shoes. Then the carriage has passed. I follow it with my gaze.

'Who is that gentleman?' I ask a fellow loiterer. 'What relation does he bear to the General?'

The stranger narrows his eyes. Perhaps my question is too earnest. We are all afraid of uttering an unguarded word.

'That is His Highness's chief adviser. I do not know his name, sir.'

But I do. Or a name he once used. Given the disreputable court of the Emperor-in-waiting who can guess what he styles himself now?

The head of the column proceeds to the Prefect's residence and the battalions that follow inspire less awe. Ranks of exhausted, grimy, wounded men, half dead on their ill-shod feet. Hungry soldiers with little left to lose, yet surprisingly orderly.

The first regiment passes. I press to the front of the crowd, seeking a single face in the ranks of tramping men. Then comes the second regiment, if that is not too grand a name for so depleted a force. Finally, the Winged Tigers enter Chunming. I can feel my breath labouring. A company marches past, then another. Suddenly I am limp with relief. Youngest Son rides at the head of his company, the same scum who troubled Wei. I almost cheer. He appears unwounded. He has no eyes for the crowd, lost in a bitter world of thought. My heart reaches out to him until he too has passed. I return wearily to the house by the ramparts and bolt the door of my room.

All the next day I sit waiting for word from Youngest Son. Without doubt he has many pressing duties: ensuring his men are fed and the wounded are tended, that new weapons are found to replace those lost or broken. Does he not owe a duty to me? One might answer that question many ways.

I descend to the garden at dusk and sit a little apart from the other prisoners. We are much reduced. Every day one of our number is arrested and dragged off to face treason charges. Not one of the accused has returned. We live in constant anxiety, afraid to speak in case some spy reports it.

The sergeant appears. I rise in a flutter of spirits. Behind him stands Youngest Son.

'Where is Lord Yun Cai?' bellows the sergeant.

His eyes fall upon me.

'You lot,' he barks at the other prisoners. 'Clear the garden. Lord Yun Cai's visitor wishes to speak to him alone.'

So they leave, casting resentful looks at me. Youngest Son watches them go uncertainly. He is dressed in full armour, dented and scuffed. A sword hangs by his side and a plumed helmet rests on one arm. When we are alone he limps up to me, then bows low as an honest son should, his eyes downcast.

'You had better rise,' I say, at last. 'And rest beside me on this bench.'

He does so. We sit side by side, reminding me of a morning when he was a boy. We sat just so, watched over by the gate gods of Three-Step-House.

'How glad I am to see you,' I say.

He looks at me sharply.

'Are you, Father? I thought you would triumph to have been proved right.'

'You refer to General An-Shu's rebellion?'

For a moment I think he will repeat his familiar tirade about the new times, the glorious new dynasty.

'It evidently pleases you to call it that,' he says, resentfully.

'No, it does not please me. It is simply best not to point at a deer and call it a horse.'

We fall silent. Night moths flit round the garden. I notice that the flower which found root in the city walls has drooped and faded. Soon the stars will come out.

'Tell me what has happened since we last met,' I say.

He tells a disreputable tale. General An-Shu's army marched towards the capital for hundreds of *li* then were met by a huge force. Step by step they retreated, fighting several battles on the way, each costlier than the last. It seems a miracle the General's forces did not break. Youngest Son says little of his own role in these affairs.

'Why do you limp?' I ask, when he finishes.

'It is nothing. I took an arrow in my thigh, that is all.'

Shadows are lengthening. I can hear the sound of tramping feet beyond the city walls.

As though sensing my thoughts, Youngest Son says, 'Our regiment has been ordered back to the front. We leave at dawn tomorrow with orders to slow the enemy advance at any cost. That is why I have come, Father, to say farewell.'

For a moment I am tempted to rail at the stubbornness of General An-Shu. Why does he not fall on his sword, or drink poison, instead of dragging thousands down with him?

'You must become a deserter,' I whisper. 'Take your horse and ride far away.'

He shakes his head.

'I cannot leave my men. I am their father. Surely you understand that?'

'This rebellion is doomed!'

His head hangs as it did when he was a boy. He is ashamed.

'I must be true to something!' he protests. 'Let it be my men if nothing else. Heaven knows I have failed everyone. But they respect me, Father, they look up to me. And they need me.'

I take his hand.

'You are young,' I murmur. 'Youth is folly. Do not feel bound by promises to a traitor.'

'No, I must go.'

The shadows have crept right across us and into my heart. I sense that certain words can no longer be avoided. Unpleasant words.

'Youngest Son,' I say, at last. 'Things have not been as they should between you and I.'

A little of his old spirit returns.

'Since you speak of it, Father,' he replies, haughtily. 'I cannot disagree. You always favoured Eldest Son from the day I was born.'

I shake my head.

'He accuses me of favouring you! I treated you both fairly. Just the same.'

'No, Father,' he snaps. 'This will not do! You were always harsh to me, never patient as you were with Eldest Son. Little wonder I was driven to bad companions.'

'So that is your excuse?'

'Because it is true!'

'You made your own choices.'

'I never had a choice, Father. I was always the wrong one, always the one who never learned his characters properly. . .'

'Ha!' I cry. 'Eldest Son was as deficient and lazy as you in that regard! To think I hoped to make scholars of you!'

Then I realise what I have said. We subside. He tugs the plume of his helmet.

'What did you expect?' he demands, miserably. 'That we would pour out verses as freely as you poured out your wine? We are different from you, Father. I am different. Certainly, I am a lesser man. But I am still your son.'

Unexpectedly, he begins to sob. A painful sound, to hear one's boy sob. I raise hands to comfort him, then let them fall. He speaks in a rush.

'Father, I am afraid to fight again! We saw such things. In one village we were ordered to punish the peasants. . . I never learned why. Oh, I cannot meet your eye. Five hundred hung by the heels from the eaves of their own houses! I was like a madman, determined to do my duty. And then in the battle which followed, we fought in pouring rain, slipping and hacking in the mud, making rafts of bodies! No one could tell friend from foe. We were all identical, just creatures of mud and slime. I left my best friend in the filth where he lay wounded. Do you remember Lieutenant Lo? Oh, he was a far better man than I! But I lost my nerve and abandoned him. I shall go to hell for that, Father, when I die.'

'Hush,' I murmur. 'It is over now.'

He is shaking.

'I crave your blessing, Father. That is why I have come. You must forgive me for what I did to that girl. I was drunk, and they all jeered when I hesitated. I had no thought. And when I went to the military academy I remembered you every day. I wanted to regain your pride in me.'

At last I find the courage to touch his knee. He recoils. His sobs suddenly cease. He sits rigid, staring forward sightlessly.

'I dreamt about Mother last night,' he says in a strange, flat voice. 'She hates me.'

'Of course she does not,' I say. 'There was never a fonder mother.'

He gazes at the floor.

'Father,' he whispers. 'Do I have your blessing?'

I do not know this broken young man. His face melts before my sight. I see only a boy. A grin of pride to reveal baby teeth falling out. I gathered all his infant teeth in case demons found them and used them to possess his soul. I kept them in a bamboo box. They still lie safe in my strongest chest in Three-Step-House. His cheeks were warm, his skin smelt of melons. When he laughed I thought of water. Bitterness fills my throat. Not against him. Not entirely.

'Perhaps I did not guide you properly,' I say. 'Perhaps I neglected you. These are harsh lessons for a man of my age. But you are young enough to start again. Many an Immortal began his life badly.'

We look up, startled by the distant call of trumpets.

'They are summoning all who must march away,' he says, tonelessly. 'I must go, Father.'

Then I clutch his arm.

'You want my blessing!' I cry. 'Foolish boy, can't you see you never lost it!'

I shake him as best I can. Such a big lump of a boy.

'I will give you my blessing in exchange for one thing.'

'What is it?' he asks, timidly.

'That you avoid all the danger you can. That you return to Three-Step-House. Then we shall start again, you and I, as though the past has never been. Time and good deeds will heal all your wounds. I shall find you a respectable wife with a strong will. You shall bear me grandchildren and I shall be a hundred times proud. And your mother will clap her hands in Heaven.'

He climbs stiffly to his knees. Lowers his head to the ground. I hesitate, then spread my palm across his hair. I can feel his warmth, his sweat.

When he rises, there is a new confidence in him.

'I will make you proud of me yet, Father,' he says. 'I don't know how, but I will.'

'Not just for my sake,' I protest. 'Make yourself proud.'

His face lengthens.

'It is too late for that.'

He leaves and I sit alone. It is quite dark when the sergeant summons me inside, so he can bar all the doors. Quite dark.

My life has become a stage of shifting scenes. Garish one moment, sickening the next and, in between, long hours of restless tedium. If the Buddha is to be believed, Chunming is a hell of my own making. All I need do is think differently, with sublime compassion, to perceive everything fondly.

Such wisdom is hard to follow when one is being whipped through the streets among a herd of prisoners to the parade ground beyond the city ramparts. There is no possibility of a riot now. All General An-Shu's army has gathered and we are obliged to witness his might. Perhaps the authorities hope to cow the city. Power never feels assured of itself without an audience.

I am on my knees. It is dawn and already haze fills the air. On one side stands the Army of the Left Fist, a ragged, loss-gnawed band of cavalry and crossbowmen, halberdiers and swordsmen. Their banners, at least, are as bold as ever.

In the middle, a shrine in the form of a low pyramid has been erected to General An-Shu's ancestors. On the other side wait the regiments who must march out to stem the advance of the Imperial forces. I scan the ranks of men for a glimpse of Youngest Son. Surely he is among them, mounted on his fine charger.

My eyes are weak from too much reading. Distances blur. I imagine him as I would wish him to be. Dignified, but with a hint of independence, marked out from the other officers. A soldier of justice, trapped by circumstances. To do so is to deny the truth. He was eager enough to serve the General before defeat followed upon defeat.

At last a procession emerges from the city gates led by the General's armoured cavalry. He rides his ivory chariot and others follow in carriages hung with bells to frighten off evil spirits. First, the Empress-in-waiting, like a goddess sojourning on earth, her silver silks catching the rising sun. Then carriage after carriage of advisers and peacock courtiers. Restless monkeys in tall hats. We press our faces to the earth as they rattle past, a dozen feet from where we kneel.

It has always been my misfortune to be bold. Or too curious. As they roll by I look up and meet a steady gaze. Then I freeze. For the eyes regarding me belong to the Lawyer Yuan Chu-Sou. His expression is startled. He leans forward eagerly. Even when they have passed he stares back as though to make sure, exchanging words with the Head Eunuch who sits glumly beside him. I am clamped to the spot as if held fast by a blacksmith's tongs.

The ceremony passes in a blur. My mind whirls with half-formed fears. Will I be humiliated, or questioned, even tortured until I reveal the conspiracy to free P'ei Ti? All the while I feel shame that I am not thinking of Youngest Son's departure. My last glimpse of him is a cloud of dust. He is lost to the cause which seduced him.

The day seems interminable after this morning's ceremony. With the arrival of General An-Shu's army all available food has been diverted to the troops. We dine on a few handfuls of millet, smack our lips over each mouthful. I am more fortunate than most, having traded what remains of the ivory writing set given to me by the Lady Ta Chi for extra rations.

At dusk, I receive a most unwelcome visitor. This time he is not accompanied by guards or underlings. He knocks at my door and enters like one who is almost polite. We nod at each other.

'Lord Yun Cai!' he says, by way of greeting.

'Head Eunuch!' I respond, bowing. 'I beg you not to find this unworthy chair beneath your august dignity.'

Awkwardly, he settles. The chair is rickety and precarious so he is obliged to clutch its sides.

'I am pressed by important affairs,' he announces. Nevertheless, he takes time to look around. 'You have found yourself a cosy little eyrie.'

He notices the view through the window, and seems surprised.

'I did not realise your room overlooks the Palace. A spy would pay a fortune for such a view. How interesting.'

His tone resembles flint.

'It can be restful,' I concede. 'The distant vista of the Apricot Hills is pleasing at sunset.'

He examines me through narrow eyes.

'You have attracted a great man's attention,' he says. 'That is why I am here.'

'Oh?'

'His Majesty's chief adviser, the Excellent Yuan Chu-Sou, has noticed you. My message is simple. A great honour for you. You are summoned to pay homage to His Majesty, tomorrow afternoon at the sixth bell, in the Phoenix Chamber.'

I try to look delighted.

'All the notables residing in Chunming have been summoned,' he says. 'It is a marvel you are among them.'

I cannot resist a little mischief at the eunuch's expense.

'So you are bidden to act as a messenger all round the city?'

His smile becomes toothy.

'That need not concern you.'

'Let me assure you, it does not, Head Eunuch of the Golden Palace.'

I'm certain he no longer possesses that title. I suspect he fell from favour when General An-Shu returned. His master can hardly have been pleased by the state of Chunming: the city is on the brink of rebellion. Someone must be blamed for failing to curb the Empress-in-waiting's excesses. I have hit the target, for he says, scowling: 'You may address me from now on as Head Eunuch of the Phoenix Chamber.'

'Ah,' I reply.

'A temporary position,' he declares. 'Between promotions.'

'Quite so.'

It is not wise to goad such a disappointed fellow. He still retains some power. His eyes flick to the view of the Prefect's residence through the window, then back at me.

'I have not seen you walking round the courtyard before the Palace lately,' he says. 'Why is that?'

Now it is my turn for discomfort.

'I have been unwell,' I say, blandly. 'Besides, I have completed the poems your mistress commanded. I require no further inspiration.'

He regards me for a long moment. How often did he see me conversing with Golden Bells?

'You delay me,' he announces, yawning.

'I beg you not to let me do so.'

Once he has gone, I count the cost of his news. So Yuan Chu-Sou recognised me and remembered. No doubt his decision that I should pay homage to General An-Shu is based upon a desire to humiliate me.

I spend fruitless hours speculating how the Lawyer Yuan Chu-Sou became General An-Shu's chief adviser. Perhaps, after the fall of Lord Xiao, he found his ambitions frustrated in the capital. Perhaps he found himself at the end of his life with a last chance for power, however uncertain. As ever, he is shadowy. Yet he remembers me. And that is enough to provoke insomnia. Surely he also recollects P'ei Ti, and by no means fondly. That is enough to make me wonder if the implements were used when interrogating my old friend.

At noon I join a select crowd before the Prefect's residence. I find a place at the rear and observe those around me.

Here is the merchant Yin Xie who owns half a ward within Chunming. All his wealth does not spare him from paying homage. Indeed, it forces him into prominence. He might be safer if he was poor. And there is Viscount Fu Ling, once the Governor of Chunming Province, obliged to abase himself as once he banged his forehead on the earth before the Emperor. Things change. And stay the same.

The gates open. We shuffle forward into the courtyard before the Prefect's residence. I glance involuntarily at the prison where P'ei Ti suffers, assuming he is still alive, and scowl at the guards.

The scene in the courtyard is hardly indicative of sober rule. Musicians and jugglers wait their turn to entertain His Majesty, some rehearsing tumbles, others applying thick layers of white and red face-paint. Groups of lesser courtiers enjoy the bright sunshine, drinking and laughing in gay voices. I watch one pursue a squealing courtesan into a stable. Little imagination is needed to guess what follows.

The crowd of supplicants moves forward, herded by eunuchs and soldiers. Once inside the Palace the revelry around us intensifies. Feckless young men in stolen silks loll against walls, their eyes glazed. Voices contend to form a hubbub. One might think His Highness was celebrating a triumph, yet there is desperation in such pleasure. They drink deeply before the cup is snatched away. Dancing girls caper for the entertainment of a dozen officers; their gaudy uniforms remind me of Youngest Son, sent on a suicidal mission to delay superior forces.

A palace servant addresses us: 'Honourable Sirs, His Highness has finished dining and will receive your homage. Once you have shown your proper loyalty, you shall be led to a side door of the Phoenix Chamber. His Highness has been gracious enough to allow you to toast his health in the Garden of Genial Twilight, where refreshments have been prepared.'

This announcement revives the spirits of my companions. There is a general straightening of dress, smoothing of demeanour. So we are to be an after dinner entertainment. Doubtless the General wishes to prove to his court that he still commands loyalty in Chunming.

One by one the notables enter the Phoenix Chamber. I follow slowly. It takes time to abase one's self properly. We are all frightened. A small orchestra plays, creating a regal mood.

Finally, my turn comes. I enter the great hall with a bowed head and am prodded into the centre. A long, narrow hall, lined with pillars and flickering candles. Afternoon sunshine filters through gauze-covered windows. Silver and gold statues, tripods and incense burners looted during the General's advance on the capital stand against the walls. The costly objects cast a net of shadows. Then I glance up.

At the far end of the room are several low tables surrounded by cushioned divans. On them sit His Majesty and chief advisers. I notice the Lady Ta Chi to his left, beguiling in her beauty. She appears terribly bored. On the right hand side of the General lolls a bleary-eyed officer who must be His Highness's brother. Then the Excellent Yuan Chu-Sou wearing the vermilion robes of a principal adviser and a brooding expression. Behind the General's chair hovers the Head Eunuch of the Phoenix Chamber. Before his demotion he would have commanded a seat among the notables.

But it is not them who make me grow still. Not them. For beside Yuan Chu-Sou sits a man I have not seen in over thirty years. His lined face is haggard, purple with bruises, yet the nobility of his features are undiminished. For all that, he appears broken, drained of spirit, and stares miserably at the dishes before him. Revulsion fills me. Shame on his behalf. Deep shame. Instead of falling to my knees, I remain standing, my eyes fixed on that forlorn figure. I long for him to look up, to recognise me. It is P'ei Ti who sits among them. My beloved P'ei Ti, dining among wolves.

The conversation on the high table slowly recedes into silence. Dozens of sharp eyes regard me curiously. At last P'ei Ti glances up and sees me.

Someone among the horse-shoe of lacquered tables laughs. Then another. Perhaps I make a comic sight, gawping at P'ei Ti. A foolish old man with an open mouth. General An-Shu looks at the Head Eunuch and raises an eyebrow. After all, it is his duty to avoid unseemly events. I expect to be dragged off, but instead the eunuch smiles slyly.

'Your Highness,' he says. 'This is the fellow who wrote those poems the Empress-in-waiting commissioned as a pillow book.'

For a moment General An-Shu looks puzzled. Then he remembers and smiles narrowly.

'A strange present at a time like this. I would prefer a hundred archers to a hundred poems!'

His court laugh appreciatively. The Lady Ta Chi's vexation is obvious. The way she regards me leaves little doubt who she blames. Yuan Chu-Sou stirs. He too examines me with barely-concealed contempt.

'It would have been well, Your Highness,' he breaks in. 'If that same Lady had concentrated on maintaining order in Chunming instead of provoking a flood of insipid nonsense from a second-rate versifier. Had she done so we might not have returned to find Chunming seething with rebellious talk. Your Majesty will perhaps recall that I advised against her appointment as proxy-ruler in your absence.'

General An-Shu grunts and the Lady Ta Chi glares at Yuan Chu-Sou. I cannot remove my gaze from P'ei Ti's poor face. What have they done to him? Much, for sure, if his courage has been worn away. Only torture could have driven him to join the General's cause.

P'ei Ti cannot bear to meet my eye. His humiliation might be my own. I discern the young man behind his wrinkles, his ardour and loyalty to the Son of Heaven. Then he glances up. It is forgiveness he craves.

I become aware the Head Eunuch is speaking once more: 'Your Highness, I suspect from the way Lord Yun Cai stares at His Excellency P'ei Ti that the two are well-acquainted. And I believe he has something he wishes to say. Would it entertain Your Highness to hear it?'

There is a general murmur of approval round the table.

'Do let him!' calls out the General's brother. 'The old man seems crazy enough for a little fun.'

General An-Shu hesitates, then nods condescendingly.

'Very well,' he says.

'Speak up!' jeers the Head Eunuch. 'Say something!'

I turn my troubled gaze to General An-Shu. His expression has frozen between amusement and habitual disdain. Perhaps that is what provokes me. I scarcely care what happens to me: I am old, and possessed by cold anger.

'Your Highness,' I begin. 'Once when Confucius was asked how a ruler should be served, he answered: *If it becomes necessary to oppose him, speak openly to his face, and do not attempt roundabout methods.*'

I have the General's interest now. A few of his friends giggle behind their hands. No doubt they expect some nimble flattery or declaration of obedience. I take a deep breath and the words tumble out. I gaze at P'ei Ti, longing for him to remember his true nature, to renounce the General's legitimacy. I cannot bear to think of him as a coward and traitor. Not him. Or the sky was never blue.

'I must tell you, Your Highness, that the Mandate of Heaven cannot be won through conquest alone. The ancient kings T'ang and Wu came to power by violence, but ruled according to the people's will. I beg you to consider, Your Highness, that the punishments you have adopted do not accord with the Will of Heaven. If you love the people, you must aid the people. You must not seek power for power's sake alone, but for how it might end their sufferings. Otherwise Heaven's mandate will always be denied to you.'

No one is laughing now. They watch me in amazement.

To my surprise, the Empress-in-waiting clears her throat. It says much about General An-Shu's court that he allows his concubine to speak so freely.

'Your Highness,' she says, her voice light and pleasing, 'I have heard that the emperors of old often instructed their ministers to debate with malcontents before the royal presence. Perhaps it would amuse Your Majesty if the Excellent Yuan Chu-Sou were to debate with this funny old man. After all, the Chief Adviser has much to say about the way I ruled Chunming in your absence. Who knows, I might learn much from his wise precepts.'

General An-Shu winks at his brother and whispers to Yuan Chu-Sou, who rises reluctantly to his feet.

'It pleases His Highness that I should answer Lord Yun Cai's puerile arguments concerning the necessity for a harsh regime. That is simply done. All know that greed and fear are the pre-eminent motives for human conduct. It follows that the just ruler must apply rewards to those who fulfil their allotted task and any deviants must be severely punished. All this was known by the greatest of our emperors. It is because we forgot the true way that barbarians rule half our ancient lands. One reward to nine punishments! Virtue has its origin in punishments, as even the simplest child acknowledges. Punishments produce force, force engenders strength, strength produces awe, awe produces virtue. Thus, virtue has its origin in punishments.'

This speech earns a ripple of applause. General An-Shu's brother bangs the table.

'You have a good adviser there,' he calls out. 'Why, the man cannot be refuted!'

Perhaps they expect me to mumble or concede. I see P'ei Ti's eyes on my face. He looks bolder than before and this gives me courage. I raise my finger in further disputation.

'His Highness is badly advised,' I protest. 'Let us remember Lao Tzu: *The highest good is like water. The goodness of water is that it benefits ten thousand creatures*. If a ruler is to deserve the Mandate of Heaven he must make the water flow. Men are not born bad. It is circumstances which make them so. The Son of Heaven's divine duty is to arrange things so men may be good. Rule based on cruelty will never achieve that.'

Yuan Chu-Sou seems vexed by my reply.

'Lord Yun Cai's argument is facile,' he replies. 'As the noble Duke Shang once remarked, if the court is full of windy scholars discoursing on the ancient kings and puffing about righteousness, the government will be plagued by disorder. The reason is simple: the ruler embodies all right and true arguments. Your Highness's word is the purest expression of Heaven's Will. Thus the ruler's duty is to rule without obstacle or impediment. To speak of 'cruelty' is a distraction which allows enemies to slip through the gate. Efficiency is not soft. The Son of Heaven's true duty is to make sure that all men are efficient. By this means one may judge a man's worth. A good man is a useful man.'

'Bravo!' shouts the General's brother, as I again raise my

finger. 'Why, this is better than watching a pair of old fighting cocks!'

The General's guests laugh uproariously. Yuan Chu-Sou scowls at me. But I notice that P'ei Ti is showing signs of agitation, even excitement.

'The Chief Adviser's arguments have been proved false by history,' I protest. 'If the ruler lacks benevolence and righteousness he shall forfeit the Mandate of Heaven, and then a new ruler with those virtues will arise to replace him. But His Highness has *not* been crowned the Son of Heaven and never will be, unless he exceeds the existing Emperor in righteousness.'

Again the laughter has ceased. I am regarded with cold eyes. Yet I blunder deeper into the swamp.

'I must tell you, Your Highness, you are not a kindly father to the people. If you desire your rule to be more than empty flattery, I would advise you to consider this.'

I have spoken a truth few dare even whisper in Chunming. I have denied the General's fatuous claim to be our anointed emperor. Now I tremble. P'ei Ti stares at me open-mouthed, whether in admiration or horror I cannot tell.

The court awaits General An-Shu's response. He tugs at his wispy beard. He no longer finds me diverting.

'Everyone knows I am the Son of Heaven,' he drawls. 'And if they do not, they shall be. . . they shall be punished!'

Yet I notice that some of his intimates find it hard to meet the General's eye. A truth once spoken sprouts many wings. Yuan Chu-Sou bustles forward.

'May I advise Your Highness that Lord Yun Cai should pay a heavy price for his impudence. Let his entire family be accorded the Four Punishments! Let a detachment of cavalry be sent to execute this order at once.'

'So be it,' intones the General.

I gasp. Reel at my folly. Eldest Son's face flashes before me. Daughter-in-law raped then executed. My sweet, happy grandchildren. Our ancestral shrine despoiled. The village burning and Three-Step-House razed until it might never have been.

Abruptly there is a screech of wood. A chair is pushed back. Porcelain dishes tinkle to the floor. P'ei Ti rises slowly to his feet. With the aid of a stick, he hobbles away from the tables laden with food. In a moment he stands beside me. An angry murmur buzzes among the courtiers. P'ei Ti raises his stick and points it at General An-Shu.

'I renounce the homage I was forced to pay to this. . . this common man,' he declares. 'An Shu is a mere traitor. This court has not been granted the Mandate of Heaven!'

Commotion breaks out. Guards rush forward to apprehend us. I turn to P'ei Ti and seize his hands. No words are needed. We both tremble. Then, as I expect to be cut down or beaten on the spot, the doors of the Phoenix Chamber are flung open and a messenger rushes in. His uniform is mud-splattered and he bears a wound on one arm. His arrival brings silence. Panting, he kneels before General An-Shu.

'Your Highness. . . grave news. The army meant to delay the enemy has been destroyed. The forces of the Emperor are only thirty *li* from Chunming!'

For a moment no one speaks. Then comes uproar. Everyone is on their feet. The General confers hurriedly with his officers and we are forgotten. I clasp P'ei Ti's hands desperately. At last guards drag us towards the door.

The door slams shut. Iron bolts clang into place. Our cell is lit by a narrow shaft of light slanting through the barred window. An earthen floor, pungent with urine and salt tears, with the misery and resilience of those who have rotted here before us. We fall to our knees, our silken clothes smeared with dirt.

In the half-light I reach out and take P'ei Ti's arm. We cannot speak, two reckless old fools together. I lead him to the brick wall and force him to sit back. Then I collapse beside him. I need his presence. It is all I possess in this vile place. That, and unsteady breath.

Breath is proof of life, a moment's ember. In the deepest distress, breath connects the inward and outward. I learned that long ago. How inevitably it comes, heedless as destiny. I close my eyes and link my arm with P'ei Ti's so that the chain of our friendship is renewed. . . Once we lounged side by side, dangling our feet in the West Lake, throwing the husks of sunflower seeds into the water until they floated way. . . My eyes close. I succumb to darkness.

I am disturbed from my stupor by low chuckling. An old man's chuckle.

'Dearest Yun Cai. . .' Coughing interrupts him. 'You are my conscience. You did not desert me.'

I could not. And that is why a squad of cavalry are riding towards Wei.

'Now I may die well,' he says. 'I owe that gift to you.'

It seems he has forgotten the price my family must pay. But it is cowardice to blame him. The choice was my own.

'I could not bear to see you crawling among lice,' I say.

Is there an accusation in my voice? I do not mean one. We are all frail.

He coughs some more.

At last he says, 'Don't condemn me, dear friend. At first I resisted, but they would not stop. Day and night. I am not used to pain.'

It crosses my mind that in the Son of Heaven's service he must have ordered torture for many. I let the thought disperse. Oh, I dare not contemplate ambiguity! Our loyalty to the Emperor must seem a worthwhile sacrifice.

'You were only pretending,' I say. 'No harm in that.'

'Only pretending. Quite so.'

'Rest your eyes,' I say, sadly. 'You are exhausted.'

Perhaps we are scheduled for a 'roasting'. Stumbling across a pit of burning coals. Perhaps for the sword or strangling cord. He lolls against my shoulder, his thin hair sticky with perspiration. May a little sleep give us strength.

I hear the sound of troops gathering. Because I am unusually tall, the square before the Prefect's residence is visible through the window. General An-Shu is lining up his bodyguard of armoured horsemen. The Empress-in-waiting weeps on the steps of her palace, waving a lucky yellow pennant. He nods stiffly to her. There is a clatter of hooves and harness. The General rides out in haste, bolt upright on his charger. Flags flutter – golden dragons upon a scarlet background, fanged jaws gaping wide – then the square is empty. I listen. The city rumbles with marching men as the entire rebel army streams out for battle in a desperate attempt to break through the encircling Imperial forces.

They said in the Phoenix Chamber that the regiments sent to delay the Son of Heaven's advance had been annihilated. Did Youngest Son perish with them? It is a question without an answer. Even if he survived, I will not outlive him.

Drums and trumpets. Tramping feet. Within a few hours the city is silent and the sky has grown dark. Bright constellations may be glimpsed through the cell window. I hear warders talking outside our cell as they patrol the corridor. Their words are indistinct. Somewhere in the prison a man screams repeatedly, then falls silent. My thoughts try to locate the cavalry galloping towards Three-Step-House. Even if they ride hard they will still be some distance away.

P'ei Ti awakes. From the regularity of his breath, I sense he is refreshed. That is something. He requests water, but we have none.

'P'ei Ti,' I say. 'I have many questions.'

Through my sacrifice in the Phoenix Chamber I may command any answer.

'What happened to Su Lin after I was exiled?' I ask, at last. 'None of your letters mentioned her. Of course, I could not bring myself to enquire openly.'

'Can you really not have heard?' he says, in wonderment. 'I thought you must know. But I suppose the intrigues in the capital hardly matter here. She became His August Excellency Lu Sha's concubine and then, after his first wife passed away, his official spouse. Even now she retains a little influence in the court.'

We fall silent. Su Lin, a great man's wife! My sweet, pretty Su Lin! I stare into the darkness.

'So she got what she desired,' I say.

'Not all she desired,' he replies. 'She never had children, except by adoption.'

'And you see her still?' I ask, eagerly.

'Rarely. When the affairs of state allow. In truth, she has withdrawn to her mansion on Phoenix Hill. You will smile to learn it is Lord Xiao's old house.'

I do not smile.

'Was she happy after I left?'

'She was unhappy for a while,' he says, reluctantly. 'I believe she struggled to present a serene face to the world. Su Lin has led a notable life, Yun Cai! Whether one may call it happy is less certain. She always asks for word of you, if that is any comfort, even commissioning an agent to report on how you fare. A strange kind of fellow, but reliable.'

At last I understand Thousand-*li*-drunk's obscure hints about a great lady. The silver he received must have paid for a whole year's supply of wine and juicy crickets.

P'ei Ti shivers as night cools. Phlegm chokes his throat and I wait as he swallows. How feeble we have become!

'What of you?' I ask.

'I have been successful. I have won high office. I have earned the Son of Heaven's favour.'

'What of sons?' I ask. 'None of your letters over the years

announced an heir.'

'There has been none.'

Silence lengthens.

'Oh, you can guess why,' he says, irritably. 'I always had other tastes, as you are well aware! Though you were far too delicate to mention them.'

'It never mattered to me,' I say.

'Perhaps not. Yet they shaped my life.'

We listen to the strange stillness in the prison.

'They are taking their time,' I say.

Then we hear footsteps approach our cell. A faint light from the corridor outlines the door and there is a rasp of heavy iron bolts.

We cower together, peering up at the door. As it swings open, I try to rise but P'ei Ti's grip on my arm holds me back.

When I finally straighten, two white-uniformed soldiers hurry into the room and take up position, lanterns in hand. A third enters, carrying a sickle-bladed spear. Behind comes a shuffling, bent figure; his moist, brooding eyes are shiny in the lamplight. He wears the same vermilion robes as he did in the Phoenix Chamber. His hat is heavy with jade badges of office, dangling from silken cords. A scroll juts from one of his sleeves.

I am glad to be on my feet, even if my shoulders are old and crooked. I would hate to meet the Lawyer Yuan Chu-Sou on my knees. But of course that title has lapsed, he is the Excellent Yuan Chu-Sou now. His word commands life or death – and agonising transitions from one to the other. I detect amusement and curiosity in the narrowing of his eyes as he watches P'ei Ti struggle to rise.

'It is a long time since we last met, Yun Cai,' he says. 'Then you waved a sword around like a little boy with his toy. I have never quite forgiven you for that. Or your impudence.'

We stand sullenly. Silence is our last weapon. One of the soldiers advances menacingly to force us to our knees but the Excellent Yuan Chu-Sou halts him with a click of his fingers. P'ei Ti flinches at the sound. I recollect his talk of torture and that Youngest Son told me General An-Shu's chief adviser was personally conducting the interrogation.

'Let them stand,' he says. 'They will be kneeling soon enough.'

Still we say nothing. Yuan Chu-Sou raises an eyebrow.

'I have come to confirm your sentence. Clemency was my first thought. After all, the Second Chancellor P'ei Ti is a valuable prisoner. Then I recollected how stubborn and insolent you both were in the Phoenix Chamber and wondered if the Four Punishments might tame your spirits. The Empress-in-waiting proposed a full 'roasting', but preparing all those coals is tiresome. So we settled on a compromise.'

The lanterns flicker as a cool night breeze penetrates the cell. All involuntarily glance at the barred window. Yuan Chu-Sou clears his throat, then announces in a sing-song voice: 'At dawn the sentence of His Majesty shall be applied. First, at Her Highness's request, the 'heater'. Then, when the prisoners' hands are quite withered away, the Four Punishments. Do the criminals wish to make any appeal?'

He longs for us to beg and grovel. But if P'ei Ti lost his courage before, he does not now. I follow his lead and shake my head.

'Very well,' says the Excellent Yuan Chu-Sou. 'As you wish. Oh, one final thing. You might imagine that the approach of the Imperial forces makes it likely you will be pardoned, or even rescued. Let me assure you, that will never occur.'

He bows with great solemnity, like a merchant who has struck a fine bargain.

When he has gone, we slump back on the filthy floor.

'How long until dawn?' asks P'ei Ti.

'Six, seven hours, at most,' I reply.

We sleep. At least, P'ei Ti does. I simply doze. There is a debt

I must pay, an obligation of understanding. And, to do so, I must go back, however reluctantly. . . It does no good to rebuke yourself, though an honest man can scarcely avoid it.

I returned to Wei from the City of Heaven to find the village stricken by plague. No one ventured from their houses as I rode up the main street on a nag barely worth eating. Bodies smouldered in communal pits, scenting cold skies of winter with the aroma of ovens. Only the foolhardy dared speak to their neighbours in case they breathed on them. I had passed through villages where beloved parents lay unburied in ditches, beside pale maidens and strapping young fellows in their prime. Their corpses mirrored my hopes.

The doors of Three-Step-House were barred and few of the servants recognised me. Those that did were afraid to come near in case I was infected. I found Mother dying on her soiled bed, and in my reckless mood, clutched her until the moment her last breath rattled out.

Father, despite his old war wounds, seemed unaffected by the plague. It is a strange fact that where I expected anger, I encountered deep relief at the sight of his only son. He never asked why I returned without office or wealth. Instead, he feverishly set out to arrange my marriage – by no means a straightforward matter in a plague-ridden district – to a daughter of a once noble family who had fallen on hard times.

I lacked the courage to oppose his choice. That marriage obsessed him, it was his last chance to determine the future. Within a month of my return I was wed to Fragrant Dawn, the go-between having cut short all ceremony – though she charged her usual fee.

Find a door, step through into the past – it was once the present. Which is more real? Do both exist side by side in time?

I close my eyes and recall the touch of a vanished woman's breasts. Where Su Lin's were small and pert, hers were round as our hill-country, and fecund. Her nipples hard and full. On our wedding night I was determined to think of her as an imposition, a duty, yet she filled my senses. Afterwards I felt guilty, as though I had betrayed Su Lin. And indeed I had.

When we awoke beside each other, neither of us knew what to say.

'Husband, are you angry with me? Do I not make my Father-in-law happy?'

Certainly she gave him comfort, I could not reproach her for that. But he was old and fading; he was disappointed with me. How absurdly jealous I felt, that he might love his gentle daughter-in-law more than his own son!

'Father, do you remember the day we both walked to Mulberry Ridge and I improvised a verse? Do you remember the lucky geese who flew over us?'

He looked at me through blood-shot eyes. A stroke had paralysed him and he was dying.

'Father, do you know what I am saying?'

Idiot-eyes blinked at me. A week later, he journeyed to the ancestral shrine he had commissioned for a thousand generations of bones.

Then I was Lord of Wei, the title inherited, but by no means deserved. I was no hero as Father had been. Yet I was determined to produce heirs, to fill the ancestral shrine. It was all I hoped for.

'Husband, we have been married six months and I am not with child. I beg forgiveness it has taken so long.'

'You beg forgiveness? Foolish woman! Such things are hardly subject to will.'

Of course, she saw no other way I might esteem her. Habits of bitterness and rancour had begun to settle in my mind. Mostly my thoughts were groping after shadows, or griping at those shadows.

After Father's death I became the reluctant custodian of our estate, obliged to contemplate the husbandry of pigs, yields of rice, the maintenance of our irrigation system. Without the help of my old playmate, Wudi – who first became head of his clan, then Headman of the Village – I would have floundered. Of course he did very well by my ineptitude, for I rewarded him handsomely. With the proceeds he bought considerable property of his own. Did he cheat me? Probably. It was a price I paid gladly.

Then, eighteen months after my wedding with Fragrant Dawn, a daughter was born.

How I loved Little Peony! At last the dammed up love within me flowed freely, a love I never felt for her mother. Pretty, lisping girl, I rebuked any who suggested she was less than a son. What plans I made to teach her to write and learn the Five Classics, as though she were a boy!

She was an artless child, blessed with round, earnest eyes and a most frank gaze. At first her unblinking way of examining my face made me uncomfortable, then I came to welcome it, for her love, guileless and trusting, lent me confidence. I would perch her on my knee and the nagging emptiness in my breast faded for a while. She was a doorway through which a life of quiet affection and laughter might be glimpsed. Her freckles were deliciously absurd. She took after her mother in eating anything set before her, then wanting more.

Yet one morning Little Peony left me and went far away. Her giggling suddenly stopped. She was just learning to talk. There is no reasoning away such sorrow. Sometimes, when I met her old nurse in the village, I would be filled with a desire to weep.

Our next child, another girl, died before her swaddling clothes were cast aside.

Perhaps that was what drove me, step by step, toward the numbness of wine. After all, it is no weakness to seek oblivion, but a kind of wisdom. In the midst of drunkenness one glimpses things otherwise unrevealed. Stars shine brighter and the moon fills one's heart. I wrote hundreds of poems no one ever read. And constantly, I neglected Fragrant Dawn.

So it was a surprise when Eldest Son was born in my

twenty-ninth year. I barely noticed him. Then came Youngest Son, an autumn child to bless my thirty-sixth birthday.

I am sure my indifference towards my sons grew from a certainty they would not live. After all, our other children had died in infancy. I could not bear to become attached to them, or mourn as I did for Little Peony. Their mother never shared my reserve. She cooed and delighted over each stage of their growing. I looked on with a hundred emotions and, in my confusion, appeared cold.

'Husband, why do you not teach Eldest Son how to hold a brush?'

I remember that conversation well. The boy was six years old. I was copying out a poem praising Su Lin, written when I lived in Goose Pavilion by the West Lake. The paper had grown mouldy in our damp mountain air. In truth, the same mould was rotting my soul.

'I have told you before not to interrupt me when I am composing,' I chided.

She put on her obstinate face. No escaping a conversation then.

'Husband, you write so well. Are our sons not to learn their characters?'

I laid my brush on its wooden rest.

'What for?'

'Because all gentlemen should know how to read and write,' she insisted. 'Honoured Father-in-law did as much for you.'

Perhaps I emptied my cup and filled another with a shaking hand.

'Madam, go away.'

As a dutiful wife should, she obliged.

But I did pursue her suggestion, every day insisting that my sons learn a new character. One might think that a man who has loved the flow of writing like his own breath, would seek to nurture the same in his sons, yet I was a harsh teacher. Each mistake was met with disappointment and rebukes. The more they dreaded our lessons, the more intolerant I became. Still I persevered and our daily lessons dragged on through years of resentment.

Fragrant Dawn sometimes criticised my methods and I would reply scornfully: 'What do you know? You are an illiterate woman.'

Once she replied: 'Perhaps so, husband, but I can see that you are crushing our boys' spirits!'

Of course I fumed and ignored her. Each time I punished them for stupidity, I was punishing myself.

Then, in the depth of winter, as frost hardened the hillsides, Fragrant Dawn fell sick. At first I ignored it. Too busy, always too busy with something. As her health failed I went the other way. Day and night I lingered by her bedside, overcome with remorse. Her spirit escaped in a rattle of breath. As she stepped from this world into the next, her eyes glittered at me – a look of distrust and reproach, I thought. She feared what would become of our sons when she was no longer there to protect them. From me, their own father! Oh, I understood her final look very well. I have never ceased to grieve over it. . .

Father! Look at me! Look how high I go!'

Youngest Son cries out as he swings back and forth on a rope attached to a tall bough in our orchard. Why don't I acknowledge him? No doubt I am thinking of something else. What it is, I cannot remember.

'Father, I have copied out the verses of Lao Tzu you wanted.'

There is a plea in Eldest Son's voice. He is trembling. At once I realise he is afraid of me, that he yearns for a slight dusting of praise as a flower needs pollen. I am torn between sadness and irritation. I glance over his efforts and say sharply to cover my own confusion, 'Much neater than usual. Do you know what the words mean?'

How could he? He is ten years old. Copying them so neatly is a triumph in itself. He bows shame-facedly, then runs from the room. I am left alone with the paper in my hand.

'They are hard words to understand!' I call out after him.

But it is too late. He has gone.

'Father,' says Youngest Son as we sit over dinner, plying our chopsticks in gloomy silence. Perhaps I am recollecting Fragrant Dawn. Or Su Lin. Or nothing at all.

'Father!' he tries again, eager for my attention. 'Today I climbed the cliff at the back of the village all by myself. My companions said that even a monkey could not do that!'

Eldest Son shoots a warning glance at his brother. I regard them both.

'It is a steep cliff,' I concede.

I have no idea who these companions are. It is the kind of thing a father should know. Soon enough I will come to learn about them, when it is too late.

'Never let anyone compare you to an ape,' I say, at last. 'Remember you are a man. After all, one should not insult monkeys.'

I smile at my own wit. He does not know how to reply. He is ten years old. Our chopsticks click and click. Everyone is relieved when the meal ends.

'Father, I have good news!'

Eldest Son is twenty-one now and already the father of a toddling boy.

'You know that piece of wasteland above Swallow Rocks,' he says, proudly. 'Wudi and I have arranged that it should be cleared. Actually, it was my idea. And I have ordered that the Widow Shu's sons should be allowed to till half of it. I know how strongly you feel that widows should receive access to land.'

He beams, expecting praise. Instead I frown.

'Who is this Widow Shu?' I ask, amazed such a person exists.

'Why, Old Shu's wife,' he says.

'That much is obvious,' I remark.

Eldest Son hovers.

'Father, did I not do well?'

Perhaps he thinks I am displeased. It is worse than that. I am indifferent to almost everything he does. He leaves, and another lonely afternoon drags towards dusk. . .

P'ei Ti has woken. He stretches, and manages a faint smile. I glimpse his yellow teeth in the starlight.

'We are still alive!' he exclaims.

'Apparently so.'

'I can feel my strength returning,' he says. 'Is there no food?'

'Nothing.'

Further down the corridor, a prisoner bellows for his mother. We huddle together.

'Yun Cai, I cannot believe my good fortune in finding you,' he says.

'You call this good fortune?'

He manages a dry laugh.

'Given the circumstances, I suppose I do.'

I stare into the dark. It is as though years of separation have never existed, such is our ease with each other.

'There is a question I must ask,' I say. 'Why did you come to Chunming Province? I can hardly believe it was to visit me.'

'No, I was ordered here,' he says. 'I have requested leave of absence to visit you many times, Yun Cai, and always His Majesty could not spare me. But at last it was granted.'

'To accomplish what?'

'Our spies reported that General An-Shu was gaining in ambition under the influence of his concubine and advisers. I was instructed to ensure Chunming Province remained steady and, if need be, execute General An-Shu. By the time I arrived the rebellion was well-advanced. My escort was massacred and

I was thrown in this prison. Of course I intended to visit you in Wei. Indeed, that is why I persuaded the Privy Council to assign me this mission. I wanted to see you again before I died.'

We sit without words. Now the dread of execution begins to clutch. P'ei Ti stirs.

'Didn't you hear?' he whispers. 'Movement in the prison.'

I listen. There is some kind of noise. It no longer seems important. I close my weary eyes and my spirit leaves me, flitting through the narrow window, flying high into the night sky. Now I see everything: General An-Shu's army resting on hillsides before tomorrow's battle; the Emperor's forces illuminated by countless campfires. Then I feel my soul being dragged back to the dark streets of Chunming, back through the window, back to this prison, this narrow cell.

'Just a dream,' I murmur. 'Just a dream.'

If so, I wake with a start. The bolts of our cell are scraping. The time has come. I close my eyes, and wait.

The cell door, swollen by damp and age, opens with a jolt. A lantern bobs, blinding us. Dark silhouettes peer inside. We cannot see faces, just shapes.

'Preserve our dignity,' whispers P'ei Ti.

I sense his deepest fear. To lose face and betray the Son of Heaven, as he did in the Phoenix Chamber. The figure in the doorway raises the lantern.

'Is this the right cell?' he whispers. 'I see no one.'

He steps in and shines the lantern, revealing us crouched in a corner. We blink like startled cats.

'Your Excellency!'

In a flash the man is on his knees. I look in confusion at P'ei Ti. Then I recognise the voice and struggle to my feet.

'Get up!' I say, filled with wild hope. 'This is no time for ceremony.'

For the man is Ensign Tzi-Lu. And behind him, holding the lantern, stands Golden Bells.

'What?' croaks P'ei Ti.

'Quick, Your Excellency!' hisses Ensign Tzi-Lu. 'Follow us!'

We find ourselves in a miserable corridor lined with closed doors. The prison is silent, its inmates asleep or too frightened to draw attention to themselves. Golden Bells' lantern casts strange shadows on the walls. He leads us to a small courtyard in the centre of the prison. Here are more lights and I gasp a lungful of cool, night air.

A scene frozen by menace awaits us. Thousand-*li*-drunk stands by the entrance, complete with his basket. Four warders kneel, guarded by half a dozen armed men, holding swords to their throats. Other warders lie dead on the floor. The Ensign Tzi-Lu looks around and listens. Stillness. No alarm has been raised. His own sword is in his hand, glittering faintly in the starlight.

'Kill them all,' he says.

At once there is a flurry of blows. One of the warders manages a thin scream – but that is hardly unusual in this place. Within moments they lie crumpled on the earth. The Ensign raises his hand for silence. Again, no sound. Golden Bells walks over to the corpse of the Chief Warder and spits on it. I glance away.

'Hide them in that cell,' murmurs the Ensign. 'Then follow us.'

He leads us to a side entrance. We wait as he unbolts it. No one speaks. I can hear P'ei Ti's laboured breath and steady his arm. Yet his eyes are bright.

The Ensign opens the door a crack. It creaks ominously. Slowly, he pokes his head outside. Whatever he sees reassures him.

'Quick!' he murmurs.

We file out into a narrow alleyway at the rear of the prison. The path smells of ordure and we soon pass a walled dung heap.

I cry out involuntarily. A corpse lies on the manure, his arms and legs splayed, eyes glinting dully at the sky. Three large pigs snuffle around him.

We shuffle through the darkness to a postern gate in the wall of the Prefect's enclosure. Beyond lies a dark road lined by mulberry trees and low houses. We are free! Can it be so easy? The Ensign barely hides his triumph. We follow him into the street and he closes the door behind him. Then my misgivings begin, for there is no sign of horses. The Ensign sheathes his sword and I turn to Thousand-*li*-drunk.

'Where now?' I whisper. 'Where are the horses?'

Thousand-*li*-drunk flaps his hands. His face is pale as mourning clothes. He is shaking. I have never seen him truly afraid before. It is hardly a sight to inspire confidence. What he lacks in courage the Ensign Tzi-Lu offers in abundance.

'Follow me, Your Excellency,' he murmurs.

It seems I exist merely as P'ei Ti's shadow.

P'ei Ti nods stiffly.

'We are wholly reliant on you,' he says.

Now begins a journey across Chunming fit for bad dreams. Every corner might conceal enemies. With each moment that passes I expect shouts of pursuit. I am filled with a strange certainty that I will meet Youngest Son somewhere in this darkness, that he will join our motley band. Under a son's protection I might feel safe. But he is far away. Or dead.

Finally, we halt in sight of the Western Ramparts, hiding in the shadow of a derelict temple. We wait expectantly.

The Ensign Tzi-Lu bows to P'ei Ti and offers us food and drink. It is strange to see a great man gobble like a beggar. I'm sure I look no better.

'We have not been able to get horses, Your Excellency,' he whispers. 'The rebels have taken every last one in the city. But I've got a ladder hidden by the walls. We'll climb it, then lower ourselves by rope. No one will know how we have left Chunming.'

P'ei Ti nods solemnly.

'Get on with it, young man.'

Our party hastens to the shadowy foot of the ramparts. A dog barks further up the alleyway. The Ensign seems to be casting about for something. We wait anxiously as he walks up and down, evidently agitated. In one of the hovels behind us, I hear a querulous voice. When the Ensign returns his head is bowed.

'Forgive me, Your Excellency,' he mutters. 'The ladder is missing. And the ropes. Perhaps they have been stolen.'

We glance uncertainly among each other. P'ei Ti's breath hisses with frustration. As for me, I sense only inevitability. For a long moment we huddle in the alley, eight armed men and Thousand-*li*-drunk, not to mention two decrepit fellows useless in a fight.

'Your Excellency,' says Ensign Tzi-Lu. 'I have a plan. We shall march up to the West Gate, pretending that you are our prisoners. Once there we shall bluff our way through and escape. If need be, we shall dispatch the guards.'

P'ei Ti and I regard him in amazement.

'That is a crazy plan,' I say.

'Yes,' says Thousand-*li*-drunk. 'Insane folly.'

'What choice do we have?' demands the Ensign. 'At any moment the warders may be discovered and a general alarm raised. Consider, General An-Shu has emptied the city of all available men. There will only be a skeleton guard on the West Gate for the Imperial army is attacking from the east.'

He sounds eager to convince himself.

'We can hide at the bird-seller's shop,' protests Thousand-*li*-drunk.

'That is not practicable,' counters the Ensign. 'We will never make it there without being seen.'

If our situation weren't so desperate, I might laugh. Our saviours look absurdly like brigands. Yet they have already proved themselves capable of daring. The question is settled unexpectedly.

'We shall do as this officer thinks best,' announces P'ei Ti. 'I have faith in his judgement.'

The Ensign Tzi-Lu puffs with pride.

It is only a little way to the West Gate. We make hasty plans. Thousand-*li*-drunk produces a tattered document which I recognise as a licence to beg. Clearly, we must pray the guards are not only imbeciles but illiterate.

Starlight and lanterns illumine our way as we approach the gate, marching in strict military style. P'ei Ti, Thousand-*li*-drunk and myself shuffle along, pretending to have bound hands. As we draw near, guards pour out of their quarters wearing the tatty uniform of the Penal Battalion. Five, six, then eight and nine, including a sergeant. Who would have expected so many?

'Halt!' calls the sergeant, one hand on his sword.

We do so.

'Special prisoners!' replies the Ensign. 'We must be allowed instant passage. Open the gate!'

The sergeant frowns.

'I have orders not to open the gate for anyone.'

'His Highness wants these prisoners removed from the city,' says the Ensign, stepping closer.

'Where is your pass?' demands the sergeant.

'I have it here.'

The Ensign walks boldly up to the sergeant. There is a sudden movement. His knife protrudes from the sergeant's throat. Blood spatters on the ground in a thin spray. Then the sergeant collapses. For a long moment the guards watch in horror. Suddenly the gateway is full of fighting men. The clank of iron on iron fills the air. P'ei Ti and I shrink against a wall. The fight seems to last many minutes. Four of our escort are dying or grievously wounded, amidst half a dozen of our enemies. The rest have fled.

The Ensign summons us over, gasping. He has taken a wound to his chest.

'The gates!' he croaks.

As his men open them, we hear pounding feet on the rampart above us, shouted orders.

'Now!' he cries. 'Now! Or rot here forever!'

We need no encouragement. P'ei Ti, Thousand-*li*-drunk, Golden Bells and myself stumble through the gateway onto the exposed road beyond. The pitiful remainder of our escort follows. It is dark, yet there is enough starlight to shoot by. Crossbow bolts land among us. The last of our remaining soldiers fall. A shaft pierces Thousand-*li*-drunk's basket. He slows to taunt the man who fired it, then another bolt appears in his exposed chest. With a short scream, he crumples. More missiles descend, they have found the range now. Yet by Heaven's will we are unscathed. Darkness conceals us. We have escaped Chunming!

The Ensign Tzi-Lu leads us into a field and we hobble over the sticky earth and hide in a stand of bamboo.

Escaping Chunming is one thing. Preserving our liberty quite another. We are a pitiful remnant.

Thousand-*li*-drunk's loss affects me deeply. I always suspected he might be an Immortal, and now he lies pierced by a crossbow bolt. His arrival in Wei every spring coincided with the plum blossom. His cryptic utterances over decades of my life have come to just this: a mouthful of dusty road.

There is no time to mourn. I survey our forces. The Ensign Tzi-Lu staunching the wound on his chest with a strip of torn cloth. Golden Bells squatting on the ground, dazed by violence. And P'ei Ti slumped against a gnarled root, evidently exhausted. As for myself, I might despair if not for one certainty. Somehow I must frustrate the horsemen riding to destroy my family. An insane restlessness grips me. To an onlooker it might seem resolution.

'We cannot stay here!' I say. 'We are less than three *li* from Chunming and dawn is coming.'

Indeed, the first rays are brightening the eastern horizon, rising above the watchtowers and walls of Chunming. The West Gate is illuminated by lanterns and even my poor eyesight detects movement. When the Excellent Yuan Chu-Sou finds out we have escaped, his rage will ensure a swift pursuit. Ensign Tzi-Lu finishes fastening his bandage.

'You are right,' he says.

I await a bold stratagem. He looks around, and shivers.

'We must find a place to hide before dawn comes,' I suggest, helpfully. 'No doubt you have somewhere in mind?'

He nods, then gestures vaguely into the darkness.

'Have you really no plan?' I ask. 'What did you expect to happen once we got beyond the ramparts?'

He peers at His Excellency P'ei Ti to check whether he is listening. But my old friend seems stupefied. This is a cause for grave concern. If he cannot walk we are lost.

'I did not expect any of this,' admits the Ensign.

Now I must be the leader. It is a strange thing, this shuffling of responsibilities.

'How far off is dawn?' I ask.

'An hour at most.'

In the midst of exhaustion I struggle to remember the land to the west of Chunming. I have ridden through this district often enough when returning to Wei, but always by the Western Highway. Only a fool would venture that way now.

As if in a dream, I recall encountering the deserters in Mallow Flower Marsh at the start of General An-Shu's rebellion. They hid there for a reason. Such places are especially hard for horsemen to search.

'I believe there is a swamp a few *li* from here,' I say. 'I glimpsed it often when travelling on the high road back to my home. We should go there, I think. As I recollect, there are many tall reeds to conceal us.'

'A few *li*?' asks the gallant Ensign.

We both examine P'ei Ti. He is breathing heavily, his eyes closed. I turn to Golden Bells who is listening to our conversation.

'Golden Bells,' I say. 'Now is the time to double your reward.'

He frowns.

'Lord Yun Cai, I've delivered my part of the bargain. More than my part. No one said anything about fighting. I should be paid what I am owed, then I'm free to go.'

I sense the Ensign Tzi-Lu's hand drifting to his sword.

'You can only be paid when His Excellency is safe,' I reason. 'Besides, you are in too deep to falter now. I promise you this, Golden Bells: act like a man and you'll never cease to be glad.'

He glances nervously at the ramparts of Chunming. I can tell he is ready to bolt.

'His Excellency will grant you land as a further reward,' I suggest. 'We discussed the matter while in prison.'

I have no right to make such a promise. Yet I have not said how much land. It might amount to a pigsty. He wavers.

'I am no soldier!' he protests. 'I don't know how I lived through that fight by the gate.'

'You do not have to be a soldier,' I say, soothingly. 'Just a porter.'

He follows my glance to P'ei Ti's slumped frame.

'Why, His Excellency is thinner than a cricket!' I say. 'And the Ensign Tzi-Lu will take his other arm.'

This is the moment of crisis. If Golden Bells deserts us now we are surely lost. Still he wavers.

'All right,' he grumbles. 'I know you're true to your word, Lord Yun Cai.'

Soon P'ei Ti sits cradled between Golden Bells and the Ensign. I am consigned to carry the weapons. If I am mistaken about the location of the marsh we might as well return to Chunming.

Casting a fearful glance back towards the city, I notice that a band of men have emerged bearing torches. We advance through stands of bamboo, clumps of mulberry trees, and every footstep leads us further from Chunming towards the mountains.

I awake from foul dreams to the music of reeds. Whenever the breeze lifts, ten thousand stalks murmur and sway. They form the walls of our womb – or tomb. We sleep back to back, hidden from the prying eyes of all but birds. P'ei Ti snores. Even Ensign Tzi-Lu and Golden Bells prop each other, utterly spent by the effort of carrying His Excellency. Only I am awake. If General An-Shu's men came across us now they could take us without the least resistance. I listen. No voices, just wind through the reeds. A yellow butterfly lands on my arm, slowly opening and closing its wings. I am too spent for further struggle and my eyes close.

A brisk shaking stirs me.

'Shhhh!'

There are many ways of demanding silence. The Ensign's tone is masterful. I freeze, but all I hear is the rustling of reeds. And then something else, indistinct yet recognisable: men's voices, close by. The four of us concealed in the hollow of reeds meet each other's eyes. How hungry we are, and thirsty! The voices recede. Golden Bells rises unexpectedly as though he means to betray our position. We stare in horror. He peers round the marsh, then bobs back down.

'Soldiers,' he whispers. 'A dozen or so.'

'Whose army do they belong to?' I ask.

'I could not tell.'

P'ei Ti clears his throat. Such is his authority, we all listen. He appears refreshed by his hours of sleep. I detect new strength in his bloodshot eyes.

'If His Majesty's army has prevailed, as surely they must, then the remnant of General An-Shu's army must flee this way.'

We digest his idea.

'That makes our position more precarious than ever,' I say.

'Not if we find His Majesty's troops,' says P'ei Ti.

'How are we to know one from the other?' I ask.

It is a good question. Not by their virtue, that is for sure. Perhaps by their uniforms, but even then one cannot be certain.

'The best thing,' I say. 'Is to find a refuge. I propose that we travel to my home in Wei Valley.'

No doubt P'ei Ti sees through my motives. He looks at me sharply enough.

'It is one of the Five Directions,' he concedes. 'At least it takes us away from Chunming.'

Golden Bells' eyes gleam. He has every reason to support such a plan, but of course he is too lowly to be consulted. We turn to Ensign Tzi-Lu. The final decision must lie with him.

'We have no food,' he says. 'No drink. We must leave this marsh soon. Why not return to Lord Yun Cai's home? We could easily hide in the hills.'

'How far is it?' asks P'ei Ti.

'A good day's walk to the foothills even if we travel on the Western Highway,' I say. 'We could follow the general course of the road, using fields and woods as cover. Once in the hills we should be able to buy horses.'

No one offers a better plan.

So the day passes. Now we acquire an unexpected leader. Golden Bells proves wily as a bandit. A true peasant, he reads the land as well as his betters might a scroll and we make good progress, seldom more than a *li* or two from the road, yet distant enough to be unrecognisable to searching eyes.

The Ensign Tzi-Lu regularly surveys the travellers on the highway. They are many. Refugees from Chunming by the look of their wheelbarrows and handcarts. Occasionally, small bands of hurrying soldiers. We take cover until they pass, then start again. All of us long to question those fleeing. Has General An-Shu joined battle? Perhaps he has already been defeated, or maybe Heaven has decided to grant him victory and he is revelling in Chunming as we trudge west. Whenever we encounter signs of habitation Golden Bells leads us on a round-about route to avoid village or house. This cannot continue. Without food we will faint, though streams and ditches provide plenty to drink.

At last we glimpse a hamlet through a stand of trees. P'ei Ti calls a halt.

'I must eat,' he croaks.

The Ensign bows submissively.

'Your Excellency, I shall purchase food in the village,' he says.

I meet Golden Bells' eye. Tzi-Lu is too obviously a soldier, and a wounded one at that.

'Send Golden Bells with a little money,' I say.

The Ensign shakes his head vigorously.

'Why should he not desert us?'

Despite the gravity of our situation, I am annoyed on the fellow's behalf.

'Because he is a *nung*, a peasant, he will not stand out as you do,' I say. 'And he has proved his loyalty. I trust him.'

P'ei Ti nods once. So it is settled. We spend an anxious half hour. When Golden Bells returns he carries a basket of wind-dried pork and steamed rice, millet wrapped in lotus leaves, pickled sparrows and cucumber. A feast.

'I told them my father is desperate for his last meal,' he boasts as he stuffs himself. 'And that no one should come near because he has the plague. They are all hiding in their houses anyway.'

I glance up sharply. Such a lie is a bad omen. No one else seems to notice, so I keep my fears to myself.

'I heard something else,' he continues. 'Something bad. General An-Shu surprised the Emperor's men as they advanced on Chunming and trounced his army.'

Our jaws cease to move. The breeze ruffles the leaves of the copse.

'Are you sure?' I ask.

'So they said.'

Our meal, delicious a moment before, tastes like sawdust.

Shadows are lengthening as we reach the entrance to the foothills. From here on there is no alternative to the road. A single ravine cuts through densely wooded slopes and the highway climbs with it. A place of dubious reputation. Five hundred years ago, a minor prince of the royal family was robbed by bandits in the ravine, taking a fatal wound when he resisted. Ever since it has been known as the Valley of White Sighs. Once through, we will find many places to hide until the storm has exhausted itself around Chunming.

'Your Excellency, are you well enough to attempt the climb?' asks the Ensign Tzi-Lu.

P'ei Ti's flush of strength is fading, yet he nods stiffly.

The entrance to the ravine is dark, ringed by huge sandstone boulders. Thorn bushes fill the gaps between the stones. A brace of cawing pheasants flutter over the deserted high road and I am afflicted by foreboding. Pheasants represent an Empress. I think of the Lady Ta Chi.

'Perhaps we should not attempt the ravine,' I say. 'It is a dangerous place. Let us find another way round.'

'There is no other way, Lord Yun Cai,' protests the Ensign. 'Besides, if the rumour is true that General An-Shu has prevailed, we must not delay.'

None of us cares to discuss such a possibility. And surely my disquiet is unwarranted. The road appears empty. We should take this chance while General An-Shu and his rebels celebrate their victory in Chunming. Still, I hesitate.

'Very well,' I concede.

After emptying the remainder of Golden Bells' basket we leave the cover of the pine trees. I find myself shuffling ahead, my stick digging into the earth. Golden Bells helps P'ei Ti along.

As we reach the entrance to the ravine, Ensign Tzi-Lu holds up a warning finger, then presses his ear to the highway. Swallows flit above our heads.

'Movement on the road behind us,' he says. 'Horses. Perhaps people fleeing Chunming.'

Suddenly he laughs. A young man's reckless laugh.

'What of it! We shall hurry.'

And we do, climbing through a narrow, twisting way, wide enough for a single cart to pass. Granite walls contain us. One may only go forward or back. Creepers and trailing plants cling to the damp walls. A troupe of monkeys shriek above us.

As the road climbs, P'ei Ti's strength falters. Soon he is being half-carried by the younger men. I must shift for myself, and continue to lead, urging them on. Half way up, I turn at a bend, marked out by a laughing stream. I have paused here before in happier days when returning from paying taxes in Chunming. The plain is clearly visible below, as is the highway, and there my gaze lingers. I stiffen, and call out for sharper eyes than my own. The Ensign Tzi-Lu follows my pointing finger.

'Your Excellency,' he says. 'Horsemen on the road. And a fast-moving carriage. No, more than one. I can see flags. Your Excellency, these are not peasants fleeing the war.'

He looks round desperately at the walls imprisoning us.

'Your Excellency, there is no time to lose.'

We shuffle and pant our way up the ravine. Now the clatter of horses' hooves can be heard clearly, voices calling out to urge on their beasts. But we are weary. P'ei Ti is being carried. My own breath rattles. Three-quarters up it becomes clear we shall not escape the ravine before the carriages catch us. They are close, driven by a haste we cannot match. Here the ravine widens into an egg-shape, bound by high walls. A young man might hope to scale the rocks, creeper by creeper, ledge after ledge. For P'ei Ti and I there is no such hope.

The Ensign's despair becomes evident in a single gesture. He draws his sword and indicates to Golden Bells he should do the same. The hoof beats are drawing close. Soon a turn in the road will reveal them.

'Stand against that rock, Your Excellency,' he barks, as though to a lowly recruit.

Then he thrusts his sword into the dirt and waits, arms crossed, smiling scornfully.

We do not wait long. Two cavalrymen wearing the uniform of the Penal Battalion trot into view, their horses wild-eyed, foaming from their exertions. They are followed by several carriages.

First comes General An-Shu's ivory chariot, though he does not occupy it. A slender figure clutches the rail beside the driver, her long hair dishevelled, her face pure and pale as white jade. The Empress-in-waiting.

In the carriages behind I glimpse frightened old men. I would laugh if laughter could bring comfort. When a tree falls, the monkeys scatter. For there squats the Head Eunuch alongside the Excellent Yuan Chu-Sou and several others I recognise from General An-Shu's banquet.

The cavalry halt at the sight of the Ensign, his sword in the earth. One by one the carriages do likewise, until the ravine is full of sweating horses and men.

A moment of long recognition follows. I cast a nervous glance at P'ei Ti. To my relief, he recollects his dignity. There will be no submission this time. He stands upright and glares like an angry judge. Above our heads the monkeys shriek and jabber. I realise they have been following our progress up the ravine.

The Empress-in-waiting regards us. The kohl on her eyelids has run, perhaps from weeping. She struggles to speak. Another two lancers trot up to join their comrades. Still the Ensign Tzi-Lu remains immoveable, barring their way.

'You!' accuses the Empress-in-waiting.

Her voice echoes round the barren rocks. A cry of wounded disappointment.

'Kill them!' she shrieks, jabbing her finger at P'ei Ti.

Unexpectedly another voice rings out.

'No!'

It belongs to Yuan Chu-Sou. His hasty departure from Chunming can only mean one thing. The battle was not won by General An-Shu. The rumour we heard was false and the Son of Heaven has been victorious. I see from P'ei Ti's expression that he comprehends the truth and the irony of our situation.

'No!' repeats Yuan Chu-Sou. 'We must take His Excellency P'ei Ti as a hostage.'

The rebels look uneasily among themselves, uncertain who is in charge. The Empress-in-waiting frowns at being contradicted but she is only a woman, her power borrowed from General An-Shu. And there is no sign of him.

'Seize Second Chancellor P'ei Ti!' urges Yuan Chu-Sou.

The soldiers edge their horses forward. Yuan Chu-Sou raises his hand to delay them.

'Kill all but the old man in blue,' he says. 'Harm him and you'll be flayed alive. Do it quickly!'

The soldiers trot forward and draw their swords. Golden Bells squeals beside me. His weapon clatters on the flinty ground. He has decided to die without a fight. It will be quicker that way. Still the gallant Ensign does not move. The flickering of his eyes betrays that he is deciding where to launch himself.

I shrink against the wall and take P'ei Ti's arm. No words are exchanged. What is left to say?

Then I become aware of a distant noise. A drumming sound. Everyone present pauses, and turns. The cavalry try to wheel their horses in the narrow space. An armoured rider appears, followed by another, and another. Their flag is the Son of Heaven's. I thrust P'ei Ti into the dirt. Hooves kick up spurts of dust. A brief clash of weapons follows, making the narrow ravine ring with noise and shouts. Horses rear in panic.

When the dust blows away our situation is entirely reversed. Imperial cavalry hold a dozen prisoners and the Ensign Tzi-Lu is wiping his sword on a dead man's robes.

*

The captives are on their knees; P'ei Ti confers with an officer who dare not look him in the face. His exhaustion has vanished. The resumption of power is like a rejuvenating drug.

I lean against a boulder with Golden Bells. Once more we are irrelevant. Perhaps we always were, for hidden within the hours of our usefulness lay a future where we do not matter. It is no hardship to resume one's natural state.

At last P'ei Ti comes over. His is a weathered face, duty and care have dried his skin to the colour of parchment. On that scroll I read a fierce determination so powerful that he seems a stranger to me.

'Yun Cai,' he says.

I remember his youthful tone. His voice was kinder when we were young.

'You have saved me,' he says. 'I honour you.'

Abruptly the ravine fills with cries of amazement, even wonder. For His Excellency P'ei Ti, Second Chancellor to the Son of Heaven, struggles to his knees before me and bows, lowering his forehead until it touches the earth. Everyone present is obliged to do the same. I drag him up, my cheeks crimson. We totter in each other's arms.

'Will we never learn?' I chide, laughing hoarsely.

P'ei Ti does not smile. He is all business now.

'I have ordered half of these men to ride with you. They will ensure General An-Shu's cavalry do not punish your family. You should accompany them in the General's chariot.'

I nod gratefully. He has read my dearest wish.

'As for me,' he says. 'I shall return to Chunming to ensure proper rule commences. I hear that the rebels have been soundly defeated and the General captured. We must part now. Remember this, old friend, that I shall honour my promise to visit you in Wei Valley, as soon as my duties allow.'

I look at the prisoners kneeling in the dirt: the Lady Ta Chi and her Head Eunuch; the Excellent Yuan Chu-Sou and the other courtiers. My own words haunt me: no man is born wicked, only circumstances make him so. P'ei Ti follows my glance and shrugs.

'I must use their carriages, there is no room for them.'

He turns to meet Yuan Chu-Sou's brooding gaze. Then P'ei Ti leans forward, clicking his fingers as I saw Yuan Chu-Sou do in Chunming, and a cruel understanding passes between the two men. I look away as the inevitable follows. There are subtleties in such matters, as in anything. Was it necessary to sever his head? No doubt it was. The Lady Ta Chi's screams, her excuses and pleading fill the ravine. Soon a dozen heads are rolled onto her silken robe and tied into a lumpy bundle. Within a few hours they will adorn the walls of Chunming as a warning. Is it cynical to detect another motive? P'ei Ti is eliminating any who might report his homage to General An-Shu.

I mount the ivory chariot and Golden Bells stands beside me. The horses are whipped forward. Swept along by a stream of cavalry we gallop towards Wei.

I close my eyes. Hours blur. When I open them the land may be glimpsed by a little starlight, occasional appearances of the moon between wind-driven clouds. General An-Shu's chariot, pulled by two fierce horses, carries me nearer and nearer to the end of my fears. I perch on a small seat, Golden Bells crouching beside me, while the driver whips on our horses. Before and behind us dozens of lancers ride in loose formation, cantering at a pace ruinous to the health of their mounts. But His Excellency P'ei Ti has issued orders. There are consequences for failing to satisfy such commands. The officer in charge is especially zealous. He rides a dozen yards ahead of his troops, drawing them onwards.

So acute is my discomfort that I have no leisure for thought, except of an unwelcome kind. Visions of what we will find in

Wei sicken my soul, but I cling to my seat and anticipate the next jolt. I dare not anticipate more. Yet I have discovered a new fear: that General An-Shu's men will not only execute my family but that my poems, my precious sheaves of poems, will burn alongside them. Ignoble to compare the two losses, yet a thought cannot help itself.

At last, toward the middle of the night, the officer calls a halt in a roadside village. His horses and men must rest for a while.

The village is silent as my chariot rolls to a stop. I glance back the way we have come. A climbing hill road, with the land falling away behind us. My eyes are drawn to the sky. Black monsoon clouds pursue us. If the rain breaks while we are still on the road it will become a quagmire, our pace a laborious trot and all hope of reaching Wei at daybreak must be abandoned. But for now the sky is clear above our heads. We must not delay here. Agitated, I step down from the chariot. At once my legs buckle and I am on my knees, panting. Golden Bells tries to raise me to my feet. I groan in protest. The cavalry officer appears by my side.

'Lord Yun Cai,' he says, embarrassed by my undignified posture. 'We have not arrived yet.'

I flash him a hard look. I'm limp as an old fish.

'That is obvious, young man.'

'Forgive me, sir, quite so.'

He looks round and orders his sergeants to wake the peasants. There is a pounding on doors and requisitioning of fodder for the horses. I remain on my knees until strong enough to return to the chariot. Then the officer is before me again.

'How far is your home, sir?' he asks.

I name the distance and he scowls.

'His Excellency P'ei Ti informed me that the enemy are a day's ride ahead of us,' he says. 'We can hardly hope to catch them, yet that is my order. This is an impossible duty!'

'Perhaps they travelled slowly,' I say.

'Well, that's easily found out.'

A villager is dragged before us by two burly cavalrymen. An old man. And quaking.

'Are you the headman?' I demand.

He nods, afraid to speak.

'Have horsemen passed this way?'

'Sir, the horsemen asked for the road to Wei,' he says.

'How many were there?'

'Thirty, maybe more.' He leans forward conspiratorially. 'They looked like barbarians to me, my Lord.'

I exchange glances with the officer. Our enemies sound like the mercenary archers hired by General An-Shu's brother. The captain does not seem pleased.

'When did they pass through?' he asks.

'At dusk.'

'Were they in a hurry?'

Everything depends on his answer. Yet it comes as a relief, for the old hetman shakes his head.

'They stayed here for several hours and cooked every last hen we own!'

Half an hour later our troop has re-assembled. The officer and I agree there is still hope. If General An-Shu's men have travelled slowly we may yet catch them before they reach Wei. They may even have camped at the head of the valley, hoping to surprise the village at dawn.

Our journey flows through nightmare. It requires all my strength to remain seated in the chariot. One wheel wobbles alarmingly on its axle. Towards dawn we leave the high road and enter the lowest reaches of Wei. The valley rolls with mist, reducing vision to a dozen yards. I pass familiar hills and slopes, listening to birds and monkeys as they greet the swelling day. The road is empty except for a confusion of hoof prints in the earth. We advance cautiously, hoping to catch the enemy unawares.

A few *li* from the village we come across the remains of a

hastily-constructed camp. A sergeant dismounts to inspect the fires and kicks up glowing embers. Dawn is spreading rapidly across the eastern horizon. Behind us banks of cloud threaten rain, almost upon us now. The cavalry officer canters over to me.

'Lord Yun Cai, you must take the rear and only enter the village when it is secure. Although we appear to outnumber the rebels nothing must be taken for granted.'

I discern from his expression that he seeks my approval. After all, His Excellency P'ei Ti bowed low before me. A cruel logic fills my mind.

'Captain,' I say. 'I expect every one of you to give up your lives to save my family. The Second Chancellor expects nothing less. Otherwise your own families will pay for your negligence.'

So I resort to the same threats as General An-Shu! The captain bows stiffly then hurries to his horse. He turns to address his exhausted men.

'Any who show cowardice shall die at my own hand!' he roars, glancing in my direction for approval. I glower implacably.

He orders the ranks and gallops up the road through swirling mist toward the village. Distorted shapes surround us. I nod to the driver and we follow at a cautious trot.

'Lord Yun Cai,' says Golden Bells. 'I can smell something.'

'Smoke,' I say, dully. 'They've set fire to the village.'

As we ride into Wei, it becomes obvious we are too late. The street is full of mist and smoke. A dozen houses are ablaze. We choke and the horses neigh fearfully. Fighting men appear through the gloom: Imperial cavalry clashing with General An-Shu's troops and, a little further on, a group of peasants dragging down a mounted archer, hacking at him with axes and spades.

Suddenly the captain appears beside the chariot. An arrow hangs from his saddle. In one hand he grips a sword, the other holds a bloodied lance. All around us are shouts, whinnies and screams.

'Where is your house?' he splutters as dense smoke billows over us.

'Up the hill! Follow me!'

I urge the driver forward. At first he refuses, then takes one look at the cavalry forming into a column. We canter up the hill and break through the mist clinging to the valley bottom. Three-Step-House is revealed and I cry out.

They have reached my home. The gate stands open and soldiers have set alight the lower buildings. As I watch, they are dragging out servants to question them, overseen by a man in an administrator's uniform. Who they seek needs no guessing. Others are climbing inexorably to the topmost house, our family quarters, swords and torches in hand. I shriek like a man consumed by demons.

'Stop this!'

My voice echoes amidst the sound of crackling wood, flames and battle in the village below. The cavalry charge forward, outstripping the chariot. As we approach the gatehouse, one of the chariot's wheels hits a pothole, bending at an absurd angle. We scrape to a halt, horses stumbling. Golden Bells and I are thrown to the ground. When I recover my breath, Three-Step-House is masked by the smoke of its own burning.

No thought now. Up the hill. Step by step. Past the gate gods and tangles of fighting, struggling men. I am beyond fear. I scale steps slippery with blood and reach the Middle House where Mother used to sew and Father held audience. An arrow thuds into the wall beside me. Ignore it. Up the next flight of steps towards the screams coming from the top-most house. Is that Daughter-in-law's voice? But she is safe in Whale Rock Monastery. Let it just be a maid's! A handful of soldiers are setting fire to the roof with their torches. Another arrow skims past. I hear a cry behind me. Then I'm running round the house to a side entrance. The air is dark with smoke. How soon my past burns! Suddenly a new terror grips me. My chest of poems! My poems will burn. I must save my poems.

When I struggle through the side door, I find Eldest Son, sheltering his sons with out-stretched arms. Daughter-in-law crouches, trying to calm the children.

'Why are you not at the monastery?' I bellow.

He shrinks back in surprise.

'Father! I thought it was safe to return.'

'Go up to the orchard! Hide in the family shrine. Everyone. At once!'

One by one the children flit through the door and up the hill, Daughter-in-law follows close behind. Sounds of fighting draw near. Eldest Son hovers, eager to join his family.

'Help me!' I command.

'Father, we must go with the children.'

'Follow me! My chests. We must save my poems.'

The corridor is filling with smoke. Coughing, I lead him into my room. The chests are safe. A great crack of wood makes us flinch. The roof timbers are ablaze.

'Throw them through the window!' I shout.

He looks at me like a dolt.

'What, Father?'

'The chests! Throw them through the window.'

'We must escape!' he wails.

That much is evident. Paper and seasoned wood melt before the flames.

'Help me lift this one!' I cry.

'Selfish old man! Our lives are worth more than your stupid poems!'

For a long second we gaze at each other, dumbstruck. Then he obeys. Together we cast the first chest through the window. The most important, containing my best work. It rolls on the grass. The second follows – legal deeds and letters. Before we can lift the third, smoke overwhelms us. Nose, throat and eyes choke with fumes.

Firm hands take hold of me. I am carried a few steps and thrust into the air. I fall with a crump on the mossy bank outside the house. Eldest Son has called a halt to my madness. A moment later he follows, coughing and retching. Smoke is our enemy now. We must breathe. He hauls me away from Three-Step-House. I can hardly see for tears. Yet my verses are safe. My legacy is safe. I have endured.

I feel drops of rain on my face, slow at first, then gathering pace. The clouds which pursued us to Wei have broken. I stare up at the grey sky. Eldest Son is holding me upright, blinking in his sheepish way. Suddenly he recoils, thrown backwards by an invisible hand. I try to pull him upright, but his weight slips through my feeble hands. An arrow has emerged from his chest! For a moment he regards me with bright, unblinking eyes. Then he falls back and his head bangs dully against my chest of poems. With a flutter, his eyes close. Rain forms silver beads on his cheeks. And all the vanity of my life dies with him.

A man rushes through smoke and rain towards us, his sword bared, slipping in the mud.

epilogue

HOW CLOUDS FLOAT

'. . . Green moss on the path seldom travelled
to Mulberry Ridge. From up here

view a hundred *li* of flooded fields
crowned by haze, circling white birds.

How many more times will this way choose me?
Once is all I beg, to say farewell.'

Hammering wakes me. For a moment I listen in surprise. Then the burden of all that has occurred disgorges itself like a white flower's seed in a strong wind. Better to close your eyes, retreat to the oblivion of sleep. Except one cannot help waking.

Thud. Thud. Thud. One of the carpenters repairing Three-Step-House breaks into raucous, unseemly laughter. I will have to speak to the foreman about that. Today my family's face depends upon the good behaviour of us all, even the servants. Everything must be correct, replete with dignity, for it is a day of rites.

*

'Did you sleep well?'

I am at Eldest Son's bedside. He lies as he has for weeks, wearied by constant pain. I fear it will never recede, though he claims it lessens day by day. The effort of sitting up brings out a sweat, surely a good sign: heat is life's proof.

'You must eat a large breakfast,' I suggest.

He stares at me glassily. His pale lips flutter.

'Yes, Father.'

'Offal of water buffalo fried in pepper and aniseed will lend you strength.'

'There are no buffalo left alive in Wei,' he says.

Answering back is a new thing, yet I am glad, for it shows spirit. We sit in glum silence. Outside the window the carpenters are bantering with my grandsons. Eldest Son's eyes narrow slightly. He has always been strict when it comes to his children's companions, perhaps because he remembers my own negligence with Youngest Son.

'They will come to no harm watching builders at work,' I say, softly. 'Consider the bees, constructing intricate hives.'

We both know how often I have been wrong. I retreat inwardly and try not to think of my poor, lost boy. Youngest Son's body – and fate – were never discovered, though P'ei Ti ordered that the survivors of his company be closely questioned. Some said he fell from crossbow bolts, others that he perished standing over the wounded when the Imperial forces massacred all the rebel prisoners. I cannot think of it. Sometimes I imagine his hungry ghost watching Three-Step-House and mourning all the years of life he has been denied. Surely he blames me. Perhaps I just blame myself.

'Will you be strong enough to appear today?' I ask Eldest Son.

He sips his cup of herbs and powdered rhinoceros horn, prepared by Daughter-in-law at ruinous expense.

'I will try, Father.'

'Ah,' I say.

In the corridor I find Daughter-in-law admonishing a maidservant for dressing lewdly. Her own hair is piled higher than Mount Taishan and decked with silver, gold and jade ornaments. Her face is covered by a layer of white powder and rouge. Daughter-in-law's stomach swells pleasingly, for in three months another grandchild will join our household. I hope it is a girl. I have had a bellyful of sons, without bearing a single one of them, except when it comes to worry.

The poor maidservant was one of those whose virtue endured an assault when General An-Shu's forces attacked Three-Step-House, but from her tone one might think that Daughter-in-law blames the girl.

'Daughter-in-law,' I say. 'You appear agitated.'

'Not at all, Honoured Father!' She produces a new silk fan and flutters it inexpertly. 'I am. . . serene.'

A fine word! I wonder who taught it to her, and at once suspect P'ei Ti. He has taken quite a shine to Daughter-in-law, for reasons I cannot discern.

'I have a question,' I say, disturbed by the wheedling in my voice. 'Is Eldest Son strong enough to attend today's ceremonies?'

She purses her lips. 'Strong enough, heh?'

Will that woman never leave off her *heh*'s? I brace myself.

'Honoured Father, who could have expected these misfortunes! His Excellency P'ei Ti has told me you risked everything, even your own family, rather than betray the Son of Heaven. Let us thank Heaven it turned out well! I am sure the repairs to Three-Step-House will be completed before winter. And Eldest Son is stronger, too!'

She is the mistress of her weapons, so I leave the field without risking a further skirmish.

Many guests have travelled to Wei for our rites. Most are welcome. I glimpse several with their families in the square below, gathered around hired carriages, awaiting the hour decreed propitious by the astrologer for guests to enter Three-Step-House.

For decades our local gentry avoided me like an unpleasant odour, but since my deeds in Chunming, and especially since Second Chancellor P'ei Ti came to grace us, accompanied by a train of secretaries and guardsmen, all taint of official disapproval has blown far away. Indeed, a story circulates that I passed secret messages to P'ei Ti while we were prisoners, urging him to ingratiate himself with General An-Shu in order to gain information concerning the rebels. By this account, I have become a wily fox directing a whole skulk of spies. In fact, I am a hero. The source of such a fanciful tale needs little guessing, yet the reward of thirty thousand *cash* from the Imperial treasury is welcome enough.

Daughter-in-law has sent down baskets of food and wine to refresh our guests in the village square, as well as fire-crackers imported to Wei at a shocking price. Sounds of mirth and carousing float through the valley. Well, let my neighbours be glad. Their noise might dispel misfortune.

I descend to the Middle House and find a pleasant scene. Two young men wearing fashionable silks perch on the steps telling stories to my grandsons. They are our guests from the capital, specially summoned.

The taller of the pair is Cousin Hong's third son and his companion is almost family too. My old servant, Mi Feng, now a prosperous man in his own right, has sent his firstborn to honour us. I loiter behind a corner, and listen.

'Is it true your father saved Grandfather's life?' pipes Little Sparrow, my youngest grandson. That boy is forever chirping.

'Many times!' declares Mi Feng's son.

I remember him as a tiny baby, crying in the courtyard of Cousin Hong's wineshop near the Pig Market. How he resembles his father! I might be young again, and Mi Feng before me. Who may explain the shuffling of moments between present and past? Yet we know what we have known, or some of it.

'All our wealth grew from Lord Yun Cai's gift of a humble inn,' adds Cousin Hong's third son. 'He sold some valuable scrolls and gave the money to my father.'

So my generous actions are not quite forgotten.

'Even so,' continues Mi Feng's heir. 'Your grandfather owes much to our own fathers. They protected him many times when he provoked powerful enemies.'

'Enemies!' exclaims Little Sparrow, relishing the word.

'Oh yes, through rash verses and the like.'

My smile falters.

'Grandfather was *rash*?' asks Little Sparrow in amazement. 'What is *rash*?'

My nephew coughs a warning but Mi Feng's heir, like his father before him, will not take a hint.

'It means, he couldn't keep out of trouble.'

'Hush!' protests my nephew. 'Remember where we are!'

Mi Feng's son laughs.

'Thankfully, there were always friends to save him.'

I shrink back against the wall, my mind fluttering between anger and acknowledgement. I feel a hand on my arm: Old Wudi stands beside me. He looks incongruous in wedding clothes, a Fat-bellied Buddha wearing gaudy silks. Yet his expression is kindly.

'Best to leave the young to their foolish talk,' he says.

We retreat to my room and I summon a flask of warm wine. He waves a hand to indicate I should not fill his cup. I lack such restraint.

'Mi Feng's son is right,' I say. 'I always relied on others to untangle my messes.'

Old Wudi is embarrassed by so much candour. I must remember our true relations.

'All has ended well enough,' he mutters.

Has he forgotten his own son's death when I ordered the cleansing of the valley? Perhaps he believes his granddaughter's marriage recompenses his family for their loss. Certainly, it raises them to the level of gentry. Mine has been a notable condescension. Yet Wudi is a man to whom I owe much and respect more than he guesses. So I talk at length about his granddaughter's beauty and virtue, and the risks he took on my behalf, as well as the honour brought to my family by her dowry, until he takes a cup of wine after all.

Several hours remain before the ceremony. I descend once more to the Lower House and discover Daughter-in-law supervising the final preparations for our feast. It is miraculous how many lucky sauces survived the burning of Three-Step-House, or so she assures me.

'His Excellency P'ei Ti is unusually wise about sauces,' she declares, smugly. 'Who would have thought it in so thin a man! I asked him to test all those to be served at today's banquet because I feared some may be unlucky.'

Such information is unwelcome. Should not I, rather than an Honoured Guest, determine such matters? It almost spoils the tea she places in my hands.

'Did he approve of your sauces?' I ask, at last.

She simpers, as though recollecting a great pleasure: 'Yes, all of them!'

I'm left to drain my cup alone.

Later, as we stroll in the woods beside Three-Step-House, I cannot help raising the subject with P'ei Ti. It is an indication of our intimacy that I approach the question bluntly.

'I am pleased you have not been incommoded by the female element of my household,' I begin.

He nods.

'Your Daughter-in-law is the gold in your treasure house!'

We climb a maple-clad hillside, paths carpeted by leaves, aromas cleansing as a soap of peas. P'ei Ti breathes in deeply, no doubt habituated to the stench of the city. Our bamboo staves click on roots veining the muddy path.

'A delectable woman,' intones P'ei Ti, absent-mindedly. 'Ah, Yun Cai, listen to the cooing of that rock dove! Truly we might be in the Blessed Isles!'

I listen dutifully.

'You have lived among us for nearly a month now,' I say. 'You have eaten our simple food. Endured a hundred dull conversations. Put up with the tedious repairs to our house – and, indeed, I am grateful for the *cash* which pays for them. But old friend, do you really believe this uncouth place equates with the Blessed Isles?'

He smiles at my agitation.

'Today is important for you, is it not?' he says, smooth as the most practised courtier.

I splutter. Today I must face all those my actions put at risk. With hindsight, the finest motives may appear madness.

'After these last few months, it could hardly be otherwise!'

He settles on an outcrop of rock, staring mournfully at the moss round our feet.

'It is not you who should reproach himself,' he says. 'Yet I see you do. Forgive me for knowing you too well. Despite all the years that separated us, you have not changed. The essence of the young man I remember stays true as a plum stone, which is to say impossible to swallow whole.'

Further up the valley monkeys are raising a commotion. P'ei Ti, sharper-eyed than me, spots a circling eagle and we remark on its majesty and strength. He is all admiration, though I point out that even lesser creatures avoid its talons, as is proved by our monkeys. The eagle will be lucky to catch one now they are watching out for each other.

'Yun Cai,' he says. 'This talk of eagles brings me to an offer I wish to make. Tell me, old friend, will you return with me to the capital? I could find a worthy position for you in the Son of Heaven's service. For too long your talents have been wasted. Think of it! We could end our days as we began. An honoured place will always await you in my house.'

I listen in amazement.

'This is something I never imagined,' I say, at last.

'Please consider it well.'

I struggle to look beyond his words, to high office and dignity, a fine home and wealth. With power, I could encourage necessary reforms, my life might end in glory, my portrait hung forever in the Hall of Assembled Worthies. I might even see Su Lin one last time before I die.

But, of course, I shall not go. The court and its follies will do very well without me; I have drunk enough poison for one lifetime. And what wisdom can I offer the Son of Heaven? Only this: I have learned how clouds float, not why. Yet once, when I was young, I believed one must always ask why.

A gong tolls in the village below and I recollect grandson's wedding. Noon approaches and we must hurry back to Three-Step-House. At the gatehouse, P'ei Ti pauses to enjoy the last traces of mist in the valley. White birds circle over Wobbly Watchtower Rock.

'Is it disloyal to my family,' I say. 'To wonder if I am just a father of drifting clouds? Everything I have ever held precious disperses, as this mist will.'

He shakes his head.

'You are quite wrong. If you could but appreciate it, you have spent your entire life taming poison dragons. As for your clouds, they are made of happy jade. Why be so morbid?'

Why indeed?

For a few hours I am the father of happy jade clouds.

Let Xi-wang-nu, Queen Mother of the West, remember us in her palace beside the Tortoise Mountains. May her thoughts wander from the Wide-wind Garden to humble Wei. Today, according to both the astrologer and geomancer, is a day auspicious for women. So it shall be for us. Xi-wang-nu's beauty surpasses beauty. Her skin is especially fine. On her jasper terrace stands a maid whose fan has the power to waft us with good luck. I have long ceased to yearn for the herb of immortality. Today Xi-wang-nu might grant it to us in roundabout ways.

At noon the ceremonies begin. I wear silks provided by P'ei Ti. His influence is boundless, and remorseless. For the last week riders have galloped between Chunming and Wei bearing clothes and other fortunate items.

Certainly we are blessed in our new Granddaughter-in-law. A comely girl, her teeth like pomegranate seeds, a sure sign of fecundity. She has a shrewd way about her, suggesting intelligence, and she reminds me of Fragrant Dawn.

Of course, my grandson is young to be getting married. Both bride and groom are just twelve years old, too tender in years to contemplate a consummation. But I made a promise to Wudi and hear only good of the girl. Eldest Son has declared himself satisfied by the dowry and even Daughter-in-law approves, no doubt glad to have a female ally in Three-Step-House – perhaps she will balance out the excess of *yang* in our family.

Eldest Son hobbles about on crutches then collapses into my ebony chair, clutching his arrow-wound with a ghastly smile. Daughter-in-law defies my expectations. I thought she might chide him for showing weakness before the guests. Instead, she cries on his shoulder until he is the one who grows embarrassed. I watch from my seat at the head table and raise my wine cup in encouragement.

After the bride has straddled herself across the horse saddle, after the customary cups of rice wine, after all and sundry have stuffed themselves at my expense, I leave by the side door of Three-Step-House and climb the hill through the orchard.

In one hand I carry a lantern, in the other a basket of delicacies from the wedding feast. Perhaps I am a little drunk. Certainly it was my intention to remain sober. Of course my expression should be sombre as I enter the pine-copse containing our ancestral shrine but the toasts I have downed make me chuckle, especially when I recall how tenderly Golden Bells sang a nuptial poem I composed for tonight's banquet, one set to an old tune, *Wind Washed Sands*. An old, sad tune. For a moment the long hall of people fell silent. Then someone called out a coarse joke and we roared with laughter. That is best. To laugh now, because melancholy must surely come later.

I reach the dark entrance to the shrine. It preserves my family's heart. A low-building, half-buried in the earth. Door of night. How easily it creaks open. I sit on the step and dare not venture further. The darkness within is absolute. I can sense Father and Mother's eyes upon me.

Youngest Son's spirit resides here, in the tablet of green jade provided for him. No one spoke of him today, as though he had never been. If I could offer my ghost to see his wayward smile again death would seem a small thing, for he would regain his chance to live beyond me and then I might feel at peace. If I could bring him back by dissolving like dew, I would.

Water drips somewhere in the lightless shrine and I pull my jacket close. Water can drip through stone.

They say distance tests the strength of a horse, time a man's character. Why should I fear Honoured Aunty and Cousin Zhi's ghosts, or Lord Xiao's angry face, or the lifeless eyes of the man I killed? And where is Uncle Ming's ruin? Or Su Lin's wilted love? Oh, that love never left my heart! Perhaps it is time to let the past go and enjoy the last days of autumn.

Sounds of celebration reach me from Three-Step-House. Am I missed? No one has come to find me. I shiver, tempted to return.

But there are others to mourn. Raising the lantern, I step into the shrine and watch light flicker on the tablets of the dead. There is poor Little Peony, who should be a grown woman now, a mother herself. Awkwardly, I lay my basket of food beneath Fragrant Dawn's tablet. Given her appetites, it seems likely she will enjoy such a gift. Do I seek to placate my own failings, so they can feed on me no more? A faint breeze stirs the pines. A sigh of wind is all her reply. And it is enough.

I step out beneath a sky lit by circling stars. Tender clouds float and my lantern gutters bravely. Someone in Three-Step-House breaks into song. It does no good to chafe, except against darkness. If I am granted another spring I shall scratch my back and doze in the sun; then I'll offer a final farewell to the Blossom God and not feel too sad. Three-Step-House will become an invisible cloud on which I'll drift away, forever and ever, haunted by nothing at all.

Author's Note

All characters and places in the novel are fictional apart from the Imperial capital, Linan, now known as Hangchow. The West Lake still exists and is admired for its scenic charm just as in Yun Cai's day.

Although there was no rebellion by a warlord called General An-Shu during the Southern Song Dynasty (1127–1279), deep tensions existed between civilian and military leaders in the Empire. Particularly when it came to winning back Chinese lands lost to nomad tribes or buying peace through ignoble payments of tribute. Within sixty years such tensions had inspired mass defections to the Mongol invaders by ambitious officers like General An-Shu eager for local autonomy.

Song Dynasty China's brash and materialistic culture resembles our own self-indulgent society in many ways. Yet in one respect – the high status given to poetry by all social classes – it seems very strange indeed. This was a world where literate men and women found it natural to express themselves through complex verse. And it was indeed possible to buy wine or tea with a sheaf of poems. It is hard to imagine another time or place where poetry has possessed such currency.

I would urge readers of this novel unfamiliar with Chinese poetry to take the plunge and sample the delights of Su Tung-po, Wang Wei, Po Chu-i, Li Po and Tu Fu – to name but a few. Excellent editions are widely available. *The Columbia Book of Chinese Poetry (from Early Times to the Thirteenth Century)* translated by Burton Watson is full of treasure.

Acknowledgements

Grateful thanks to my agent Jane Gregory and everyone at Gregory and Company, especially Stephanie Glencross and Jemma McDonagh. Thanks also to the many people kind enough to read an early draft of the novel: Steve Powell, Angie Turner, Carole Pritchard, Dr Vicky Fogg, my brothers Rich and Phil, as well as my parents, Jim and Dori Murgatroyd, for all their encouragement. Thanks to Bob Horne for inspiration over the years. Antonia Crowther's generous assistance has also been much appreciated. Finally, thanks to Ed Handyside for his editorial advice and making this book possible.